Pauline McLynn grew up in Galway and started acting while studying History of Art in Dublin. She has played many stage roles, but shot to fame as the inimitable Mrs Doyle in *Father Ted*. Her other television work includes *Aristocrats, Bremner, Bird and Fortune* and, most recently, the hugely popular comedy series *Jam and Jerusalem*. Pauline has read several *Books at Bedtime* and her appearances on cinema screens include *Angela's Ashes, Quills, Gypo, Heidi* and *An Everlasting Piece*. She has also written the extremely successful comic novel featuring Dublin private detective Leo Street, *Right on Time*, and the highly-acclaimed *The Woman on the Bus*.

BRIGHT LIGHTS AND PROMISES

It's not easy being the mother of a twelve-year-old boy who's in love with his babysitter and having trouble at school. Nor are matters helped by the unexpected arrival of an elderly mother who's suddenly footloose and fancy-free. There are times when Susie Vine wonders how she'll ever survive. At least she feels secure at Arland & Shaw, London's leading theatrical agency, where her clients love her almost as much as they love themselves. But, as the New Year beckons, Susie feels there's something missing. Then the man who broke her heart comes back into her life and she's forced to ask herself whether she was right to leave him all those years ago. Or is the man for her waiting in the wings elsewhere . . . ?

PAULINE McLYNN

BRIGHT LIGHTS AND PROMISES

Complete and Unabridged

CHARNWOOD
Leicester

First published in Great Britain in 2007 by
Headline Review
an imprint of Headline Publishing Group
London

First Charnwood Edition
published 2008
by arrangement with
Headline Publishing Group
London

British Library CIP Data

McLynn, Pauline
  Bright lights and promises.—Large print ed.—
Charnwood library series
  1. Theatrical agents—Fiction 2. Single mothers—
Fiction 3. Parent and child—Fiction
  4. Man-woman relationships—Fiction
  5. Love stories 6. Large type books
  I. Title
  823.9'2 [F]

  ISBN 978–1–84782–310–6

Published by
F. A. Thorpe (Publishing)
Anstey, Leicestershire

Set by Words & Graphics Ltd.
Anstey, Leicestershire
Printed and bound in Great Britain by
T. J. International Ltd., Padstow, Cornwall

This book is printed on acid-free paper

For Richard Cook
my biggest critic
my greatest supporter

This one would not have
happened without him

1

'Are you telling me that my son being robbed at knifepoint is something I should just get used to?' Susie Vine asked, her voice shaded with disbelief and sarcasm.

The weekend had started early with the theft of Milo's mobile. This was the second time in a month and set to become a regular occurrence, if the dour police officer was anything to go by. Statistics about the robbery of school kids bounced off the shabby station walls, mingling with spent breath and an air of vague hopelessness. Susie honed her mind away from the fact that she should be at the opening night of a new West End play later, supporting a client, doing business.

'Sadly, this is modern life,' the constable went on. 'And there's no real hope of getting the phone back.'

She wanted to scream: the fucking phone is irrelevant. My twelve-year-old son was held up by a thug from a neighbouring school wielding a carpet knife. What are you going to do about it, you moron? She stemmed her annoyance, realising it was largely the manifestation of guilt about missing the show and an unfair resentment at Milo for impinging on her work.

'Mrs Vine,' the officer continued.

'Miss,' she corrected.

Did she detect a hint of a smile across the

1

cop's lips? Or was she hunting for something that didn't exist, nuances of the expected slight. After all these years it was pathetic if she was. Besides, this guy didn't look old enough to have that sort of baggage built in; the remnants of a past judgemental age. Even more of a relief was that she didn't seem old enough to be his mother, a modern pitfall avoided. Even some of the staff in her building were beginning to look like children in her eyes and she did not want to go down that dark road just yet. Thirty-six was too young to be feeling so old.

Milo sat hunched over the table sweating in his school blazer, trying hard to come over all hard and nonchalant. She stretched a hand across his back and for once he didn't shrug it off. She could feel his tremors through the fabric and thought her heart would shatter.

'Officer, I am deeply concerned that this sort of thing can happen on a crowded street in the middle of a big city. Is there some programme in place to tackle the problem?' Her voice was on its highest horse, an impressive sound, she liked to think.

'We are doing our best, I assure you,' the police constable said frostily, picking up on Susie's tone. 'The schools themselves have to take some responsibility. Perhaps if your son or one of his friends was prepared to identify a culprit, we might be able to do a little more. He did say it was a pupil of Saint Vitas that attacked him.' He looked expectantly at Milo.

'Vitas HATE Morning Star,' Milo muttered, actually in some awe at the ancient tradition he

2

had invoked. Beyond that he offered nothing.

'We'll have to think about it,' Susie said. 'The last thing we want is Milo being victimised for grassing someone up.' She nearly laughed at her words, too many television cop shows. She turned to her son. 'Where were the others while all this was happening?'

'They ran off.' He caught her expression. 'Mum, don't blame them for that. I'd've done the same.'

She let that go for now. 'We'll discuss it later.' She squeezed his shoulder, trying to take any sense of warning out of the statement. She didn't want Milo retreating on her. He was adept at disappearing before her eyes while appearing to stay in the room. 'As for identifying the creep who did this, we'll consider that too,' she told the policeman.

She gave their home details and her work address and numbers.

'Arland and Shaw?' the cop asked. 'What's that?'

'We're an agency.'

'Oh?'

Here we go, she thought. She assumed Milo was raising his eyes to heaven.

'It's a theatrical agency. We represent actors.'

Now they had his attention. 'Anyone famous?'

Susie rattled off a few names, soap opera stars, a hard chaw in a police procedural and the latest movie ingénue.

'Anita Fay,' the policeman repeated. 'She's great.'

Wait for it, Susie told herself, and try not to smile.

3

'I don't suppose I could have her autograph?'

'Of course,' Susie replied. 'I'll get her to send you a signed photo.'

'Oh, not for me,' he insisted. 'My nephew is a big fan. His name is Gabriel, same as myself, funnily enough.'

'What a coincidence. I'll pop that in the post to you, Gabriel, and in any case we'll be talking about this incident further I'm sure.' That's rhetoric there, she wanted to point out. I don't mean there's any other option but further action, whatever that may be. But as she spent most of her day banging her head against other brick walls real and imaginary she decided to leave it for the time being. She was not entirely in charge here. Let the idea stew, stagnate and hopefully begin to grow like a fungus that had to be dealt with.

Susie and son left the stuffy building, stepping out into the still air of a balmy September evening. Milo had slung his enormous schoolbag onto his back and Susie's arm now only reached halfway across, encountering canvas before books before him. They needed to match their mood to the sunny weather.

'Young man, I think our only choice at this point is to indulge in pizza as therapy.'

'That makes sense to me, Mum.'

'I may have to have extra ham and an egg on mine.'

'Hard day then?'

'Much like your own, Milo.'

She wanted to reach out and kiss the mangled grin he gave her, but as he was now approaching

4

teenagerdom that would have been tantamount to a war crime. Instead she steered him to the high street and pizza and another odd start to a weekend. She was already practising the excuses she would issue later and the accompanying platitudes to make them palatable to her client.

★　★　★

Valerie Vine wrestled with the Chubb lock, painfully aware of the echoing sounds of her efforts throughout the stairwell. At sixty-six years of age she could expect to get away with this outside an apartment that was not her own, looking as she did both matronly and well off. When I turn to my devilish life of crime that will stand to me, she convinced herself as beads of exasperation broke out on her forehead. She could not fathom how any thief was expected to get through this door when she had such trouble using a key for it. Which was probably the point, she conceded, but that didn't help her. If she were the swearing type (she was not) she would have coloured the air blue there and then.

Footsteps clanged through the building and she heard an approach. She redoubled her efforts and jangled at the lock in one last frantic effort to get through without embarrassment.

'I can help you with that,' a light voice said. 'You are Susie's mother, aren't you?' The girl was a tiny wisp swaddled in bright red wool and a continental accent. 'I'm Isabelle,' she explained. 'Next floor up. I babysit Milo sometimes.'

'Of course. We met at the summer garden party.'

The girl expertly jiggled the keys and pushed open the heavy door. 'I'll help you with your bags,' she said, though Valerie doubted she could hoist much, being so elfin.

'Would you be a dear and drag in that number? Dodgy wheel so it can be a nuisance sometimes.' She congratulated herself silently on her tact, and was taken aback to see this minuscule Isabelle drag in the wheelie as well as the overly large Gladstone she had appropriated from her husband. If Susie was here, she thought, I'd get a lecture on underestimating the modern woman and living in the past.

The apartment stood calmly waiting for them, the darkness hinting at a home of cottage pies and scented candles. Isabelle clicked on lights familiarly while Valerie headed for the kitchen.

'Tea or something just a little stronger?' she asked. 'It is Friday, after all.'

★ ★ ★

The waitress scanned the restaurant while wringing her hair tightly into an elastic band. There was a healthy teatime crowd, most of whom would disperse in time for the ravenous had-too-many-Pinot-Grigios-after-work crowd and on into the Friday-night regulars. She tied on her white apron and crossed her fingers in hope of a tip-tastic night; funds were low and she had her usual raft of impossible bills to pay. She fought the urge to daydream about a ridiculously

6

well-paid job bathed in glamour and fame. All in its own good time, she hoped. The door opened and a blast of heat hit the air-conditioned cool in the pizzeria. A well-dressed woman came through, briefcase first, trailed by a uniformed boy near doubled over under the weight of his schoolbag. Something about the woman ticked a box in the young waitress's brain but fled the moment she tried to pin it down. She grabbed two laminated menus and approached them.

'Table for two,' the woman said. 'Non-smoking.'

And that's when she realised that this was Susie Vine, agent with Arland and Shaw. She stifled a basic instinct to tell the woman that she was about to graduate from RADA and would love her to come to see one of the showcases planned over the next few months. She felt like a giant cliché: the drama student moonlighting as a waitress to pay her fees. Sometimes the truth was too hackneyed for words and this was one of those times, she decided. Instead she ran through the specials and took a drinks order for a large glass of the house Chianti and a Coke.

She made sure to walk away with poise and a straight back and resolved to sharpen up her voice and diction for the duration of the agent's stay. She would play the part of the waitress with style, élan. Often the maid's parts were pivotal in the plots of what some of her classmates called 'snot-rag drama', the comedy of manners with fops and archetypes posing about a stage uttering brilliant epigrams and being quite vacuous. She would make her mark before this über agent, perhaps be snapped up that very night?

She remembered that one of her teachers, Mr Roe, told her not to daydream so much. Hard graft, that's what he said it was all about. Well, she could do that too, had proved so far that she could. It wasn't easy holding down an evening job and attending classes nine to five. In this last year they would perform whole plays too and host showcases, so that was to be even more work piled on. It was exciting and exhausting and she wouldn't swap it for the world. She redoubled her efforts to be the perfect Waitress One. She checked that her nametag was straight and prominent and went to fill the order.

All of this was lost on Susie Vine who could think of little but her first long slug of wine and an enforced early night in with her son rather than schmoozing a first-night crowd. She could watch the soap she had recorded featuring a new young actress she'd just taken on. After a dissection of the phone incident, of course, and possibly stern words about Milo's coterie of friends. She wondered how the play was going. Perhaps she should have asked for a pint of vodka.

★   ★   ★

John Forbes shucked out of his costume. It looked quite ridiculous lying on the seat without him inside. It was a Roundhead's uniform for the period piece he was filming. He replaced it with his own uniform of white T-shirt and jeans.

8

His mobile phone chimed out to tell of messages left and trouble to be dealt with. He sat heavily into the cushions of the small Winnebago that was his home while he was on set. A knock on the door was followed by the fresh face of an assistant director delivering the call sheet for the following day. He hated these six-day weeks.

'Not great for you, I'm afraid,' the girl said. 'It's a six-thirty pick-up in the morning. Sorry.'

'Showbiz,' he sighed. 'If only the public could see my fabulous lifestyle, eh?' He smiled wearily at the AD. 'Thanks, Phoebe. If I have to hear bad news it's always best for you to break it to me. It somehow lessens the blow.'

The girl beamed and continued her journey around their little circle of caravans to break more details, good and bad, to the other actors on the shoot.

John stretched and grimaced. He had spent the early part of the day on horseback, then filmed some heavy love scenes in the afternoon. All were long and technical, somewhat boring too and he was now feeling the strain. Pretending to make love, to prescription, was one of his least favourite bits of this job. He was not getting any younger and he lately found he had to watch what angles were planned for intimate scenes. It wasn't so much vanity as trying not to scare the public with a less than perfect physique. He was in good shape, very good shape, but age had crept in where it was supposed to naturally and he no longer had the body of the twenty-year-old he once had been. This wasn't a problem for Richard Fine, the other male lead, who had no qualms about buying a younger self, using Botox or the knife. 'Whatever keeps the jobs coming in, John.'

The great irony of the shoot was that, because of the weather they would experience between now and the end, they were filming backwards. All of the summer scenes were set a decade on in the story. When they got to the end they were at the beginning. So, after a long and gruelling shoot he was supposed to look ten years fresher.

Right now all he could contemplate was a long iced Scotch, a massage, a bath and an early night. No wild partying for him, he mused. No cocaine-fuelled romps with nymphettes. Fact was he had never really got into that scene, though he was always popular with the ladies and certainly would not die wondering what all the fuss was about. But marriage, two kids and an expensive divorce had curtailed any of show business's wilder excesses and at forty he almost felt he'd become staid. Christ, he was tired if he was letting himself indulge in a paean for a life he'd never wanted. He braced himself. Eight more weeks of the Cavaliers and Roundheads to go, then a rest, followed by the horror that was Christmas.

He hauled himself out of the seat and into the company car that would take him home. He wanted to lose himself in the soft leather and snooze but seven messages awaited. He hoped none of them required immediate action because he was beat. The first voice he heard was Roma's. Problem. End of the massage, the bath and possibly the Scotch. His heart sank as he reached for a pen to jot down the list of those he must call. He needed help. At one stage of his life he might have facetiously said he needed a wife, but he now knew that was precisely what he did not need. Some class of Sherpa or indeed an actual slave might fit the bill better. Anything but another emotional drain.

★ ★ ★

Susie waited until they were halfway through their pizzas before bringing up the problem of Milo's mates.

'So they ran off and left you?'

Milo shrugged. 'Yeah. I guess.' He barely opened his mouth as he spoke, delivering the garbled lazy diction of all of his age group, the words almost unintelligible from mere sounds: 'yareyegez'. Then he stuffed his mouth to avoid any further conversation.

'That's not the first time, is it? I'm really worried that these are not good friends for you to have, Milo.'

He gave her a 'Muuuum', to indicate that she was too old and fuddy to understand the vast complexities of being twelve-going-on-thirteen now, and a bloke, and that he couldn't bear to discuss any of this with her. Milo preferred silence during their meals, which wasn't usually a problem as his mum was often preoccupied with work. There was too much focus on him this evening. He willed her phone to ring.

'You'll have to tell your father about it,' she said. 'I'll be phoning him tonight to bring him

11

up to speed and I'm sure he'll want to talk to you over the weekend.'

Milo studied the table and nodded, trying to ignore her words. He didn't want to go through it again. He had been frightened witless when the thug from Vitas had waved the knife at him. He was still surprised he hadn't shat himself.

Susie looked at her son's dusty face, streaked with city grime. She knew that he would let himself forget what she had just said and that would simply make it go away. It was an enviable facility but not ideal for building a moral code. Milo lived for the moment and the sooner he forgot the ones he didn't like, the better for him. They continued to eat in silence, clearly preferred by Milo.

Susie wondered again about sending him to Morning Star. In truth, there hadn't really been any choice in the matter. It was the best of a bad bunch of second-level schools that had offered her son a place. He wasn't a stupid boy but he had absolutely no interest in academia and really only wanted to slack off and have fun: at his best executing pratfalls to make people laugh, and there were precious few tests in that for GCSEs. Morning Star had seemed a decent enough place. The school marched the legs off its boys, wore them further down with sports and taught them to mess about on boats. They had a neat uniform with a cute beret and middle to low standing on exam results. Milo had known Adam from primary school in Clapham, although they had never been very close, but Rafe and Gregory were new acquaintances made at Morning Star.

And even though the term was only newly under way, already they had trouble. He had friends from sailing but those classes were mainly at weekends and only sometimes on week nights. The rest of the time he was with the Morning Star entourage.

He was so easily led, she realised. For instance, he thought nothing of bidding for ridiculous items on eBay, prodded on by the others and desperately trying to amuse and impress them. This had come to light when Susie's credit-card bill showed up the transactions and he was now barred from going on the Internet at home unless he had adult supervision. It wasn't always possible to regulate what he did elsewhere. She had begun to feel a bit helpless about the whole thing. She had disciplined him fairly over the years. He hadn't had any childhood traumas he needed to work out of his system through some sort of rebellion. He was simply a weak boy with no ambition other than to be popular. She was going to have to try a new approach but had no idea what that might be. She watched him pack in his meal, thinking some table manners wouldn't go amiss. Her boy had matured so incrementally she had hardly noticed his approach to adulthood, yet here he was on the cusp of hormonal mayhem. She drained her wine and reluctantly decided against another, signalling instead for the bill.

'Come on; let's get you home. Your dad is calling for you early tomorrow.'

She paid and left a decent tip and failed yet again to notice the pretty waitress as she smiled her biggest smile and thanked her in her best Received Pronunciation. She had played her part too well and didn't attract any undue attention as a result.

★　★　★

Valerie Vine closed the door after the tiny Isabelle left and found herself all too alone in her daughter's apartment. Suddenly the weight of the past week got to her and she began to cry. The cry rose to a wail. And as suddenly as it began it stopped again. She wiped her eyes. Foolish, foolish woman, she admonished. Pull yourself together, you ridiculous old bat. Worse things happen at sea. But her heart was broken and she really felt nothing could mend that.

★　★　★

Susie watched what she ate for most of the week so that she could splurge at weekends. It wasn't that difficult a system to maintain as she usually spent at least three nights at a show or a premiere or a press night and they happened hot on foot of work, so the dash was from office to venue with no break in between. It was expedient to grab an apple or a banana in lieu of a meal and as long as she had plenty of chewing gum to mintify her hunger-breath she was fine. As an agent she worked a nine-to-five day, five days a week and was available either in the office or on her Blackberry for America to call when it woke up, first New York then Los Angeles. Her

14

list comprised mostly young talent, a handful of whom were creating heat, peaking the interest of the movie and television moguls of the New World. Oh, and she was also available twenty-four/seven on her mobile in case of client burnout or producer paranoia or casting-director angst. All told it was a way of life as much as a career. And most of the time she loved it. Enough of the time she loved it.

She struggled up the stairs of their block, groaning to Milo about how stodgy she felt. He ignored her, that being weirdo women's country.

The first sign that they had been burgled was that the Chubb lock was undone. Oh God, no, she thought, not this on top of Milo's phone, there's only so much cop action I can take. 'You stay here,' she instructed her son, sounding a lot braver than she felt. She pushed open the door and said, 'Hello?' which struck her as ridiculous the moment it left her mouth.

'Is that you, darling?'

Susie swore, silently. 'Mum?' Had she forgotten a planned visit? She didn't think so.

Valerie appeared around a corner. 'I let myself in, sweeties. Well, I had some help from that nice French girl who lives upstairs.'

Susie couldn't help but notice that Milo's face blanched, while his ears went pink, at the mention of their neighbour.

Her mother went on oblivious. 'Now isn't this jolly': a fact not a query. She hugged Milo and kissed his head. 'You are a grown man,' she exclaimed. 'And you are far too thin,' she told her daughter. 'I've opened a bottle of red.'

Susie felt a stab of agitation. This had been a bitch of a day and so far she could see no let-up. 'Milo, you need to get out of that uniform and I'm afraid you'll have to have a bath too, even if there is a risk that you'll dissolve.' He had loved a nightly bath until he hit age ten when suddenly it was taboo. She had been banished long before that in case she saw him naked. He was too big to carry to the bath and throw in, so long negotiations took place with him resorting to creative time-wasting and more and more stupid excuses as to why he couldn't wash himself. No clean towels. Towels too high in the cupboard for him to reach. Stool too heavy to drag to the airing cupboard to reach the clean towel shelf. And on, and on, and on. Tonight he shuffled off with a trademark unintelligible murmur. She'd give him a few minutes then check he was doing as he was told. The battle was ongoing and each side vigilant in its stance. I'm a five-star general, Susie reminded herself. I am the Mum. I have to win this skirmish or the war will be lost.

She followed her own mother into the living area, looking right and left for her scruffy old terrier. They had to sneak him in, as rules did not allow the keeping of pets in Berkshire Mansions. No sign of the mutt. As her mum placed a hefty tumbler of wine into her hand, Susie asked, 'Where's Toby?' and her mother fell sobbing into an armchair.

Eventually she parted with, 'I had to have him put down this morning. Cancer. Inoperable. Oh Susie, what am I to do?'

Susie felt like the original heel. She had arrived like thunder, openly bringing all of her day's frustrations with her, and had failed to notice her mother's distress.

'Mum, I am so sorry.' The older woman was curled against the arm of the chair and awkward to hug. Plus she had filled Susie's glass so full there was danger of spillage if they tried to negotiate an embrace. Susie knocked back a measure as she digested the information then said aghast, 'What will we tell Milo? He's known Toby all his life. He's never known a world without him.'

★ ★ ★

'I HATE her!' Flora was screaming down the phone now.

John Forbes took a deep breath. 'May I ask why?'

'She's a complete bitch and she doesn't want me to have any fun because you left her.'

In a nutshell.

'Flora, be reasonable. You cannot go to an all-night rave in Oxford. You are fifteen years old. You are simply too young. And this has nothing to do with Mummy not wanting you to have fun. She loves you. So do I. But there are limits to our indulgence. We cannot allow this trip.'

The fact that Flora could sing really well now stood to her as she ululated her misery. Loudly. Then, 'Everything is shit since you left, Dad. Please come home. Please.'

Things were shit before I left, he wanted to

say. But he never would. And anyway he knew she was playing him. When he had lived with the family she was never done telling him what a crap dad he was and how unhappy he made EVERYONE. And that wasn't just her opinion in case he wanted to know: EVERYONE thought the same thing. And he was a pig to make Mummy cry. And all the girls at school pitied her because she was so unhappy. And it was tragic how bad EVERYTHING was.

Time to get tough. He hardened his voice. 'Look, Flora, it really is time you grew up a bit. Both your mum and I have been very, very patient with you. In fact I'd go so far as to say we've spoiled you, and far too much. It stops right here. Do you hear me? You will be grounded without your allowance if you keep up this pathetic routine of hysterics. Do I make myself clear? And you won't go on the school trip to Rome either. So I suggest you toe the line, young lady, or face the consequences.'

She was so silent he thought she'd hung up. Then he heard a gulp and the sound of the telephone hitting the table with a clang.

After a pause his ex-wife spoke. 'Whatever you said certainly calmed her down, in a weird way.'

'Brought her to her senses more like. I threatened a grounding with no pay or school trip.'

'Ouch.'

'I presume there's a boy involved.'

'Oh yes, a flaky piece called Nicholas Huntsford. Mad for some skirt, I think. Well, you'd know, you were a teenage boy once.'

'Is there *any* way we can get her put in prison?'

'In the olden days I suppose we could have packed her off to a nunnery.'

'We have lost all of our best traditions.'

He could hear a muffled roar from the other end.

'I think she wants us to know that she never asked to be born.'

'Lovely. So some things never change, it seems. How comforting.'

★ ★ ★

Reginald Darwin hated Fridays. At his advanced age he didn't relish the idea of a weekend of inaction; he already had that most of the rest of his time. He was a scrupulous man and so did not need to spend Saturday or Sunday cleaning up in preparation for the coming week. He did all of that as he went along. Habit was a bugger but he was a creature of the same and could not change that at this late juncture. His shirts, socks, underclothes, jackets and trousers were all pressed and accounted for in their appointed places. His shoes were polished and standing to attention. His crystal and silver glistened on the sideboard. Carpets were vacuumed, floors washed and porcelain pristine. He looked at the small mountain of books by his favourite chair and failed to muster up the interest to start another. As it was, he was reading three novels simultaneously and delving into a history of Stalingrad for a second time. He needed a job to stimulate him. But that very thought sent him rummaging for the Scotch.

Settled again, he found he was perspiring slightly to think of work. He did the usual bits and pieces available to the elderly actor still able and willing to work. The grandfathers, the lordly statesmen, the mad old scientists and so on. But more and more he found himself praying for television or film work where the parts were small and the lines unchallenging. He just couldn't seem to retain much in his addled brain any more. Oh, this was his dotage and no surprise, but even the crossword was proving trickier these days and he didn't want to give in to the notion that he was headed for utter decrepitude. He had no interest in that whatsoever. His was always an active life both physically and mentally and that was the way he would have it stay, thank you very much.

Since his beloved Claire had passed on two years ago he had felt his own time slipping away from him. Part of that was the grieving process, of course. He had lost himself for a while, which was natural after losing the partner of forty-five years. She had been so ill for so long in the latter years, he needed to rest up as much as anything else after her time came to forsake the world. He had been exhausted, he found, by the sheer act of willing her alive for so long as much as the nursing. It was almost a relief to see her peacefully off and to take to his bed to rest. Some had put this down to depression but Reg thought it more likely that his batteries had needed a full recharge. This was not to diminish the grief. Oh yes, it had hit, and hard. But he was made of the stern stock that got on with life as long as it was allowed. And he did.

Perhaps there was a good documentary on one of the channels? He unfolded the television guide. Bloody glasses missing now, he thought, fumbling about. Where the blinkin' hell had he put them? Such a ruddy Catch 22 situation: he couldn't find them if he wasn't wearing them because he was short-sighted and couldn't see far past his large Roman nose to look for them. Oh, he was wearing them. Dotage, he thought again, shaking his head. He clicked on to the news and saw an item about bird flu. Well, let it come and get me. If I caught this famous deadly H5N1 I'd probably forget I had it. He chuckled at the idea that sheer forgetfulness could negate the virus. He raised his glass and toasted new and thoroughly alternative cures.

★ ★ ★

Milo took the news of Toby's death better than Susie could have hoped. He was clearly more concerned about how upset his gran was. They hunted out old photograph albums to see pictures of the dog as a pup. In one Milo was a baby lying on a blanket by a red and yellow spotted ball and opposite was a four-legged bundle with perky tail even tinier than the ball itself.

'And he'd grown by then,' Valerie exclaimed. 'He was so small I could carry him around in my pocket for the first few weeks.'

21

'He was a great dog, Gran.'

'He was good value, yes. A mad little chap. I'll miss him.'

'Have you told Grandad?'

'Oh, you know that man, he never answers his phone so I left him a message.' She avoided Susie's eye. She could have added that he never answered his phone to her, in case she was being what he termed needy. And that she had tried his number many times before giving in to the answering service. Susie had lectured her before about 'poisoning' Milo to his grandfather so she was careful not to be too negative in his presence. How she would have loved to let loose. That, however, might have led to banishment from the apartment and she did not want to be alone again in a hurry. She had had it entirely with being alone. Hot tears welled again but she blinked them back. That was another thing she was thoroughly fed up of: crying. She hugged Milo close and smelled the peppermint shampoo from his hair.

'You off to your dad's tomorrow?'

Milo nodded. 'Will you be here when I get back Sunday night?'

Again she avoided her daughter's eyes. 'I hope so, dear.'

Well, now I know the answer to one of my questions, Susie thought.

The apartment was a well-appointed, quite luxurious space that reflected Susie's healthy salary. They had space for visitors. It was incumbent on Milo, as a twelve-year-old, to host sleepovers for his friends. So, his room had a double bunk and lots of inflatable mattresses.

Valerie was installed in the bottom bed and Milo in his usual top spot. Susie oversaw the washing of teeth and the saying of goodnights, then kissed her two charges and left them to their dreams. She decided to have a quick shufti through the recording of the soap from earlier. She fast-forwarded to the scenes featuring her client and was happy with what she saw. The girl needed more camera experience but she acquitted herself well and didn't stick out. She looked pretty and sounded good and with some halfway decent storylines she'd be dangerous and highly employable.

She mooched around the apartment switching off lights and yawning, then went to her room and followed her nightly regime. She changed into a silk nightgown and proceeded to her small en suite where she removed her make-up, washed her teeth, toned and moisturised her face and neck, slathered on hand, foot and leg hydrators and returned to snuggle into bed. This was her sanctuary. It didn't matter what she looked like or what she wore. It was a reward at the end of every day and she looked forward to it, deserved it. She climbed between her crisp, pressed sheets and savoured being alone and pampered.

The rafters of the old building stretched rheumatically as a wind whipped up outside. How many lives have you shepherded? she thought. How many seasons have you endured in your care of the world? A substratum of sound was emerging now. Susie stiffened as she recognised the sounds of a woman in agony. This was happening with regularity and she worried that the tenants next door had chained up a poor unfortunate and were torturing her. In fact it was merely rough sex and the woman was a screamer but the sounds were so distressing that she had considered calling the police as a precaution on more than one occasion. The papers were full of stories of people found dead after months or even years and she didn't want to live with the guilt that she could have saved a life and had not. She sweated to hear the noises and felt dirty. There was no more mystery to it than that a couple was having intercourse next door. After so long without, Susie felt uneasy intruding in any way on their dealings. She reached for earplugs and stuffed them in. Maybe she just needed to get laid. She grunted derisorily. She definitely needed to get laid, no maybe about it. Must put that on my 'to do' list, she chuckled, that'll get it sorted. Not.

★　★　★

Valerie's eyes grew accustomed to the dark. She watched Milo's round shape above her shift and morph. The springs of the bunk bed stretched and recoiled. He snuffled in his sleep. Then his legs began to thrash gently. Dreaming, she thought. Perhaps he was winning a marathon. Maybe he was being chased. Then she heard him laugh and imagined the thorough pleasure he was experiencing; no laugh was ever so good as the one we dreamed.

24

Her toes missed the feel of Toby's fur. She should never have allowed the dog onto the bed but he was company and better than any hot water bottle. He always began the night on top of the covers but by morning when Valerie woke he was underneath. It was so lovely to look into his trusting face each day and to know that he thought the world of her. He never found her clingy or irritating, as her husband seemed to. He didn't find her boring when she discussed current affairs or the many Amnesty International campaigns she wrote letters for. He didn't think her ridiculous for going on marches to highlight wrongs, even if they were local ones only attended by a handful of bored housewives and some crusties. And he never, ever criticised her cooking, even if it didn't contain meat.

She was beset by worry and panic. She breathed slowly, deeply, to calm herself. She felt alone, vulnerable. She was suddenly very afraid of dying. And then she realised that an even worse thing would be to lose another of her small circle of intimates. There was no way she could lie here and let this mood strengthen, she knew the dreadful consequences of that and the days she would lose to worry and despair. She slid noiselessly from the bed and went in search of warm socks. Then she intended to drink a pint of water to ward off the effects of too much wine. She really must not let herself get this drunk again; it provoked all sorts of havoc in her and life was tough enough without bringing that upon oneself.

Susie's mind would not slow down. She lay with her eyes closed and went through a list of things she would need to chase up for an hour or so tomorrow. She had left the office in a dash because of Milo and hadn't quite cleared her desk. It had been a horrible day and she didn't enjoy replaying it in her head. A movie everyone had worked hard on had folded when the finance had fallen through. She had done a demon deal for one particular client but the agreed fee had never made it to the magical escrow account, where fees for actors were posted pre-production and where the money would have been untouchable no matter what the outcome of the overall financial package. So, when the movie collapsed they were left with nothing but the bittersweet taste of what might have been. The client had been sanguine. 'For an hour there I was actually quite rich,' he said. 'It felt good.'

Show business was no business on this occasion. If the film makers were particularly tenacious and got a break from somewhere, they might get the project back on track in the future. In her experience, when a film missed its moment it was usually dead in the water. Some producers and directors were savvy and brave enough to recognise this and let it go, in spite of what might have been years of work to get it to this point. Others were not and could not let it go which sometimes meant the end of a career whiled away on a dead duck or a very dated and inferior work when the movie finally emerged.

The hardest lesson to learn was to know when to quit. She had called most of the people who needed to know of the film's demise but there were a few loose ends that needed chasing.

She sat upright. Her laptop was still at the office. No wonder her shoulder felt so relaxed. She hadn't been hauling it around in her bag all evening. Well, that meant a trip into work for sure the following day. If the office was burgled between now and then she was done for because she had a lot on the computer that she hadn't backed up. Bloody Milo's bloody mobile phone. She had left so quickly she'd paid naff all attention to her usual routine. She shifted uncomfortably, her mind whirring. Dammit, I'm not going to be able to get back to sleep now. She got out of bed and into a bathrobe, then crept to the kitchen to make hot chocolate. Great, this on top of pizza and lashings of wine, I am going to be a spongy heap by Monday. A blue shadow fell across the stainless-steel hob as she sloshed low-fat milk into a saucepan.

'Could I put my name in the pot too?'

Mother and daughter sat awkwardly on the sofa not wanting to make too much noise yet willing idle conversation to work off some of the stillness of the wee small hours.

'I'm so afraid of dying or losing someone close,' Valerie said, wondering at her blunt honesty. Well, it was out there now. 'I'm feeling a little abandoned at the moment. I know that's probably unfair and also not quite the case but I can't help it.'

'Oh Mum,' Susie said, wrapping an arm

around her shoulder. 'We're here for you, you know that.'

'It's so long since someone hugged me,' Valerie said. 'No one thinks to touch old people. Why is that?'

2

It seemed only five minutes since John had closed his eyes. The hated bleep of his electronic alarm stirred him and he knew that if he didn't swing his legs out of the bed immediately and make to rise he would go back into a deep sleep and be late for collection. He staggered blindly to his kitchen and the espresso machine he had paid a fortune for. It was his lifeline on these impossible mornings. As the machine spat forth hot caffeine, he scourged himself between hot and cold water in the shower. Sleepiness departed, muscles unlocked and humanity tried to peep out at another day. His buttocks and thighs were sore, as predicted, from horse riding the previous day but all in all he could have been in worse shape. He wiped the bathroom mirror of condensation and checked his red-rimmed eyes and stubbly chin and cheeks. A quick shave and some eye drops and he was ready to sit at the breakfast bar and savour his coffee, a fine Blue Mountain Java. If he hadn't needed it so much he might have paused to think of exploitation in far-off climates but he did so need this so he made a remote vow to adjust to another brand, if ethics called for it, just as soon as he had something resembling a normal life again. For now, it was background guilt and he could manage that.

A buzz on the intercom, the squawk of the

driver's voice and he was off again. He hit the day as sunrise began to streak across the sky in shades of orange, pink and blue and thought, all over again, that legions of adoring fans would never believe the length and mundanity of most filming days. He longed to be back in his bed sunk in the arms of some wondrous dreams. He thought of the other actors being spirited across London to the set and those already preparing the site. Caterers were frying and grilling, boiling and baking the first of the day's meals. His tummy rumbled. They had been blessed with good cooks on this shoot. A film crew marches on its stomach and nothing fomented disquiet more than bad food. He had been on other jobs when whole sections had refused to work because of poor catering. Production assistants would check the trailers were aired, warm and ready. Wardrobe would be laying out costumes and make-up putting on their own faces before the challenge of tired actors arrived.

He smiled at the London sunrise and slipped happily into a short, stolen sleep.

★　★　★

Susie rose early as much through habit as desire. Today was no different although it was officially down time. In a way, there was no such thing since Milo joined her life. She stood before her lounge window and the narrow view of Clapham Common, which she loved. The stealthy crawl of an urban fox took her eye as it skulked from shelter to shelter in the trees. Soon the

30

stick-throwing dog walkers would appear, then families off on their weekend jaunts. Cyclists would whizz by, and around the edges, constantly, the city's cars thrummed and sped regardless of the hour.

She shouted to Milo again, warning that his dad would be here soon and they would miss their boating time if he didn't give it some wellie. Her head throbbed, as much from yesterday's vexations as the amount she'd drunk last night. Valerie sat at the table demolishing an apple. Noisily. It occurred to Susie that she didn't much like watching people eat.

'You know these organic apples are head and shoulders better than the tasteless, cheaper nonsense in the supermarkets,' Valerie said between mouthfuls.

The return snipe was a reflex action. 'I agree. But let's not forget that those particular ones are imported from America and the air fuel alone to get them here probably negates all of the good health and environmental kudos we're hoping for.'

'You're very negative this morning.'

That rankled Susie. Steady, she thought, this is the classic mother-daughter wind-up. The remark was innocent enough, no need to read great theses into it. 'Milo, now!'

She caught her mother making a little face. 'What?' she demanded.

'Nothing, dear, really.'

I am tired and cranky, Susie thought, mustn't take it out on the others. Much as I'd like to. 'Sorry.'

'A little snooze when Milo is gone and you'll be right as rain for the day.'

'I really need him to eat before he goes.'

'I'll get him, you rustle up his breakfast.'

They got half a bowl of cereal and a pancake into Milo by the time the bell rang. Chris Falucci stood huge and handsome in the doorway a moment later, ready to take charge of his son. Valerie was quiet but for the niceties of weather and hoping all was well with Chris's other family. She really didn't know what to say to the man and never had. Susie's relationship with him had been a little too unorthodox for her mother and father, and the fact that Chris had a gangster's name and was of Italian extraction confirmed for them that they were better leaving well enough alone. Their other children had made conventional marriages so they could afford one maverick, they supposed. And the union had produced Milo who was more than enough compensation for a little family notoriety.

Susie took him aside briefly to say, 'I'm going to trust you to tell your dad all about your mobile phone and those friends of yours.' She thrust a banana into her son's hand and looked at both of them, amazed at how like his father Milo had become. They were dark and brown-eyed, mischievous and stubborn.

'How did you get so big?' she asked, making to tousle his hair.

He pulled away saying, 'Mum, don't start that again.'

She wondered if they would ever return to the

32

time when a hug and a kiss were normal, everyday events.

Chris looked back to wave, a sight that would probably have melted most women on the planet. All Susie could think was that men were a luxury item that she could ill afford. Of course there was Max, but he was another proposition and she didn't have the energy to go there right now. She smiled wanly at the disappearing men in her life. Leaving Valerie to battle with the dishwasher she allowed herself an extra hour in bed, alone, which was as close to decadence as she ever got these days. She ignored the Bigger Issues. Milo's ability to reject awkward ideas was not taken from the wind.

★　★　★

Reginald regretted his courtship of the Scotch bottle from the moment he opened his eyes. Not that it had taken much to bring on this hangover. It never did any more, which was another down-side of age, he felt. He remembered hedonistic days on national tours when a bottle of Scotch a day counted as nothing. In fact he knew still-eminent actors who had been famous for downing a bottle during the day, turning in a performance, then sculling another before bed. He had never truly been a member of the school of utter soaks, nor had he wanted to, but he could certainly hold his drink when required. In those days there was no shame to drunken high spirits, as they were seen, as long as the work got done, and somehow it did. Not that he was nostalgic for those times. There had been moments, yes, but when one looked back and realised that a decade of memories was largely missing from one's life, it was hard to justify those good times he heard and read about but couldn't quite remember. He popped some aspirin and prayed for a swift death. When it was clear that would not be today he padded to the kitchen to brew some weak tea: leaves in a pot not bags in a mug, naturally.

He had also spent an unconscionably long time in bed. It was now past noon and therefore long past time to wash, dress and get the papers. Saturday and Sunday were days for the full range of broadsheets and at the rate he was going he would have made little inroad on the news by the time he was due to leave for the theatre. A friend was taking a part in a Beckett play at the Barbican and he was on a promise for some time to attend.

He wasn't sure if he was looking forward to the content of the evening. He liked his Beckett funny but some directors only went for the bleakness of vision. Reg liked to laugh with old Samuel's death and failure and the tiny unwanted triumphs of the ordinary, like breathing, or simply being. Of course Shakespeare had said it all first, hadn't he? 'To be or not to be, that is the question.' Reg's voice was a rasp, so dehydrated from that demon drink. He was no great fan of water but he sipped a lukewarm drop and tucked into his sweetened tea.

He had played Hamlet once, touring to schools and universities in the regions. Had a lovely affair with his Ophelia. Nice lass named Moira who had the good sense to chuck in the life and marry a rich consultant. Had he broken her heart a little? Time dimmed the edges of memory or sometimes the mind didn't want to remember at all, particularly the petty cruelties that darkened the shine on a life. The closer one came to a day of reckoning the harder it was to admit to regrets, especially if they had been hurtful to others. He had met Moira once more, oh, twenty years later, and hadn't recognised her at first. Different hair colour, different shape, a different person really which was only to be expected when one thought about it. She seemed thoroughly happy with her life and was sanguine about ditching her Art. 'Well, if you remember, Reg,' she said, 'I wasn't very good at it anyhow. The business was better off without me clogging up the ranks, although I'm sure Equity missed my humble dues for a while.' He was starring in a popular soap at the time and for a brief moment he thought she might have slept with him again, happy life or no. When he thought about it later he couldn't decide whether it would have been for nostalgia's sake or the fact that he was mildly famous. He never did find out, for the moment passed without incident and they went their separate ways again. He wondered if she was still alive.

★ ★ ★

Susie was not the only agent in the office that day. Mitch Douglas was worrying the phones and swearing gently. She waved at him and he was unsurprised to see her as she was to see him. There were never enough hours in any day to look after all of the details of all of the situations their clients were involved in. Mitch had charge of corporate appearances by clients and voice-over work. At any hour of the day or night people needed entertaining somewhere in the world and Mitch often had the performer they were looking for. He had the job everyone else avoided. Ten pissy, circular phone calls might yield one job, well paid or not. At the same time he brought in as much money as any of the others, which meant, pound for pound, he was punching well above his weight as an agent.

'Trouble in gig paradise?' she asked.

'A last-minute pull-out from a big insurance do tonight so I'm trying to shoehorn one of ours into the breach. Logistical nightmare.

The wonder was that more of the staff wasn't playing catch-up. What was interesting was that Jay Burns was at his desk. He almost never worked later than his allotted hours, or if he did it was from home or his Blackberry while travelling loudly to some trendy destination. Susie disliked Jay. She hated the ultra-male, testosterone-fuelled shit he spouted to all. She hated his sharp suits and designer sunglasses. She hated his expensive, witty shirts and just-gay-enough shoes. There was no denying that he was very effective and did great deals for his clients but it was no excuse for being a pathetic human being. And she would never forgive him the day he leaned over her desk and said, 'The only reason you don't like me is that when you look at me, you recognise yourself.'

It was always interesting to see the office without its full complement of staff and bustle. When the company had moved here several years ago it was a minimalist marvel of aluminium and dark wood, stylish and calm. They had collectively decided to operate a neat-desk policy and started with all of the good intentions of pioneers, but the design and beautiful materials could not halt the march of paper. Every space quickly became dominated by it. A great volume of scripts came through the door or was delivered each day electronically and transferred to print. Then stacks of reading matter and scripts to be disseminated to clients became mountains on all available surfaces. A regular cull only just kept the behemoth within manageable limits. The teetering volumes had nearly reached problematical proportions again and Susie skirted them gingerly, aware that they would pack a mighty bruise if they toppled onto her.

The laptop was sitting patiently atop two scripts on her desk. She took a moment to wonder if that was exactly where she'd left them. Something didn't seem quite right. She was probably being fanciful, Lord only knew why. She stowed all three items in her bag and should have made a bolt for the door there and then. She couldn't resist checking her voicemail on the phone then email on the big desk Mac and even neglected snail mail in the tray, and ninety minutes later she was still replying. My own stupid fault, she reminded herself, but these were the old habits that died hard and the reason she was worth every penny of the fifteen per cent the agency charged for her services.

Her favourite item from today was an email from an American director who was chasing an exciting young client, Craig Landor, for a movie he'd written and hoped to direct.

From: marty@direkshun.com
To: susie@arlandshaw.co.uk
Sent: 27 september 03.00
Subject: Glory Days

Dear Susie,
It was lovely to meet you over the phone today. As you know I really feel Craig is the actor for this movie. The subject matter, a pioneering scientist in eighteenth-century Wisconsin, is unusual and will certainly challenge him in ALL the right ways. The movie has everything IN SPADES! — historical relevance, morality versus progress and a great love interest. I really believe he will respond to the script. I am also anxious to have your feedback too, of course. I would love to meet with Craig and wonder if we could schedule that in for the near future? I am in the process of putting my production team together and will be in London soon. My producers are EXCITED that such a name as Craig's be attached to the project and I know that backers will realise his potential too. His

star will RISE EVEN HIGHER through this project.

I look forward to hearing your thoughts,
Marty

It wasn't the dooziest of all the emails she'd ever got about how her clients would benefit from the magnificence of a project but she had a feeling that this correspondence could grow, pushing language to new infinities. She noted that the email had been sent at 3 a.m. his time and wondered if that was after that extra sneaky bottle of wine (at home — no one in Los Angeles seemed to drink to excess in public any more) or coming down off a coke binge. His script wasn't bad, needed polishing, and she had a meeting with Craig to talk about it on Monday after he'd read and thought about it over the weekend. The guy's track record was reasonable, with a brace of independent hits under his belt and one ill-judged but harmless mini blockbuster that everyone had seen but no one really remembered. This project had possibilities and possibilities always made her tingle. She smiled a happy smile and decided to call it quits. Mitch waved again as she left. Jay continued to ignore her. It was exactly how she liked it.

Saturdays were predictable. There was always one more thing to be done at the office then it was home, via the supermarket and dry cleaners, to tackle the wash pile and organise everything for the week ahead. And there always seemed to be dinner to eat at a friend's house. As she came back through the apartment door she heard

Valerie chatting. She called out, 'Susie, Max is on the phone.' Val handed over the phone and said, 'He can't make tonight.'

'I'm sure he can tell me that himself, Mum.' She went to her bedroom to finish the call.

'Sorry about that, she got it out of me almost without my noticing,' Max said.

'She's a mother, it's one of the skills.'

'So listen, Susie, I'm sorry for the short notice.'

'Don't worry about it, although this is the umpteenth time. If we're not careful people will think we've split up.'

They both laughed at that, knowing it to be true. She expected him to comment, make a joke, but he didn't.

'Everyone took that rather badly last time, as I recall,' she continued. 'Hence our present arrangement.'

In fact their friends wouldn't hear tell of them breaking up and it was easiest to capitulate and pretend they were reconciled. It wasn't such a bad deal, actually: she had arm candy and an occasional bedfellow and Milo had another adult bloke to hand.

'We should probably talk about it soon,' Max said.

'But not now, I have a woman on board who likes to eavesdrop through several sets of walls.'

'So,' her mother said, after she had rung off and replaced the phone in its cradle.

'So,' she returned.

Susie could hold a silence. It was a tactic she used when manipulating a deal or a decision out of a client. Valerie was her match, holding her eye while she was at it.

'What?'

'Has he stood you up terribly?'

'I think we're both a bit long in the tooth to be talking about standing the other up but yes, he has. It's no big deal.'

'Sophie and Phil's tonight, I believe. How are they?'

She gave in. 'Would you like to come along, then you can ask them yourself?'

'Oh no, no, I really couldn't impose.' She did a flustered flutter of the hands.

'You could.'

Valerie took a moment, as if mulling it over. 'Well, if you think it would be all right?'

Now it almost looked like Susie's idea. She quashed the smart remark which would have borrowed another and on into a typical family row full of hollow retorts and years of over-familiarity.

Val had rearranged the kitchen and gathered a row of cleaning products on the countertop. 'Mum, why are these out especially?'

'You might want to stop using those lines, dear. I'm afraid those companies have terrible records of animal testing or polluting the environment. I can give you a list of alternatives.'

'I assume we'll finish these, now that they're here.'

The wrinkle of Valerie's nose revealed this was the wrong answer. 'That's up to you, dear.'

Susie muttered an excuse about being too busy to pay enough attention and how shameful that was, to which her mother said, 'Time is something I have plenty of. I can care for all of us.' It was a perfect mixture of martyrdom and priggishness guaranteed to make a daughter boil. It also suggested she wasn't going anywhere soon.

★   ★   ★

Sophie was married to Phil and they had a house full of squishy sofas and children off the south side of Clapham Common. This was a pleasant stretch of the legs across the greenery from Susie's apartment on the Pavement in Clapham Old Town and not as much of a challenge as the schlep to Islington to visit Tasha and Jan. The brisk momentum of the walk created a tiny self-generated breeze and blew away any cobwebs that dared take up residence. Susie had opted to bring two bottles of Prosecco, keeping matters Italian for the inevitable bowl of pasta at their hosts. Weekends were carbo-centric, hence Susie's salads and chewing-gum regime Monday to Friday.

Susie had taken care to dress her favourite gloves into the front pocket of her handbag because Sophie and Phil had brought them from Florence for her last birthday. They were a fine, red leather with black dots and Milo called them her ladybird gloves. They poked out, looking jauntily exquisite. Valerie had taught her children to send thank-you cards immediately after a party or a kindness shown and to always wear a present of clothing to the appropriate house or in the company of the person who had gifted it. Simple manners, she said, and it cost nothing. Hence Susie's childhood was scarred as she was forced regularly to wear a hideous brown jumper to her Grandma Vine's. She always prayed fervently, there and back, that she would not run into a friend and be disgraced forever. Her brother and sister never gave her grief about it because they had similar items they were doomed to sport so they adopted an honour-amongst-thieves code. Her joy was unalloyed the day it fitted her no more. It was replaced by a striped nylon blouse that made her hair stand on end and gave little shocks to anyone who touched her. This was her introduction to the idea of swings and roundabouts.

They were greeted at the door by Maya, fourteen going on forty, and assaulted by the twin smells of garlic and cream. Susie's tummy rumbled delight like a traitor savouring the Judas kiss. Maya took their coats and scarves and made conversation when pushed, answering every question on an upward inflection, which was annoying but ensured that she never sounded as though she was giving an opinion, merely answering with another question and therefore unlikely to offend. Milo had a similar affliction, adding an interrogative curl at the end of sentences that indicated a subject was so interesting, a question should be asked about it. It was the badge of their age and an excellent fobbing-off device.

Phil enveloped the women and made a huge fuss of Valerie whom he had not seen in a while.

Susie double-kissed the assembly and went in search of glasses for the hooch. Sophie was red and happy and, frankly, looked pregnant but Susie desisted from inquiring about that, having been wrong on more than one previous occasion, which had led to Sophie obsessing about her size and threatening to go on hunger strike. It suited her to carry some weight, in the way that it had done nothing for Susie when she was big.

'Look at your lovely nails,' Sophie sighed. 'And your shiny hair.'

'If I had to do anything more than type by way of manual labour I wouldn't be able to keep these talons so pristine,' Susie explained. 'And the tresses have to be kept in check too. Have to look groomed and shipshape. All part of the job.'

'How's work?' Tasha wanted to know. 'What should I be seeing?'

'The latest incarnation of *Blithe Spirit* at the Albery is a total triumph and my client Gavin Frye is superb.'

'And might you have told us if he was even just a teeny bit ordinary in it?' Jan teased.

'Not even if he was awful would you hear me utter the word,' she admitted. 'Happily he is tremendous in the play and it's a great night out, even for a jaded palate like my own. Highly recommended.'

'Well, that's the culture sorted till Christmas,' Tasha told her partner Jan. 'We don't go to the theatre often enough. But it's an expensive mistake if you get the wrong show.'

Sophie covered her ears and let out some 'Wahs'.

'What?' Tasha asked. 'What did I say?'

Phil laughed. 'You uttered the C word, the bad C word. Soph has decided to get into her annual tizzy about the season to be jolly, in spite of the fact that she's brilliant at it and it's months away and everything goes swimmingly every year.' He put his arms around his wife's waist and she wriggled away, slapping him gently as if he'd embarrassed her. It would have been gag-making in any other couple but somehow they got away with it, probably because they had never once had to cover up a single secret from one another or pretend to be anything they were not. Susie was so used to them together that she didn't envy this world she'd never had or a situation that seemed a million miles beyond her still. This was Phil and Sophie, for goodness sake: an everyday miracle.

'What have you been up to, Valerie?' Jan asked.

Susie held her breath a moment, wondering how much of the truth her mother would part with, but Valerie had been too well bred to poop on a party and simply said, 'Oh, you know me, endlessly on a quest to rid the world of badness. I'm deeply into an Amnesty campaign to end gender violence at the moment. And the local cinema is under threat from developers. My right hand has practically fallen off with all of the letters I've written in the past fortnight.'

'Repetitive strain injury,' Jan said. 'I get a bit of that from thumping a keyboard all day. Mind you, I won't save the world doing my job whereas you just might doing yours.'

Valerie shrugged. 'I wish I could say it was

entirely altruistic but the truth is that it keeps me busy.'

They sat at the patio table to pick at antipasti and Sophie hauled a tray of food into the den where the children had been banished.

'Jan thinks we should have a kid,' Tasha said. No one got too excited to hear this. It was a perennial idea though it usually sprouted forth for Christmas like a showy poinsettia that would dazzle, wither and be forgotten by 2 January. They were early this year.

'But I thought you weren't even allowed a cat in your building,' Valerie remarked.

Tasha snorted. 'I think they'd make an exception for a baby, even if it did belong to two such shocking lesbians as ourselves.'

Valerie reddened. She had meant to be amusing and now felt gauche and old. 'I didn't mean to offend,' she stumbled.

Jan hooted. 'Oh, you didn't, Valerie. Tasha just loves saying the word lesbian. Gets some sort of weird kick out of it. Or perhaps she's not convinced that she is one.' She arched a mocking eyebrow and got a pimento-stuffed olive in the face.

'Now, now, children,' Sophie said as she returned, 'play nice.'

'Do you know what I've always wondered?' Phil was asking Susie. 'You know all of those lookalike pictures on the back of acting newspapers? Well, some of them don't look remotely like the star they're meant to be impersonating and surely if it's a photograph then they're going to take it under ideal conditions and be the most like the person that they can be and then pick the best one of those to print and yet there they are looking nothing like the famous person, so what's all that about?' He was pink and out of breath.

'Well, Phil,' Susie began, kindly, as if explaining a religious mystery to a child, 'you know the way not every carpenter is a good carpenter, much less a great one, yet they still advertise their services? I guess you could say it's a bit like that.'

'Good answer,' Sophie said, clapping.

'Yes,' Susie smiled. 'I hadn't given it much thought till now but I must remember that reply. That could see me through a number of sticky moments. Well done me.' She raised her glass and made a toast then bawled for pudding, at which point she realised 'I am pissed' and said as much. A tiny, bat-shaped wine stain appeared on her peach-coloured blouse.

'I love it when you're not being perfect,' Sophie said, passing the salt.

★   ★   ★

Actors and their guests milled about the bar, all watching one another to see who was watching whom. Or at least that's how it seemed to Reginald. He stood in line to be served and was delighted and horrified in equal measure as a woman allowed him to take her turn. It was a classic illustration of age before beauty and he hoped no one he knew had seen it. He took his chance all the same and ordered his small round, asking the young woman if she would like anything while he was about it. She declined politely, saying she was in company, and he went on his way knowing from her expression that she couldn't decide whether she recognised him from somewhere or he reminded her of her grandfather. He hoped neither was that bad an option. Could bear an uncanny resemblance to Hitler, then where would he be?

He sat at the table with some old comrades and they threw about some business gossip including the scandal that an old mucker of their acquaintance had disappeared to America for a few months and come back looking remarkably younger. Plastic surgery was the only answer.

'He looks like he's had a stroke, of course,' Reg's pal Arthur said. 'Can hardly squeeze a sentence out he's so frozen in the face. Hilarious.'

'Has it improved his chances of getting cast?' Reg asked, not knowing what to make of the situation.

'No, he's still a mediocre actor. I think that will always be his cross.'

'Oh, agreed. It's just that I never knew he was so vain.'

'Old age does terrible things to a man, let alone an Actor.' Arthur delivered the word in two very separate sounds, Ak-Tor. 'I don't think he could deal with losing the pretty-boy aspect he had in his youth, though I must say I thought his face had recently taken on some character in spite of the fact he's an idiot.'

'Nice voice.'

'Yes. Made a fortune in voice-overs down the years.'

'Hope so. Wasn't he married a few times? Bet the few bob came in handy for alimony and the like.'

Young actors from a new play streamed in laughing and making an entrance. Reg smiled indulgently. 'They carry an invincibility about them, don't they? As if they will live forever. Anything else is unthinkable in their vitality. Good luck to them.'

And he meant it.

★　★　★

Valerie lay in the bottom bunk, wondering at her predicament. I am a grown woman, in the autumn of my years, and I am sleeping over in my grandson's bedroom. In effect I am holed up here, a fugitive. It's hardly the most dignified position to be in at my age. Yet there was comfort in it. Susie was next door, Milo would be home later and the others were only a bell away. All except for Alistair who had stopped returning her calls. He probably thought he was being kind, in the long run. They had been separated just short of a year now. He had left early in January, probably acting on a New Year's resolution. If so, it was the only one he had ever kept. He still didn't get the idea that she liked to talk to him, to relate a day's events. And she was beginning to twig that he didn't care how she spent her time, to put it mildly, probably hadn't for longer than she cared to guess at. In fact, the creeping suspicion was that he found her boring. She must be the slowest human being in the world not to have noticed this before now.

They had seemed well matched when they married. The sixties had hit London with colourful decadence, but their edge of the Devon coast was largely unaffected. She was the child of old-fashioned parents, as was Alistair, and neither one was after fireworks although they had their certain frisson she was sure. He was solid husband material and she was destined to be a perfect mother. They were handsome together, as the family album attested. They would have their children and the companionship and support of the other and a large group of friends to share their lives with. These were the aspirations of their place and time, and decent ones too.

After rearing three children, seeing them off into the world, they settled into their deserved, quiet later life. It was more than a shock that her dependable Alistair had just upped and left. The man was sixty-four, for crying out loud. How would he manage? He couldn't boil an egg, let alone cook himself a meal. He probably thought a special house fairy brought clean shirts. Had he lost his mind? There was no one else, he said, answering her first panicked question. He just wanted to be alone. He couldn't stay a day longer.

Had she missed years of signs that this was their destiny? Or did the situation present itself of a sudden even to him? Could she have prevented it by changing, because it did seem that she was the main cause of his leave-taking. He said as much. She appeared to drive him to the brink of exasperation. There was no other woman to blame. No one new had come between them. There was no one to hate but herself. She was cheated of another figure to obsess about. She was the only one she could point a finger at, if Alistair's version of events was to be believed. It wasn't much to show for all those years of marriage, the sacrifices, the compromises; all so much wasted time if he was to be listened to.

The shame in the face of her peers was excruciating. She could hardly leave the house in the first weeks of her abandonment. If she had been widowed, at least there would have been a structured course to follow, but this was uncharted ground of the most hurtful sort. She didn't know how to proceed so she hid. There in her idyllic cottage, roses climbing along the trellises and arches preparing to bloom cheerily for a season, daffodils waving to the passers-by, she was singular and bereft. The world was burgeoning with possibility but she was finished. Any kindness shown exacerbated her condition, and was such a painful indicator of her plight that she stopped answering the door to callers and more often than not hid behind the telephone-answering machine she had so opposed letting into the house. She also suspected everyone of wanting to grub over the details of her straitened circumstances for general gossip and trusted no one as a result.

The one thing she did not let herself do was

51

descend into her dressing gown. It was tempting to go the route of looking as wretched as she felt so that he would know how devastated she was, how utterly torn apart. But she was also proud. She rose, bathed and dressed every day, taking great care with her make-up. The last thing she would allow was to give anyone the satisfaction of thinking she had let herself go. And thus she was also prepared and looking good for when Alistair came crawling home begging to be taken back. She bought waterproof mascara at the supermarket in the next town along on a late-night foray to stave off any streaking if tears accompanied his return. She wished all outings could be kept to the dead of night when she was sure the other oldsters in the village would be asleep or drunk and unaware of her movements. The power of the pre-dinner gin and tonic or sherry along with wine for digestion was her greatest ally in other people's houses. She avoided alcohol as it made her maudlin while she was drinking and panicked when she was hungover. She tried to steer a boring middle course between emotions she had control over so that the ones that hijacked her could be dealt with a little easier. It helped but it didn't mend her problem.

She didn't tell the family for two whole months and would have left it longer if Milo hadn't spotted the inconsistencies of his grandfather's supposed whereabouts. First to swoop was Chloe, self-appointed matriarch of the children, doing her best Angel of Mercy impersonation. Her face got into a prim aspect during this routine and her expression seemed to add the word 'poor' before a name in a way that annoyed Valerie more than usual so she sent her packing. Tim was chosen by Chloe as the next to be dispatched. Big, stolid, dependable Tim; the eldest of her brood. He didn't have the vocabulary for the job and only succeeded in standing by the fireplace wringing his hands and looking as if he might burst into tears. He singed his best trousers quite badly, actually, and Valerie made a note to replace those. She rallied long enough to convince him that she was fine and waiting for their father to come to his senses, which he would, as they all knew in their heart of hearts. In the meantime she was simply avoiding the village bitchery by lying low. He bought that version of events and Valerie bought some time.

She warded off other attempts to help her, or interfere. Days would pass without speaking to anyone, broken only by accidental spells of chatting when caught out in the front garden or walking Toby. When these occurred, the conversations consisted of light words strung together about mundanities and the weather. She made sure to keep things that way. A talk with the dog was usually a fairly one-sided affair, which they both enjoyed enough to repeat regularly. Somewhere along the line she gleaned that Alistair was living in the rooms above his office and began to pester him with requests to come home. She phoned often, sometimes spoke to him though he rarely engaged in conversation. She wrote him letters. She tried to detail the substance of their marriage and how it was too awful for him to throw it over as he had. She listed the reasons they should be together still. She dished out a lot of purple prose, finding it best captured the importance of her message. Occasionally he left her a message, to the tune that she should get on with her life as he was with his. He continued to pay the bills and, ever practical, paid her a healthy allowance. She would have preferred to have her husband back.

She began to fantasise about Alistair becoming ill and needing her. He might have a heart attack and ask for her as the ambulance wailed on its emergency dash to the hospital. She would rush to his side and they would never speak of what he had done, only that he must live for both of them. Or he might discover a lump on his neck and need her support through the tests and eventual chemotherapy. She would buoy his spirits and make him laugh in spite of the seriousness of his predicament. This scenario needed work, as the idea of Alistair laughing volubly would necessitate a complete change of character, though of course crises brought out the best in people. Whatever the case, he would realise that he could not manage without her, that she was the fulcrum of his world and the reason he was now still alive. She would nurse him back to full health after his stay in hospital, or help him die with dignity, whichever diagnosis came to pass. They would quietly rediscover their old ease and the happiness he had so foolishly thrown up, however briefly.

Little by little, as it became clear that daydreams were simply that, she began to accept her new status and to get busy again. She had to. She eschewed group activities but took up causes that involved correspondence. And as long as she had Toby to walk and to talk to she could get from one end of the day to the other. When he became so ill so suddenly, she was frightened beyond her comprehension. This had been nowhere on her agenda, never a part of the sickness fantasies. She couldn't imagine how to continue without him, though she had no problem planning Alistair's funeral by then. And on the terrible day of her little friend's death, as she held his body and felt his last breath escape and his warmth start to chill, she reached a zenith of despair. She left his remains with the vet to be disposed of, went home and knocked back two swift sherries. Then she watered her plants, stored her plate, cup and saucer, packed her bags and headed for London. Which was how she came to be here on her grandson's territory, washed up and at retirement age. She had no plan of action, just enough clean clothes to last her a fortnight. It was only as the train pulled into Paddington that she realised she hadn't even considered going to any of her other children. It hadn't occurred to her. They could make of that what they would. And they would, she supposed.

*　*　*

Susie was shocked to wake up in her bed the following morning, fully clothed and made up, her head banging like a battering ram. How had she got home? What had she said, done? She reeked of soured cream, garlic, and vinegared wine. She tried to waylay her aching head by tracing a plaster crack across the old ceiling, testament to the aches and trials of its two hundred years of service. She was ferociously uncomfortable, lying there with her heart racing, bathed in perspiration, but unwilling to get out of bed. Her head thundered and her thoughts were unmanageable. She led a controlled life, carefully modulating events in her work, and had so little time to invent situations in her life that didn't already exist, a full-fledged hangover was an exotic but unwelcome sensation. Actually, agony sort of got there better as a description of what she was feeling.

Groaning, she remembered dominating the conversation last night, roaring about the government and the arts, irrespective of whether the others were even interested in the subject. She really had no manners. Oh Christ, she'd even cried. What was all that about? What had she been weeping for? Please don't let it have been about something I was trying to keep secret. Everything seemed impossible now. Every decision she had ever made was wrong, very wrong, the worst kind of wrong, disastrous. She was an unfit mother, daughter, friend, agent, human being. Dung below a farmer's boot. No, that was organic and useful. She was less than that. A twisted, rusty nail sticking into a naked foot, infecting a system and killing the host? Yep, that was the territory she now inhabited. If she didn't get some paracetemol into herself rapidly her head would burst open and end this trial there and then. That would be a mercy to her but create many difficulties for those innocents left behind. If Sophie could see her now she wouldn't be calling her anything like perfect. She moaned aloud; oh, this too, too solid flesh. Somewhere she was sure she could hear bells ringing and it might have been at a church or it could be in her head or perhaps someone was listening to an obscure bell concert on a classical station in an adjacent apartment. One way or another she wasn't enjoying it.

She tried to move but the bed had claimed her. Come to think of it, gravity was probably at the back of that. Sneaky stuff, always there but never seen, the intangible that keeps us on this earth while all the time trying to get us back into the ground, from cradle to grave, and a lot of sagging bits of body along the way unable to resist its pull. She thought of her breasts and their march south, in spite of the best in brassiere engineering that Marks and Spencer could provide. The eyes and cheeks, chin and neck plied with firming creams and manipulated in ridiculous exercises to tighten and tone. They hadn't much hope against gravity. And the larger expanses of thigh, bum, upper arm? No chance whatsoever.

She couldn't put it off any more. She had to get out of bed and try to assemble her errant and now septic life. Milo would be home later and she couldn't have him see her like this. She would have a gentle milky decaffeinated coffee, something to whack the pain and a nice soak in the bath. And she had work to do, scripts to read. The show must go on whether she felt like shit or not. That's entertainment, she muttered as she put one foot in front of the other and crept out of her room.

'I wouldn't put a naked flame anywhere near me,' she said to Valerie. 'I think I may be toxic and inflammable which is one deadly combination.'

'You don't look your best,' Valerie conceded.

Susie fixed them both a decaff and even tried to nibble on a bagel but its very chewiness defeated her. Later, she promised her tummy, though it didn't kick up much of a fuss about not being fed. Seemed content to be fighting with the liquid for the moment.

'Do I need to do a round of apology phone calls?' she asked her mother.

'No, you're fine. You were just overtired and a bit loud.'

It wasn't exactly a comfort to hear this but Susie allowed a modicum of relief to seep through.

'Is anything the matter?'

Susie was so not up to this. 'Why do you ask?' She must be mad not to have stanched the subject there and then but her mind was mangled with pain and a straight thought was beyond her.

'You were crying.'

'I always do when I'm pissed. It's like a release valve is loosened and I let rip. I think I must like the feel of it. It doesn't mean anything. It's just letting off steam.'

'Are you sure?'

58

Deflection was the answer here. She sat opposite her mother who looked red eyed and forlorn. 'Are you OK?' she asked, turning the tables nicely.

Valerie inhaled a jagged breath. 'I'll be fine. I miss Toby. He was good company. Well, a presence at least. I get into a state sometimes wondering where I went wrong. Here I am, alone, and it's my own entire fault if your father is to be listened to. Not that he speaks to me any more.'

Susie didn't have it in her to dissemble. 'Look, Mum, Dad is a bit dull. You're not. He couldn't keep up. And when he realised that, he tried to diminish you, to get you to lessen yourself. When that didn't work, he left. He couldn't sit staring at his own inadequacies and defeat or failure, as he saw it, in his marriage every day so he baled out. He is quite a selfish man, you know.'

'Did I make him into that?'

'No, Mum. We make ourselves. You can't take the credit or the blame for Dad being Dad.'

'He told me I was needy.' Valerie was wringing the hem of her turquoise cardigan.

'You aren't any more needy than anyone else I know. He took you including him so totally in all aspects of your life to be that. He was inactive and a bit boring, or maybe bored. Who knows? Who cares? I think he was a coward to leave like he did. And a bit of a bully to try to lay the blame firmly at your feet. He has to deal with himself now and he's welcome to that. I love Dad, you know that and so does he, but he is a bit of a lump.'

'What if he finds someone else?' Valerie burst out. 'Where will I sit at his funeral?'

Susie smiled. 'Let's deal with that if and when, shall we?'

She was secretly delighted with her mum for imagining that she would outlive her spouse. It showed spirit. Now they just had to get her an interest and a new lease for this long life she intended.

'Oh, I read a couple of those scripts you brought home yesterday,' Valerie said. 'I hope you don't mind, only they were just lying here and you know how curious I get.' She passed them to Susie. 'The first one, *My Year of Hell*, has nothing to recommend it. Trite, badly written, wooden characters and ridiculous situations.' She saw Susie smiling. 'I presume we'll be seeing it in a cinema this time next year.'

Susie laughed. 'Probably. The producers have already signed two Hollywood names and if they get the tax break they're after they'll shoot here in March, padding out the cast with British actors.'

Valerie shook her head at the intricate folly of the movie world. 'The other script is *I-Dentity*.'

'I've just been sent that. Is it good?'

'Oh, yes, I think so. It's set in the near future, a fable about what happens when fashion and vanity lead most people in the First World to stop having babies and simply clone themselves instead. It's frightening and funny in equal measure and quite savage. There are some fabulous parts for actors. Most of them get to play a few versions of themselves. I can think of a number of your clients who'd be excellent in it.'

Susie saw an opportunity to be kind and keep her mother busy. 'Mum, could you jot down your notes on both scripts and I can use them along with mine for making decisions about who to push for the jobs.'

Valerie made a strange, popping noise. She sounded as if she had burst with delight. 'I'm ahead of you there,' she said, handing over four typed pages.

★ ★ ★

Milo arrived home in a fanfare of tall tales and sporting a new mobile phone. To head her off on a rant he said, 'Dad's programmed it to block all of the numbers you banned last time.'

'I hope he's paying you for that out of his pocket money,' Susie said to Chris.

When he said, 'Oh, that's all sorted,' she knew Milo was not.

'It's not as if he carelessly lost the last one,' Chris pointed out. 'He was robbed at knifepoint.'

Susie felt like a complete chump. Chris was right and Milo must have been traumatised by the experience. But she couldn't let it go and an unhelpful motherly pride made her say, 'You spoil him,' in a general remark designed to make a point and save face. Who's the child here? an annoying inner voice asked.

Chris Falucci gave his trademark shrug, the one that said, 'How can I help it if I'm a great guy and everyone loves me?' It made Susie boil. She waited till Milo had gone to get ready for bed before saying, 'It's no wonder he places so little importance on his things when you are so ready to replace them whenever they go missing or he gives them away. I realise this latest incident is different but in general he has no idea of responsibility. You really are going to have to take all of this more seriously. You are ruining him. I know you mean to be kind but you can't buy him, Chris. You have to earn him.'

She surprised both of them with her vehemence. She had spoken in the wrong on this occasion but in general the point held and she had wanted to make it for ages so she couldn't find it in herself to be sorry for the outburst when he did his best hurt and disappointed walk to the door to leave. 'I don't care if I've ruined Christmas,' she said, to tell him she was impervious to his wiles.

He couldn't let that go. 'Susie, you should chill. Don't make out like I'm some sort of enabler helping an alcoholic or something. You're over-exaggerating. I just want to know that we can reach Milo at all times.' He paused to give his coup de grâce full weight. 'Don't be such a drama queen.' Then he left before she could take the situation up a notch.

Drama queen? Oh, he knew where to hit all right. She walked back to the kitchen and reached for the white wine.

Susie Vine had been an actress. This was Chris Falucci's jibe. He should know. He had employed her in some of his radio productions. This was how they had met and grown to know one another, then tumbled into bed together and how their son Milo had come to be conceived. Susie realised that acting could not support her and a family, however small. She would not hear of a formal, long-term commitment to her from Chris, especially if it was simply because of Milo. He needed to love them both unconditionally and she would never be sure that he did and hadn't been forced into a corner if they had set up house then.

The other salient fact of her life was that, in her opinion, she was talented but she wasn't special. She became an agent. She had been playing that part ever since.

Those were the bare bones of it and however she dressed it up or down, it seemed to her to smack of defeat. She hadn't been good enough to be an artist so now she was a facilitator. It was leech-like and seedy put that way. She'd heard all the actors' jokes about agents: her personal favourite was, 'An agent is the person who resents you getting eighty-five per cent of their earnings.' She had failed creatively. To hand it to her, though, she was a very good agent and there were times when she wished that were enough. Tonight it was not.

⋆ ⋆ ⋆

Reg didn't visit his London grandchildren as often as he'd like any more. There was a time when it would have been automatic to go to his elder son's house for Sunday lunch or supper. All that changed with the divorce. He no longer felt comfortable turning up at the house, though he

63

was always welcome. He felt awkward. He didn't want to seem to take sides. He regretted not seeing his grandchildren grow more. He was missing out on valuable developmental material and therefore couldn't keep up with their moods and mannerisms. There was a distance between them now. It was like meeting familiar strangers when he encountered them after a break. His son's decision to leave had impacted hugely on everyone else in the equation. He couldn't help but blame him for the remove he now experienced from the children and relations between father and son were strained as a result. It also meant that Sunday could string into a long day.

He found talking to his eldest strange now too. They didn't discuss family much, given circumstances. That left them with their shared profession: acting. When his son had followed him into the business Reg had been torn between pride and worry. It was hard to graft a living. John was talented, though, and hard-working. He proved himself time and again. He had never asked his father for anything but advice, working various jobs to meet his fees. He gave cracking performances in all of his graduation shows and Betty asked Reg's permission to take him on at Arland and Shaw. That made him feel odd in the extreme.

'You must take him if you think he has talent,' Reg had said to her.

'I don't want you to feel in any way strange about it,' Betty said. 'Nothing fucks a family up more than professional rivalry.'

'It won't come to that,' Reg assured her.

It hadn't. But there came times when Reg had to warn John off interfering on his behalf, encouraging him into jobs or suggesting him for them. 'Let the director choose me, son. I don't need any favours. I don't need any nepotistic help.'

He didn't.

'I have been long enough in this business to look after myself.'

He had.

'But thank you.'

John had taken his mother's maiden name for work to distance any idea that favours would be done simply because he was Reg Darwin's boy. He was John Forbes and a star in his own right. Oddly, they had never played father and son on stage or celluloid. They joked that they found that hard enough in real life.

3

Susie liked to be at her desk no later than nine o'clock each day and Milo was supposed to leave home at 8 a.m. to be in time for school. He was old enough to travel on his own now or with his mates. He had to be allowed to grow up. She had to give him his chance and not suffocate all personality and possibility out of him by keeping him too close in a safety that made her feel better than it did him. She thought she could do with a book like *A Duffer's Guide to Parenthood for the Single Woman* but as far as she knew, it hadn't been written yet and the moment it was it would be out of date. Susie thought it important that Milo should get streetwise and independent, though incidents like the knifepoint robbery shook her. We cannot give in to the thugs, she told herself, but she worried all the same.

She had intended a lovely send-off this morning because of his tough end to the last school week. Milo had other ideas and instead they had one of their regular rows. He couldn't find his gym kit.

'It was washed and put back in your room. What happened to it then is down to you.'

His voice hit high doh. 'I can't go in without it. It's not my fault it's missing.'

'Milo, I'm telling you right now that if this is a ploy to skip classes it's not going to work. I don't care how late you are, you are going to school and that's all there is about it.'

'You don't care about what happens to me. If I go in without my proper uniform I am gonna be in big trouble, you know.'

He stomped off and made plenty of noise ripping out drawers and clanging through his wardrobe. If it hadn't been his sports gear it would have been his uniform jacket, or beret or an English book. The list had so many permutations it was probably endless. Susie quickly scribbled a note explaining his lateness and thrust him out of the door when he had got his gear together. Valerie offered to go with Milo if he'd like, which he didn't, and her availability calmed Susie's nerves a little.

'Was I impossible when I was his age?' she asked her mother.

'All of you Vines were.'

Susie left enough time for Milo to have got his train then went to the same station to catch her own. It would have made sense for them to walk to the Tube together every day but she rationed that. She didn't want to embarrass him or smother him with too much attention. Today she was so worn out arguing with him she couldn't feel guilty that he had loped off alone.

The offices of Arland and Shaw were on the north side of Oxford Street in a modern block of glass and steel and took up the entire fourteenth floor. Susie had a corner spot and a fine view of the city's roofs from the Post Office Tower to the north to a fraction of the London Eye to the south. A full roll call of staff was drinking takeaway coffees and quickly catching up with correspondence. Susie smiled and chattered her hellos to the company. All but Jay Burns seemed glad to see her. He wore his perma-scowl and was probably kicking himself gently that he met her eye as she waved. Hardly even a minor victory but it made Susie chuckle and she took it to mean she was in for a good day.

The office had a feel of being open plan. After the enclosed reception area a client or visitor could be led into the central space, which radiated off an island hosting plants and comfortable seats, for an informal chat. All of the cubicles had windows and a view of the city and were fronted by glass doors with blinds which were generally left open unless an agent was hosting a private meeting. A large staffroom with a long table held bigger, more formal gatherings.

Farrah, their receptionist, was delivering the post. Susie could tell from the size and shape of the envelopes that it was the usual mix of scripts and CVs accompanied by head shots of prospective clients. She opened the chunkier packages, weeding out the expected scripts from the speculative ones and left the latter with the unopened CVs for later. These were unimportant to the main thrust of her day but she would get around to them when time allowed.

Susie was accustomed to the noise of other agents talking on the phone or to one another and it was no more than a background hum to her now. She whizzed through any pressing correspondence and got together her report for the agents' meeting, which took place every Monday at noon. Then, for an hour (and often through the lunch break) the staff reported, boasted and justified their positions. This weekly open confession was vital, competitive and exhausting. Susie loved it.

Lola Stein perched on the edge of Susie's desk. 'I think I'm adoring the Ice Queen look.'

Susie always liked dressing for work in smart, structured clothes. Today she wore a charcoal-grey, linen trouser suit and crisp white blouse. It was her uniform and part of the signature she brought to a situation. These were the costumes she wore to represent her clients who in turn would become characters in the dramatic web, that second oldest profession in the world. But as Lola had pointed out, the difference between 'art' and 'tart' was a fine one. 'We are all whores, it's just a matter of price,' she explained.

'Elaborate, pray,' Susie had urged.

'It's like if I ask you would you sleep with me for a million pounds and you say yes, then I say, 'Right, now that we know you're for sale, let's haggle.' '

Lola wanted information. 'Any action over the weekend?'

'Aside from Milo being mugged, which you know about from Friday, no. Oh, and my mum's come to stay. Big fat chance of me seeing any other unusual action. Have you lost your mind to dream of such a thing?'

'You are going to have to start coming out with me.'

'What? You're going to bring extra competition with you for the few single men left in London? Even if it is me.' Susie had begun to see herself as a safe woman, a mother with responsibilities who had no time and little inclination to take on a new relationship. Then she remembered a salient detail. 'And anyway, what would Max think?' Max was handy in so many ways. She could summon him at will and invent whatever she liked about their weekend. She used him as an excuse to cry off social events she couldn't face. She brought him to the ones she didn't want to speak to anyone at. He was the perfect man, the perfect affair; he never got in the way or lost her sleep or needed much cosseting. She could love the idea of him yet not see him. She presumed he used her in much the same way.

'Ah, yes, Max. The boyfriend we never see.'

'He exists.' Susie found herself saying this defensively as if it was untrue. She needed to be careful of her tone. It didn't need to be so definite, so telling.

'Oh I know, I've met the man and very nice he is too. But to be honest, Susie, you might just hire the same guy each time you have to produce an escort.'

What's brought this on? Susie wondered. 'What's brought this on?' she asked.

'Ignore me. My period is due and the way things are going I'll never have to worry about missing one ever again. I'm crazily jealous of anyone who's got a partner and my parents have given up on me finding one. Next they'll get mad Aunty Zelda to match-make me and then I am totally scuppered. Her taste in men boils down to anything human with a penis and a pulse. Oh,

70

and Jewish, of course, so the penis will have to be circumcised.'

'I'll ask around, see if Max or any of his buddies has a friend. Does he have to be of the Faith?'

'You know he does. I may be the black sheep but I'm still my mother's daughter and my papa's princess. And there is no way I am letting my cousin Ruth get her nasty, red little hands on the family silver.'

'Don't you have notes to get together?' Susie asked, looking pointedly at the clock.

'Piece of cake, sweetie pie. I am shit hot at my job, it's my life that's in chaos. What about the cop on Friday? A possibility?'

'We all love a man in uniform but no, not even a maybe.'

'Would you have been his mother or an older date?'

They encountered a lot of young men and Lola liked to grade them accordingly.

'Strictly speaking, an older date but more realistically the babysitter.'

Lola sighed. 'Maybe the staff meeting will lift me. I can goad Burns.'

Betty Arland was the Arland of Arland and Shaw. The co-founder of the agency, Rosie Shaw, had stepped down after a mild stroke five years ago. 'Delighted to get away,' she told Susie. 'Got very fed up of looking after all of those lovely actors. In loco parentis and all that. Now I grow orchids, which are every bit as cranky as clients, and take in lots of stray animals and they are so much more grateful than most of the dear

71

luvvies I used to represent.'

Betty was some sixty years old, always wrapped in clothes rather than dressed in them and smelling of Chanel No.5. It was entirely possible that she had invented the pashmina along with the chain that holds spectacles around the neck. Her fingers were encrusted in rings of every size and sort. According to Betty, her husband Jack didn't ever think about what to give her, he just bought rings for every occasion. 'If he doesn't die before me I may have to grow extra fingers,' she would say. Her management style was the same as her agenting: brisk, fair and ruthless. It was good to know where one stood in life and the grand scheme of things, and one always did with Betty. Her manner was direct, her speech acid and peppered with expletives that her crystal-posh accent made acceptable if still shocking. She presided over six other agents, an accountant and Farrah. It was a tight ship and everyone was expected to work hard and look after fifteen to twenty clients each, which also meant sourcing a lot of work.

Arland and Shaw was all about actors and this distinguished it in the modern game. Many other agencies spread themselves, covering directors and designers also. Arland and Shaw had built up a reputation for managing really good actors. Each agent worked on a specific list, concentrating on their talent rather than sharing it.

The staff gathered in the meeting room, each gravitating to his or her usual spot. Susie sat beside Mitch Douglas who offered her a Vitamin X, as he liked to call it.

'I'm fine for Xanax at the moment,' Susie told him.

She wanted to reach out and smooth a tuft of his hair that was sticking up and out at an odd angle but it looked too stubborn to be dealt with by anything but the sturdiest gel. It gave him a winsome, surprised look that made her want to hug him too. Again, she resisted.

Lola sat opposite, principally to make faces at Mitch and Susie, and Jay Burns planted himself beside her. He was always a floater and they posited the notion more than once that he was deliberately trying to freak out the other members of the company one by one each Monday. He had yet to succeed. Susie never understood why Betty had asked him to join the company. His agenting style was quite American so perhaps she thought that would add to the mix at Arland and Shaw. Susie hated the snide way he treated her, as if he felt superior. The last two full agents were Nell, who worked from home two days a week, and Dave, married with two young kids and constantly sleep deprived. They both sidled in just shy of being late.

The company went through the reports. They had some actors going into pantomime for the Christmas season, had leads and supporting actors in many of the big West End plays, more touring, and several clients were finishing shoots or about to start on them in the New Year. All round it was a good showing for Arland and Shaw, with an unprecedented seventy per cent of clients working or about to begin work. There were some interesting productions due to come on-line soon and they looked forward to those.

'We must not get complacent,' Betty warned. 'January is always the doldrums and now is the time to put our names out there for that and any of the fuck-few jobs that are still going. But well done, all, I am very pleased.'

The bonus signs lit up in everyone's eyes. This might be a bumper year.

Susie checked her watch. She had missed lunch. Good, she had more than enough spare calories flying around her body after the weekend's excesses. She remembered the Anita Fay photo for the cop and entrusted the mission to Farrah. The agency had a box of signed artist memorabilia and Farrah was an adept forger of dedications and well wishes. Susie flung a stick of chewing gum into her mouth and began to read *I-Dentity*. She sped through it, enthralled. She turned to her mother's notes. It was a pleasant surprise to discover that Valerie had a touch for nailing the faults and strengths of a piece. There was a salty quality to her analysis and a lack of pretension that gave further credibility to things she liked and cut through what she did not. She was concise in her précis of the plot and characters. Her overall judgement was opinionated but sound. Altogether very helpful.

Susie made her list of candidates for the American film first and copied it to the office. The other agents would add theirs and then a full list would be compiled and sent to the casting director. Later, they would send CVs and head shots of those chosen to meet for the jobs.

The second and far more exciting prospect was the near-future fable, *I-Dentity*. She gave that a lot of thought and finally decided to talk to Betty before ringing the producer to see what the state of play was and to tell him how good she thought it was.

'I think we could follow the American way of putting together a partial package,' she told her boss.

'How many other agencies have this?'

'That's the thing, none so far. They've deliberately kept it small so they can work with who they want rather than be pushed around by investors too much. I believe the producers accessed a lot of soft money from friends rather than hard money from the banks. I got my hands on the script through a contact in a publishing house that is considering the writer's first novel. She asked to see more of his work and he gave her this, which he's in development with. I spoke to his agent and they are looking to attach the director Noel Parks. So now it's time to nail the money down and from there a cast. I've bought us a few weeks maybe.'

Betty looked impressed, which was gratifying. 'Story?'

'Cloning has become the norm for the First World in the near future. Society has decided in its vanity to reproduce itself with clones for exact similarity but also to preserve women's figures. A female police chief is hunting a notorious criminal who has cloned himself twice so there are three of him running around and DNA from the crime scenes is no help as they all have the same, so which of the clones does she want or is it the original guy? In the meantime she's infertile and wondering about cloning herself to have a baby. There's a thriving black market in faulty clones, which are sold on illegally for the services industries in a kind of slave trade. An academic clones herself so that she can concentrate on her groundbreaking research and the other her can fundraise for the work. One man kills his clone because he realises he's a complete bore and the question then is did he kill himself or another entity? Is it murder or a new kind of suicide? That strand is both grimly hilarious and heartbreaking, I think. And so on. It's Philip K. Dick meets the darker Ealing comedies. I've done up a synopsis for you and a breakdown of the characters.'

'Good.'

'We have more than enough good actors to cast the leads and the parts would really show their talents off beautifully.'

'I agree, but we don't want to piss off a casting director down the line who might want to put their own stamp on it.'

'No, but if we get in there first with this idea and are there from the beginning as the production is pulled together and the finance raised, I think we'll be in a very good position and no casting person in their right mind would change, say, the leads if we suggest a winning combination.'

'True, if we pull it off.'

'We have the talent, why not try?' She let the idea sink in, then, 'We would have to offer them someone like John Forbes though.'

Betty laughed. 'He would sweeten any package. Let me read the material, then we'll talk again.'

★ ★ ★

Reginald was uncomfortable sitting in the too-low sofa of the hotel room. It hadn't escaped his notice that he was meeting a man about a job in a room rented by the hour. A video camera was pointed at him from a tripod behind the young writer/director's head and the casting director, a hippy-chick named Cassandra, was twiddling with some buttons.

'If you would just say your name and agency, Reg, that would be great. Then give us your profiles too. Many thanks.'

He did as he was bid.

'As you're not going to read for us,' she simpered, pushing some blame onto him for this, 'I hope you don't mind if I leave the camera rolling for our conversation, just so our producers can get the full flavour of you?'

He nodded acquiescence.

The young auteur was running his hand through deliberately unruly hair and looking as if he didn't know where to begin with getting to the very nub of Reginald, as a man and an actor. His gaze was worried and earnest and he clearly fancied himself. Reg took an instant dislike to the kid. He felt himself clam up. Not looking too good for the meeting, old chap, or for getting the part.

'Reginald,' the youngster began. 'You know this is the crucial role of our leading lady's father, a man of the old school's unyielding beliefs and so on?'

'Yes, I've read the script.'

'Did you enjoy it?'

'Oh, yes. I think it will make a handsome piece of television.'

'Thank you,' the director said, as if the thing was already made and he was waiting for his BAFTA nomination.

'How do you feel about the notion that he may have abused her in her childhood?'

'That sort of thing happens. It's an integral part of the story and I think it works as written.'

Reg could see frustration growing in the young man's eyes. Suddenly he realised that the dislike was travelling both ways and the director was looking to get rid of him on camera. Reg was thwarting him by being so reasonable. Now things were looking a whole lot more interesting. Reg went from not caring about this mediocre job to really wanting to get it. He had something to prove now.

The director did the classic chin rub. 'Reg, I hope you won't mind me saying this, and please take no offence, but I'm not *getting* you. You know?' He left this bombshell unadorned, happy that he'd delivered it with an enigmatic twist, the 'I know what I'm talking about and if I have to explain it to you then you are not of a like mind or intelligence' sort of theme.

So Reg did something that surprised even himself, he offered to read. Which he did, brilliantly. There was an audible silence afterwards in the rented-by-the-hour room. He was tempted to say, 'See you on set,' as he left but resisted.

He wondered how long they would take to make their decision and if he would actually accept the part when it was offered. He grinned. Life in the old dog yet.

★   ★   ★

Milo didn't see the point of school in general and thought it unnecessary and cruel, but he was trying hard with his French. He had an ulterior motive with that one. His dream was to conduct a proper conversation with Isabelle from upstairs in her native language. Then she would see him not as the young kid on the block but someone she could really talk to. A pain jabbed his heart whenever he thought of her but he assumed that was part of the price he had to pay for his affections. It wasn't easy. The main problem with his dreamed-of communication wasn't the grammar or vocabulary, though these were issues, it was his French accent. His teacher, Bowler, was the only one he could speak to and learn from but that meant asking questions in class and Rafe was merciless when this happened. He would corner Milo after and tease him with stupid phrases like, 'Oooh, Missyoor Bowlair, *je t'aime*,' followed by kissy-kissy noises. He got accused of being gay for Bowler, which was a thought that nearly made Milo faint it was so gross.

Rafe backed up his accusations with the fact that Milo was left-handed. His gran said it meant he was artistic but that was further trouble because according to Rafe being arty was the ultimate proof of being a batty boy. A bit rich coming from the son of architects, but there it was. Roger Fulton in Year 8 was brilliant at drawing and endured a campaign of slurs until he started selling filthy pictures. Now he was nearly a millionaire and no one ever mentioned his supposed gayness.

Thankfully, Milo was not prone to blushing and that stood to him. People couldn't see it but the heat generated within him through embarrassment had to be like a meteor entering the earth's atmosphere. He couldn't believe his luck that it didn't show in his face.

The other thing he had over Rafe was that he was a head taller than him. He had thought nothing of it until he almost lost his temper with Rafe one day after a particularly hot session of insults and when he loomed over the other boy he thought he saw a shiver of fright, just a flicker. It was enough to calm him and to trust that when he stood a little too close to Rafe and told him to shut his gob, the other boy might leave him alone, at least for a time. So today when Rafe started up and Adam followed suit, Milo simply shoved Adam aside and thrust his face towards Rafe, growling, 'Bog off, Shorty.' When he turned around he was sure Gregory was wiping a quick smile off his face. 'Très bien,' he said. Then Milo became meek again, blending into the river of boyhood streaming by to the next class.

Just as well because Rafe's older brother Vince hove into view. He was a big lump of youth and hung around with a selection of other beefy types. He thumped Rafe across the head and said, 'Runt, you got money? I need some.'

Rafe searched his pockets and came up with one pound fifty, which earned him another hit, this time a jab into the chest.

'More next time, you tosser.'

His flunkies all laughed and looked like Orcs, Milo thought, as he hugged the wall and gazed at his trainers. Then they were gone, leaving behind a horrible smell of smoke and body odour and bad breath. Maybe his dad had a point about washing.

Rafe was pink with embarrassment and degradation but laughed as if his big brother just cracked him up. Milo could see his primitive brain clicking through the options that would allow him to save face and satisfy his low threshold for revenge. Rafe reached casually into his satchel and located his compass. Then he walked off, jabbing sneakily at any leg he came in contact with in the swarm passing on its way along the corridor. The noise of so many boots and shoes on wood almost camouflaged the yelps and cries of pain. Milo tried to block them out further. He didn't want to get involved. No point in drawing too much attention. No need to stick out. He couldn't wait to be a grown-up and not to have to think about such things. And he couldn't wait to get away from Rafe. That was one messed-up individual.

Susie met Craig Landor in the Soho Hotel for coffee and a powwow. He had chosen the venue and it didn't surprise her. He knew it would be full of media types, it always was. He was hot right now and wanted to be seen and noticed. Susie nipped in the back door from Flaxman Court and ordered a latte. Craig arrived through the front from Dean Street, sashayed past the enormous cat sculpture in the foyer in fabulously tight jeans and leather bomber jacket, greeting everyone with a million-dollar smile. Oh, let it be so, Susie wished, feeling the twinkle of possibility in this nascent star. She liked the way it tripped along her agent's nerves and synapses. Fifteen per cent of that would do nicely.

He kissed her on both cheeks, which was nice but unnecessary; I am the help here, after all, she thought. Then he opted for a red wine. 'I'm resting, as you know, so I can have a few blow-outs.'

He wasn't the only one. While Susie was waiting for her client, who was his fashionable ten minutes late, she'd heard lots of young guns doing business by phone as they sipped the first of many celebratory drinks. She had been here last week at morning elevenses and a group of lads were getting started on the port. She didn't like to think what had gone before to warrant such an early kick-off. She was reminded that the world never sleeps.

She spotted an agent from a rival firm on her mobile at the bar, cradling a glass of clear liquid which Susie didn't mind betting was vodka. When Craig saw her he said, 'Isn't that Polly whatsher-name? Off her tits on coke too, I'd say.' He was probably right. Polly had also had so many facelifts that no one really recognised her any more, which was probably handy. It must be great to slip in and out of a room unnoticed if one wanted to, Susie thought.

Craig relaxed against the wall where he had a good view of the narrow bar and where he could be seen easily by anyone who wanted to admire him. He wasn't so much an attention seeker as a sensible actor using his time in the limelight. She liked that about this client. He was interested in the process and was easy about exposure. Not everyone was able for that or bothered to engage in it. He'd recently had a success with the television series *Fun Zone*, playing a troubled, self-harmer. The series was gritty, moving and an indictment of the health system. Even Milo liked it and asked for autographs for his friends. Craig had emerged a star. A short film was garnering prizes on the festival circuit and a feature was in post-production, surrounded by great industry whisperings. Everyone wanted a piece of the buzz.

They got down to business, Marty's movie *Glory Days*.

'I like the script. Great part for me. How likely are they to get it made?' he wanted to know.

'How long is a piece of string?' Susie answered. 'Sorry to answer a question with a question but there's no way of knowing. You should meet with Marty and see if you rub along. And if you do and you're still up for it, we'll attach your name to the movie and see what emerges. It's not usually a speedy process, as you know, but this is relatively low budget and I think he fancies it to be a bit of elemental film-making, so who knows? In the meantime we have some concrete offers. There's that new play at the National?'

He shook his head. 'I've had a read and it's basically the same territory as *Fun Zone*. I'd be repeating myself. I don't think that's the right move for me now.'

'Agreed.' Susie was relieved. A lot of the time actors had to make decisions based on pure economics but Craig didn't seem concerned by that. 'How about the radio play for the BBC?'

'Yes to that. Shame it's only three days.'

'Chekhov, though, nice to have a classic under the belt.'

He laughed. 'Yes, dahling,' he said in plummy tones. Craig's normal accent was soft Geordie but he was a good chameleon and could turn his hand to most things. She took time to admire him herself. Dark, tumbling locks, grey-green eyes, slim physique with just enough muscle tone, all topped with a killer smile that could switch to a heartbroken frown in an instant. He oozed charisma. She had signed him up after a fringe show at Edinburgh and it was part of the thrill of her job to know that she was now managing what was potentially a major career. It made her wonder too; why couldn't it be the same for her women clients?

The struggle for a female to hit the top flight

was harder than for her male counterparts. Generally, they had to be younger, thinner, and prettier when they started out. Especially if they wanted to be in the movies. And entirely so if they were trying to cross over into the American market. Five thousand hopefuls arrived in LA every day wanting to be part of the Hollywood dream. The competition was truly frightening and the casualty list high. Being able to act was only a small consideration.

Unless someone was funny. If the actor was joke shaped, they had the chance to be different, to be bigger, plainer even, because talent was of the essence then rather than looks. The whole business was a minefield at one end and a rubbish tip at the other, with an infested snake pit in between.

And so goddammed exciting.

* * *

Flora turned up on set mid-afternoon. The production had moved on to a heath in north London and John Forbes couldn't figure out how she'd found him; he wasn't sure even his agent knew where he was that day. Good detective work then from his daughter but behaviour that was not to be encouraged. He didn't bother to hide a look of plain annoyance.

'You better have a very good reason for being here,' he growled.

She switched on the waterworks. 'Dad, don't be angry with me. I'm so unhappy.'

So far, so recognisable.

He started to dial her mother's number. She grabbed the phone from his grasp. 'No, don't call her. Please, Dad. I just want to be with you for a while.'

'Flora, you really know how to pick your time. In case you hadn't noticed, I am up to my eyeballs in work and this is the last thing I need.'

'I am always the last thing you need these days,' she wailed.

He really couldn't let this escalate. He sat her down and crouched before her. 'Flora, cut me some slack here.'

'I miss you so much.'

'I know, baby, but this isn't the way to go about showing it. When this job is done I'll have time off and we can see plenty of one another then. How's that?'

She sniffed and nodded and he hoped the worst was past. Flora might be the most annoying daughter in the world right now but she was also his little girl and the awful feeling that he was failing her was cracking his heart in two. His son Quentin, younger than her by over a year, employed a policy of ignoring him. He was so successful that sometimes John wondered if he had actually blocked the fact that he no longer lived with them from his consciousness. He accepted his father's appearances, not with any acknowledgement but equally without histrionics, and there were no reports of him missing his dad at other times. This was probably just as worrying but John found it a blessed relief for the time being. He would deal with the psychological trauma later, if there was any at all.

Thing about Quentin was he was a phlegmatic chap who got on with things. Perhaps when his hormones kicked in properly they'd get a rough ride but until then he was almost a comfort, especially in comparison with his sister.

He wondered how this ridiculous scene looked: him in Roundhead armour, Flora in a school uniform. Man, the tabloids would have a field day with this one given less than a tiny percentage of a chance.

'Come on, you might as well meet the gang while you're here and we'll organise a car home for you.' Seemed Quentin's practicality was a chip off the old block; in one movement John Forbes was squelching any scurrilous rumours that might emanate from the set and getting shot of his daughter Flora.

From: susie@arlandshaw.co.uk
To: marty@direkshun.com
Sent: 1 october 17.45
Subject: craig landor

Dear Marty,

I have just talked to Craig and he would be happy to meet with you when you are here. Let me know the dates you have planned and we'll set something up. In the meantime I hope your production plans are coming together.

Yours,
Susie Vine

Her mobile beeped. Lola texted, 'TJ was

almost nice to me earlier! What's going on?' TJ stood for The Jerk and represented Jay Burns in all correspondence between them. Susie texted, 'Pathetic attempt to spook you! Ignore!'

A reply to her email appeared ten minutes later. Someone was up and busy on the other side of the world.

From: marty@direkshun.com
To: susie@arlandshaw.co.uk
Sent: 1 october 17.55
Subject: craig landor

dear susie,

I am so glad to hear that fantastic news. As it happens I will be in London next week and would love to meet with you and Craig then. I can really feel the project taking flight now and I just know we will make a GREAT movie, full of passion and beauty.

Please advise when and where would be good for you.

Thanks again for your help,
Marty

Lola approached, looking worried. 'I'm freaked out since that *thing* gurned at me.'

'Relax, Lola, it was probably just a facial spasm.' She took a quick shufti around the office. 'I presume he's gone for the day?'

'Oh, yes, loudly. Dinner with some financial dick friend of his.' She looked thoughtful. 'He's probably got lots of single friends, if they're anything like him.'

'Don't go there.'

'I'm a desperate non-housewife! My vibrator is worn through to the batteries. Oy vey.'

'Some day your prince will come and so will you and you'll live happily ever after.'

Lola tugged on Susie's lapels. 'You have to promise me that or I'll get mad Zelda to put the evil eye on you.' Her face was wild and she looked as if she was telling the truth.

Susie's intercom buzzed and Farrah asked if Lola was with her. 'She's got a call on line three from Eleanor Macklin.'

Lola gave an over-the-top groan. 'Nooo. Tell her I've left the country, or I'm dead. I am so not in the mood for a fucking client.'

'Er, hello. Lola?' The client. Lola had no room to manoeuvre, so she did the next best thing, she was honest.

'Ellie, I can't lie to you, I am having a bitch of a day. Let me get back to my desk and you can go through me for a short cut while I put heartfelt words to my remorse.'

As she moved off she whispered, 'Do you think Farrah did that deliberately?'

★ ★ ★

As Susie swayed on the Tube later she wondered if she had let herself get lazy or unsociable, or was it just that she didn't have those pheromones any more? The magic ones that got men all excited? Or, if they were still in there, knocking about, she wasn't exuding them. Had she lost whatever attraction she once possessed? She certainly wasn't raising any glances from the tired men around her in the carriage. No one offered up his seat. She'd probably have refused it anyhow, embarrassed by the blatant good manners or worried about what payback might be expected of the good deed. Well, none of this lot needed to worry about a surfeit of those. Chivalry and steady boyfriends must have gone out of fashion while she was busy elsewhere.

She walked along the Pavement from the station, enjoying a cooler temperature to the oven of the Underground and the earlier scorch of another fine day. A handbag called to her from the window of Oliver Bonas but happily it was closed and the danger removed. She popped into the butcher to get the sausages Milo loved. Bangers, mash and salad for him and Valerie, simply a naked salad for Susie this evening. She was looking forward to a night at home, but even this involved some work; she had a new script to read and another television programme to watch featuring one of her clients as a real-life murderer in a documentary re-enactment of a famous trial.

The apartment seemed eerily quiet, even with all the windows open, then she heard laughter from Milo's room. He and Valerie were enveloping letters and chatting happily as they went. Susie stood on the threshold, an interloper, intruding on a private party.

'Milo has come on board my campaign for Amnesty,' her mother said. 'He's also shown me how to use his computer to type the letters up and print them out. And I'm learning about the wonder of the interweb. He says I could become a Silver Surfer.' She looked to Milo for confirmation that she'd got her lingo correct.

He gave an easy, 'Internet, Gran, but yup.'

'I'm exhausted just hearing about it,' Susie said, trying to sound cheerful. 'What sort of pupil is she?'

'Quick,' Milo admitted.

'Desperate to learn,' Valerie qualified.

'Just as long as Milo isn't hogging the computer. He's only allowed an hour on the Internet under supervision. He knows why.'

Her son looked cutely sheepish. 'I can't be trusted,' he told his gran, without much shame.

Valerie nodded as if she understood his problem.

'Dinner in twenty,' Susie announced. As she made her way to the kitchen she heard suppressed giggles follow in her wake. She felt like a fusspot and a spoilsport.

★   ★   ★

John Forbes decided a summit with his ex-wife was in order so he had his car drop him at his old home in Highgate. His call for the following day allowed him a lie-in till nine o'clock and he was heady with freedom. He rang ahead to make sure his name was in the pot for dinner. He had an expensive Chablis in his bag. Any more might engender fighting talk and that was the last thing he needed at this juncture.

It was strange to round the corner and confront a house that was no longer his home, but familiar like an old, neglected friend. It was a better place now that he wasn't in the day-to-day mix. Flora didn't think it was happier but he knew it was, or would be ultimately. His marriage hadn't been one of screaming rows, quite the contrary. But silences had a way of poisoning an atmosphere too. Admitting this was the bravest moment of his and Roma's lives, he thought. They had reached a natural end, ground to a halt.

Flora beamed to see him again so soon. Quentin looked through him. All was as he knew it. Two fluffy balls yipped out from the kitchen to greet him. They both wore bows.

'Weren't those dogs sissy enough without making fun of them?' he called out. He bent down to pat them. 'Hi, guys, how's it hanging?' They were called Romulus and Remus in honour of their human mum, Roma.

His ex-wife appeared, looking edibly gorgeous. Long blond hair, physique sculpted by the gym and regular tennis and golf, skin glowing with health and expensive treatments and moisturisers. Oh wow, just as well he was over her. If he could control the fact that he was alive and a red-blooded male he might get through the evening without making a pass at her and an ass of himself.

'They love those ribbons, asked for them especially in their ickle doggy voices. The ones I can't resist.'

'So that's where I went wrong. Wasn't dog enough.'

'Don't joke about it,' she warned lightly,

kissing both of his cheeks and relieving him of the wine. 'You haven't earned that yet.'

He had been the one to leave. Apparently he still deserved admonishment for that. He wondered when the faux blame game would end. It was their own Cold War, complete with the diplomatic trappings of clipped niceties and meaningless waffle designed to soothe and salve. They were communicating very deliberately and always aware of the tightrope they found themselves on in these post-divorce days.

Flora clung to him all evening until she was forced to go to bed. She tried her best to entertain in such a forced way that everyone felt sorry for her by the end, herself most of all. Quentin gave a backing soundtrack of sighs and mocking snorts. The dogs clambered for knees, both of John's. It was a festival of guilt, if he wanted it to be. But he didn't so he rose above it.

'Flora needs stability,' Roma said when the kids had disappeared. 'Most of the time she doesn't know what she wants, of course. She's cursed with raging hormones on top of a broken home. I think you'll have to formulate some sort of system of seeing the kids regularly. We never did sit down to figure that out.'

'It's tough with work,' he grumbled.

'That's an excuse not a solution.' His wife had distant German ancestry and it showed in her brutal analysis of any situation, all the more cringe-making when it involved the personal.

'I'll draw up a schedule for now until Christmas,' John promised. 'That'll give us something to go on with.'

'Have you seen your father?'

'Not lately.'

'You should.'

'Yes, I know. It's awkward. Have you?'

'He phones. I don't think he wants to impose.'

'That's my dad: last of the gentlemen. Would die rather than embarrass anyone.'

He was massively on the back foot now and he didn't like it. Roma reached for a second bottle of wine. 'So, are you seeing anyone?' Too light, too indifferently delivered.

Time to go.

*   *   *

Susie's client got to her just as she was about to dial. She did her best to calm her down. 'Anna,' she said. 'You were great. The programme was lacklustre, certainly, but you came out of it with honours.' This was close to the truth; the programme had in fact been execrable, her client had been fine. 'No, there's no damage done, believe me. Now calm down. Remember you are rehearsing the new Diane Bennett play and the whole of London is looking forward to that. Everything else is icing on an already fine cake.'

'You have a very smooth manner,' Valerie said after she'd hung up.

'I'm in charge. I can't be seen to panic. Besides, it really won't matter at all to Anna. She'll ride this one out. And I really didn't think she did too badly.'

'No. Quirky-looking little girl. Nice voice. Charming presence. Made the murder aspect all the more chilling. The girl next door gone bad.'

Again, her mother had got to the nub of things. Things that didn't involve her own emotional life, that is. Objectivity was elusive there. It was for most people, Susie knew, including herself on that list.

* * *

John Forbes had not been seeing anyone. The media attention after his break-up with Roma was a chastening experience. The split had been as amicable as anything of that nature could be. Regret was his abiding memory of how he had felt. When he realised that a feeding frenzy was upon them he was glad it wasn't due to an infidelity. There was nothing extra-spicy to hide. The lurid details of his marriage, mostly imaginary, were hard enough to read about, let alone if they'd been accompanied by descriptions of an affair. Photographers dogged his every move and those of his beautiful wife. He now used the term 'vulturazzi' to describe the creatures that crawled out of the earth's recesses to follow them. He thought they might leave the children out of the mix and for a while they did, but when the story was just a filler on obscure pages leading up to the television section, some bright spark thought to reignite the not-so-sordid tale by publishing a pixillated photo of Flora at a school fete. The picture was taken from a huge distance and all of the girls blurred to the point where it was unclear which of the miserable teenagers was his daughter, but it was a step too far. This sort of intrusion was totally unacceptable and bordered on the illegal. He had his lawyers send some strongly worded letters and eventually the fever cooled. He had made certain to lie low since. Not that he didn't have dalliances, he did, but these were so short and discreet as to be invisible.

He'd asked Betty why the papers continued to be so interested in his personal life.

'John,' she'd replied, as if indulging a child, 'you are living the Dream.'

He whined a demurral.

'Don't be a cunt, darling,' she instructed, sharp as whiplash. 'You are an aspiration to your many fans. Your life is perceived to be ideal compared with that of Joe Public. You've got it all: the beautiful wife, two adorable children, the trophy house, money in the bank and a fast car to swank around in. You're glamorous. Don't disappear up your own arse trying to deny your good fortune, or complaining about it, even if it has been bloody hard work, as you and I know. It appears ungrateful and churlish.'

He had grunted wearily at that. At the time he was scrabbling around to find a flat he could afford that wasn't too skangy. Not that he'd have to sleep on the streets if the letters from fans were anything to go by. Men and women of all shapes, sizes and mental conditions wrote to offer a bizarre range of services to their hero. The most worrying were those from people who seemed perfectly sane. Get a life, he wanted to tell them, but as he didn't have much of one himself then he refrained from lecturing. He autographed photos with their names on and Farrah posted them with specially printed thank-you slips. He hadn't approached his dad for a room and Reginald hadn't offered.

Betty was adamant about one point. 'You must maintain dignity during this, John. That would be most helpful. Remember, the public want to believe that you live a life larger than their own. And that it's possible for someone to make it. You do have some responsibility there.'

'As you so eloquently put it, don't be a cunt.'

'Precisely.'

Whether this was true or fair, he took her words to heart and tried not to disgrace himself. So far he'd been successful, even if it made for a predictable work-filled existence. To be honest, he didn't have the energy for anything more. As his cab pulled into his complex in Hammersmith, he felt old and knackered.

4

The baby who died defined Valerie and therefore Susan. He was third after Tim and Chloe. Valerie's body had nurtured him for the requisite time and all preparations were made at home for his delivery. The children were as excited as she was. She assumed Alistair was similarly thrilled. Looking back now it was hard to tell for sure. Perhaps he thought then that they would issue a child every two years. The contractions began on cue and her womb thrust him forth. But on the way they were both betrayed. The baby's umbilical cord wound around his tiny neck and strangled him. The more Valerie pushed him out, the less air he got and so he perished. Her treacherous body had loved him too much, wrapped itself around him too tightly and hugged so hard that precious breath was denied him. His name was James.

Valerie was plunged into a circle of hell far beyond Dante's vision of rings and inferno, lower than Gorky's depths and into God's own biblical terrain of anguish and torture. She could not be consoled. She lay facing the wall in her hospital room. She refused food. When she was discharged she took to her bed at home and her husband moved to the spare room, unable to deal with the zombie who had been returned to him. The children crept around the house. A neighbour came to make meals and clear away the baby things that had been amassed. The doctor prescribed Valium and Valerie lost four blessed weeks in a drug-induced fug. Finally her mother came to stay. She was a stern woman who had never heard of depression and therefore would have no truck with it. She stopped the pills and got Valerie out of bed to wash, to walk outdoors, to play with her living children. Valerie hated her for it.

James haunted her thoughts. He was the child who might have been, the boy who never had a chance. She blamed herself for killing him. She tried to engage with Chloe and Tim but she was millions of miles away from them in her mind. James was always in the room with her, hiding where no one could see him but her. The rustle of a curtain as he ducked from sight. The creak of a tread as he stole upstairs. She wrote him notes and the occasional poem. When Chloe asked her who she was speaking to one day, she realised she had given too much away. It was time to store James safely and deal with the corporeal reality all around her. Gradually normality impinged, colonised, and the family began to believe she was better and back. But Valerie was preoccupied in a way none of them suspected; she had a plan. She wanted another baby.

Those next nine months from conception to birth were the most nervous of Valerie's life. This filtered down quickly to the rest of the household. Sex became immediately taboo in case of miscarriage, not that Alistair was much of an animal for it anyhow. He was stoic in her rejection but slept well and complained less. Tim and Chloe spent the time wide-eyed and fretful, aware that momentous events were upon them again but unsure what that meant or what their place was in this approaching new order. No one enjoyed the gestation and the relief of Susan's safe arrival produced the kind of noisy joy that frightened all but the Vines.

Susie, the longed-for child, was treated with gossamer hands until she began to talk (early) and demanded that people stop tickling her. She made sure they knew she didn't like it, was having none of it. There were other items not to her liking; mashed turnip, for example. Banana she loved. She took to her feet without bothering to crawl much (it was clearly a waste of time and effort) and tore around the house and garden like a dervish. She appeared to have many more lives than the resident cats, which was just as well considering her pioneering outlook on life. She devoured new experiences. No need to write notes or poems to this one, she wouldn't stop to listen. Speed was her theme. To top it off, a rogue gene from somewhere in the mists of family time had thrown up auburn hair.

She started school aged four, got fat and placid, and let the others push her around. But Valerie could see her size them all up. She was biding her time. And by then she had taught her mother how to divide herself equally between her children and not to concentrate on mollycoddling just one. She had James in her heart still for any of that carry-on, Susie seemed to say. Valerie was chastened but happy. They had made it through.

★   ★   ★

Susie was on the phone to Craig Landor talking about Marty and his movie when he mentioned that he'd met Jay Burns in a bar a few nights before.

'He seemed anxious for me to read some film about cloning,' Craig said.

Susie's blood stopped.

'Then he said he couldn't show it to me because I was your client and that it was a shame because there was a perfect role in it for me.'

Susie felt her muscles lose their definition and go cold. She cast her mind back to the Saturday Jay Burns had been in the office unexpectedly. She had thought her desk was slightly askew. Her head began to buzz a warning. She signed off to Craig, assuring him he was missing nothing so far on that front. She looked across the open office floor and saw Burns's tousled dark mop bent over his landline. He had taken the cloning script, copied it. Cloned it! And now he was developing it too.

Arland and Shaw agents worked on their own client lists not on general projects which was why, up till now, she was the only one who had *I-Dentity*. He had stolen it from under her before she was ready to bring it to a more general agency level.

She buzzed Farrah and asked her to hold all of Jay's calls, as she needed some quality time with

101

him, say fifteen minutes. She walked over to him slowly, pacing her breath and pulse. The important thing here was not to let him see how rattled she was. She would gain nothing by accusation. It was imperative to keep the upper hand.

'Jay, I've just had a very interesting conversation with Craig Landor. He tells me you were touting a film script to him, a script I hadn't mentioned to him yet.' She wanted to scream, 'A script you had no right to read.' Instead she smiled and sweetly said, 'If I didn't know better I'd say you were finessing my client.'

Stealing clients was a total no-no in their world of thieves. An actor had to move of his own volition and that happened every day of the week. But the Americans had introduced the notion of finessing: a rival agent runs off at the mouth about a script or a series and how perfect the actor is for it and is utterly shocked their own agent hasn't mentioned or pushed this, then clams up as he's said too much. He is negative without being negative. He is now in second position. The client is increasingly unhappy with his or her representation and a move is almost predictable, to the rival agent's stable. Lola said it was akin to paedophiles grooming children; a nasty comparison but one that Susie was allowing in her imagination now.

Jay Burns didn't have the decency to look abashed. He just shrugged. His eyes never lost hers, daring her to challenge him. She began to sweat. It was clear he wasn't going to say anything at all. Susie gave him full beam wattage and tsked as if he'd been very naughty but not a lot more. Before she could turn away with dignity, and subterfuge, intact, his intercom buzzed and Farrah told him he had a call. This was all of five minutes after Susie had asked her to hold those for fifteen. Burns turned away, ignoring her, and took the call. She began to fume. She tried to get back to her desk without stumbling which was difficult as her knees were rubber and her heart hammering up a storm in her chest. She wasn't sure of what had just happened but it sat badly with her. She needed to talk to Betty, to untangle the situation. Worst of all, she no longer had advantage with her package idea, even if it was a member of her own team who had undermined her.

⋆ ⋆ ⋆

Reg liked to drive his fast car fast. It was his one big luxury. The Mercedes soft-top two-seater was most younger men's 'affair car' but he felt those times were over for him and he used it to fuel other thrills. Today's jaunt was to visit an old friend who was immobile now. He stocked up on goodies in his local food hall and some of the latest bestsellers. He inched through London's sprawl for an hour, cursing traffic, then he opened up the engine and let rip down the motorway and onto the typical English roads that feature in all good movies set around a grand old house in the countryside. The day was a strange, hazy grey. Occasional birds twirled sleepily from the trees. He saw pieces of indeterminate road kill. He passed one massive oak tree, which loomed after a tight corner. Must have been there for centuries. Some flowers were resting at its trunk so he supposed a motorist or two had met their maker there. He had seen Famke K's Road Shrine art and he wondered if the artist knew of this place. He slowed down a little. No point in becoming another statistic even at his late stage of life.

As he settled into Margaret Le Bute's room at the Grove Retirement Home, he commented that he knew so many of the residents it was like visiting a rehab for alcoholic actors.

'Hard to find any other sort of actor of our vintage,' she commented, offering two fingers of pale sherry to oil their wheels.

Margaret's room was a trove of sparkling memories. Her many awards, including two BAFTAs, were lined up on the window sill beside an angry-looking mother-in-law's tongue. Photographs decked the walls, from social scenes with other stars to stills from her movies. The air was spiced with her scent, a cedar and sandalwood essence with a sharp, citrus undernote. As far as he knew the house of Cardin had created it for her and they still sent her batches regularly. Scarves and precious silks hid the plain functionality of the institution's furniture. She sat like a diamond mounted in a strange and wonderful setting, perfectly made up and stylishly dressed. She had always been a looker and the years had not diminished that. He knew she still had her hair coloured and set once a month and bought clothes from upmarket catalogues and the big department store websites. She was the very pineapple of perfection and he told her as much.

'You are well,' she announced, raising the sherry to her lips.

'More or less.' His hands felt like lumpen hammers around the stem of the delicate crystal. 'And you?'

She arched an eyebrow. 'Not as nimble as I once was.' Margaret was confined to a wheelchair. She got straight down to business then. 'Well, we'd best get through the deaths first.' Her mordant sense of humour was one of the things that appealed most to Reg.

They listed their fallen comrades, one of whom Margaret was certain had been murdered by his lover. 'It just seems a tad convenient that he died of oxygen privation due to apnoea in his sleep.' She devoured detective novels and had all the lingo. She said she'd seen every kind of death imaginable in those. If it can be imagined, it can happen, was her verdict.

'He was a cantankerous old bugger,' Reg said of the dead man. 'The wonder is that he lasted so long, if you ask me. Speaking of which, I saw Arthur in *Endgame* at the Barbican. He was one of the parents in the dustbins.'

'Place for him.' Margaret sniffed. 'If he'd been the mother in the bin rather than the father you'd have had the pleasure of seeing him die.' She had never forgiven Arthur for being a terrible George to her Martha in a production of *Who's Afraid of Virginia Woolf?* back in the sixties.

They dissected the latest slew of television dramas and Reg fessed up any gossip he thought she might not have heard. She had a wide circle of correspondents so he had to be on his toes to bring fresh news. It depressed him to see so keen a mind hidden away. She professed to love her home and said she had endless hours of fun teasing the other retired entertainers. But at the back of those dancing, violet eyes was a woman who was running headlong towards boredom, and with that would come true ageing. When the mind gave up, the body had no option but to follow.

They ate a high tea hybrid of the home's fare and his own offerings. They drank Earl Grey and aired more reminiscences. As usual he told her she should write her memoirs and as usual she promised to. He drove back to London even faster than on his outward journey, fleeing the faces of the forgotten and his own inevitabilities. He hated his mortal decay and time's cruelty.

★　★　★

'I really think you are overreacting.'

Susie had masticated her words for an hour before approaching Betty's office and had spewed forth with eloquence and venom.

'I will concede that Jay Burns has been opportunistic in taking the cloning script and seeming to begin work on it but I don't think there is any need to jump the gun and assume a dark, ulterior motive.'

Why was Betty being so fair to the weasel? He

106

was a sly shit and he was up to something. Had she learned nothing from her years in the business?

'Let me mull it over and perhaps come up with a suitable way forward for everyone.'

Susie Vine led a controlled life. She held her emotions close, carefully regulating all aspects. She was safe hands. This Burns situation bothered her as nothing had in ages. She was scarlet hot with anger. At that moment her safe hands could have snapped the Jerk's neck and ripped his head off. She couldn't understand Betty's reluctance to act immediately, if only to haul the fucker across the coals. Betty was asking her to remain calm and say nothing to anyone. Was the oldie losing it? Susie didn't want to think that but what other option was left to her if Betty didn't nip this in the bud promptly, as she so clearly should?

★   ★   ★

The weekend in the Clapham apartment was fraught. Milo went with his dad as usual, leaving Susie and her mother together. She couldn't settle. Valerie gave her sympathetic glances that only riled her more. The last thing she needed was help to get out of this funk but that's exactly what Valerie wanted to offer.

'I think some air would do you a power of good,' her mother announced.

'Air won't cut the mustard, trust me,' she snarled.

'You should get out. Perhaps we could go for a

meal. It doesn't do to stay cooped up.' When she got no reply from her daughter, she added, 'You're knocking years off your life with this sort of behaviour.'

She might have been addressing a teenager.

Max cried off his second weekend in a row and Susie was glad because she was poor company while this preoccupied. She cancelled them both from a soirée, citing bad and contagious colds. She did feel like she'd come down with something. She felt terrible. She was obsessed with Jay Burns and what he might do. Eventually she told Valerie what was bugging her. It calmed her somewhat, enough to go around the corner to Gastro for dinner with her mother and try to tease out some other topics.

'It is so unhealthy to dwell on negatives, Susie.'

'You should know.'

Valerie sighed, which took the place of the words, 'Very mature.' 'I'm just trying to help,' she said.

'Mum, do you have any idea how important my job is to me? It's my living, it's how I earn the money to support me and Milo. I cannot afford for anything to go wrong with it. You don't understand the sort of pressure I'm under and until you do you'd be better off keeping any half-assed advice you have about it to yourself.'

Valerie dropped her head and pudding passed in silence.

Susie relented, feeling worse now than she had earlier. 'I'm sorry to be such a grouch. I know I shouldn't take it out on you. I really am in a state about this and I can't explain why.'

'Perhaps you see this man as a threat.'

Susie was not going to get into this sort of job analysis with her mother. She held her counsel this time.

Valerie smiled. 'I bet you're just as ruthless as he is.'

It was a good time to change the subject. Susie asked about life in Chittenham.

'It was all so different after your father left. I didn't know who to trust, or if I could turn to anyone. I suddenly felt like I didn't have any friends, just acquaintances who would treat me like the village freak show, picking over my bones for news of failure. I even got afraid for a while. That grew very tiresome, I can tell you. I was afraid of everything: life. It was a very lonely time. And when Toby died I felt like I might disappear altogether. That's why I packed up and came here.'

Susie had nothing to offer that would sound anything but trite. She imagined they made a sorry-looking pair, sipping their cafés au lait and looking downcast.

'Of course, only the lonely are truly free,' Valerie said.

★   ★   ★

On Monday morning hell broke loose and tore up the offices of Arland and Shaw. Jay Burns had left the agency to start up his own company. And worse was to emerge. He had taken Farrah with him.

'Now that's what I call a crisis,' Lola said.

Mitch remarked that it would be a two-Xanax day for him. First time since his thirtieth birthday the year before when he'd gone into a decline at how old he felt and looked. He became a bit unhinged about skincare.

Betty was grey as she called Susie into her office. She pulled her pashmina around her as if to ward off further evil. Her rings glittered but her hands looked wrinkled and frail. 'I was wrong and you were right. I apologise.'

'It gives me no pleasure to hear this,' Susie admitted. 'Right now all I can think about is how to maim the bastard.'

'We will have to rise above that for the moment,' Betty said. 'A more immediate concern is that we have no arsewell first fucking point of contact now that Farrah has been lured away. Traitorous bitch. Never truly liked her but it's a bit late to be admitting that. I've put a call out for a temp to take on mission control but that is bound to be unsatisfactory. We'll need to recruit a proper replacement. Something to think on. Right, let's get through the staff meeting and formulate some sort of response to that ungrateful little fucktoad's actions.' She had some colour back in her cheeks by the time she got through that.

Everyone around the table was shellshocked. They fussed with notes, unsure where to begin. Betty took the meeting by the scruff and began to issue instructions. She told Mitch to take the minutes and Dave to answer the phone when it rang.

'I can't believe he didn't tell me he was going,' Lola muttered.

Susie had quietly suspected that her colleague hadn't been fully committed to reviling The Jerk and this seemed to prove it. 'Believe it,' she told her. 'The guy is an asshole.'

'Time is not on our side so I'll make this brief,' Betty said. 'We have been ambushed. I want you all to consolidate your position with your clients. I do not want any more defections or even the chance that Burns might act the predator and poach some other talent along with what he's brought with him. Everybody's priority today is to shore up the lists. And for fuck sake sound positive. We are still a great agency.'

Susie began her calls with Craig Landor, who was relaxed and untroubled. 'I'm happy where I am,' he said, to which the only reply was a heartfelt 'thank you'.

All of the agents went through their paces, sometimes thrilled with the support of their clients, sometimes tortured by ditherers who took the time to worry aloud about their careers and monopolise their representative's attention.

A trade magazine rang for a comment so Arland and Shaw issued a press release congratulating Jay Burns on his initiative and wishing him luck in his new venture. In the nicest possible way they pointed out that he was a very new kid on the block and the company directors hoped he would have even a fraction of their success, naming their top clients and all of the projects they were currently involved in.

'If that doesn't make him spit I don't know

111

what all,' Susie crowed.

The staff took turns in charge of the phone system. No one had any appetite so lunch was a non-event. The camaraderie was terrific. Everyone was doing his or her bit for the war effort.

'The good news,' Lola confided to Susie, 'is that I have cystitis.' When she saw her bemusement, she added, 'Sex. I got some at the weekend.'

'Bless you for trying to make me feel better,' Susie said.

The atmosphere in the office remained jumpy. Susie used the time between calls on her shift to sort through the bizarre mix of post that had come for her clients. It was therapeutic to filter out the craziest or most upsetting of the items before forwarding the harmless stuff. Today Craig Landor was the subject of most of the requests. Some were for autographs, some for signed photographs. Packages held gifts, mostly underwear or small cuddly toys, often both. There were two offers of marriage and one lunatic circular warning of hell's fire which was so badly put together and punctuated Susie longed for a return address so she could offer some advice on layout and a spell-check. It was a cowardly tract designed to frighten the unshielded, citing biblical passages and the consequences of ignoring them: 'IMMENSE DANGER (sic)' and 'Strange Curses' which sadly weren't elaborated on, as they might have provided a laugh. There were also sad letters from people who identified with Craig's character in *Fun Zone*, telling of their own problems. A lot of those didn't seem to realise that he was an actor and had taken him on board as the troubled young man he had played on the box in the corner of the room.

A casting director rang to offer support. 'I'll be honest and admit that I will still have to deal with Jay Burns, but you really are better off without him. I've always found him unneccessarily tricky to work with and I thought he skewed the tone of Arland and Shaw.' She paused. 'And if you say any of that to another human soul I will have you stoned.'

Susie was handing over to Betty when Valerie came through the door. She had completely forgotten a half-baked notion that they might grab a coffee that afternoon.

'Betty, I think you met my mother before?'

'Oh, that was ages ago,' Valerie said. 'I wouldn't expect you to remember.' Valerie had, in fact, been terrified of Betty.

'Of course I remember. How are you?'

Valerie shook the outstretched hand wondering what to say next. 'I'm on my way to visit the British Museum.'

'More than the rest of us natives do. Fuck knows the last time I was there.'

Valerie was agog at the selection of client photographs.

'That's our agency Wonderwall,' Susie explained.

Valerie pointed at a portrait of screen legend Martin Moore. 'I loved that man. I thought he was the sexiest hero ever when I was younger.'

It was faintly strange for Susie to see her mum come over all girly about a matinee idol.

'Mmm,' Betty murmured. 'I repped him for

about a decade. Terrible man for sticking his cock into young flesh, I'm afraid, preferably male, but great fun for all that. Takes all sorts, I suppose.'

Valerie looked as if she might gag but Betty was oblivious.

'Those on that side are clients who are no longer available,' she went on, 'the ones who are resting permanently in the hereafter. Damn all commission from them now, though an odd repeat fee arrives sometimes, which reminds one of how good they were and how missed.' She sighed. 'And how wonderful life was before total buyouts became the norm on contracts.'

★　★　★

Milo's embarrassment squeezed his muscles tighter and tighter to near-paralysis. There was no way they should be doing this. Curiosity and morbid interest in what grown-ups 'got up to' won the day. He took the binoculars from Rafe and tried to keep his hands from shaking. He trained them on a second-storey apartment south of the roof of the science building where they were crouched. A man and a woman were doing unspeakable things to one another. Adam had shown them a dirty mag he'd found under his parents' bed so the sight of naked flesh wasn't a shock. It was a different matter altogether to see the naked flesh animated. Rafe supplied a continuous stream of questions. 'What's he doing now? Is he sticking it into her? Is she moaning?'

114

'We're too far away to hear that,' Gregory pointed out.

The man was indeed banging his penis (which was huge and a strange, reddish-purple colour) into the woman as she lay beneath him, her legs wrapped around his torso.

'They're fucking like animals,' Rafe hissed.

Milo knew from his biology book that this was intercourse, but what word could possibly describe a man pushing his face into a woman's private parts? Milo thrust the binoculars back at Rafe and tried not to vomit. Rafe looked, cackled and said, 'That is so gross,' before passing them along the line. Over their shocked breathing they heard boots on gravel and threw themselves flat onto the roof until the heavy steps were gone.

'I'm out of here,' Milo said, glad of the chance to end their spying and escape.

* * *

Susie almost didn't recognise her home. The sofa had been moved and some large houseplants lounged new and shiny leaved in pots around the wall. She had killed so many of them before through neglect, she already felt like a murderer just looking at them. It depressed her. She remembered Lola refusing a dish of deep-fried whitebait in a restaurant once, citing 'too many lives on one plate'.

Milo and Valerie were in his room playing a computer game, which she didn't inquire about. The last time she'd asked her son to explain the difference between his two favourites he'd said, 'One is guns and the other is more kung fu and knives.'

'What happened out there?' Susie asked.

'I had a little tidy-up, dear. I hope you like it.'

Susie supposed she wouldn't be able to find anything for a week. She took refuge in her bedroom.

Milo knocked on her door as she was getting out of her office clothes and into a shamefully comfortable tracksuit. She had made plenty of vague mental promises that she would go to the gym but even wearing the gear might do at a pinch, she hoped. Milo mooched a bit before getting to the point.

'Mum, did you see Max over the weekend?'

'No. He cried off again. Why?'

'I think you should talk to him, that's all.' Milo wouldn't look up from the floor and she happened to know it wasn't that interesting. She saw it every day and it wasn't exactly scintillating, floors so seldom were after the age of three.

'OK, I'm officially intrigued. What would he have to tell me, do you think?'

Milo looked as if someone had his balls in an ever-tightening vice grip. He was sorry he'd started this conversation and didn't know what had possessed him to. Why not leave well enough alone? Any time he drew attention to himself, it went badly. He couldn't backtrack, much as he wanted to. Crikey, saying anything to your mother was worse than pressing the send button on an email: there was no getting it back. Might as well lash it all out now. His palms were sweaty and his throat dry. If only he could have enlisted his gran to do this, but she didn't know the true situation. He took a deep breath and blurted, 'He's met someone.'

'Yes?'

It was as if the information didn't compute. Were adults wilfully stupid sometimes or just naturally dim always?

'Max has a girlfriend.'

A light seemed to come on. 'Ah.'

When she nodded, he knew she'd grasped the info and he padded from foot to foot, awaiting an exit point.

Susie couldn't help herself asking, 'Have you met this new . . . girl?'

Poor Milo's anguished tweenie face begged for release as he shook and grunted 'No' in horror at her last suggestion. It was a vast tub of worms and shit and he was glad to be able to tell the truth. No, he had not met this new girlfriend.

His mum frowned. 'Then how do you know?'

'Max told me.'

'Man-to-man?'

'Um, yeah, I suppose.' Please let this end.

'Thanks for telling me,' she said. 'Now I'm sure you've got homework so off with you and do it.'

He fled before she'd finished the sentence.

Susie sat on the edge of her bed feeling extremely celibate. It was never going to last forever, she reasoned, but now her perfect camouflage was blown. She'd have a bit of grace time after she publicly admitted single life. Then

117

she would be a market commodity again. She was stunned, she realised, which wouldn't have been her prediction for what she'd feel when this moment arrived. She'd thought she'd be cool and accepting but she wasn't. She was mildly jealous, which floored her. Suddenly she wanted to know all about this other woman. The worst-case scenario was that she was tall, thin, beautiful and brainy. This foxy minx was hopelessly attractive to men and every woman wanted to be her. Her fabulousness was suddenly such that Susie's mind couldn't compute an actual image of her, just an amorphous loveliness that was heartbreaking and disgusting all at once. She hated this faceless hussy with her virtual talent and physical perfection. She was unreasonably agitated to be officially back on the shelf.

Her discomfort would not lift. She didn't like the silence in her room. All day she was surrounded by phones ringing and beeping, other voices doing deals, the clatter of a busy office. Travel was noisy. Foyers of theatres and cinemas bustled. People talked at her from stages and screens. Radios played in cabs. This lack of a soundtrack was intolerable. She thumped her pillows a few times but the dull whumps did nothing to fill the void. She liked expending a little of her negative energy though. She went in search of bustle, which was Valerie banging saucepans, and listening to *Just A Minute* on Radio Four.

★   ★   ★

Milo lay on his bunk avoiding homework. He hadn't liked that last scene at all. He wasn't cut out for the role of bad-news giver. Adult relationships were clearly nightmares, full of pitfalls and disappointments. His dad was happy enough but he was actually married and that seemed to remove a lot of the trouble with going out and socialising in search of a partner, as far as Milo could see anyhow. All the people he knew of who weren't hitched or had been and were now divorced seemed to be less settled in their lives, always complaining about the lack of potential partners or how hard it was to meet anyone. He really didn't understand what the fuss was about. And also in a city of so many million people just how hard could it be to meet someone? The weirdest situation was his gran who was separated and staying with them. He'd never heard of grandparents separating before. They were too old for that. Grandparents were quiet and spoiled you with money behind your parents' back. He didn't think it was possible, at their age, to still be having sex. Surely. He really, really hoped his gran wasn't going to go on the hunt for a man. He didn't think he could deal with it. She was way too ancient for that caper. He had a horrid flashback of a man and a woman through binoculars, so close in magnification that he could make out hairs on the man's shoulders and both their pubes. It made him feel faint and very guilty.

The more he thought about it, and it made him incredibly uncomfortable to do so, the more he vowed never to have anything to do with anyone romantically. He might even have to give up on the beautiful Isabelle. If other people's experiences were anything to go by, it all looked like far more trouble than it was worth. He was glad he went to a boys' school and didn't have to deal with the opposite sex much. They scared him a little. He just couldn't figure out what went on in their heads, whatever about the fact that they were differently constructed too.

Rafe was full of stories about his sisters who sounded totally awful. Worst was when they were 'on the blob' according to him. Then they were bitches from hell. Milo knew from biology that this was menstruating and he preferred that way of describing it. It involved buckets of blood and mysteries like tampons and sanitary towels. The whole thing made him feel queasy and unclean. He didn't think he had a lot in common with girls. Couldn't have. He didn't think he had a lot in common with anyone, really. He hoped it all got easier as it went along: life, school, friendships. And the whole girl problem. Though he really didn't see how it possibly could.

★ ★ ★

'Number-one worry is that her name is Stacey,' Lola said of the temp sent to fill the gap left by Farrah's defection. 'She's also far too jolly. I wonder if she's on something. Oh, and that new version of *Othello* is a train wreck. I give it a fortnight, max.'

'Have you read this interview with that

120

mange-ridden, shit bag Burns in the paper? Seems he's the saviour of show business and only just escaped from here with his integrity intact. We tried to suck his soul out of him.'

'Susie, loath as I am to back him up in any way, what he suggests is that he was stultified here because we're so backward and old fashioned.'

'Oh, right, that makes it OK.'

'I hate it when you do passive-aggressive. I prefer just aggressive.'

Tuesday brought the sort of fallout from Jay Burns' exit that no one had foreseen: he had not taken all of his clients with him. The unfortunates involved had read of his departure in the paper the previous evening. They rang to worry, complain and demand satisfaction. Betty divided them between the remaining agents, which was how Susie inherited a mercurial young man called Rod. He had made the crossover from modelling to character acting but in truth still made a living from both. Susie had met him on a handful of occasions and hadn't made up her mind about whether he was chronically shy or playing mind games by letting everyone else run off at the mouth and seeming eloquent by comparison when he gave of his pith. She had no idea why Burns had left him behind as he worked constantly and had a high profile. Rod knew the answer to that one. 'I told him he was a wanker week before last.'

'Which he was, is and ever will be.' Susie wasn't usually so upfront with a client about business rivals but she wanted to get that off her chest.

Rod rewarded her with a wide flash of perfectly maintained teeth. He was a picture of blond-haired, blue-eyed youth.

'Rod, neither of us was expecting this situation but if you'd like me to I'd be happy to represent you. I'll understand completely if you decide to move on.'

'No, no, I'm content to stay. In fact, I'm sure this will be much better for me. I never really got on that well with Jay. He always tried to be too blokey with me.'

'I've had a quick look at your file and I see that Rocket sunglasses are wondering if you'd be the new face of the brand worldwide but there's no indication as to where the deal is at right now, so does that mean you're not interested? It would be a lot of exposure but that would be reflected in the fee, I'm sure. At the end of the day it's advertising, but classy enough, I think. How do you feel about doing something like that?'

He was amazed. 'First I've heard of it, to tell you the truth. I think the brand is hot. And if they pay, I haven't got too many objections to some fantastic shots of me saturating the world.' He smiled again and Susie forgot she'd ever had a problem talking to him.

Instinct told her that the scenario didn't feel right. Why wouldn't Burns have told his client about this? Unless . . . an idea formed in a cortex so when Rod excused himself for a few moments she took the opportunity to make an emergency call to Rocket. As she suspected, Burns was pushing someone else for the contract.

Susie was silk-smooth as she verbally gestured

that aside as piffle. 'Your first choice is here with me at Arland and Shaw and I feel confident that we can do business.'

Suck on that, Jay Burns. She arranged a meeting with them to scope the campaign, ballpark figures on money and whether they would be tolerable to deal with. She would meet Rod afterwards to discuss whether they would go further.

'*A demani*, Svengala,' he said, blowing a kiss in the air as he left.

Her heart fluttered in a pleasant way, which she dismissed as hopeless sentiment. It made her chuckle all the same. Lola sidled by her desk to ask, 'How did you get that hottie while I ended up with a clapped-out radio soap star with an inflated view of her gifts? She rang this morning to give me an earful about agents' morals. I can't wait to fire her ass.'

'How long has she got?'

'She's out next week unless there's some act of God in the meantime and I can't imagine what would be good enough to keep her on my books. Cut and thrust. Push has come to shove. I love it. Speaking of pushing, I may have to kill Stacey. She's putting through every call and when I tried to introduce a weeding-out procedure she laughed in my face and told me she'd never remember all the information.'

'Yes, I've had to endure a little too much mirth too. Let's give her the benefit, shall we? We're a bit up the Khyber at the moment.'

'I preferred it when it was just us against the world yesterday.'

'But you hated having to put on silly voices so your clients wouldn't know they had you at hello.'

Lola shivered at the memory. 'One last chance for the laughing cow so, but I'm mean as a snake and anything could happen if she even smiles at me one more time.'

Susie popped her head around the door of Betty's office to remind her that she had a meeting of the PMA. Betty looked fit to chew iron.

'Not only is Jay Burns a smegmatic fuckpig, this Stacey thing is a fucking nightmare, darling. Doesn't know her tits from her Wonderbra. If she tells me one more time that no one died I will kill her and then someone will very much have died.'

'Hang in there.'

'I may be hanging in here when you get back,' she warned. Her phone buzzed. 'Christ only knows who she's chosen to put through this time. I actually talked to someone on a cold call selling fucking insurance this morning, in the midst of all of this fucking mayhem.'

As Susie walked past Mitch, she heard him say, 'My friend, I cannot get you arrested right now.'

'I hope you didn't actually let your client hear that,' she remarked. 'Telling the truth is not a luxury we can afford at the moment.'

'There are times when it's tempting to let some of the special people we represent know just exactly how special they are. But no, I disconnected before he got that gem. If he had heard, I'd have been treated to him heaping even more of his hose on top of me. I'm not man enough for that.'

'They've broken you.'

'Oh yes, yes, they have.' He shuddered. 'Do you remember when I first came here? I took every call for a fortnight.'

Susie nodded. 'It was hilarious. You were so eager. Apparently I was too, back in my own good old, bad old days. Imagine.'

They paused a moment to remember their splendid naiveté then with another shudder they moved on.

The Personal Managers Association was formed by a number of agencies so that they might pool information and weed out bad deals. The concern today was that a series being filmed by a private company for transmission on the ITV network was offering below the odds of Equity agreements and trying to do away with residual sales commission for actors. The production company's sharp practice had just come to a sticky end whether it knew it or not as the Association drafted up figures and terms that they would accept for clients and vowed not to budge on these. Many of her peers at other agencies wanted to know about the Jay Burns situation but Susie remained smiling and enigmatic, wishing him luck. She did point out that he hadn't joined the PMA and someone should get him to as it wouldn't do to have a rogue elephant trampling all over their good work. 'He's a bit of an individualist,' was all she would part with.

She heard the phones ringing off the hook before she got into the office. Stacey was busy entertaining two motorcycle couriers and obviously had her hands full.

'Answer those, would you?' Susie barked. 'What are you lot waiting for?' she asked the couriers.

'They need scripts copying and bundling up but I can't do it 'cos I can't leave the desk.'

Susie's back stiffened. 'Strange, the last person in this job managed all of that with no problem.' She stalked off to deal with the copying issue, but not before hearing Stacey's voice say, 'Wonder what their last slave died of?'

Susie went to Betty's office and said, 'Either she's out by six o'clock or I am. Can you ask the temp people to send us another?'

'My pleasure.'

Dave was thumping the photocopier. 'This used to work with our telly when it went on the blink.' His eyes were crimson holes in an ashen face. 'I loaded it with paper and I think there's enough ink but the bloody thing refuses to budge.' He looked on the edge of his reason.

'Keep going, champ, you're doing great.'

'Please make Stacey go away,' he pleaded. 'I can't take the good humour and her entire lack of feeling for the job.'

'Consider it done.'

Lola was speaking on her headset.

'They loved what you did,' she said into the phone. 'Really loved it.' She looked at Susie and made a Pinocchio gesture with her hand to denote her nose growing from the lie. 'They

126

especially asked me to tell you that. But unfortunately they've decided to go another way.'

Susie recognised the spiel. It was probably three-quarters true and it was important to keep a client's spirits up with praise in the face of rejection, but Lola could never resist an opportunity to roll her eyes metaphorically to heaven. When she finished the call she buzzed Stacey and said in a stern, not to be misunderstood tone, 'Hold everything for me till I tell you.

'I am freaking well exhausted with this day,' she told Susie. She grabbed some nail varnish and began to paint. 'I need some Me Time.' She flicked through a newspaper, awkwardly ringing items while trying not to smudge her varnish.

'You looking for a new job?' Susie asked. 'Joke, by the way.'

'No.'

It was odd for Lola not to be voluble in explanation so Susie paid more attention to the newspaper. It was *The Jewish Chronicle* and clearly very interesting and indeed full of gems if Lola's expressions were an indication of content. Susie looked over her shoulder and saw that she was ringing death notices.

'Oh, Lola, I'm sorry. Did you know these people? Were they friends?'

Lola snorted. 'No. I realised today that I might not be cut out for this life of ongoing crises so I'm looking for my get-out route. I'm taking the details of the younger widowers. They'll be desperate for company in a few months' time and it's a better shot than having Zelda set on my case.'

Susie had genuinely heard it all now. And not in a good way. 'You have reached a new low.'

Lola shrugged. 'Get real. It's a jungle out there. I'm a survivor.'

'You are a bad pop song made flesh.'

Lola refused to rise to the bait.

'Humanity hangs its head,' Susie said.

* * *

Valerie went through the pile of post again. This morning it had contained a letter from Milo's school. Now that was missing. She called her grandson out to the main room, not wanting to approach him in their shared ground of his bedroom, his lair.

'Milo, I think you should put back the letter that came for Susie from Morning Star.'

He looked appropriately blank.

'Milo?'

He shrugged at the unimportance of it all. 'It's just my attendance record. It comes every month.'

'I'm not going to ask why you've hidden it because I can guess it's got some late arrivals that you'd probably prefer not to explain. I'm asking you to put it back.'

He was good at staying silent and intractable, she had to give him that.

'Just put the letter back and take what's coming to you. It really is the best way in the long run.'

128

'That is so easy for you to say. You don't have to take the flak.' He managed a high-pitched tone on the complaint that reminded her he was still a child.

'Milo, you have to take responsibility for your actions.'

He stomped off to his room and returned with the crumpled envelope, unopened. He obviously knew what it had to say.

'Thank you. I won't mention any of this, of course.'

'It's so unfair. Like, sometimes the Tube is late, or my Oyster card needs topping up.'

'Save it for your mum.'

★ ★ ★

Office pressure was getting to Susie along with a shapeless dissatisfaction she couldn't put her finger on. It was an itch she couldn't reach to scratch. She found herself deliberately sticking people with her bag, which was heavy with scripts, and poking her elbows into other bodies that dared share her path. She boarded the Central line to go to the theatre in Shepherd's Bush. The aura around her darkened as she found herself wedged between a smelly armpit and a man who had eaten a lot of raw garlic yet still streamed with a head cold. Every time she inhaled she imagined microbes entering her nose and tubes, into her lungs and multiplying. Her eyes watered, her throat tickled with germs. There are times when I hate my life, she thought. And this city.

She was going to this play to check out a young actor who wanted representation. She had seen him give quirky and creditable performances in his graduation show and a fringe production three months ago. Milo's dad had cast him in a Shakespeare on radio and was raving about him. Susie worried that he might be a bit mannered. She hadn't announced her attendance and hid at the back of the tiny theatre hoping to stay anonymous and ready to be delighted.

The play did nothing to lift her. She had seen it described as anxious modernism somewhere and it certainly delivered all that. Video projections moved self-consciously on the walls of the theatre and a score of atonal music and medical machines was manipulated by a live DJ through headsets the audience wore on only one ear. It was a meditation on loneliness today and the attendant grief that it brings to a life, apparently, but ruined by pretension and a lot of very noticeable acting. There was way too much of it. In a small space subtlety was afforded but ignored by this production. She blamed the director mainly and thought she should be taken out and shot for leaving a clearly talented cast so exposed. Here they were over-emoting for England. It was the Olympics of shakes, tics and gestures, of long faces and longer sighs. Susie thought that they were either out there with no direction or too much of it. Whichever, it did none of them any favours. Inevitably someone tried to kill himself. Susie was right up there with him by then.

The play completely missed the point. Loneliness isn't just being by yourself in a room, she wanted to shout. It's being busy but never truly engaging with all of the activity. It's not allowing the self any space. It is an ego-less place. It's actually also a bit of a bore. It's a lot like my life, she could have told the playwright. She was left exhausted and low. But, hey, only the lonely are truly free.

5

Muriel was not the respite they had hoped for. She was starstruck, for one. She clutched her impressively displayed chest and squealed when she saw the Wonderwall. 'Oh. My. God,' she exclaimed, her delivery clearly indicating that she was a fan of popular American sitcoms. She pointed at various actors' shots, calling them by their on-screen names if they were in long-running series and wondering if she could ring to ask them for their autographs. They talked her down and put her off that terrible idea.

'Two words,' Lola said. 'Frying pan and fire.'

'It's three words and all of them have plunged me further into despair. Bad enough that I have to start the day bawling Milo out of it for consistently turning up late to school. I'm as wound up as a very wound-up thing and it doesn't feel good. The sooner we recruit proper help the better. I'm not sure I can face into another week of this.'

'Show business as usual, tararaboomdeeay,' Lola declared, without much enthusiasm. 'I need a husband not a career.'

'No you don't.'

'Eventually I will dwindle into a wife.'

'I am going to admit to being impressed. That's a quote from *The Way of the World*, isn't it? Congreve?'

'Yep. I had a client in the production at the

Nuffield in Southampton this summer. Hearing that gem nearly made the awful train journey acceptable.'

'I'm still not allowing the sentiment. Now, get on with it.'

They were waylaid by the arrival of a large bouquet of flowers for Lola. She preened until she read the card: Jay Burns had sent the floral tribute. 'Why does the only man in London to show some interest in me have to be that putz? I am being chased by one of the Untouchables. Says here he wants to have dinner with me now that we work for separate companies. I should do such a thing? What a day. Already.'

She paused for a think, which everyone recognised as trouble. Then she wondered, 'Should I not lead him up or down some garden path, spend lots of his money on pink champagne and trinkets?'

'Absolutely not,' Susie insisted. 'That would be consorting with the enemy.'

Lola did not look totally swayed but yielded to sense. 'OK, these have to go.' She gestured at the roses. 'Dave, do you want to take the flowers home for your wife?'

'And risk being accused of having an affair? I think not.'

Lola was close to withering as she asked, 'Where would you have had the time or the energy for an affair?'

'Good point. Thanks, I'm sure she'll love them.'

The romance, such as it was, reminded Susie of a situation that needed dealing with. She didn't think she should be the one to initiate proceedings, however. Then again she never did these days when it came to emotional digressions. Not that there were many. Or any. It was ridiculous that her son had told her that she was officially single. Admittedly her set-up with Max was far from conventional. She hummed and hawed, while flicking through the CVs of next generation's wannabes. It was an easy diversion and one she could have done in her sleep. Most went to the left-hand pile and would be answered with a standard letter, the bones of which read, 'Thank you for your interest in our company. At the moment we are not taking on any new clients. Good luck with your career.' In the pile on the right were the ones to watch and if it was someone she recognised and whose work she liked she might even meet with them.

'I went to the play at the Bush,' she told Lola.

'And?'

'Strong, but wrong. Did no one involved any favours.'

'For me, that's the crap bit about being a professional. I hate having to go to a show to check out why it sucks, instead of just basing it on my finely honed intuition.'

Susie located the CV of the young actor she had seen over-act for England in the *Grief* play. She gave him the standard 'good luck, but not for me just now' treatment. In light of the agency's situation, it was pertinent.

All of these decisions she could make using only part of her brain but the side that dealt with relationships was harder to press into service. She prevaricated about whether she should be

134

the one to confront the truth and force them both to admit to the sham. After all, she wasn't the one who'd found someone else and upset the cosy, rosy apple cart. Happily, she was saved having to act by a phone call from Max. She wondered if he had wasted as much of his morning trying to decide on a course of action or simply drumming up some courage.

Susie should have helped him a little, she knew, but preversion took hold of her soul. She decided to torture him for choosing this mythical goddess she had constructed and made him spell out what she already knew in very plain terms. She employed as much silence as she could get away with on a phone without Max wondering if she'd been cut off. He faltered beautifully on his end but got through his prepared speech.

'The thing is, we've had a really good run out of this arrangement but it was never going to last forever. One of us was bound to meet someone else.'

She wondered if he'd practised it, carefully choosing words that would leave little margin for misunderstanding yet not hurt unnecessarily. And so far he hadn't actually admitted he was the one to jump ship, which was a lovely touch. She hummed to let him know she was still listening.

'All right, the thing is . . . the Thing is . . . I've met someone.'

Susie couldn't resist it. 'Are you dumping me?'

'Well, it's not exactly dumping, is it? It's not as if we've been, I don't know, together, truly, for a long time, now is it?'

She imagined a thin line of perspiration rolling down his rather nicely sculpted back. Ah well, she'd have her memories. Then she pointed out an obvious. 'Now that my mum is staying at mine you'll have to come over in person to break up with me. Otherwise she'll think you a terrible coward to do this over the phone.'

This broke the ice and she was glad to let up on the pressure. She hadn't enjoyed it quite as much as she would have liked. They both laughed at the idea of a face-to-face split but it suited the farce they had created and he agreed.

'Of course, I could meet you in town for a drink and do the same, that would be face to face,' he pointed out, after they arranged for him to visit on Saturday.

'Yes, but this is a lot more satisfying.'

'For you.'

'For me,' she acknowledged.

'I still can't figure out how I became the bad guy here. I have to go over to yours to break up from a relationship that doesn't exist.' She could sense him shaking his head in amused perplexity.

'I am a smooth operator,' she reminded him. 'And if you don't turn up I'll tell everyone we know you broke up with me by phone.'

'Yeah, that would be bad for my image. Text is a lot more fashionable these days.'

She found herself hoping that he'd miss her.

★　★　★

Valerie had done as much to the apartment as she felt able to. She had cleaned and dusted, vacuumed and polished. The laundry was up to date. She had de-cluttered, shifted furniture and bought some plants. Susie hadn't altogether been thrilled with the streamlining but Valerie had wanted to help, to pay her way. She needed to get out now. London was full of sights and amazements and she should visit them.

The still, city air was over-sweet with the smell of uncollected rubbish. In Chittenham she would have sat in her back garden breathing in the crisp aroma of late autumn as it tipped into winter. Here she felt surrounded by concrete and traffic fumes. She travelled on the Underground, aware that she stuck out. She paused before the ticketing machines. She read the notices. She was unsure of which turn to take. She was an outsider. Young men in hoodies all seemed to have bad intentions. They shouted their banter loudly, ignorant of the glances of the other passengers, or perhaps enjoying their effect. No one would challenge them on any ground. She listened to the content of their talk and it was vacuous at best. She shook herself mentally. They couldn't all be villains. It was time to be less fearful.

No one noticed her sitting mouselike in the train. No one noticed her walking the streets. She was completely anonymous. She would traipse the National Gallery until her legs and feet hurt. She would drink overpriced coffee in the West End. No one would see. She looked around at the city, aware that London was magnificent but not always beautiful.

She needed to be home at a certain time for

Milo when he got back from his late clubs and extra lessons. The French girl from upstairs usually took charge if Milo was to be home before Susie from his extracurricular activities, and sometimes he visited friends. For now, Valerie would be there and hopefully save Susie some money. She wanted to be useful but really she would admit to feeling largely purposeless. No one truly needed her. She was, in fact, pointless.

★ ★ ★

Lola entertained the company with a preview of her weekend. Her niece's bat mitzvah was the highlight but it meant a gathering of all of the dysfunctional Stein family. Her brother was too mean to hire the local hall so they were going to accommodate the party at her parents'. Everyone had to be in situ before nightfall.

'It's the Jewish equivalent of a blood sport, or certainly the way our family celebrates it is,' she told them. 'The wives hate each other, my parents aren't getting on and I'm the family disgrace. The children are little shits, particularly the bat mitzvah girl. I intend to get very drunk to ease the pain. My brothers will almost certainly join me in that and we'll get pissed and aggressive and have a massive argument about what will happen when Mamma and Papa die.'

Her phone beeped and she paused to read a text from Jay Burns.

'Wants to know if I'll meet him for a drink after work. Who is this bozo kidding?'

She sent the reply, 'Fuck off, you troll,' but

consensus was he'd find that a turn-on as if she was playing hard to get.

'The man is a pervert,' she reiterated, but didn't seem altogether displeased.

Susie's afternoon passed slowly, in a fog of abstraction. She found concentration hard, glad that she didn't have to pull off any pyrotechnical brilliance for a client yet also annoyed that she was getting hardly any satisfaction from her work. Then something crossed her desk that she could get her teeth into. A client, now based in America, was starring in an unexpected low-budget hit for a big company, made last year in Cornwall. Susie had done the deal and ensured that bonuses were in-built. Twice these had come through because of the film's popularity. The movie was really close to achieving the figure for his third bonus but the company refused to round up their figures in good faith. It had annoyed her for weeks. Now they wanted him on a publicity tour of Germany. She was feeling mean. She emailed his publicist in the US.

From: susie@arlandshaw.co.uk
To: darleen@informers.com
Sent: 4 october 3.15
Subject: german publicity

Hi Darleen,

I've been mulling over the situation with Will Funge and the proposed media tour. I think the company are taking the piss so I feel we should tell them where to go. As it happens, Will's wife is due to give birth soon and I can't be arsed asking him to take time out to go to Germany. Can you take it from here bearing all that in mind?

Thanks,
Susie

She felt a little better to have vented some spleen.

★   ★   ★

Milo was cleaning his football boots on the building's rather grand marble staircase outside their door. Unusual that he would do the job without her prodding him for an hour or more, and even then he'd avoid it and settle for a row before school about how he couldn't do phys. ed. with his kit in the state it was in. He had slicked his hair into a quiff with an evil-smelling gel and wore the collar up on his rugby shirt. A smile tried to edge across Susie's lips. She halted it immediately. 'I like that look for you,' she said breezily. His ears reddened like neon tomatoes and she wondered if she'd said the wrong thing. If he was out here he was lying in wait for someone and Susie could guess whom. He was seeing less of Isabelle now that Valerie was ensconced with them. Her presence was impacting in all sorts of ways. It broke Susie's heart and gladdened it in equal measures to see her little boy take his first steps into manhood. Didn't half make her feel old, though.

'Have you seen Isabelle, by any chance?' she asked breezily.

'No.' He gave that the upward twist that wondered 'why?' and exuded cool.

'Just need to talk to her about something. I'll call and ask if she could hang by this evening.'

He was suddenly done with the boots and in the door ahead of her. He dumped them in his room, grabbed his mobile and stationed himself casually in front of the television, playing nonchalantly with his phone, ready to receive any visitor.

'No homework?'

'Done.'

Hard to believe, but she didn't have the strength for the full metal jacket of another school-based argument.

Milo checked the whereabouts of their guest and asked, sotto voce, 'Is Gran staying long?'

'That's a very good question.' It did raise an issue. 'Would that bother you?'

He thought a moment. 'No. She's cool.' After a pause, he added, 'Don't think she'd want to stay here. We're not that much fun.'

From the mouths of babes.

'We'll get fun,' Susie promised. She was usually so exhausted from her long hours, fun was hard to drum up. This shit didn't get any easier. 'I know what'll make you laugh,' she said. 'Max has to come over tomorrow to break up with me so that your gran can witness the event and feel sorry for me, and believe we were still going out in the first place.'

'Oh man, that's complicated,' Milo said. Then he grinned and Susie felt it might all work out yet.

Isabelle arrived for payment and instructions for the coming week. Valerie noticed the awkwardness in discussing this in front of her and said they should continue as if she wasn't there. She didn't announce a departure date. Great, Susie thought, now I'll have two idle teenagers under my feet.

'*Ciao*, Milo,' Isabelle trilled in her fabulous French accent as she made for the door.

Milo gave a mangled, self-conscious 'Chow' in return, clearly uncomfortable with the trendiness of the phrase and aware of his mother's averted gaze. Women were impossible.

There was a strange and palpable silence in the apartment in the wake of Isabelle's perfume. 'Did you have enough to eat?' Susie asked.

'Yeah.' He didn't seem to have opened his mouth at all there.

'How was school?'

'OK.' He gave a tiny shoulder shrug with that one.

'That good, huh?'

'Yeah.' Totally without irony.

Time to call it a day. 'I'm wrecked, so if it's all the same to you guys, I think I'll have a bath and an early night.'

They didn't seem pushed either way. She left them to the television. As she steeped under bubbles she heard their chatter, though couldn't make out words. Why was it he had plenty to say to his grandmother but not a lot to her, his mother? She would never get on top of this parenting lark.

The absurdity of her life threatened to

142

overcome her. Lola was facing a weekend of endless family politics and so was Susie. Her son had a lot more to say to everyone else in his life except her. Their day-to-day relationship was based on argument and fractious negotiation. She was about to let a boyfriend, with whom she was not in a romantic relationship, break up with her for the benefit of her abandoned mother who was living indefinitely in her pocket.

⋆　⋆　⋆

And so, goodbye to another fleeting week, Reginald thought as he sipped his first whisky of the evening. Where did time fly to? There seemed to be less and less of it as the hours disappeared without him noticing some of them at all. At least if he was working he could mark the passage with performances or ticking off his scenes in a movie as they were filmed. Who needed retirement when resting as an actor felt like just the same thing? He didn't like to be idle as much as he'd thought when younger and looking forward. He didn't understand the race to retirement at all, the obsession with wanting to become obsolete. He had known one man, content in a perfectly acceptable desk job, who talked of nothing but how he would fill his days when he was free, then reached his departure level and walked himself to death for want of something to do.

He looked at the empty chairs in the room. He missed his wife. He missed the company above all. She had been a quiet, persistent support.

When she spoke, everyone listened. And if she had a criticism, Reg took it on board and dealt with it. She had disapproved of some of the more sozzled of his friends and he had distanced them. Most were dead now, courtesy of their demon, so she had been in the right. He reckoned it was some sort of impenetrable irony that she should also precede him having devoted so much of her life to lengthening his. Here he was, left alone and in good health for a man of his years.

He hated the phrase 'for your age'. What the hell did that mean? In his head he was a scant thirty-five. Yes, the world and his lifestyle had marked their territory on his face and body. Such was life. Not a lot to be done about it. And though he felt death would be a terrible bore, he knew it was on the cosmic cards for him and felt no rancour about that. Perhaps not just yet, he told himself. 'Cudgel thy brains no more about it', as the Bard said. There was Scotch to be savoured, a steak to be seared, books to be devoured and thoughts to be teased out. Andrew would be pleased. His younger son was a nutritionist, of all things. 'Your side,' as Reg constantly told Claire. Had told Claire. As Reg had constantly told Claire.

* * *

Milo wanted the ground to open very quickly right now and swallow him whole with no chance of ever returning him to this dank and awful earth. His father had chosen to talk about wet dreams and other stickiness. There were no

144

words to express the horror of this conversation. Well, his father was talking, Milo was dumbstruck. They'd gone through physical issues before. What to do with his weeny when he was done peeing, pulling his little hoody back over the tip, that sort of thing. Simple stuff. That was years ago. Now he was expected to wash more often, even his hair, use deodorant and keep a roll of loo paper beside his bed in case of accidents. Worst of all, Milo knew what his dad was talking about. Adam, Rafe and Gregory were full of it too and he was terrified he'd get the wanking bug just by listening to them. As it was he was plagued by thoughts that muddled his brain and did funny things to his privates. He'd have preferred if everyone would keep it all to themselves too, the way he had tried to till now. Privates private and don't draw attention to what should be kept hidden.

It was total agony to be expected to have something to say about the embarrassment of growing up. His anus was clenched. That was one good thing about school, having the proper names for things, and they were nearly always better than what Rafe and the guys wanted to call them. It was epically hard to have to do this boggy maturing thing. Apparently all of the horrible stuff was natural. How could that be true? And why hadn't anyone found a cure for it by now? He nodded a lot as his dad droned on, man to man. He even nodded at the questions, but that seemed to do the trick. I can outwait him, he thought, he can't talk about this forever. Or could he? It was probably what people referred to as quality time. Uh, no, he had news for them: this was in no way, shape or form good quality shit.

'If you ever have any questions at all, Milo, ask me. No matter how silly or trivial you might think they are. I went through all this. I can help.'

'Sure,' he mumbled. Let that be an end to it, he begged silently. He wondered if his mum was having a better time.

★　★　★

Max arrived shortly after lunch to go through the ritual of breaking up. Susie found herself oscillating between nervous dread and the urge to laugh. It was like giggling at a funeral: appalling but impossible to stem. Max affected a vaguely brusque manner for Valerie to remember when she thought about the afternoon, so that she could decide in retrospect how clear it was what he intended. As it happened she was preoccupied with her newest discovery, the Internet, and left them to their own devices after a short bout of small talk. They grinned about this and agreed that she probably thought she had a lot more time to catch up with him.

'And it's not like I'm disappearing altogether,' he said and they both regretted that he had, because that was close to what would happen now. They would see less of one another and that gap could only grow.

Susie made coffee in the kitchen and said, 'It's all right, you don't actually have to put it all to words, tempted as I am to make you.'

'Milo texted to say he was sorry to be missing it. He has more than a touch of your perversity.'

'That's ma boy.'

The silence between them wasn't all that comfortable. Too many things were happening simply by being in the wake of this break-up.

'I'll stay in touch with him,' Max said, voicing one of the big concerns.

'You don't have to, but it would be really nice if you did. You've been one of his role models for years.'

'I'd like to think of myself as more of a friend.'

'You're that, to both of us.'

'What now?'

'You mean me?'

He nodded. 'Without me as camouflage.'

'Guess I'll have to go out there. Or maybe I won't bother. I don't really have the time, Max. I was never that interested in the pursuit of romance, if that's any sensible way to describe it. It's all so undignified and toe-curling. If it's not there, you can't manufacture it.'

'Susie, you should have a string of men dangling. It's easy to get out of the habit of trying to meet someone.'

'You got lucky,' she pointed out.

'I made myself lucky. I put myself out there. Not in any hungry way, just became available. It worked. Let yourself have some fun.'

'That seems to be a running theme in my life now, people telling me to have fun. It's not as easy as that.'

' 'You know, I think maybe it is.'

Susie felt a sudden lurch. She was losing her comfort zone. She began to feel afraid of what lay in wait for her without Max. Above all she hated to lose control over the situation. Control calmed her. It had rules and a predictable course. Max, with his easy-going nature, and factual bulk, made her feel safe. Now she was to be alone, jettisoned in a world she had successfully avoided for ages. She didn't want to be single, no more than she wanted to be half of a couple. Not unless it was on the brilliant terms she'd had with Max, with more regular sex. Being alone wasn't the same as being single in London. Single meant prey, alone was peaceful. With Max she'd had the peace, and peace of mind, and none of the exposure to the meat market. She wanted to cling to Max, to solidity. The future was a bewildering place. But Max had only been an interim arrangement in a meanwhile that had stretched into years and nothing that good lasted forever any more. Which was a shame, as she saw it at that moment. Some people study culture by what's thrown out, she remembered: garbology. She was surplus to requirements now. What did that tell the emotional garbologists?

His last words were, 'I like it when you let your hair go curly.' Her hand rose to touch her tresses. She hadn't tamed them today. They were wild. Out of control. 'Loosen up,' he might as well have said.

When he stepped out through the door she actually shed tears, which was unexpected. It wasn't exactly as if he'd caught her by surprise.

Good moment to approach Valerie with the news, she thought, but even the sluttish actressy remnant of her brain vetoed such subterfuge. Over the top, morally, it advised. Weird, as morals had hardly ever reared their heads above her low-set parapet during her brief career. Everyone's lives were available to be plundered for tics, habits, emotions, details. It was a matter of practicality; to dissemble well, one had to seem entirely sincere. What a many-edged irony that was. According to the old saying, acting is all about honesty, if you can fake that you've got it made. When she had composed herself and set a sad face, she told Valerie that she was single. 'Sophie said to call her when it happened,' her mother told her. 'She wants to come round.'

Am I always the last to know anything important? Susie wondered.

She had no time to dwell, though, as Sophie was about to pounce. She was consumed with trying to remember all of the little lies she and Max had told to disguise their situation. These were proving far harder to recall than the larger subterfuge, which was broad strokes all the way. Sophie opened with, 'That rat Max,' allowing the trashing of Susie's ex to begin. She defended him on some points but had to allow others, otherwise she might have been lynched for the huge lie they had perpetrated on their pals for so long. It felt good to bitch about men, harmless actually. Valerie joined in with aplomb, telling Sophie all about her own single status. Sophie was appalled and laid into Alistair too.

'Is this some clichéd scene of women enabling

women?' Susie mused aloud.

'It's certainly women getting drunk on Sancerre,' Sophie said. 'I think that's probably a modern cliché too.'

'Good enough, so,' Susie declared. 'I wouldn't be able for anything ground-breaking at the moment.'

'No, no,' Valerie agreed. 'Leave that to the pioneers for now. I haven't the energy to do more than whinge about what's come to pass. It's far more enjoyable anyhow. We do, however, have to get back to saving the world on Monday.'

A detail surfaced in Susie's addled brain. 'How did you know that Max was going to break up with me?' she asked Sophie.

'Ah. Phil met him and his new paramour in a bar in town. He said Max looked almost relieved to be caught.'

I'll bet, Susie thought. And then she couldn't resist asking, 'What is she like, this new bird?'

'Well, bearing in mind that Phil was describing her to me, his wife, and a best friend of the soon-to-be ex woman friend, all he would part with was that she was tallish, a redhead and 'all right if you like that kind of thing'.'

They groaned at this.

'So in other words she's gorgeous,' Susie concluded.

'I would think so, yes.'

'Hand me the bottle, I am moving on. We are about to take this up a notch.'

It was a relief not to have to lie any more about Max. She felt a little foolish that they had allowed it to go on for so long. But the arrangement had suited its time and she hadn't wanted anything more. Was it so wrong to hanker after a quiet, uncomplicated life? To be left alone now and again?

* * *

Valerie got the full story of the disastrous receptionists at breakfast. She laughed at the stories of ineptitude then made an announcement. 'I'm thinking I should look for a job,' she said chirpily.

This was interesting and a little scary. What location had her mother in mind for this new departure in life? She could take an educated punt. 'I presume you mean here rather than Chittenham?'

'Well, yes. It's less than half formed as an idea, I'll grant you, but I can't see myself rushing back to Devon in a hurry. Now, I don't want you to be worried, I wouldn't be under your feet all the time. I just need to find a way to make a living then I can get my own place.'

'Oh Mum,' Susie sighed. 'You have no idea how expensive London is, do you?' She sipped tea for breathing time. 'I know this will sound harsh but you're also beyond retirement age and don't exactly have a range of skills to tempt a prospective employer.'

Valerie was totally crestfallen.

'I'm not trying to rain on your parade, Mum, but it's tough out there.'

From some depth Valerie got extra puff and rallied. 'Well, listening to you I was aware of the fact that I could run a desk like your front office. I'm a mature woman with good social skills and I ran your father's business on and off for forty years. How different could it be?'

'I suppose you're right,' Susie conceded. Her mother was pleasant with people and fairly calm under pressure. She had some old-fashioned experience and could type. None of this was world-stoppingly shattering. An idea had seeded itself all the same. If she paused for analysis she might not act on it. Her mind felt too exhausted to thrash through the possible outcome of her actions. She occupied her mother with clearing away the dishes and used the phone in her bedroom to call Betty.

'It's out of left field, but I wondered if Valerie might see us through while we advertise for a proper office manager? That way we have a controllable menace at our beck and call.'

'The devil you know,' Betty commented.

'Exactly. She used to do secretarial work for my dad before the Ark set off to sea and, if we talk her through the phone system and the basics of the computer, the rest is pretty much standard.'

'Good. Yes. She's a solid person? Organised? Not easily thrown?'

'I think so. We can fire her if not.'

'Right, well, beggars and choosers at this stage. You bring her up to speed and I'll ask her in for a chat. If all goes well I'll jettison Muriel first thing though we'll need her for the changeover and no doubt she'll need time to get her signed client photos together.'

'One last thing. I don't think we should tell the others she's my mother. Perhaps we could say she's a friend of yours? I wouldn't want anyone feeling awkward about that or thinking they can't criticise her because of me.'

'Understood. Put her on, would you, and I'll ask her to come in.'

Sweet Mother of the Divine and Suffering Jesus, what have I done? Susie wondered. My mother is about to join the agency, however temporarily, at my behest. I must be mad. Well, bring it on. I thrive under pressure and shuffling details and possibilities.

Valerie came through the door ashen. 'Thank you. Thank you,' she said.

'Don't be so sure. You have to get past Betty first. And if you do you'll find I am a slave driver, a very hard taskmistress. Get yourself ready for a crash course in Arland and Shaw.'

The tutorial took place at the table fifteen minutes later. Susie sat eating satsumas, relishing the burst of juice as she pierced the membrane of each section with her teeth and saliva mixed with satisfaction and vitamin C. The zest filled the air with sweetness. Valerie was armed with a notebook and looking anxious but thrilled. Susie began.

'Acting is essentially lying for a living. Cynical, I know, but true. It's all pretence. And agenting isn't all that different. It's showmanship and brinkmanship and basic haggling so that someone else is paid well for their lies. And we like to think that we represent some of the finest liars in the country at Arland and Shaw. We tell

153

the clients what they want to hear, keep them sweet, then we praise our talent to putative employers and raise the bar incrementally over negotiations till we have the price we want, and the employer has perhaps an even more inflated view of the artist they've bagged. Basically, as long as they're convinced they've got the best for a good price, be it high or low, everyone is happy. A lot of smoke is blown up everyone's skirt and the buzz is created. We take our ten to fifteen per cent and move on to the next negotiation.

'I suppose the difference between our style of agenting and say the Americans is that we would say 'I love your work' whereas a US agent would be much more likely to ask 'Where do you see yourself in five years' time?' It's a bit more aggressive. But it's all the language of love, in a perverted way: I love you, I love what you do and I'm going to get you the best deal I can because I believe in you and I will kill for you in there and defend you to the utmost against anyone who wants to fuck you over. That sort of thing.

'We can go totally one-on-one if required, arrange for the client to be dressed, made up, accompany him or her to media interviews, veto subjects, issue press releases, walk them into VIP gigs, all of that. Hold their little handies if that's what they need. As long as they're doing the work, delivering on screen or on stage, we are there to look after most of the rest. We have a management style. In Los Angeles, a successful actor will have an agent, a manager, a lawyer (sometimes more), a publicist and so on. Here we tend to have all that to hand if needed. It's a slightly slower pace and less litigious. And the money isn't as astronomical. As yet.'

Valerie looked a bit boggle-eyed, punch drunk with information, but gamey all the same.

'We should fix up the box room for you. It's tiny but we could make it really funky and comfortable. And it'd be your own space.'

'As long as I wouldn't be in the way?' Valerie checked.

'Don't be ridiculous,' Susie said, wondering if it was all that crazy a suggestion. Her little two-person unit had expanded by thirty-three and a third per cent suddenly. 'What's to happen with Chittenham?' she asked.

Valerie could have kissed her for not calling it home. It didn't feel like that any more. 'I think it's time for your father to take some responsibility there. Hopefully he won't over-water the plants. Other than that there's not a lot he can do to mess things up any more than he has.'

There was a harder edge to her mother now that Susie decided to leave unexplored. Small wonder that she should feel resentful of a husband who'd upped and left. A man who hadn't the decency to move more than a few streets away. It must have dented her mother's pride horribly, after so many years of support, and left her self-confidence next to non-existent. And what effect had it had on her love for this man? She must have had her feelings ripped apart for her, without ever having deserved it and certainly without expecting it.

155

Susie loved her dad but he could be stubborn and impossible and she was never certain that he heard any of what she said to him. She was glad to be able to abdicate the next task without any guilt and to know it was in better hands than hers. 'I'm guessing that's one phone call you'll get some pleasure from making,' she said to her mother, smiling. 'I'll leave you to it.'

She went to the box room to try to figure out where all of the rubbish she'd acquired was going to go. Time for a de-clutter, like it or not. These things were best pushed on a life unawares, leaving no time for faffing about. They needed space now so she would be vicious. It might prove gloriously cathartic. She was free of a significant other and about to streamline her life. The important thing was not to start reading anything that looked at all interesting or to look into photo albums. These could be piled into storage boxes under her bed. Anything else that hadn't been used in over a year was getting the boot.

She opened up a huge black plastic sack and began to chuck in all of the so-called useful things they had accumulated but didn't need. Another bag of actually useful and recyclable items would be for Oxfam. She remembered a time when Milo was a child and she'd decided to get rid of lots of his old toys. She'd made a pile of the halt and the lame, then had to sneak them out the door rather than let him see her discard creatures with only three legs or one eye. She worried about what message she might be sending him. Parenthood was a minefield and no manual could help or solve its puzzles. It was the leap into the dark that could not be put off. Fingers crossed and jump, and hope and pray that you don't fuck it up.

★　★　★

Valerie took time to compose a beautifully worded statement for her husband. Reality, however, rarely lives up to expectation and so it was that she found herself giving her announcement to an answering machine. She made sure to sound upbeat and indifferent and in the end was thoroughly pleased with how things had gone. She might not see the place she had once called home for a long time but that didn't bother her. So much the better for perspective to set in. She realised if Alistair got sick à la her fantasies, she would now feel annoyance at the disruption. She would be busy with other matters and enjoying them. For his own sake he'd better not fall ill because she was by no means sure she would dash to help him, as things now stood. What a liberating feeling it was to be utterly selfish. A steady pulse of excitement beat in her craw.

First up, she'd have to see about the curtains in the box room. Hideous. In fact, if she wasn't mistaken she'd actually bought them as a present for poor Susie years before. Her daughter had been forced to hang them rather than hurt her feelings. What had possessed her? They were the chintzy ghost of Valerie Past and they had to go. Funnily enough, Susie didn't object for long and

157

the window was soon naked.

'Toby would have loved this,' Valerie said, nonsensically. Pulling herself up, she asked, 'What's the word for that? Giving animals human thoughts and so on? Anthropo-somethingorother, morphism?'

'I don't think I have a brain cell big enough to remember that. You'd best hang on to it for both of us.'

'We need to talk about rent,' Valerie stated.

Susie laughed off the suggestion.

'I mean it. If I'm to be a working woman I'd like to pay my way.'

They tussled over this in a good-natured way, then agreed on a price that left Valerie with her dignity but wouldn't leave her broke. I'd better get this job, she thought. She relished the prospect of independence. She would open her own bank account, get her very own credit card instead of having to share one with Alistair. She wrote National Insurance number with a question mark beside it on the pad. She must look that up. There was so much she hadn't paid attention to about her own life, her own self; details that didn't really add up to her exactly but which had a bearing on who she was, or who other people thought she was. Even people in government offices who had never met her and never would. To someone out there she was a number. Only that. Again, this felt oddly liberating. She would stick with the solid, official facts; everything else was up for grabs.

6

Lola eyed Susie suspiciously.

'Not what you think,' Susie told her. 'Max broke up with me on Saturday. I'm single again.'

'It suits you. You should have let this happen ages ago. I like the hair, I think.'

Susie had left her mane to do its own thing, merely using two combs to hold it behind her ears. Milo had eyed her quizzically before leaving and said, 'You look pretty, Mum,' unable to put his finger on what exactly he saw that was different about her.

'Yes, it's a change. I think we'll be seeing a few of those. How was your weekend?'

'No one died,' Lola said in a flat, dark tone.

Valerie emerged with Betty from her office. Betty asked for their attention. 'I am pleased to announce that my friend, Valerie Macintosh, will be taking up the position of receptionist and office assistant. I hope you will all make her welcome.'

Susie took in her stride, awarding herself good marks for her acting. She hadn't lost all of her performing gifts, by any means. Valerie, for her part, played a good role, but then she was also too nervous to dissemble much. She was so overwhelmed, Susie might as well have been a stranger. Betty led her to reception.

'There are two phone lines that clients use to get to us, the rest is for the general public.

Muriel will talk you through the computer and then we'll leave you to get on with things,' Betty said. 'A lot of what we do is excellence through guesswork so don't be afraid to ask questions.'

Valerie had been thrust into the midst and there was nothing Susie could do for her. The birdie had to learn to fly alone now. She kept an eye out for trouble in the first hour but Valerie managed any task given. She was slow and careful but a pleasant antidote to the giddy antics of the temps. Susie felt trepidation and pride.

The other surprise was Marty who had come to London to meet Craig Landor. They rendezvoused at the Soho. Susie had expected a man in his fifties who tried too hard to be younger in outlook and dress, possibly an ex-hippy or ex-biker type, ex something anyhow. Wrong. In spite of a long CV, Marty was barely out of his thirties and neatly turned out. He wore small round glasses that gave him the look of a scholarly, tall hobbit. The lazy hooded eyes looked gullible behind his geeky specs but when he began the Gatling gun critique of his trip, a shark with a sense of humour emerged. He was excellent company and cute in spite of features that could not have worked alone but somehow were more than the sum of their parts when put together. An interested smile adorned his face when it was at rest and it put everyone at ease. They passed some pleasantries and then Susie made her excuses. She'd arranged to call Craig in thirty minutes to see if he needed rescuing. As it happened he did not and was about to go to eat with Marty.

On her return Susie went to Betty's office. 'I want to start moving the cloning project on,' she told her boss as she stood before her desk. Then she had a pace. Her tail was up.

'Agreed. I've looked at the material and it's fucking wonderful. I want to send a copy out to John Forbes today to see if he's interested. I'm certain he will be. Other than that we need to circulate it in the office and get suggestions for all the major parts so that we can package this one up tighter than a gnat's arse.'

This was the buzz they lived for, the excitement of making a job happen, urging good work along. They were making a difference now and it was the sort of fulfilment Susie wanted from her job.

Valerie hardly noticed her daughter's return to the office. She was a blur of action now, printing off copies of *I-Dentity* for John Forbes and the other agents. A courier was dealt with in the midst of the packaging of the scripts and a phone call patched through to Lola. Susie went to her desk and her butt had hardly hit the chair when her mobile rang. The number came up as 'parents'. Not any more, she thought.

'Susan, I'm worried about your mother. I think she may have flipped.'

'Dad, long time no hear,' she said pointedly.

'Yes, yes, there's no time for sarcasm. Your mother is obviously losing her mind. She left a most extraordinary message for me saying she has a job in London and isn't coming home. I think the dog's death may have sent her over the edge.'

'You don't think that maybe you are partly responsible for that, if it is indeed the case?' She could see Valerie through the glass partition. She was gesturing happily at Dave, sharing some quip. She certainly didn't look like a woman on the edge or gone over it into the abyss. Far from it.

'You'll have to bring her back immediately,' her dad continued, ignoring his part in any of Valerie's troubles. 'She's clearly not well.'

'Dad, I have never known her to be so well. She has landed a top job here at the agency and everyone loves her. I'm delighted to report that she is a new woman and having the time of her life. How are you?'

'Susan, I can tell from your tone that you're angry with me. I suppose that's understandable. I don't want to discuss it with you as I'm sure we'll simply argue in circles but suffice to say I didn't see the point of continuing what had become a posturing charade.'

What a charming way to talk of a long and, until now, happy marriage. 'Dad, there's no easy way to say this. She's not going back to Chittenham any time soon. Still, look on the bright side, it means you can move back into the house.'

She heard him give a harrumph on the other end, which she recognised as annoyance. It was hard to feel in any way sympathetic towards the man. Too bad if things weren't to his liking any more. She made her way to Valerie's desk to tell her about the latest instalment in the family saga and heard Lola coaching on the nuts and bolts of the business, as she saw it.

'Can't act,' Lola was pronouncing. 'In the same way as some animals cannot swim.'

'Hope that's not one of ours,' Susie commented.

Neither of the other women replied and Susie thought it best not to delve. She jotted a note on a post-it and said, 'Something you can have a look at later.'

As she walked away she heard Lola continue, 'Impossible, like trying to nail jam to a wall.' Susie hoped Valerie had a filter to sift through the good and the unrepeatable.

Reginald Darwin passed through on his way to Betty's lair. Susie saw so much of John Forbes in the older man. They were both tall, elegant almost, though Reg was thickening as men of his years did. They both had excellent bone structure and tumbling heads of hair, but what really pierced were the eyes. Pale, wise, grey. Her heart warmed a little to think of John. He had once had the good manners to ask her out. She made it clear that he was a client and off limits. It was only later she realised she should have cited her boyfriend Max and John should have mentioned that he wasn't quite divorced then.

★　★　★

Betty had left a message for Reg to phone but he rather fancied a trip into town so he presented himself in person. A delightful new receptionist made him a good cup of Earl Grey while he waited for Betty to finish a call in her office.

163

Valerie Macintosh complimented him on a recent 'Book At Bedtime' he had read for the BBC. They had a lovely chat about literature in general. She was a fine-looking woman with a lively mind and he'd almost forgotten the purpose of his visit by the time Betty came to collect him from his comfortable perch. He followed his agent as she wove through the desks and smiled at the other familiar faces, all of which looked thrilled to see him.

'You've been offered the part,' Betty told him from the business side of her desk.

He was momentarily puzzled. 'Which one?'

'The movie is called *The Summer House*. The young director you met recently? He was blown away by you.'

Reg laughed. 'I was sure he hated me on sight so I socked it to him, as they say.'

'It worked. So much so that he's working on a rewrite in order to feature you even more.'

He couldn't hide his delight.

'All to the good. More days filming, more money in the bank.'

'I think we should hold off saying anything until we see the new draft of the story, what say you?'

'Oh yes, let's have them very eager by the time we strike a deal. Well done, Reg. I wish all of my more mature actors had some of your get up and go, not to mention talent.'

He was thinking about that when he had an idea. 'They need a wife for me, don't they? If they haven't already cast it, how about suggesting Margaret La Bute? And before you say it, no, she isn't dead. She's simply mouldering in the Grove Retirement Home.'

★　★　★

Lola had news. 'I ran into The Jerk. He was full of talk about a film called *Highway*. Know anything about it?'

'Can't say that I do,' Susie admitted.

She asked Betty, who shook her head. 'Not something that's ringing a bell. So the slimy fuck-heap is up to something. Think you can investigate?'

'I know the very woman to ask.' She went to Val's desk. 'You've been working your way through anything Jay Burns left behind, haven't you?'

'Yes. I'm also getting some computer types in to see if we can recover any files he wiped before he went.' She saw Susie's expression and added, 'Milo's idea. He'd make a very good spy.'

'I'm more interested in a script called *Highway*. Have you come across that at all?'

'Oh, that's quite an interesting one. I've done you a little report.'

'You're a marvel, do you know that?'

'Not at all. I'm just interested.'

'And I could kiss you for it.'

'I really do think that would make people suspicious.'

Valerie was completely deadpan. Susie knew now where Milo got it.

She waved Valerie's report at Lola. 'I have the low-down on TJ and his big plans.'

'Make with the details.'

165

'Valerie found it. It's *My Beautiful Laundrette* meets *Thelma and Louise*.'

'I am surrounded by the gay. I wonder if I'm a magnet for it?' She waved her talons in a 'more, more' gesture.

'It's an actual car journey from Land's End to John O'Groats, and a metaphorical coming out of age. Great parts, well written, funny, touching. Apart from a slightly schmaltzy ending, it's really good.'

'We are so going after it.'

'Oh yes. Valerie will distribute synopses and a cast breakdown and we can draft our suggestions and begin the stalking.'

'One more intriguing thing on the Burns front,' Lola drawled. 'Apart from a vaguely dirty email waiting on-line for me this morning, there was also a single, red rose on my desk. No outside delivery involved. How did he manage that?'

'Jeez, of course, he's probably still got his pass for the building and the office. We'd better get the codes changed. He probably knows everything we're up to if he can get in here and onto the computers. We'll make Arland and Shaw a fortress, then continue to be immensely successful, which is the only answer to any skulduggery and show-business espionage.'

'Agreed. OK, my latest Jewish haiku:
Jewish voodoo.
Mention a career in acting,
And watch for chest pains.'
Susie gave the appropriate groan.

★   ★   ★

Valerie was glad to know that her message had got through to Alistair. That is to say he had listened to it. She wasn't sure there was any 'getting through' to him any more. She could imagine his face creased with an uncomprehending frown. It wasn't good to picture him, or her lost life. She thought it might be useful to list his faults, to steel her resolve, to be her own woman. His annoying peculiarities would help her stay strong. He always slurped the first two drinks of his tea even though it was never piping hot as he couldn't handle the scald. He never liked food at the correct temperature, wanted it tepid, like his tea. It made nonsense of her efforts at making a meal to a recipe when he let it congeal before trying it, usually heaping on salt before he even tasted the dish. In winter, he favoured a cardigan of indeterminate colour, from which he picked lint absent-mindedly and, equally without noticing, piled into small pyramids on the armrest of his favourite chair. He peeled his nails. She would have preferred him to chew on them, which would have had honesty to it. He couldn't sing. Not even one plausible note. Yes, that would do for now.

★ ★ ★

Margaret La Bute rang Reg to tell him of her job offer. 'Seems the young director chap is a fan but like most of the known world he thought I was dead.' She laughed, a smoky rasp along the telephone wire. 'Sometimes it feels as if I am.'

He heard the echo of the corridor at the Grove

167

Retirement Home and the distant cry of a bewildered, old man.

'Thank you, Reginald. I know it was you who engineered this.'

'You are a great actress with a lot still to offer.'

'Bless you for your faith. I can even use my wheelchair, which is a mercy. Old age is so bally tiring. It's a drag, really. Inside I am so much more.'

Reg could feel tears welling and was afraid they would tell in his voice so he made his excuses and rang off. He went to bed bothered by the notion that, no matter what age you are, life is a trial, a puzzle with no easy answers. It can also terrify.

★　★　★

Susie had missed a call from Craig Landor but his hoarse and slurred message led her to believe he had partied long and hard with Marty. The thrust of the message was that it had all been a success and she should go ahead with her end of things.

From: susie@arlandshaw.co.uk
To: marty@direkshun.com
Sent: 7 october 6.45
Subject: Glory Days

To Whom It May Concern:

This is to acknowledge that Craig Landor has responded to the project provisionally entitled

168

GLORY DAYS, to be directed by Martin Reed.

He is happy to attach his name to the lead role of 'Joshua'. This is of course subject to the usual conditions of availability, contractual negotiations surrounding his fee, shooting location and final screenplay approval.

Yours sincerely,
Susan Vine, agent for Craig Landor

They were in business bed together.

Across the room, Lola was putting through a call to a client with the words, 'Could you tell Mina her agent is calling? No, I'm her agent, not her angel.' She covered the mouthpiece and looked over at Susie. 'Although . . . ' she said, smiling.

Arland and Shaw, Angels to the Stars.

Lola put her head onto her desk to steady her heaving body. From a distance, it looked a lot like crying.

7

Christmas was coming and Milo Vine had money problems. He needed funds for presents. His allowance was fine but he had to use a lot of it on keeping up with the lads and the games they had on their mobiles. If they met up in the morning to get the Tube to school, everyone had to have a Danish pastry. On the way home it was a can of Coke. These things cost hard cash but they had to be got somehow. Nothing was worse than sticking out, being different. His life's mission was to blend. So when Rafe bought something, so did the rest of the troupe. And it was usually Rafe who led on those things. Life was different for him. His parents were incredibly busy architects and didn't seem to mind what he got up to. Not that Milo's mum wasn't busy too, but she noticed a lot more than Rafe's parents. Plus Rafe's house seemed to be full of loose change. He just picked it up wherever he found it and it all totted up. Apparently his dad didn't like coins jangling in his pockets and decanted it onto shelves in their huge house. Rafe was sorted. Adam was inclined to take money from his mum's purse and she rarely noticed. On the few occasions she did, he pleaded a stolen Oyster card or low credit on his phone. It worked fine. Gregory was more in Milo's position but it was no help to know that. When Milo had been caught using his mum's credit card on eBay, he had in fact been trying to get things cheaply.

He definitely didn't want to go through that kind of grief again. She had been crosser than he'd ever seen her, that time. In fact he was ashamed of the whole incident but that wasn't something he could ever admit to his mum. She spotted a chink and niggled away until she'd broken through. She was way too nosy. Intrusive was probably the word he was looking for, he thought. It had taken ages to get her to realise his room was off limits unless he was in it and even then she couldn't just come barging in. He blanked the eBay incident and tried to block out her words too. If he promised never to do it again and ignored the fact that it had ever happened he could erase it from his memory. But every so often he would remember his mother's face full of anger and disappointment and he would cringe all over again. He paid back what he owed from his pocket money but that left him incredibly short now.

He needed enough to cover gifts. He desperately wanted to get something beautiful for Isabelle, something that would match her. That was bound to be expensive. He had no idea what girls really liked. He couldn't ask his mum for advice. He couldn't ask any of the guys. He didn't want his dad to know either. His feelings for Isabelle were his own and he held them close like treasure. He probably wouldn't even let Isabelle herself know. Ever. He didn't see how he could. That would be way too embarrassing. He hoped the right gift would take the place of all that. He was back to his most basic problem: money. He needed enough for Isabelle, his mum, Dad and his gran. It was a nightmare. He needed a job.

★ ★ ★

Susie's father, Alistair, was not pleased. 'I thought this job was supposed to be temporary. It seems quite permanent to me.'

Susie knew how he felt. It was hard to believe Valerie was still here. If anything she was entrenched with no sign of a move. Still, now was not the time to break ranks.

'She's a valued member of the Arland and Shaw family,' she said, primly.

'There is no need to take that tone with me, Susan. I worry about your mother. What about Christmas?' He delivered the last stroke as if it was the winning gambit of a lawyer in a courtroom.

'What about it? You surely didn't think she'd host you a dinner with all the trimmings as if nothing had happened?' She paused for an answer, expecting a denial of the notion, but got none. 'Did you?' His silence confirmed that he had. Susie was astonished at his thick naiveté. 'Honestly, Dad, you are the end. You walk out on the woman and then expect to cherry-pick occasions when it would be nice for you to hook up.'

'I thought it would be nice for her,' he insisted. The sincerity in his voice was real. The man was an idiot with no feeling for human relations.

Numbers were his thing, always had been. And jigsaws.

Susie took a deep breath and let her mind take over before her mouth opened to give him what for. One thing the job helped her with was diplomacy. She rarely shouted at a client or a producer, preferring to get her way through dogged reason or just doggedness. Though there were moments when she longed to let loose.

'Dad, you really haven't thought this through at all, have you?'

'I'm sure I don't know what you mean, Susan.'

'Would you like one of us to be with you in the house?' She realised that was a bit open-ended. 'One of us kids,' she qualified. She had to stifle a giggle. The 'kids' were all grown-ups now with families of their own.

'No thank you, dear. I can manage it all until your mother comes to her senses.'

There was no getting through to him. Susie signed off as politely as she could but wanted nothing more than to wring her father's stubborn, unfeeling neck. She needed to talk to her sister and brother about their parents' situation. Christmas was fast becoming a concern in all manner of ways. Valerie was clearly staying in London but someone would have to see to Alistair. She suspected that he wouldn't totally mind being left to his own martyred devices in Chittenham but who knew when that might return to bite the family backside? Best fix it for one of the others to take him; she reckoned she was precluded from that by sheer dint of Valerie living with her now.

She dialled her sister who told her, 'This is one almighty crock of shit.' She didn't normally use this sort of language and it skewed her speech patterns in an almost cute way. Then again, Chloe, too, had a teenager in the house and some of her daughter's wisdom and lingo might have permeated.

'I think Mum is happy here so we don't need to worry there. It's Dad who's the more immediate problem now.'

'Stubborn old git.'

And this from a daddy's girl, Susie thought. What was the world coming to?

'Wouldn't it be great if Tim offered to take him?' her sister said. 'Though I don't think the lovely Amelia would be too pleased about that.'

Chloe did not get on with her sister-in-law. It seemed to spring from a fight between two of their children years before which neither mother wanted to let go of. Each thought the other was rearing savages and dragging the family down.

'What are the chances of them taking him?' Susie asked, genuinely interested. It really would be a handy solution to Christmas.

'Dunno, let me check. Now, to more important things. I need a trip to London to do some shopping and to check up on Mum. How does next week grab you?'

Susie knew enough to realise that this was a done deal; Chloe was merely doing her the courtesy of informing her. 'What day did you have in mind?'

'Will you have room for me now that Mum is in situ?'

'Sofa bed in the main room do you?'

'See you Thursday.'

Susie sighed and gave in. Her sister was visiting, no point in fighting it. She thought about her parents. They had looked after their children for years without too much complaint. She supposed it was only right that positions be reversed. But, as her younger self had been fond of declaring, no one asked to be born, so were they just paying now for their parents' selfishness in mingling their genes to reproduce and perpetuate themselves? They might argue this was to advance the human gene pool though that was a bit lofty. Perhaps it was plain carelessness. Whatever, it was payola time. She chuckled lightly to herself. She intended to make Milo suffer too when he was her age. Something to look forward to, for sure.

Valerie came to Susie's desk with details on a pink post-it. 'There's a company manager going berserk looking for you. He rang twice while you were on your last call. Seems he's just lost his Aladdin and he thinks you have the perfect replacement.'

'Show me the money,' Susie said in her best Tom Cruise.

She established that the actor in question was available but only interested if the run was short and the money fantastic. 'Nothing', he told Susie, 'is so like a pain in the arse as panto.' She thought he was too young to have such an opinion but he pointed out that he was chorus in many a local show in his youth. 'I learned a lot from the older ladies of the dance corps so I'm grateful but this time I'm only in it for the money.'

She didn't convey that sentiment to the theatre man on the other end of the phone but stressed that family commitments might keep her guy from travelling to save the day, unless the price was right. She thought it was by the end of the conversation and a quick call to her client confirmed that hunch. She had rarely done a deal so quickly and it was all the sweeter for it. She jotted the details on her invoice pad for accounts to follow up then asked Valerie to email CV details and a photograph for the Aladdin programme and also to get her boy's measurements to the costume department at the theatre soonest. She broke the good news of decent wages to the actor, who took the time to thank her for her work. So many of her clients didn't think to.

* * *

Milo didn't want to be a part of it at all. He felt they were giving enough of a bad time to Miss Rivers by simply ignoring her in biology class or sniggering whenever she tried to teach them about reproductive systems. Even the life cycles of the amoeba or a fern were treated with a nasty hilarity that made him uncomfortable. It only took one of them to start and the whole class followed suit. Miss Rivers dealt with it by almost ignoring them back, but there were moments when the tears in her eyes threatened to spill and that made the pack snigger even harder. Milo couldn't bring himself to look at her as a result and he felt certain this meant she thought he was a ringleader, guiltily avoiding eye contact. Now Rafe wanted to post a horrible assessment of the teacher on a website. Anonymously, of course. That guy didn't even have the guts to put his name to the torture.

Milo finally plucked up some courage and said, 'I don't think this is right.'

Rafe scoffed. 'Of course it's not, that's why it's so radically brilliant. Whoever got anywhere being right or nice?' He looked to Adam for back-up and got it.

'We should give her a chance,' Milo said. 'She gets a really rough time from us as it is.'

'Yeah, right. Have you gone soft in the head, big man? Maybe it's since you got gay for Bowler?' Rafe's face was twisted into an ugly little mask. Milo couldn't watch it any longer. He started to walk away.

'Stupid fuck,' he heard from behind. The voice was low but calculated to be just audible. 'Stupid, big, faggot fuck. Taking it up the shitter from Bowler.'

He wheeled round, his head raging and face burning. Crimson flashed through his brain. He didn't trust himself to put words to the anger, because any stumble would be pounced on. Instead he smacked Rafe in the face and left him with blood pouring from his mean, pointed nose. The other boy howled and threw himself to the ground, curling up as small as he could to look put-upon and vulnerable. Milo instantly regretted the violence. He didn't know where to put his body or how to arrange it. He had to get away from here.

Gregory fell into step beside him. 'Well done,' he said. 'He deserved that. I'd get ready for trouble from Vince now, though, and probably the headmaster too.'

Milo's heart shuddered and headed south. He swore to cover his panic. Even if Vince treated Rafe like dirt, they were brothers and would band together now. With Vince came his gang of foul-breathed friends, all eager to impress their leader. He was so for it on so many fronts. He would have to phone Mum before the school did and he didn't expect her to be too proud of his latest scrape. It was time to come clean about a whole range of things, he reckoned, and he hoped the truth would stand to him.

★   ★   ★

'What's Betty up to?' Lola wanted to know.

The blinds in the boss's office had been pulled more than open for days.

'Not a clue,' Susie admitted. 'She is being very furtive, which is worrying.'

Mitch came over. 'Couldn't help but hear. Don't know if you've noticed but Nell has had a few solo audiences with the Maestra.'

'Grim,' Susie agreed.

'I'll pump Valerie, see if she knows anything.'

Susie felt uneasy that her mother might be privy to what Betty was planning but not tell her.

'This coffee sucks.' Lola gurned her face into the shape of a burst cushion. 'I think our Miss

Macintosh has snuck in some worthy brand that tastes like civet piss.'

'She's big into fair trade and organics,' Dave offered as he went by.

'Which I applaud unless it tastes like cack, which this does,' Lola pointed out.

'How do you find her?' Susie asked.

Mitch took this up. 'Initially I thought she was an odd choice for the job, at her age and all that, but she's doing fine. She seems to know her stuff. She's quite slow though.'

'Have you noticed she's been reading a lot of Bernie Brillstein?' Lola said.

Mitch laughed. 'Yeah, she said we should have known Jay Burns was bad news because any man who walks you to the lift with his arm around your shoulder is not to be trusted. That's our Hollywood guru, Brillstein, isn't it?'

Susie nodded. She had seen Valerie devouring one of his tomes at home and on the Tube and muttering about how the little things matter most. She'd also declared that there is no such thing as a good divorce. Susie wanted to think it was a reference to the Burns defection from Arland and Shaw but she had a nagging suspicion that it was horribly ambiguous.

'Dave adores her since she snuck in a little afternoon nap for him. He's positively giddy with the extra rest.' Mitch stretched and yawned. 'I could do with a snooze myself. I went to a screening of a new sit-com last night expecting a few taster episodes but they showed the whole shebang which made it one long evening. Not much in the way of laughs either. Three hours of agony, though it felt like a year.'

'The clients are responding well to Valerie,' Susie said. 'She talks to them and listens to their worries.'

'Whinges,' Lola corrected.

'You love those guys and gals,' Susie said.

'Yes, but the minute they find that out they'll eat me alive, pick over my tired, single bones and leave nothing but a dry husk behind.'

'It's one way of losing weight,' Susie mused.

'But back to Valerie,' Lola said. 'I think she may be our way in to solving the Betty mystery.'

'Speak of the devil,' Susie said as Valerie approached with a worried look on her face.

'Milo, er, your son, is on line three and he sounds upset.'

★ ★ ★

Susie really didn't particularly care for the other parents that Milo's friendships brought into her orbit. It was incredible to think of all of the people throughout the country thrown together simply because their children attended a particular school. Neighbours could be avoided; not so school parents, or indeed teachers. Rafe's mother looked pinched and disappointed all the time and was in complete denial that her son was anything but a minor saint. Susie had tried to talk to her about the credit-card problem when Milo had used hers for eBay but she denied that her household had that problem, although that's exactly how Rafe was managing his games habit, and intimated that Milo was a low, cheating liar

180

to boot. The other parents fell in line with this although Gregory's dad seemed to lean toward thinking Rafe a bad influence too.

She and Milo sat facing a wall of hostility while the headmaster, Mr Stephens, paced the room ranting about discipline and morality. The man loved the sound of his own voice and more than once Susie had wondered if he was auditioning for her. He had actually asked about voice-overs, in a stretched query about what she did and the oddness of it for an ordinary man like himself, all the while affecting a faux modest boom that displayed his base notes melodiously, or so he thought. In fact, he had an adenoidal layer of ugliness to his voice that Susie associated with bullshit and pomposity.

Susie felt fifteen again, in a world of zits and Clearasil and Batiste dry shampoo, waiting for her turn to speak, heart painful with each thump in her chest, knowing that she and Milo would be denied justice. She could see it from his point of view. When Stephens drew breath she said, 'I do not in any way condone what Milo did and he is abjectly sorry for his behaviour.' She paused to let him nod miserably on cue. She didn't care at that moment if he meant it or not, just that they be seen to toe the line. 'However, in mitigation, he was very clearly provoked.' Rafe's mother made to object but Susie raised a hand to stop her and said, 'I won't stand for any escalation of this situation and I must make it clear that I expect you other parents to have stern words with your sons about the need to forgive and forget this and move on.' Milo had told her how vengeful he thought Rafe and his older brother would be. 'Anything else is savagery.'

The room smelled of stale disinfectant and mould.

Stephens was furious to have the moral high ground taken from beneath him and began to froth ever so slightly at the mouth.

'Ms Vine, I hope you are aware of the severity of this incident. Your son assaulted a smaller boy, physically injuring him. Who knows what the long-term psychological effects may be?'

Rafe's mother squeezed her eyelids together hard, trying to force a tear to roll out. She accompanied it with a few quick catches of breath as if she was trying very hard not to have a breakdown. She played the victim well. Susie wanted to reach out and slap her noisily. I know just how Milo feels, she thought. She jerked back to the lecture, as Stephens said, ' . . . no choice but to consider suspension.'

She let out an involuntary 'What?' and looked to the room for support. Group cowardice was about to win the day when Gregory's dad said, 'I wonder if that's a little excessive. Boys will be boys and all that.'

Milo thought it sounded like freedom. Time off? Result. In what way could Stephens possibly think that suspension would be a punishment? Adults and their logic would always perplex him.

'We cannot be seen to condone violence,' the headmaster said, sanctimoniously.

'Clearly not,' Susie agreed. 'But surely detention would be more appropriate?'

Milo couldn't believe his ears. How could the woman on his side be letting him down like this? Not only was she rejecting a perfectly acceptable way of dealing with this as far as he was concerned, she had now also offered a substitute punishment and it was so nothing that was making him jump up and down with joy. Incarceration was what she was proposing; imprisonment within the walls of this hellhole, leaving him a sitting duck for Vince, Rafe and their vengeance, which he imagined as more and more biblical as the moments ticked on. He was scaring himself with these florid imaginings and wondering how he could leave London and avoid them, possibly for the rest of his miserable life.

Stephens let out an enormous sigh, as if he ruled the world and no other person could understand the horror of what he dealt with every day as he toiled selflessly for mankind. He looked at the wall for inspiration, lost in his unfathomable thoughts and decisions. After giving the room ample time to admire his gravitas, stature and sheer stoic wisdom he pronounced detention for the rest of the week, and a thousand lines as an afterthought.

What century does he live in? Susie wondered as she murmured what might be taken as gratitude and bundled Milo out the door. The last thing she wanted was a recriminatory chat with Rafe's mother who was giving Stephens a bit of an earful. She glanced at Gregory's dad and mouthed, 'Thanks,' then steered herself and her son roadward, praying for a black cab to swish them away from this smelly, depressing place.

Valerie was waiting at home with an anxious face.

'Detention and lines,' Susie announced. 'He can count himself lucky after doing such a thing.'

Milo's voice rose. 'I only hit him once. He's stuck his compass into lots of people loads of times, you know.'

She cut him off before he got into any more detail. 'It's not about levels of who did what,' Susie said, exasperated. 'It's not a bloody compare and contrast exercise, Milo. You have to take responsibility for your actions and you have to realise that you were wrong to do what you did. You also lowered yourself to Rafe's level. I really think it's time you stopped hanging around with him.'

'No problem. He is so going to kill me anyhow. Him and his brother Vince. They are totally going to feud with me now. I'm dead.' Then he surprised and embarrassed himself by starting to cry. 'I'm afraid, Mum.'

Her heart ripped with the ferocious love a parent is gifted. She put her arms around her son's quaking shoulders and he let her. She never wanted him to know a moment of unnecessary anguish. 'You're not to worry, sweetheart. We'll get through this with cunning and brains. And besides, no one gets to my boy without going through me and I am one mean bitch right now.'

She pulled back and made to wipe his face but he got his sleeve to it first. His eyes sparkled with tears and the beginnings of laughter. 'Language, Mum.'

Valerie confirmed, 'Those idiots really do not want to mess with the Vines.'

Milo's mobile rang and he answered Gregory with a series of 'yeahs' and an 'OK'. 'Greg is going to call for me tomorrow.'

'Great, you can both walk me to the Tube,' Susie said.

When Milo was settled in bed, Susie fretted openly about what was to become of him.

'Oh really,' her mother exclaimed. 'You'd think the lad was guilty of gross moral turpitude the way you're carrying on. No child is ever an angel.' Before Susie could protest, Valerie continued with, 'You certainly weren't. I seem to remember the wholesale raiding of orchards and allotments all over town when you were young. And if I might point out, as I did then, that was some family's food you were stealing.'

It hadn't seemed like that to Susie when Mr Fentham had chased their intrepid gang, pockets bulging with apples and pears. And they always ate every one of them. But she had to admit that Valerie had a point. Still, her exploits hadn't involved bodily harm to anyone; aside from the time Mr Allerdice fell and sprained his ankle while in pursuit. And once Ellie Worthing fell through a glass cloche and had to get stitches in her bum but everyone said she deserved it on account of she was a clumsy heap and always holding the gang back and the grown-ups told her it was the wages of sin. She had to sleep on her tummy for a fortnight and was the butt of

185

every joke from then till Christmas that year. Poor Ellie Worthing. That's what everyone called her. Whatever happened to her?

'It's not behaviour that can be condoned in any way, no matter what I got up to when I was a kid.'

'Agreed, but do keep a bit of perspective.'

'I don't want him to turn into a delinquent. It happens so easily. And I feel guilty enough that he doesn't have a dad living here and that maybe he's missing out. Especially now when he's facing into being a teenager.'

'Is that what this is about? Your guilt?'

'I don't know. I haven't ever thought about it like this before now.'

'Well, do us all a favour and try not to reach any ridiculous conclusions that don't make sense just to justify yourself or maybe even to punish yourself in some bizarre way.'

Susie was left with mouth open as Valerie took herself off for an early night. When had her mother become the wise counsellor? And if her mum was so clued up, why was she in such a mess? Susie found herself muttering into her pillow half an hour later about parents and how unfair the world was. Then she had a vision of a much younger Susie doing the same and she began to laugh. The kid within was never far away.

* * *

'And that's a wrap,' the first assistant director called. Four blessed words of joy. The cast and crew applauded, some hugged. They were done, on this leg of the production at least. Time to party. Small gifts were exchanged. John Forbes presented his dresser with a bouquet of roses and gave a bottle of single estate vodka to his make-up lady. They cracked open a bottle of pink fizz and toasted making it out the end of another shoot more or less in one piece each. Then he packed up and went home to shower and turn around to go to the celebrations. He looked longingly at his sofa, imagining a few beers and falling asleep in front of the television. Instead he scrubbed up, doused himself in delicious cologne, had a stiff drink and left again. I am an itinerant, he thought, as he got into yet another car.

They crept into central London in a misty fog. The Christmas lights shone through the cotton wool of the weather. Window displays were decked with glitter and temptation. Late-night shoppers smiled wanly at others laden with parcels and bags. There was a damp camaraderie among the ghost figures as they shuffled from place to place, eager to find the perfect offering to cheer their loved ones, to show how much they cared.

The party had kicked off in a hotel that had once been law courts. The main room devoted to their shenanigans was already filled with rowdy technical types who had come straight from packing up equipment and sending it back to whatever base it lived at. They were still in their working clothes, with the odd concession to the party and venue, usually a better pair of shoes than they'd worn on set. They were sculling back free booze and hungrily scarfing the nibbles offered on huge trays by the harried staff.

One of them greeted John and indicated the trendy, miniature cone of fish and chips in his huge hands. 'There'd've been a riot if this was the normal scran on the job, eh, John?'

He grabbed a white wine from a passing platter and immediately regretted it. Anti-freeze probably tastes better than this, he thought, and went in search of the public bar. Besides, if he stuck with beer he'd last longer. Tiredness permeated his bones and fibres but he had to go this one last leg of the journey. He was clutching a pint and returning to the official do when he was accosted by a gaggle of female fans and dragged to stand at their patch by a huge potted plant to pose for photos and sign autographs. Each wanted a kiss, and all were getting progressively wetter. They were decked out in bling and tinsel and well the worse for wear. He was in the middle of office party hell. Trying to prise himself free of their grip was proving tricky when a hulking camera loader from the production materialised and rescued him as if he was his personal security. He felt like kissing the man in gratitude but that wasn't likely to be appreciated so he shook his hand when they were out of sight of the gaggle.

'Thanks. That was a close one,' he joked.

The man thumped him across the shoulder and told him not to mention it.

'My life was beginning to roll before my eyes and it wasn't looking well shot or acted.'

'Were you playing yourself?' the loader asked.

When John nodded, he added, 'Too close to the story to be able to give it socks. Get George Clooney next time.'

Clutching his pint, John made his way back to the main room. He thought about the wretches who'd populated this place until recently. There was a gag in there at the expense of lawyers but he was too bushed to hone it. The weirdest part of the new arrangement was that the holding cells had been transformed into small snugs. Bizarrely, the loo was still in situ in each, now holding a pot plant, and surrounded by drinkers laughing and making jokes.

'I think this is where Oscar Wilde was tried,' an assistant director mentioned as she passed by, hands balancing plates full of snacks.

'I'm sure he'd have approved, somehow,' John observed.

She offered him some of the minuscule bruschetta heaped with different toppings.

'It must have taken someone hours to fiddle these up,' he laughed. He declined the morsels, saying they might set him on a roll of eating and pointing out that however many he had of these delights he'd never feel full. 'Denial is the way forward here,' he assured her.

'You have a lovely way with words,' she said. 'Have you ever thought of writing something?'

Was this a factual compliment accompanied by a genuine question or a come-on? And was it age that made him quake at the thought of brushing off an advance? He was knackered. All he could think of was a long sleep, alone. Clearly it was time to effect an exit though he had barely arrived. It would be much better to leave early and remain enigmatic. The important thing had been to turn up and be seen. His duty was almost done. He excused himself and sought out the director who was ringed by producers. Super, he could knock down all of the pins in one shot. They exchanged praise and platitudes, most of them heartfelt, and when he thought he'd fulfilled his remit as leading man and team player he slipped away without further ado.

It was early yet, for London at Christmas time. Rowdy parties spilled out onto the streets. He was glad of the distraction. He always hated the goodbye at the end of a job, leaving people you had come to value, or even hate, but need for the short, intense time of collaboration; moving on into an unknown, no matter how many details of the future were pencilled in in the diary. It was as precarious as life itself. He was rudderless now, living alone. It exaggerated his solitariness. He liked that some of the time. But with the passing of another year suddenly upon him he was reminded of how much he missed his mother; a good woman the world could still benefit from. He needed to see his dad and contact his brother. He had ignored his family, using work as an excuse not to engage with that strand of his life.

He hailed a black cab and was amazed that no one stepped in ahead of him to snatch it. As he rattled around in the back of the car he tried unsuccessfully to avoid thoughts about his own little family unit, the people he had helped make.

He was losing touch with them, letting work interfere with being a dad. He needed to take stock. Another year was drawing to its close, another set of resolutions ready to be drawn up and broken. Was this the splendid fallibility of man? Or just another almighty fuck-up? He had to let his mind rest and take a meaningful break. Otherwise he would be of no use to anyone, least of all his family. He let the twinkling lights lull him. Thank you, he muttered to the passing street and revellers. And good night.

★   ★   ★

Milo spent a largely sleepless night worrying about what waited for him at school. He twirled and tossed till he was wrapped tight in his duvet and unable to move his arms. One of his greatest phobias was to be held down without possibility of protecting himself so his discomfort was multiplied as his heart raced and glands poured forth fear and sweat.

He extracted himself and sat on the edge of his bed. His mind was a mess of fearful premonitions and his exhaustion fuelled ever more gothic versions of the physical and psychological vengeance about to be visited on him. He tried to plot his day ahead so that he would see as little as possible of Rafe's brother Vince. He was banking on Rafe staying at home to be nursed for his injuries and of course use the time to plan his revenge. Milo wondered if he could persuade his own mother to allow him to stay off school. His eyes stung with fatigue and worry. He slumped into his pillows and tried to calm his breathing. He nodded off a few times only to jerk awake in terror as he realised that morning was inching closer even faster if he dozed. He switched on his reading light and tried to stay awake to stretch his time at home in bed and in safety.

As a milky winter dawn fingered its way through his curtains, he began to sob lightly. He could see no way forward in his life. All that he could look forward to was misery and pain for the rest of his days at Morning Star. Years of despair stretched before him and he had no idea how to deal with that.

8

Susie Vine was cranky. She wanted to be with Milo, to supervise his day at school, to protect him from bullies and the neglect of his overworked teachers. The weather matched her mood. An icy cold had become the norm, spiting hands, face and feet. It was mean spirited and so was she. She felt her lips tighten and dry in spite of lashings of salve. Her nose dripped. A damp mush of bodies jostled through the Underground and onto packed trains. Everyone smelt bad. They steamed up carriages. Susie had risen in the dark and it would be dark when she made for home again. It was a depressingly repetitive routine.

At the office, she growled at the others and got through her messages in double-quick time, issuing curt replies that would normally have had a little more guff attached. Her heart was elsewhere today. The peripheral constructs of her job, the petty embellishments, were beyond her. Her vision was clouded by the remembered sight of Milo sloping miserably off to the Tube, shoulders hunched, expecting the very worst that life could throw at him. A difficult client rang to whine about not being seen for a Channel 4 series. Susie gave her short shrift, which dissipated the paranoia and led to a fairly civilised discussion about where they should try to go with her career in the New Year. A tactic to remember?

'She might stop calling me her secret agent now,' Susie remarked to Lola.

'Tell me about it. What they don't know is that we care every day. That's all we do. Even when we really do not feel like it. I wouldn't do it for people I love, but for some of these bozos I lie and exaggerate and all I get back is that I need to give more. Thank the elements we're getting a break soon. Mind you, it means spending time with family and that's just as tragic as dealing with some of the fruitcakes we have on the books. I need to get laid again.'

Susie groaned. 'Wish something as simple as that could solve some of the shit I have to deal with.'

'Simple? You really have been away from the scene too long. It's bitch eat bitch out there, over slim pickings I may add. There are times when Jay Burns looks like a viable prospect.'

'You will never go so low as long as I have breath.'

'Actually, we would make a lovely lesbian couple, if only you weren't a goy.'

'Nobody's perfect.'

'True.'

Valerie came through with a package, looking the very essence of efficiency.

'You know what?' Lola said. 'That woman is opinionated.'

Susie's antennae went up. 'How so?'

'I caught her advising a client who was in to collect some audition pieces about what to wear to it.'

'Oh dear.'

'Oh no, the advice was good and said client was delighted with the attention. Looked like they thought they'd got their money's worth.'

'Hallelujah.'

'Yeah.'

Dave walked by. 'I was at *The Misanthrope* last night. Excellent. Go see.'

There was a lull in the work and Susie was still fidgety with worry about Milo so she took a break to pound the treadmill in the building's basement fitness centre. Some queries had stacked up nicely by the time she returned, calmer and thinking straight. She spoke with an advertising agency about the possibility of a voice-over campaign for one of her actors. The company gave a lot of babble about punching up the funny in this series. As long as you punch up a decent fee as well, Susie thought, you may have my client and we won't need to come to fisticuffs. A producer at the BBC wondered if another of her charges would be interested in a dramedy he was planning. Susie stanched a groan. She had been fine with the original description: comedy-drama. It had ticked all of the right boxes for her. But like every language, this was a living thing and terms changed all the time, however foolishly. The producer was interested in new blood, particularly an actor he described as geek chic. He wasn't far wrong. The young lad had a lopsided face and wonky, huge hair. He could make people laugh just by turning up. They arranged for a script to be sent and a meeting set up.

Chris Falucci rang with a request out of left

field. 'I was wondering how you'd feel about letting me use Milo in a radio play?'

'I hadn't ever considered that he might want to act, to be honest, or even be able to, more to the point. He could be a woodener, you know.'

'I don't think he is.'

'Have you asked him about this?'

'I sort of scoped it with him and he seemed keen, or at least I think so. You know how closed up he can be even when he's jumping for joy about something.'

It was good to know she wasn't the only one he seemed to clam up around.

'When would you record?'

'Weekend after next.'

'Ah.' Susie laughed. 'This would be a handy way of having your access and working at the same time.'

He sounded phlegmatic. 'You got me there. Will you think about it?'

'As you know, he's been in a bit of trouble at school recently and I have no intention of seeming to let him away with that. But the experience would be good for him. If I can get a licence from Lambeth for him, and he still wants to do it, I'm cool. But you'd better ring me then to do the deal. I am his agent, after all.'

'My balls have already shrunk.'

That was nice to know too.

★ ★ ★

Mad Dog Maud was the Morning Star sports master. He was built like a tank and had a bad

196

attitude. Nobody crossed Maud. The rumour was that a foolish boy called him Maudie once, decades ago, then spent the rest of the term on crutches. No one ever called him Maudie again. Another report was that Maud had fiddled with Jason Farthing but Milo seriously doubted that. Mostly Maud looked at them with such belittling scorn it was hard to imagine him enjoying any contact with his classes, let alone getting up close and personal. Milo had managed to get past Assembly without encountering either Rafe or his brother. Gregory scouted the hall and reported that they were both present. Milo nearly wet himself there and then on the parquet flooring. His bowels felt painfully loose and his knees didn't seem reliable. Now he was skulking in the gym changing room, hiding out until he had to join his class for games. He heard Rafe's reedy voice threatening horrible retaliation on 'that homo Vine'. He was not going to be able to avoid him too much longer.

Maud appeared at the door and roared for them to muster. They lined up and he chose teams to practise rugby passing and rucks. Rafe drew his finger across his neck and mouthed 'You're dead' at Milo. Milo flipped him the bird and tried to look hard. They began to run and tackle as Maud shouted verbal abuse designed to spur them on. What Maud threatened them with was as frightening as the prospect of Rafe getting close. Eventually Rafe managed to make contact, grinding a foot onto the bony side of Milo's heel. Rafe howled in delight, Milo in pain.

'Up, Vine, and shut it, you're not a girl,' Mad Dog said.

'Or is he?' Rafe sneered as he strutted off.

On the next offensive he managed to kick and bite Milo. Next came a punch to the kidneys and a vicious pinch to the thigh. Maud seemed to see all of this but did nothing to stop it. He operated on the principle that whatever didn't kill you made you strong. Milo began to retaliate by lashing out wildly but he caught a few of the other boys also by accident. Rafe sneered again and muttered insults. Then, just as Milo recognised that he was going to have to take his opponent down at least once or face an endless barrage of hurt, Rafe launched himself forward so fast he lost control of his momentum and crashed into the climbing frames that lined the sports hall walls. He turned once with a surprised look on his face and fell to the ground unconscious. Maud actually seemed to smile, muttered, 'Idiot,' and sent Milo to the office to order an ambulance.

As the class watched the vehicle leave with Rafe, Milo was torn between joy and victory. He couldn't believe his luck. Rafe had been taken out of the equation. That left Vince to deal with. It was too much to ask of Fate that he have an unfortunate accident too but Milo kept his fingers crossed just the same. When he turned to go back in, the school windows facing the road were filled with a canvas of the curious faces of pupils and teachers. Morning Star looked like a strange Art Happening.

The story evidently shifted shape throughout

its telling in the hallways and classrooms. By the time Milo heard its latest incarnation it featured police intervention and a possible murder charge. At the break Vince sought him out and Milo thought his time was up. He knew enough by now to realise he had two options. He could let Vince belittle him publicly, perhaps even hurt him physically, or he could attack first. There was a lot of honour at stake on both sides. He was in the process of toughing it out, pulling himself to full height, like a cat caught in a corner magnifying itself to its enemy, when Vince said, 'My brother is only a spaz. Someone had to teach him a lesson. Good on you, mate.'

Milo wanted to explain that Rafe was the architect of his own doom but that would have spoiled the moment and with it his new status as hard man. Instead he nodded nonchalantly, increasing his credibility.

'Bummer about the detention,' Vince said.

''Snothin'.' Milo shrugged. 'Lines too.'

The heavy gang shook their heads at the punishment a righteous dude had to go through. 'Later,' Vince said, and not in a bad way.

That night, Milo reported events truthfully and waited for a response he couldn't even begin to predict. His mother merely nodded. 'Remember you have lines to do tonight. Your dad spoke to me about the radio play he's doing soon. He thinks you're right for one of the boys. I assume you know what I'm talking about?'

Milo's limbs and innards seized up. He could so forget about doing that with his dad after today's events at school. He could taste the disappointment in his mouth and feel it travel to his stomach when he swallowed.

'In spite of your recent conduct, I think it's a good idea too. Lambeth Council is willing to grant you a licence to do it, so you may, as long as it doesn't interfere with your detention. I'll talk to your producer and get back to you about the fee.'

He was pretty certain he was goggle-eyed, smiling too to think he could borrow against this for Christmas. Relief was a marvellous feeling, and his dad was a genius and a gentleman. Then his forehead creased. 'Are you going to charge me a commission for doing this deal?' he wanted to know.

His mother considered this, giving him another unreadable stare. 'If you buy me a takeaway from my favourite Indian I'll call it quits.' She shook her head and laughed. 'Will work for food. Who knew?'

'Deal.' He held his hand out to shake on it and they did.

Milo floated off to his room and began his lines. It had to be painless after the day he'd had. He would write 'I must never harm another human being' a thousand times. He was under strictest instructions to do these neatly, legibly and with great care from the headmaster. He got through fifty paying some attention, then found he had done fifteen more in a soporific trance. He'd enjoyed floating off and the lines were passable. He didn't think there was much that could dint his good form. He decided to experiment. He wrote another line, ten lines away from the last written on the page, then filled in all the 'I's from the top down. He did the 'beings' next and moved around the other words as if filling in a square. He would have liked to use coloured pens to relieve any tedium but that might look like rebellion designed to bait more punishment. He stuck with blue. The action was soothing and after he had done three more squares he stacked the pages neatly and settled in for the night. There was no need to avoid sleep now as it didn't matter how quickly morning came.

When he dreamt, it was of a brilliant blue sky lit up by a giant rainbow that Milo knew travelled all the way around the world's horizon, joining up again to make a wondrous ribbon of colour.

★　★　★

The days began to deconstruct as less and less work was required. Few productions wanted to do a big deal so close to a holiday but inevitably some offers snuck through for the New Year, which was good for some and disappointing for others. Susie found herself making the usual slew of calls on a variation of, 'I'm afraid it's not going to work out this time. They loved you, but they're going older on this one.'

Valerie was interested in the language used, as always.

'It's not a lie,' Susie explained, truthfully. When Valerie stared her out she allowed, 'Sometimes it's an exaggeration.'

'Seems like semantics to me,' Valerie said.

'Yes, but it works and everybody keeps their dignity.'

Valerie felt as if she'd regained some dignity too. She had adapted to this new situation well, she hoped. If there was one thing that could be said about the members of her family, it was that they were adaptable. Except for Alistair. While the thought of him provoked a pang, she wondered if it wasn't mere nostalgia and that she somehow thought she should feel something of a regret, of longing for the past. She couldn't say she missed him now; she was too busy for one thing. But it might have been nice for him to see how well she was doing. How needed she was, not needy. She was close to happy again. It was a nice place to be, a good place.

Valerie couldn't help comparing everything about London to her life in Chittenham. She thought of what they might be doing at this time of year, had she not been abandoned. Probably a round of scintillating trips to the Cock and Feather, her treat when Alistair decided they needed one. Choosing from the overpriced specials misspelled on a blackboard in the landlord's illegible handwriting. They promised more than they ever delivered. Diners were accosted by what she'd once heard called puppy porn and green welly fascism, a cliché of tweedy Albion. The car park even had a space for a horse and cart, for goodness sake, as if anyone ever fetched up in one of those any more. It was a crazed tourist theme almost entirely for locals, since they rarely had much in the way of the real thing, foreign visitors. Instead there was a steady stream of the retired English who wandered the back roads of Britain discovering a country they probably didn't want to know anyhow. They arrived anxious and damp in winter or broiled and fractious in summer. There wasn't that much to see in the town: a mediocre church with a graveyard full of unimportant remains and an ugly Victorian town hall and clock tower that threatened rather than delighted, she felt. She was probably being a little harsh on it all, but it was bound up in much more disappointment than she was ever likely to burden others with. No doubt she would see the place with new and kinder eyes some day. But not soon, she hoped. For now, she was of the city. She had a new chance, a second shot.

The phone lit up and she chirruped, 'Arland and Shaw, Valerie speaking, how may I help you?' then patched Chris Falucci through to Susie.

'We'd better settle on a fee,' he said.

'No. Haggle,' Susie explained.

Chris groaned. 'I should have known this guy would have a dynamite agent.'

Susie chuckled. 'Flattery won't get you a discount. You want the best, you pay for him.'

'I feel like I've been ambushed.'

'It's what we call an attactic. Now, to take things up a notch, is this play a dramedy?'

★ ★ ★

Susie appeared to have entered a loop of correspondence on Marty Reed's system so she began to receive interesting emails. Most informative was the one about a different project to *Glory Days*, the movie intended for Craig Landor. Her understanding had been that this would be Marty's next project and all of his attentions were devoted to it. If this latest round robin email was something to go by she was mistaken.

From marty@direkshun.com
Cc ALL
Subject: Tanzanian Project

Hi everyone,
    This is an important email so READ IT.
    I had an interesting conversation with Skip Floris yesterday. As you know he is the man trying to get our Tanzanian movie properly into pre-production. Now, the man is the best, as we know, but it transpires that he is expected to do this on a budget of NADA, ZERO, NOTHING.
    Eh, HELLO, people. Is no one out there doing his or her jobs?
    The Tanzanian movie is a huge undertaking and will require two units to bring it to a level above a TV movie, and also a fully trained stunt unit which will have to be prepared soon to be ready for shooting when we agreed. We cannot use untrained extras and hope for the best. Skip has not been given his budget for this, which is totally unfair to the whole project as well as to Skip. And everyone seems to be acting as if this is okay.

Ever since I was persuaded to step back from GLORY DAYS I was under the impression that we were all pulling in the same direction and rooting for the Tanzanian project. If it is to happen we need to take action NOW.

So, I need to start hearing back from you all. I need answers to my emails. We need to start communicating, people! Because for the last month I have received nothing — no phone calls, emails, no discussions, no decisions, NOTHING.

I know you are all busy but if you are all on board for this project still I NEED TO KNOW. And if we are still go on this we need to get a budget to Skip so that he can hire the crew we need to MAKE OUR MOVIE.

Silence gets us nowhere.

We cannot operate in a vacuum!

Marty

Susie stared at the screen delighted to have been mistakenly copied into the correspondence. Knowledge was her greatest ally. Well now, Marty, what are you up to exactly? Where do my client Craig Landor and *Glory Days* fit into this little schedule? I shall watch this space.

She decided to use the multiplicity of the movie world as an excuse to talk to Betty. The blinds were open and the boss was receiving.

'I thought it would be good to meet with the producer of *I-Dentity* in the New Year to see if there's anything else we can do to move the project along. She's already delighted that so many of our clients have shown such an interest in it.'

Betty shot her a sharp look. 'Yes, dear. That all goes without saying, doesn't it? So what are you really here for?'

'You've been acting strangely. You seem to be having secretive meetings. I was wondering if there's anything I should know.'

'I'm worried about where the agency is going. We've been staggering along since Jay Burns left us and I intend to do something concrete about that after the break and it may not be popular. That's about all I'm prepared to part with at the moment.'

'Should I be concerned about this?'

'I don't think so but it's all down to perspective, really.'

Susie had been in the business long enough to know that there were only three options open to Betty if she felt the agency was compromised: one was to fold, one to sell up and the last was to expand. Suddenly knowns were shifting to unknowns. Susie didn't feel secure about the future.

'There was one other thing,' Betty said.

Bring it on, Susie thought. Pile it high.

'How would you feel about Valerie staying?'

★   ★   ★

John Forbes hadn't organised Christmas properly in years. Bachelor days had meant going home to his parents or on a sun holiday when he could afford it. When he'd been married he'd relied on Roma to do the necessaries. He'd muddled through the initial stages of being single again as shambolically as was allowed but it was time to up the ante. Now he was having to decide what teenagers might like and what an ex-wife would find acceptable but not mistake as a token of any desire to return. He even harboured notions of cooking one of the family's meals but that amounted to a swoop on a Marks and Spencer chiller cabinet closer to the time.

Roma was pushing hard for him to stay over a few days and he hadn't decided yet whether it was part of an elaborate ambush plan designed to compromise him and get him to take up full husbandly duties again or simply the practical detail that transport would be difficult around the hub of the festivities.

Perhaps you're flattering yourself, a little voice suggested. Perhaps, he conceded, but reluctantly and only because he knew he was human and while he had a pulse he was prey for Roma, even if she was merely proving her point that she could have him whenever she wanted. He would have loved to deny that this was possible but sometimes the beast in his trousers got the better of him and he didn't want to take that chance over a festive and drunken season. The pursuant complications were a nightmare to contemplate. He would go home to his apartment each night. He hoped.

He settled on a small abstract painting for Roma, which he felt covered all of the right ground and didn't give off any signals that could be misinterpreted. He asked the youngest member of staff in a trendy high street shop what his daughter might like. She pointed him to a short dress with 'star' written in sparkle across the chest and told him to accessorize it with a bag and sunglasses. 'At Christmas?' he asked. She shot him a pitying look and said, 'Trust me.' He did and had the gifts wrapped.

This left the Boy.

He was Quentin's least favourite person in the world bar none and even the best gift ever was going to be met with disdain or ignored altogether. He resisted the urge to buy a boy-toy that he might have liked himself, knowing that his son was no flat and would see it for what it was immediately, and went instead for a skateboard with all of the safety stuff the incredulous sports shop attendant recommended. The sales assistant knew he had a live one here and milked it for all he was worth. From the very little John could make out, it was good stuff, nothing too geeky or embarrassing, and he hoped that would count for something.

He totted up the balance after the spree and figured he'd get back a mere fraction in socks and aftershave. Them's the breaks when you're a heart-breaking, leaving kinda guy. They had never been much of a family for competitive present-giving anyhow, though Roma liked things to cost, so nothing had changed there. Divorce and separation meant money and he was shelling out. Them's the rules. He didn't ever imagine they'd change. Hell, maybe he'd get a few books or vintage movies too to soften the blow. From now on he needed to work all the hours and jobs available to support this expensive lifestyle. Resting was not an option.

He'd always wondered why the period when an actor was unemployed was called that. His experience of it was that it was fraught with the certainty that one would never work again and that one's career was over. Resting was the last thing it was. He'd like to meet the man who'd coined that and shake his hand for getting away with such an outrageous principle and description. And he imagined it was a man. Well, Shakespeare's women were played by boys for centuries, for instance, so it had been a man's world for aeons. Women had more logic and brutal practicality than to call the thing 'resting'.

The thought made him realise he hadn't bought his father a gift, and he'd better sort out things for Andrew and his family. He rarely saw his brother, which was a shame. Life just seemed to be an endless round of work with barely enough time to learn lines and move on. It would be good to have time to sit back and assess. On a whim he bought Betty a small pin from Tiffany's and swung onto the street bearing the signature blue bag. Women looked envious of the bag, men jealous. He still had a gal he could buy jewels for. Roma would have his guts if she knew.

★ ★ ★

'Have you seen the price of the champagne here?' Sophie shrieked. 'Even the wine is prohibitive.'

'Welcome to my world. Besides, it's my treat so drink up and enjoy.'

'You have no idea how exciting it is to be out of the house. Alone. This might as well be Australia, it's such a difference for me.' She had finished her first glass in double-quick time and was tucking into her second. 'Will we see anyone famous?'

Susie shrugged. 'Possibly.'

'Ooh. Is my lippy on straight? Any on my teeth?'

'Sophie, people will think I'm giving you a dental examination if you don't stop.'

She sniffed her armpits. 'Not too bad,' she judged. 'I'll spritz them with whatever fancy perfume is for sale in the loo later. Now, how's work?'

'Valerie is probably going to stay on.'

'How do you feel about that?'

'I don't know. She loves the job and she suits the agency. Turns out everyone knows she's my mum.'

'How did they rumble you?'

'I ignored her too much. Plus, apparently, I look very like her, which I cannot see at all. And they put the Devon connection in. It all added up to one thing.'

Sophie didn't comment.

'So I do look like her.'

'Yeah.'

'Only to be expected, I suppose. I can't really object to her keeping the post. I think of all the times I berated her when I was a teenager about being a slave to the family and Dad. I always wanted to know why he got the job and the hobbies and she got the servitude.'

'It was generational, Susie. She went from the shelter of her father's house to her husband's with no period of independence. We didn't have to do that because our mothers did and we were spared it. We could be our own kind of feminist on the back of others, and change the rules as we went on.'

'And now that she's got out and made something of herself I'm carping on about it.'

'You've helped her do that. You were the one who suggested her in the first place.'

'I guess.'

'Do you remember how you felt when Chris married Corinne? You were afraid Milo would like her more than you.'

Susie nodded. It had been a bad time. She'd felt even more alone than usual then. She had been a very single parent. She still was.

'And when they had their children, you were afraid that Milo would want to live with them, to have that sort of family.'

'Are you doing some sort of parable thingy here?'

'In a way. My point is he never wanted any life but the one he has with you. He loves you. He values you. He needs you. The same goes for Valerie. You're not losing her.'

★   ★   ★

Reg stood by his large picture window looking out at the milky soup created by fog and darkness. It rendered the windowpanes opaque. He wondered if it was possible to capture the vapour in a jar for all to see and wonder at. If he let it in, would it cloak his furniture and paintings in eerie mist, perfect for a ghost story or supernatural thriller? Would it cloud his lungs as he breathed it in? Would he relish its unsettling density? On such a night he should take Poe down from the shelves and give him a whirl. He could barely make out his own features in the glass, with electric light behind him and foggy night before. It made his face look younger, as if he had a portrait in his attic ageing steadily while he stayed vibrant and beautiful.

'Silly old man,' he chided. 'Such fanciful nonsense.'

In fact, he looked a lot like a fuzzy John Forbes, which made perfect sense and didn't involve anything darker than biology and DNA.

He nursed a whisky, determined not to drink too much tonight. Christmas would be upon him soon and he supposed he should hang a bauble or two to mark the season. There would be a pleasant round of parties and a warm feeling of bonhomie for all. That was the plan. He would go to Andrew this year, as John's situation was a tad overwrought. He must ring his eldest and ask after his filming and what his plans were. He was not pleased that he still felt a residual annoyance that John had changed the status quo between himself and his grandchildren. John had done what he thought best. It was wrong of Reg to let selfish concerns impinge.

Andrew had married an elegant but unremarkable woman. She had borne them a clutch of unruly children whom Reg enjoyed greatly in small doses. He had never been a kids' man, even with his own when they were little. There would be turkey and low-fat mince pies, cheer, tears and fisticuffs. Everyone would have a good time. Andrew and Heather were perfectly happy in their self-produced mayhem and it was hard not to be affected by that. His beloved Claire had approved.

She had also approved of John's decision to enter the business, citing the fact that it was his destiny and that his talent would out if it was there to do so. It was. Reg was glad she hadn't lived to see the divorce.

★ ★ ★

Sophie was slurring now and bright pink from champagne and freedom. 'How are we going to find someone new for you?'

'Lola says there are no available men in London any more so I'm happy to stay single and die lonely. I don't have the time to meet anyone or the inclination. And I certainly don't have any available time to keep seeing anyone once a connection is made. I'd need to work with the person to guarantee seeing them on any regular basis.'

'I thought you had a strict no-colleagues policy. Isn't that why you wouldn't go out with that gorgeous actor, whatshisname?'

'Yes, the policy still holds. And John Forbes is

213

whatshisname's name. Anyhow, it would be even worse to go out with a client as opposed to a fellow office type.'

'Susie, life is short and sometimes nasty. We snatch at happiness wherever it presents itself or we die wondering and alone. Rules are made to be bent, at the very least. Cut yourself some slack.'

'I am so not listening to you or taking your pissed advice.'

'You know I speak only wisdom.'

★ ★ ★

It had been the makings of a lark to sign up for this radio play but anticipation and reality were two very different things, Milo realised. One was filled with jittery excitement, the other a jittery dread. He made his way to the studio at Maida Vale, then became hopelessly lost in the labyrinthine corridors leading to the recording area, even though he was following a production assistant. He was disorientated. They seemed to be underground and very far away from civilisation. They didn't encounter any natural light on their way and he expected to see strange sightless creatures scurry past chased by a roaring Minotaur long forgotten by London and those living above ground. The assistant chattered on as if this was the most normal place in the world.

Milo clutched his script. He had marked his lines in yellow highlighter and thought the fluorescence would help lead him out if he became trapped in this strange maze. He had run through his lines with his mum last night but was nervous of saying them aloud with anyone else. He was playing a nerd and he had to wrestle with the word 'peripatetic' early on, which he was so not looking forward to. At least he sort of knew what it meant now though he couldn't envisage a scenario where he might employ it at Morning Star. That would be, like, the gayest of all gay utterances. He thought of Rafe and decided this would be a cakewalk compared to dealing with him. Well, he would try to use that to get him through today.

The assistant peeked through a door and beckoned him. She pointed into a vast cavern. 'This is where the orchestra play and record,' she said. Large cello cases lined the wall like enormous sarcophagi, mummies within waiting till nightfall to stagger about dripping bandages and inspiring terror. Who would want to be a security guard in this place? They continued along the long corridor accompanied by heating pipes high on the wall, covered in padded silver foil. It was like a jaded spaceship. At the end, and a very long way from the start of their journey, they came to an inexplicable and useless lobby, turned right and entered a room furnished by chairs that looked as though they'd come from a mental home.

His dad was surrounded by real actors and as they turned to look at him, Milo knew they smelled an imposter. His sphincter jabbed him and he wanted to dash to the loo. Before he could bolt, his dad began to introduce everyone.

Then he called the gathering to order to read through the script. Great, they had been waiting for him, he was the last in as well as being the rookie. Milo staggered through somehow but was left with the distinct impression that he was totally the worst member of the cast. He got a few laughs, which was odd in a good way and it bolstered him enough to stay seated and not dash screaming from the room when they were done.

His father brought him to the sound box where the engineer 'drove the bus', so that he could get the full flavour of the production and see how everything worked. On the way his dad put his arm around his shoulder and said, 'Well done, that was great. You're going to be just fine.' Milo's mouth was too dry to put much of an answer to that.

He was agog at the process. Outdoor atmosphere was sometimes created simply by using one of the specially designed rooms. Other times the engineer played in traffic or a playground from the 'grams' on his desk. Inside the studio, a mouse was re-created live by another sound person wearing a glove with buttons sewn onto the fingertips and clattering it along a board. A square box of different doors and locks was wheeled around to wherever it needed to be used and a row of different bells and knockers made the sounds of people coming and going.

Scene by scene they committed the play to posterity and when Milo went in to record, he found new quirks to add to his lines and swelled to hear his dad's praise. One of the other actors told him, 'You're a chip off the old block,' and he almost burst with happiness to hear it. He didn't know how he would ever return to school or normality again. Here in this windowless, magical place he felt more alive although it was all make-believe. It was the sort of pleasure he got from sailing, but here he could pretend to be someone else all day and get paid for it. Whoever invented this was a genius.

When it was all over, they passed along the corridor again and saw that the orchestra had arrived. The cello cases were open and empty. Around the corridor and the pit within, men and women staggered cheerily, smelling of punch and wearing tinsel in their hair; happy, festive zombies.

★   ★   ★

Chloe's visit was brief and chaotic. Susie had dreamt of leisurely lunches with her and Valerie, or ruthless shopping while on the other end of a Blackberry in case of a work emergency. Then Chloe hit town like a tornado and Valerie disappeared. It sat oddly with the fact that she had recently become such a permanent fixture in Susie's life at home and work. She probably should have been relieved to be shot of her for a while but instead she was agitated and couldn't work out why.

Chloe was sharp as a tack. 'Take that look off your face, baby sister, I'm not trying to steal her.'

'Why do I always think of you at a distance as

being softer, more empathetic, a yummy mummy type?'

'Magic.'

'The power of the dark side, more like.'

'Sticks and stones, et cetera. Now, what exactly is your problem?'

Susie was too embarrassed to put words to it. 'It's too stupid and I feel like a spoiled child even thinking it.'

Chloe filled in. 'You feel like you've been dumped.'

'How come you're so good at this?'

'I have a teenage daughter. That species cuts to the quick. Every accusation in a teenager's life can be issued in one fundamental sentence. It's very hard to deal with but I'm learning. So, am I there or thereabouts with my theory?'

'Yes. I feel a bit left out. I don't know where I stand.' She wasn't proud of the admission. She also knew she was supersizing a problem that didn't warrant it because she was uneasy about other issues, particularly Betty's plans for the agency.

'Susie, you are a ninny. Honestly, if Mum doesn't stop singing your praises to me I might have to throttle her. The woman never shuts up about you. And the reason she seems a bit distant is that she's trying to get you something wonderful for Christmas to thank you for all you've done for her and she doesn't have a lot of money so it's taking up a lot of her mind space.'

Susie felt like a dolt.

'What she is not talking about is Dad. That can mean one of two things: one, she is in denial about what he's done or, two, she is planning to take him to the cleaners.'

'I'm not sure I mind which of those it is.'

'Me neither. She did part with one gem that she says is from some American she's reading, about not being afraid to make tough calls.'

'I know who she means. He also says there's no such thing as a good divorce. He's talking about business but I think Valerie finds him an inspiration on all levels.'

They digested this.

'There's not a lot we can do about that for the moment. As to Dad's festive plans, apparently he intends to move back into the house, purchase a stuffed crown of turkey for one, some ready-to-cook sprouts and a tiny plum pud, and spend the time doing the jigsaws he hopes we're sending him. After the Queen's speech, of course. Gawd bless us every one.'

'He's actually quite a straightforward type of chap, isn't he? Comfortingly dull and easy to manage.'

'Yes. I'm inclined to leave him be, maybe swoop for a day before New Year's. And before you ask, there's a do at the Cock and Feather to ring it in and he's going to that for his seasonal two pints of Oakham. The man is on fire.'

★   ★   ★

The countdown to the end of another year was a catalyst for change and so it was that Lola lost a male client before the break.

'I was inches from a clean getaway,' she

219

moaned. 'Clear record for the whole second half of the year until Mark Ali turned up looking haunted. Things were going too well. I'm a Jew, I should have seen it coming a mile off. I am a card-carrying, doom-laden fatalist. It's my calling to know that shit is coming down the line.'

'Not necessarily,' Susie pointed out. 'He's of that age, isn't he? Mid-thirties, thinks he should be doing better and that a change of agent will sort it? Worried about himself.'

Lola nodded in resignation. She rose to magnanimity but it wasn't easy. 'Hope it works for him. He's good.'

'At least he came in to tell you face to face, didn't just phone or write.'

'Yes. I got the whole 'it's not you it's me' break-up spiel.'

'The language of love,' Susie said. 'It's what we deal in.'

'It's beginning to get on my chest that I have to listen to the same scenarios in both my professional and personal life, and neither is yielding a screamingly orgasmic time.'

'I know,' Susie sympathised. 'The rules of engagement are messed up.'

★   ★   ★

John Forbes had the classic actor's anxiety dream that night. He was waiting in the wings of a large, packed theatre ready to go on, only he had no idea what show he was in or what part he was playing. A hum of excitement resonated through the theatre from both cast and audience. Just as his turn came to enter and speak lines he did not know he was suddenly sitting in the stalls saying to the person next to him, 'This is where I come on,' while suddenly realising that he was in the wrong place for that and should be back in the wings although he still didn't know which show was being performed. He woke terrified and drenched with sweat. I'm supposed to get that dream at the beginning of a job, he thought, not after I've finished one.

9

It had become traditional for Arland and Shaw to host an informal drop-in day for clients close to the Christmas break. The staff cleared their desks, set up some cheery lights, lolled about chatting to visiting clients and sneakily took any calls that needed dealing with. The festivities usually kicked off from mid-afternoon but a few bottles would be cracked open by then. Valerie was first in line to greet the guests and also to put more faces to the voices she spoke with daily. She directed Craig Landor through after a chat about him being a Chelsea fan. She thanked her good fortune to have a grandson with identical footballing taste. She knew little extra bits about a lot of clients now from brief conversations as she introduced herself and put them through to the main office.

Reginald Darwin brought some handmade chocolates and Valerie couldn't help but wonder why she couldn't have one like him at home. Actually, she was too busy, distracted and happy for that: a wonderful rule of three, if she understood Lola's directions on that. (Lola had declared someone uppity, fuckedy and twatmost while illustrating her point.) Poor Alistair, with his dull life and tiny prospects, happy with the village chiffchaff. Chittenham was another world, another universe. London would chew him up without a thought and this business would cough him out like a hairball. She was pleased with the image. She belonged to one of the Great Cities of the World now. She connected people from so many different places, helped them in her own tiny way by facilitating calls and booking meetings. She was a player. And in the process she had rediscovered her resilience.

She had power too. If she didn't like a caller's tone she made it difficult for them to get to their chosen target. She was particularly punishing on bad manners. She might be the lowly reception-ist but treating her like dirt was tantamount to snapping fingers at a waiter and not to be endured.

Rod Ferguson was fidgety and full of talk about the Rocket website. 'I had a look at it and I was wondering if we should get them to dress me in their Matador range?'

Susie could only think sparkling boleros and little Mickey Mouse hats but kept that to herself. 'If you'd like that, I'll have a word with them. As long as there are no strings attached to your wearing their clothes I'll be happy enough about it.'

'It was Valerie who put me on to it,' Rod said.

'Really,' Susie inquired. What have you been up to, Miss Macintosh?

'She's sparky for an old bird,' Rod went on. 'Very enthusiastic. But I nearly laughed when she called the Matador stuff men's casuals.'

'I know exactly what you mean. That phrase says slacks and polyester shirts somehow. We cannot have one of the brightest and most handsome men in the country dressed in beige. Can we?'

Rod helloed past her shoulder and when she turned, her mother was standing with a strange look on her face. She knew Valerie was thinking about her father, Alistair. He was a casuals man when relaxing. He had several worn-out suits for work but descended into bland slacks and sweaters in his leisure hours. She lightened the moment. 'Macho might have been a better title for the range. What do you think, Valerie?'

There it goes again, thought Valerie. I am being sentimental about Alistair. The shit effectively ditched me and he deserves all he gets, even if it is only unkind words or comparisons. Clearly he's a habit that needs to be purged, like smoking.

A cadaverous actor named Harvey Bolt was wheeled over. He looked permanently ravenous, possibly for human flesh. He was usually the first client in and stood by the canapés shovelling food into his mouth, as if no meal could ever fill him or bulk him out. A whiff of imminent death or suicide followed him about and he did well playing the sick, the sick-minded and often the dead brought back to walk the earth. When Harvey was eating, and Susie had rarely seen him when he was not, it was important to stand out of range or direction of his mouth, as he tended to speak with it full and spray. Betty stood to his side, laughing at something he had said, or perhaps it was that he had spurted a mangled olive onto Mitch's back as he'd rushed by. Mitch had been quick but not quick enough.

Harvey smiled and she noticed his teeth were covered with black fish roe. He looked as if he had eaten the very soil he'd been buried in. Susie drank a litre of water to make up for her earlier champagne and the fancies it was visiting on her.

'What will you do?' Susie asked Lola.

'It's Hanukkah for us. The Festival of Lights. So we'll fire up the menorah and probably eat Chinese food on the twenty-fifth. It's not prescribed by the Torah, by the way, but it is fried in oil, which reflects the miracle of the lamp that burned for eight days instead of one, and it's not too hard for it to be kosher either. Here endeth the lesson, daughter.'

They were debating the merits of deep-fried turkey and being a little cruel about some of the lesser performances they'd seen during the year when John Forbes walked through the door, and for a moment Susie lost her train of thought.

'I had almost forgotten just how gorgeous that man is,' she confessed to Lola.

'Bloody hell, yes. Has my make-up gone mushy or am I still presentable?'

'Perfect. Me?'

'I'd let you out.'

'That'll have to do.' Susie gave in to the notion that she was drunk enough to care. John Forbes was so far off the scale in terms of romantic interest it didn't bear trying to find words to cover it. But she still had a pulse and a gal couldn't let the side down. Ooh, this was definitely the bubbles talking, but, you know what, it's Christmas, what harm? John Forbes seemed to be standing looking only at her, as if absorbed. She probably had some ridiculous expression on her face that he was trying to fathom, or perhaps he was transfixed by her swollen, blotchy face. She didn't want to disgrace herself any more so she raised a hand as if all was normal and wiggled her fingers in his direction, before wafting off to make sure Valerie was coping out front.

'I'm fine and dandy, dear. I enjoy this job.'

'Good. Rod told me you had information on the company that owns Rocket sunglasses.' Great, back to normal.

'Yes. I just thought it would be interesting to look up their past campaigns. Rod seemed very excited about the clothing range.'

'That's fine. But you might run that sort of thing by me next time. No harm done, but just something to remember.'

'Oh, right.' Valerie nodded. 'Would you like a chocolate? Reginald brought them.'

Lola came out to say, 'Is it me or is Rod Ferguson a little too up today?'

'He's young. Who knows what he's on.' Susie shrugged. ''Tis the season, after all.'

'Wonder if he'd share.'

'Don't even think it. Remember, you are one of the zookeepers.'

'Why couldn't I have had some talent? I'd love the acting life.'

Susie refilled a few glasses and John Forbes finally got her to himself. 'Didn't you used to be — '

'Fat,' she finished for him. 'Yes, as you know I was the Susie that ate this Susie.'

'Straight-haired was more where I was going,' he admitted. 'I like this style better. How gay is it that I know about hairdos? And it's none of my business and probably awfully pass remarkable of me to mention it at all.' He looked mortified, as if he had spoken well out of turn and had even surprised himself.

He had. Truly he had. He could not believe he had made such a hash of an opening remark. This was hardly the gambit of a man who was supposed to be smooth with the ladies. He was like a ham-fisted teenager, tongue-tied and foolish. 'I wonder if we shouldn't start this conversation again.'

She laughed. 'Are you flirting with me?'

'Is it that obvious?'

'I'm just checking because I'm not sure I'd recognise it after so long. And I suppose I'd be horribly disappointed if you weren't.'

He was divine, no doubt about it. But he was an actor and their business was to bamboozle and make people love them. 'Betty tells me you like *I-Dentity*.' Business was a good place to be.

' 'Like' is hardly at the races. It's wonderful. I was thinking only this morning it would be handy to clone myself. Then I could send that me home to my ex-wife and children. Roma could treat me like shit but the kids would have a full-time dad on the premises.'

He wanted to kick himself. He couldn't resist making sure she knew he was still very single. Admitting he was a rubbish dad hardly sweetened the package. He was an idiot and there was no way this woman would ever be

227

interested in him. 'Hi, Dad.'

Reg looked at both John and Susie as if he knew exactly what was going on. But, as he'd often explained to John, that was a good tool of the trade. 'Enigmatic wisdom is the look to go for, especially if you have no bogging idea what's going on. Keeps you out of all the reviews. No mention is better than a bad one. Very handy.' This was the only advice John had ever got from his father. He counted it as increasingly excellent stuff as the years went by.

Susie was light-headed. 'So,' she said, failing to add anything else on to the statement. She was saved further embarrassment by Milo's arrival.

Betty made a fuss when Valerie told her about his radio job. 'Our newest and youngest client,' she declared. She brought him across the agency, introducing him to everyone along the way. He could hardly string two words together with excitement. He struggled through his thoughts on the orchestra in the Maida Vale studio and John Forbes told a racy story about a percussionist. Milo felt mildly embarrassed, grown-up and included.

Clients came and went, Susie stuck to soft drinks, deciding it was not the day to try to figure out life's meaning. John asked if he could phone her.

'You are persistent, I'll give you that.'

But she left without giving him her number. It was Christmas and she wanted to leave work with a clean sheet and concentrate on her family. There was no point in allowing a situation that could go nowhere. She had done that in her life before and it was a waste of time. It was flattering to enjoy John Forbes' attention but there was no point in encouraging it.

* * *

Waking with a start was beginning to grate on Susie. She found a new wide-awake time at five thirty the following morning did nothing for her mood or the slight hangover trying its best to invade. She went quietly to the front window to check on the weather and was gratified to see a white fleece on the common. She became mesmerised by the flakes of snow flurrying to the ground. Softly they twirled, tiny balls of fluff. It was unbelievable to think that they were water, essentially, or at least a version of. The candyfloss of water, perhaps. The fancy made her giggle. She opened the window and put her head out, letting the cold clear a passage for her mind to relax in, then stuck her tongue out and let flakes land and melt. Her skin tingled, scalded by its inability to tell extreme cold from burning heat. She breathed in the icily refreshing air. She felt cleansed. When her upper torso began to tremble from the cold she pulled back into the heated room and allowed a pleasurable thaw to take hold. She sat to enjoy the sensations in her favourite armchair and must have dozed.

She answered an insistent phone to a blubbing Debbie Jenkins. 'I've just been taken apart in the paper for my Glenda,' she wailed. Before Susie could even cluck she went on with, ' "The most wooden and charmless performance I have had

the misfortune to see in many's the long day.' '
Susie knew enough of actors to know this
slighting phrase from the review had been
learned off immediately and was not being read
to her from the offending review.

'Debbie,' she soothed, 'the critics don't matter
a damn to you or your show. *The Wizard of Oz*
is a classic. If anything, this reviewer is probably
trying to find a fault to justify his or her
existence. Critics trade in disapproval. The
people will come and that's all you should care
about. It's the audience that matters.'

Debbie was snotting for England on the end of
the phone. 'I know the bitch that wrote it,' she
admitted between moist snuffs. Susie waited for
an explanatory punchline and got one. 'I slept
with her future husband when we were at drama
school.'

'I rest my case.'

Debbie honked and cleared her throat. 'It was
only once and he was useless, but elephants
never forget. This woman has never let a bygone
go by. God, I better get some more sleep. We
have three shows today.'

'Sold out?'

'Oh yeah, way in advance.' She chuckled
rustily on the other end. 'This must be the only
profession in the world where the concept of
selling out is a good thing. Sorry for the
blow-up, I just had to let off steam. It wouldn't
do for the Good Witch to go on like the bitch
from hell. The munchkins are easily spooked.'

'That's what I'm here for. If you can't tell me,
who can you tell?'

'Thanks, Susie.'

'Don't mention it. Have several good ones today, and then lots more.'

Three shows, Susie thought, aghast, as she hung up. Debbie was on a good but unremarkable wage for the run. There are days when I'm glad I didn't stick it out. She looked at the clock on the cooker and gave a groan. It was only eight o clock. She shouldn't have answered her mobile. Being available at all hours was taking on an unappealing bent if this was to be a trend for her panto babies. And she was only on ten per cent because it was theatre, and ten per cent of a small fee was even less than a very small thing, as Lola was forever pointing out. A yawn overtook her as if to reinforce the point, so she shuffled to her room and tucked herself back into bed. She was glad to be somewhere under a duvet and nowhere over the rainbow.

★ ★ ★

Margaret La Bute rang with the news that Charlie Morley had died in the night. 'We always lose a few to pneumonia during the cold weather,' she said. 'My mother called it the old people's friend.'

'I didn't know he was at the Grove.'

'Latterly, yes. He became too much of a handful for Eugene and was gifted to us.'

Reg hated the end of the year for precisely this sort of news. An entertainer died and was later remembered at the BAFTAs. All too often his friends' photographs showed them in their prime

231

and in black and white, such was their age. Often, too, they would have to have an explanation posted under the photo to denote their status as actor, director or writer because the world had moved on and the majority no longer knew who they were. He went to his scrapbooks and found them, himself and Charlie, in various and varied motley: Rosencrantz and Guildenstern, as heroes of the Somme in a movie that was sometimes shown on daytime TV, much later on stage as the Sunshine Boys, in Leicester if Reg wasn't mistaken.

Charlie had been one of the last of the flamboyant actors, much taken to wearing a cape and carrying a cane. 'Dear heart,' he would greet. He gestured profusely and bemoaned the arrested teaching of Latin to the younger generation. To the best of Reg's knowledge, Charlie hadn't learned Latin either but loved to pick up a phrase or two to bandy about. He was fond of uttering on *vitae humanae speculum* and would graciously talk of all of human life if pushed to downgrade, explaining gently as he did that he had not gone for a totally literal translation and was slumming it somewhat. He did his best to be different and exotic, as he felt all conjurers should be. He enjoyed the sheer exuberance of his art and the celebrity it afforded. He always wore a dickie bow, even in private, and favoured hats above a bare head. He lived large. There weren't many like him left, if any at all. Charlie's favourite quote was from *The Picture of Dorian Grey*: 'I love acting. It is so much more real than life.' For all his theatrical campery, Charlie was hard-working and practical, like all actors. He gave performances that came from an inner well of bravery that all good performers drew on. Without risk, there was nothing to be gambled or therefore gained. That was why actors opened up and left themselves vulnerable. Even the losing could be glorious.

When had he last seen Charlie? A fact of any actor's life was that you spent most time with those you were working with and, in spite of best intentions, rarely socialised with other friends or colleagues. For goodness sake, he hardly saw his own son John and they were both in the same business. Yesterday was the first time he had clapped eyes on him in an age. They had lost touch. When had he last seen Charlie? Claire's funeral, he realised. It seemed to Reg that as life went on, a person spent more and more time going to funerals and less and less to birthday celebrations or weddings. Funerals weren't always po-faced or entirely unhappy, of course, but the experience of marking mortality always diminished those who felt they were next over the top of the trench. Now he would see Charlie off. He felt discountenanced, bereft. It was lonely, getting old. His universe was shrinking. His points of reference were changing, disappearing.

He flicked about the channels on his television to distract from his morbidity. He flashed past a programme about young beauties on an island, so called celebrities, expected to pair up for the viewers' titillation. What had they done to deserve the exposure? What were their talents?

Could they not meet people on their own time? Could love be manufactured for the spurious delight of an audience? Was it not the most important strand in a human's life: to love and be loved? How could that be rustled up artificially for mass entertainment?

A purple bear sang inane songs in a false and condescending voice.

Tourists were being bombed in Turkey.

A news bulletin ended with an item on a mathematician who had calculated an equation to predict when the immortal line 'Are we nearly there yet?' would occur during a car journey. A representative of a car manufacturer enthused as if the automotive industry's atom had been split. He explained cheerily that it meant they now knew which features to add to their product to combat back-seat boredom. Reg could see the cash signs 'ker-ching' in the man's eyes.

He didn't recognise the world in which he lived. A pain began to thump behind his eyes. His blood pumped steadily, spreading the ache throughout his head, beating out its point. He took two aspirin and went back to bed. He hoped a sleep might chase the headache off or at least let him wake with a less grim outlook on life.

⋆　⋆　⋆

Valerie intended to use some of her time off to gen up on agency work. She had taken home old contracts to study the wordage and what that meant. She had a pile of scripts to read. She could access office files from Milo's computer to study CVs and learn what everyone had been up to. She intended to know more about these people's careers than their own mothers by the time she was done. She alternated between scripts and other work to keep it fresh. Milo stirred and she pointed him towards muesli and the television.

'I love Christmas,' he said, flopping into the sofa. 'Great movies and I don't have to get dressed.'

Valerie looked at him, stewing in his pre-teen juices, and smiled. Every so often she read him a passage of a contract, usually stuff that hardly made sense although it was more or less in English. The sections covering the future life of a film or television series were nothing short of fascinating. Here the language mentioned 'formats known and unknown' in 'territories known and unknown' in 'the known and unknown universe'. So, if there was life on Mars, the companies had covered the rights to sales. Plus they had covered their backs on the rest of creation, just in case. It was fabulous legalese and devious, really.

Susie presented a bleary face, looking for tea while she ran a bath. 'My system is taking the opportunity to crash, I think, now that I have time off.' As she nursed her mug she asked Valerie why she was working. 'This is holiday time, Mum. And while I'm at it, why are you so fresh?'

'I didn't drink yesterday. I didn't want to miss a moment.'

'You are a marvel, Mum.'

'No, just sensible,' Valerie stated.

Susie searched her face for a barb but didn't find one. She had a vision of her mother smothered under a tower of paper, not unlike the scenario threatened in the office when things got out of hand and a cull had to be called. 'Let me know how you get on.'

'Of course. One last thing. How would you feel about describing agenting as a posh version of pimping?'

Susie lost some tea in a spray of disbelief. 'You and Milo have been watching way too much MTV.'

* * *

John Forbes was in flux and that felt as bad as it sounded. He went over the events of yesterday afternoon without deciding whether he had been an ass or hadn't made enough of a fool of himself to be dismissed as drunk or silly. He was pretty certain that he had left his dignity with the umbrellas at the door and probably forgotten to retrieve it after the party. He certainly didn't feel full of it now. He was low, cringing to think of his attempts to keep Susie Vine's attention. At least it had happened in front of his acting family. With his profile he might have expected photographs in a tabloid if he had made a fool of himself in public. Small mercies.

What affected him about this woman? That proved nearly impossible to pin down. There was no one single thing that could explain the attraction. She simply floored him, like a boyish crush, delivered out of some blue area of mystery. This last embroidered fancy made him clench his teeth and grind them in embarrassment. But he could not get her out of his idiot head. For the first time in an age, he felt uncontrollably horny.

He tried displacement in the form of checking lists of things done and to do. He intended to pass Christmas off with all of the t's crossed and i's dotted. Otherwise Roma would spot a fissure and widen it with sarky observation and ridicule. She had highly developed skills for spotting vulnerabilities. God, if she got wind of his latest silliness she would be merciless. On no account must he present himself with the possibility of Roma getting under his skin, be it on the personal or practical levels of his life. He spent a sweaty hour wondering how to deal with his other problem, namely the Cape Horn promontory south of his navel. He went for a long walk in the snow.

$$\star \quad \star \quad \star$$

Susie felt refreshed and enthusiastic after a delightful supplementary snooze followed by a soak in a bubble bath. She had lazed in the water thinking up such philosophical gems as suds were the feathers of the water world. They could now go into the file made earlier where snow was the candyfloss of the water kingdom. Both bed and bath were miraculous in their ability to calm and console. Sometimes life's pleasures were tiny and incomparable. Valerie and Milo had mucked along nicely without her and now they were all having a lazy lunch while planning which shops to hit.

'I think we should make a rule not to spend too much money on gifts,' Susie said.

The others nodded but she knew she was talking to herself. She had made an effort, now let the games begin.

Valerie was looking particularly sprightly. 'I can't believe that my first Christmas in London is a white one,' she enthused. 'I thought I might throw myself onto the common and make a few snow angels then head to the shops. Any takers?'

Three sets of hands went up, including her own.

'You've got to dry your hair,' she told Susie. 'You'll catch your death if you go out with it wet.'

'Yes, Mum.'

Inevitably snowballs were chucked about and the Vines had to go home to change outfits before presenting themselves to polite society again.

As they ventured forth a second time Susie took a call on her mobile. 'Sure,' she said. 'I'll pop in later.' She swore as she disconnected.

★　★　★

Reg was silently berating himself in the bookshop. He really needed to branch out on his gift giving. Every year he ended up spending a fortune on books and recordings. This time out he would try to buy one fewer item here and replace it with a game, possibly educational, or a toy, at a pinch.

It didn't work out that way and he still bought out the store, and then had to go even further afield to bolster his selection in other directions. Can't help myself, he thought, I love words and the worlds they create. He pitied any child who grew up in a house that was not groaning under the written word. Happily a few adult tomes fell into his basket, little treats to savour later. He really needed seeing to as he had just broken his rule that he wouldn't buy one other book until he had finished reading the untouched stacks at home. A man should have some bad habits, he reasoned, thinking he was probably paraphrasing Lady Bracknell. With a pang he remembered that Charlie's ambition had been to play her but he never did get to. He's in acting heaven now, trying out with the best of them, Reg thought. Break a leg, old faithful.

He could smell coffee from a café smack bang in the middle of the shop. He remembered days when to lift a book off a shelf meant you had to buy it. Now, customers were encouraged to take the item to the café and leaf through to decide whether it was for them or not. A sign over the coffee machine told him that geography is a flavour. He knew this was snappy and, at a stretch, true within the parameters of the world created for such a soundbite. But it made him uncomfortable all the same. He was uneasy with trendy attempts to bamboozle the populace with clever marketing ploys. He shook himself. He was becoming the stereotypical grumpy, old man blustering about days of yore and how they were somehow better because they were simpler. Not always so, he knew. Still, there were elements of modern life that were nonsense. He should at least be allowed to blow on about them.

He was leafing through a junior atlas when a breathless type with a pink face asked him to sign a copy of *Holidays Abroad*, a comedy hit from six years ago and the last time he had graced a stage. It was a rambling mess of a farce but very popular on the amateur circuit because of its large cast. His name was on the original cast list printed at the front. Reg wondered if his new fan was pink from meeting him or had simply run all the way from the drama section in the nether reaches of the store.

'When can we expect to see you perform again?' the woman asked, susurrantly.

'I'm making a small film in the New Year,' Reg told her. 'Very gritty and upsetting, so it's not a comedy like you've got there.' It felt good to have news of work to report.

'I am sure you will be your excellent self,' she told him.

I do hope so, he thought, as he watched her retreat. 'Thank you,' he called out before she rounded the corner. What a nice thing to happen to a chap.

★ ★ ★

Chris Falucci hung by in his giant car and collected the Vine entourage to go to the Morning Star Christmas concert. 'Where's your mum?'

'She had business to deal with. She said she'd

meet us there.' It was clear that Milo didn't expect her to.

His father swore and reached for his mobile. 'I'll be in the car when you're both ready,' he told Milo and Valerie as he walked away. He got Susie's answering service. 'If you miss Milo's night I will never forgive you. I can't speak for our son. This is typical you, Susie. You expect everyone else to dance to your tune, but you conveniently change the rules for yourself.'

Milo didn't want to talk on the journey in case he gave away any of the details of the evening. He would only part with the information that this year would be the best, if the older boys were to be believed. He was nervous but excited and admitted that much. Chris played a radio station pumping out carols and seasonal fare. They sang along to 'Let it snow, let it snow, let it snow.'

'I have never seen so many taxis,' Valerie said as they drew close to the school.

'Parents of the pupils. It'll be tough getting a cab in south London tonight,' Chris told her.

Milo craned his head at odd angles trying to see into the driveway of the school. This had been closed off to parking for the evening so they drove around a bit before finding a handy spot. When they returned they saw why and gasped at the beauty of it. The car park was filled with papier mâché snowmen formally arranged in rows like the Chinese terracotta soldiers. Milo explained that every boy in the school had made one so, like snowflakes, no two were alike and of course Morning Star didn't have nearly as many as the Chinese as a result of them not having that many pupils so there were just four hundred as opposed to four thousand and they hadn't expected the weather to match so the men were resting on a bed of gardening fleece but the snow had added a brilliant backdrop and each snowman was waterproof which was why they were a little bit shiny. He was breathless imparting the information and clearly pleased as punch with the school's surprise for its visitors. They were stunned at the sheer scale of the project as well as its audacity.

'Your mum is going to be blown away by this,' Valerie said.

'If she makes it,' Milo said.

He waved coolly to other passing boys. When pressed he pointed out his snowman. It was wearing his old scarf from last winter but now that he had a school one he didn't think his mum would mind, would she? She thought he'd lost it and they'd had a bit of a barney about it. He'd get it back when the exhibition was taken down. Though everyone said it would be totally radical to leave it up all year round but then the teachers wouldn't have anywhere to park and that would be a pain for them so the snowmen would have to go but in the meantime they were really cool.

They loitered, unwilling to leave the magic outside, but Milo finally ushered them in, got them seated and dashed off importantly to take his place for the musical end of the evening.

★　★　★

Susie needed to take in a press call for a recently released movie. She went to the venue, a mid-town hotel, to check that her client had everything she needed. The actress was enjoying a Renaissance on the back of the film's success after two decades in the wilderness of a daytime medical soap. The event was a disaster. The client had been put in a room with a full mini bar and had proceeded to work her way through it. All of it, if her bloodshot eyes were any indicator. She was also flushed and slurring gently.

Susie hauled the publicity monkey aside. 'How many interviews have you allowed her to do in this condition?'

'Just three.'

'Just? She's barely conscious. That's it. I'm calling off anything else you have lined up.'

'You can't do that.'

'I can. We're done here.'

'It's part of her contract that she does publicity.'

'Read my lips, lady, No More. Now organise transport to take her home.'

She eventually poured her client into the back of a car and checked her watch. The hotel concierge had an hour-long waiting list for a taxi and advised her to try her luck out on the road. If she could hail a cab now she might just make it back to Clapham for Chris's pick-up. She soon realised she hadn't a hope. Snow sprinkled from the sky and the streets were lined with shoppers desperate for taxis. She decided to go straight to Morning Star by tube so she trudged to the

243

nearest station and wedged into the mass of bodies heading home. The air was fetid with the sweet smell of alcohol-stained breath.

Progress was slow and uncomfortable. Trains were packed and Susie only made it on to one on her fourth attempt. Stops were lengthy and they stalled regularly in the tunnels waiting for the train in front to clear. A heavy man trod on her left foot and it ached painfully.

The closest station to the school was a fifteen-minute shlep when the weather was clement. Today it was not. The snow was quite heavy now, building as slush on the street and causing slippery conditions. She dialled in for her messages and heard Chris sounding tightly furious. Great, the tension ratcheted up another notch. She would have missed the start of the concert by now. Milo would never forgive her. She began to run which came as a sprinting waddle as she tried to maintain balance. She could picture Milo's disappointed face and in that moment she wanted to lie down in the snow and cry.

★   ★   ★

It was like he'd always known she wouldn't make it. Her work always took first place. It didn't seem to matter what time of day or night it was, she was always taking calls and arranging things for other people. He was the last person on her list, the lowest priority. He played his first piece badly. He could see Gregory looking at him, wondering what was the matter. He made a hash of 'When the Saints Go Marching In', his trumpet in charge of him and not the other way around. He had been looking forward so much to showing his mum the snowmen and playing his pieces. Now it was all a mess. It was good his dad was here, and his gran, but it wasn't as good as having his mum here too. Milo choked back tears.

★ ★ ★

A police car pulled up alongside on the road. Oh what now? she thought. What extra shit can be heaped on to me?

'Is that you, Mrs Vine?' a man's voice asked.

Susie approached the car.

'Gabriel Potter,' the policeman said. 'You sent me that lovely signed photo of Anita Fay.'

It was the cop they had talked to about Milo's stolen phone a few months ago.

'Where are you off to?'

'I'm late for my son's school concert because of work and the weather.'

'Hop in. We'll get you there. Morning Star, isn't it?'

'Yes. Oh thank you, thank you, thank you,' she said scrambling into the back seat.

She was still babbling thanks and praise as she got out and dashed past the snowmen in the parking lot. Please don't let me be too late, she begged of any Higher Power that cared to listen.

She got to the assembly hall as the entire school seemed to take to the stage, many of them armed with tambourines.

So this is why he wanted one of those, Susie thought. She jumped up and down to attract Milo's attention. When he saw her his face lit up, sweeter than any other reward in the world. She waved to Valerie and Chris as electric guitars started to play the first notes of 'Rock the Casbah'. A tranch of boys filled in the vocal and the tambourines jittered lightly into percussion. Violins entered the mix, young boys sawing away happily. By the time the chorus arrived, a slew of piano accordions were jigging through the melody and the result was a tumultuous celebration of The Clash. The tambourine boys shifted their jangles this way and that in splendid and uniform formation and the guitars, voices, fiddles and accordions married into a Gypsy-inspired delight. It was a total triumph that had the audience singing along and standing by the end. They screamed for more, demanded it, and got an encore. Susie's throat had seized with emotion to see her boy so animated and she felt she might bubble over. The exuberant joy was nearly too much to bear. This was the sort of spiritual enlightenment Susie was sometimes missing when she went to other performances. She was letting herself get cynical, inured to the magic. She must watch for that when she started back to work.

'That was close,' Chris muttered.

Way too close, she thought but didn't admit to it. 'I had a client in trouble. And I made it. Let's not build this into something it's not.'

'Promise me you'll think about what happened and try to see it from Milo's point of view.'

'Yes, yes, yes. Don't be such a downer, Chris.'
He bit his tongue. 'Right.'

'That is the best thing I've heard in years.'
Valerie said hoarsely. 'The snowman art is the
best thing I've seen in years.' She fanned herself
with a programme.

'Perhaps old Morning Star isn't the dumping
ground we thought, after all,' Chris said. 'Let's
go shake the hands of the teachers who inspired
this.'

'And tell Milo how great he was,' Susie added.
'He's a star.' He's my star, she thought. I must
always remember that.

★   ★   ★

Susie sat on the edge of Milo's bed, squiffy and
loquacious. Milo smiled indulgently, happy to
fight sleep yet enjoying the fact that he was safe
home and tucked up and could nod off whenever
he liked.

'Do you ever miss having a dad here with us?'
Susie asked out of nowhere.

That got his undivided attention. 'What?' He
couldn't figure out what odd angle this had
come out of. Again, the adult brain was
bewildering him.

'I just hope that we've been OK all this time,'
his mother said. She was pressing on the duvet
like a cat padding a cushion. 'I know you might
be different from the majority of the boys in your
year because your dad has another family,
another life separate from us. It doesn't mean we
don't love you as much as they're loved.'

This was embarrassing talk now. 'I know all that.'

'I don't like to think that you've been denied a normal family life.'

'Don't be mad, Mum.' He couldn't figure out why adults constantly made problems for themselves, especially when they were a bit drunk. They needn't. In Milo's experience, problems always found you out, you didn't have to go looking for them.

Susie was rambling a little now and even she knew it. She clutched at a final straw. 'It's the small things too, like you've got no one at home to talk to about football.'

Milo actually snuffled a laugh at that. Bonkers, adults were a bit bonkers.

She was continuing. 'Football,' she tried again. 'And so on.'

'And so on?' he repeated.

Susie wasn't sure if he was confused or ribbing her.

'Do you feel different to the other boys?'

'Only 'cos I'm me,' he admitted, truthfully.

Jason Fleck had an actual dead dad, now that was different. Maybe even too weird to fathom. He seemed OK about it, most of the time. Lots of the guys at school had divorced or separated parents. Jason was the only one who had a dead dad that Milo knew of so far. Oh, and he'd heard that Des Parker in Year 9 had a dead mother. That must be way weird. Milo looked at his mum and his heart went funny to think of her dead. He reached out his hand and squeezed hers. 'We're fine,' he told her.

'You're sure?'

'Sometimes you're just nuts, Mum.' There was no way to varnish that truth.

She ruffled his hair and kissed him on the cheek, mumbled about bed bugs biting but he was gone off by the time she'd finished.

Valerie handed her mobile to her as she returned to the living room. 'You missed two calls,' she said.

Susie checked caller ID and saw that it had been Lola. She dialled the number. The busy sounds of fun on Lola's end made the conversation hard to hear. Eventually Lola got to a quiet corner. 'I'm in a bit of a scrape here,' she said. 'I think I might be about to do something really terrible.'

'How terrible?' On Lola's scale this could go from bad to catastrophic.

'Very terrible. In fact, I might have done a little bit of unintended snogging already.'

Susie had a sick feeling in the pit of her stomach. Somewhere her cunning put together the scenario in the city centre bar. 'Does this involve that jerk Jay Burns?'

Lola's silence was enough confirmation. 'Do not move back into his orbit,' Susie ordered. 'I'm sending in the troops. I repeat, do not go back to his company. Even if your champagne is there.'

'I'm not that stupid,' Lola snorted. 'I have that with me.'

'How did Jay Burns find you?'

'Accident.'

'But not fate, Lola. Remember that. This is an unhappy turn of events, that's all, not a sign that you are to have anything more to do with that man.'

'I made him spend loadsa wonga on me,' Lola said, giggling.

'Stay there till someone comes for you,' Susie ordered. 'Oh, and happy Hanukkah.'

She thought quickly and dialled Mitch. 'You live in Soho. Tell me you are partying there too right now.'

'But of course. 'Tis the season.' It sounded like a two to three Xanax day for ol' Mitch.

'We have a bona fide Arland and Shaw emergency. Lola is falling prey to Jay Burns in a bar on Brewer Street.'

'Christ,' he swore. 'Officer down.'

'Correct. Go rescue.'

'What will my reward be?'

'My kind words for a month and a magnum of bubbles.'

'Done.'

'Don't forget to spill some very red wine on whatever festive shirt he's wearing.' She turned to Valerie. 'This job is exciting.'

'It is, isn't it?'

'I think we love it, Ms Macintosh.'

'I think we do, Ms Vine.'

10

Reg was subsumed beneath a tangle of two boisterous children. A third was yanking on his trouser leg. The noise level was beyond decibels that a human was normally asked to endure. Bony limbs jabbed him vigorously. He was entirely aware of his post-Christmas paunch. It was all terrifically satisfying.

'Boys, please leave your grandfather be,' Heather begged.

They paid her no mind.

'Grandad has whiskers,' Finn said in wonder. 'They're grey.' Another amazing fact. 'Crinkles too.'

Albert dropped to the ground and went in search of a bow and arrow Santa had been foolish enough to bring him. They agreed it could have been worse, say if Santa had brought the drum set he had been so taken with for the boy. Santa had almost succumbed to the idea of a recorder for Finn too in the mistaken notion that it would foment musical curiosity. Mrs Claus made a guess at the racket and they abandoned that strand of thinking.

Reg was wearing a shirt and matching socks the boys had actually chosen for him. It was fire-engine red, which was their favourite colour. 'I need to perk up my wardrobe,' he told Heather and Andrew. 'This is a sign that the children think so too.' He was about to take the eye out of all who encountered him in London.

Hayley fell onto her bottom, having tried hard to climb onto his lap, which she could see was where all the action was taking place. She hated to be left out. He would have helped but was pinned beneath his eldest grandchild. He also knew that she would have been insulted. She was a very determined young lady and liked to do things solo. He was amazed each time he saw her lower the edges of her lips determinedly, trying to figure out how to achieve her plans. When she did she was so like her grandmother, the late Claire, that his heart gladdened and pained in a seizure of love. This is it, he thought. This is why we are on this earth. This is our continuity.

Andrew said all three bore unmistakable traits of Reginald. What a miracle that some of him could be part of these little gems of humanity. He wanted to hug and kiss them hard but each was an independent spirit that eschewed being held down, mussed or slobbered on. They were too busy. They had a lot to learn and do. During these early years they would learn more than ever again. There was a lot of cramming they must devote themselves to. He wondered where his childhood accomplishments were within him, if indeed they were still in him at all any more. Each time he remembered a scene from his youth or a memory long forgotten he wondered if that particular brain cell was giving up the ghost and tossing its treasure forward for another to take up and hold safe.

Albert climbed up again armed with the bow and took aim at random targets around the room. Hayley began to beat Reg's leg with a well-gummed, soft toy she favoured. It seemed to have been a rabbit once.

'All right, you monsters. Off your grandad.' There was a yell of protest. 'Now. Spit spot.' Andrew began to haul them off, prising sticky little hands from his father, trying to control the wriggling masses.

Heather gave Reg a mock exasperated look. 'I keep hoping they'll end up with some of your manners and a little proper grammar, but there are times when I wonder if I'm asking too much.'

★ ★ ★

Roma surprised John Forbes. She filled the house with parades of people. She kept the proceedings busy and social. He had expected her to toy with him, to seek out weaknesses and enjoy some torture using these against him. He thought he would be the butterfly she would pull the wings off after a few days. Instead she hosted drinks, brunches, lunches, afternoon teas and full-blown dinners. Each evening she arranged for a car to take him home. She was the perfect hostess with the mostest. She had a different outfit for each event. She looked divine.

Flora, for her part, had as many friends over as she could get away with without needing police crowd control. They spent their time sniggering in corners or blushing as they asked him questions. It became clear to John that teenage girls didn't play together, they lurked in groups. It unnerved him slightly but he reckoned his daughter would protect him, at a push, so he tried to relax with the thwarted adoration and curiosity. She wore her sunglasses constantly, filled the bag with a lot of heavy items and passed her dress around for admiration. 'I can only, like, wear that once in front of these guys this time out, Dad,' she explained. It seemed as if there was a code involved that he would never understand so he didn't try.

Quentin looked on as bemused as John himself. They were living in a festive commuter station with a lot of strange specimens traversing the territory. The two male Forbes were often found sitting on the bottom of the stairs cuddling a dog each. John didn't tangle with attempted conversation at these times. When his son wanted to talk, he would, and in his own good time.

A specimen went by that John just had to ask about. 'Is that a guy or a girl?'

'He's an Emo.'

'Oh, a guy. Is that his name?'

'No, Dad.' According to Quentin's tone, John was a total fool. 'His name is Corey. He's an Emotional.'

The boy had long lank hair and was wearing black loose clothing. He seemed to be a fluffy kind of Goth.

'Right, so,' John said and returned to silence.

The truth was that he wasn't expected to play any part but that of guest, like the other visitors. Roma didn't pass him off as anything but a very ex-husband. He served drinks but he didn't absolutely have to, as he would have in the past.

He didn't wonder if there would be enough beer or wine, Roma handled that. He didn't look at dwindling hors d'oeuvres and think to refill platters, those were already looked after. It was a doddle. He met people he hadn't seen in months. He heard gossip and tall stories about mutual acquaintances. He fielded queries about any 'famous' actors he'd worked with. He told some jokes. He made sure not to draw untoward attention to himself or to dominate conversations.

Quentin finally said, 'That Mark Hill is the one she's seeing.'

He felt all blokey that his son had been frank with him. He imagined they had achieved a father/son bonding. He was glad to be spoken to at all, of course. He knew better than to push it. In the silence that followed, as they both heard the gears in his head crunch and creak, he did have the thought that his son might not have parted with this information entirely in a helpful way. Now he felt like a stranger in this house. His son was scoring points off him and his wife had found someone else. A part of him wanted to think good on her but instead he was leaning towards the notion that nothing hurts like a loved one doing well. That gave him pause. What form did this love take? He was not in love with Roma. He felt a great affection towards her, but carefully, as she knew him well and which cards to deal when managing him. It didn't help that he had developed a fixation with a seemingly unattainable work colleague, which was what he thought Susie Vine probably was in his world.

Now that his ex-wife had a partner, serious or otherwise, he was made to look altogether single and he wasn't sure how he sat with that. As for Quentin, he didn't know what to say to him. Was the guy a little shit or simply tipping his dad off? His face was a cipher. John stood up and brushed some crumbs off his new, pink cashmere sweater, a gift from Roma. 'Better go check this fellow out,' he said and disappeared with his tail somewhere between his thighs.

He engaged the very pleasant man called Mark Hill. The only aspect keeping him firmly with tongue in cheek was that the other chap was a tennis coach and, more specifically, Roma's tennis coach and as that was one of the top ten movie clichés for a romance, it relieved him.

Later, after he got home in the car his ex-wife had arranged, he reflected on the days that had just passed and realised that his former house now belonged to others. He sat with an Armagnac, vowing that he'd only have one or two. He tried to ignore the very fact that he had just thought 'one or two' which left open a window of opportunity to get blotted. He examined his surroundings. His bachelor pad seemed sterile. What did it contain that immediately declared 'John Forbes'? Nothing that he could readily spot. It had come furnished. He had not added anything but bottles of expensive booze, bedlinen and some toiletries. What made this home? As he followed this line of self-goading, it looked increasingly like more than a two-Armagnac night. His pride was dented. He was due a wallow. Nobody is better at punishing personal failure than the self. He poured the self another.

★ ★ ★

Valerie had sent Alistair a cardigan for Christmas. It was in his regular beige hues but had sprinklings of russet and gold in the weave that might jolt him around. She figured he could do with that. They had phoned on the day so that Milo could thank him for the books and money he had sent him, and Susie for her fountain pen. He had donated money to charitable causes in Valerie's name, as she had requested in a terse fax she penned one lunchtime when she got mad as hell at his actions. She spoke with him for one and a half minutes, mostly checking that he had watered the plants and would watch the garden for slug and pest damage when the daffs were trying to get through. He thanked her for the cardi and said it made him look quite rakish. As she hung up, Susie had more sense than to ask what the phrase 'Oh goody' referred to.

This time last year Valerie had been getting ready to see in another New Year at the Cock and Feather with the usual, disappointed cronies eyeing one another and wondering who would pass away in the next twelve months. They clocked the others' cricks and wrinkles, the sagging chins, tissuey skin, baggy eyes, rheumy from too little to do and too much time to do it in even with the help of regular nips of gin and sherry to dull the tedium. She had thought nothing of it, hardly noticed the decline. She was a happily married woman who had given three wonderful human beings to the world and was eking out her retirement with dignity in a picturesque corner of Albion.

That was another world. At the time she could have no inkling of what her perfidious husband had in store for her. She wondered how long he had planned his leave-taking and the subsequent destruction of life as she then knew it. It was nearly a year since her abandonment though not the length she had been in London and yet the time she'd spent in Devon alone with Toby rolled by quickly in her mind. All she knew was that now she was in a much better place on all levels, except that her dog was dead. She would have atrophied in Chittenham until death and never known what she was missing. Now she was vitality itself and full of new knowledge.

She hated to give Alistair credit for much but he had really done her a favour, in the long run.

★   ★   ★

Milo had agonised over what to buy Isabelle. In the end he plumped for a gift set from the Body Shop. It seemed uncontroversial and wouldn't exactly set alarm bells off in any adjacent adult heads. Last thing he needed was to tip them off about his scrambled feelings. Or, worse, to let Isabelle know. Smellies seemed neutral, a gift between friends. He hoped she didn't think he thought she smelled bad. She did not. She was sweetness itself as far as he was concerned. He meant it as a pampering gift and hoped it would be accepted as such and not misunderstood. Writing a card to go with it was hell incarnate. He practised a message and his writing on a pad for nearly an hour before he trusted himself to have a real go.

His heart was enlarged and at the top of his windpipe, beating painfully, as he handed over the brightly wrapped package and attached envelope. He tried to scratch out a vocal greeting with it but his mouth was too dry to form any recognisable words. He felt he might lose consciousness for being such an idiot. She had beamed a smile that nearly carried him off and stowed the gift to open at her home. He'd had to give it over early, before the official celebrations began, because she was going home to Lorient for the break. Now he would never know what she thought of it as he hadn't witnessed the uncovering of same. She had given him a calligraphy set and airily suggested he have a happy holiday and perhaps use it to do her a drawing in the future. More pressure. Now he was tortured trying to think what would be a good subject and hoping it wouldn't be too cack-handed when he went to do the bloody thing.

He needed to get cool in the New Year. He needed to learn the means by which to chill. He wanted to be hip and capable of coherent speech around this woman, in English to begin with, whatever about her native French. He wished she had been at the school concert or seen his groovy snowman. Timing was another skill he put high on his wish list. As far as he could see, it was a hard nut to crack but the essence of calm and cool.

He had so much to learn. He needed to raise his status around here. To begin with, he would get good at darts with the board his gran had given him. Then he could amaze his friends as well as Isabelle. He went off to practise.

★ ★ ★

Andrew Darwin watched his father leave with regret and a slight worry. Well, there was a major and obvious worry on top of all that. Reg drove a car a man half his age would wet himself over, twice as fast as any man half his age would dare. When challenged he would point out that his driving licence was clean and his faculties excellent, as long as he remembered his glasses. He whizzed out of the driveway to a chorus of his grandchildrens' goodbyes.

It had been a marvellous addition to have him here with the family to celebrate Christmas. He proved best by a mile of the bedtime readers. It would be difficult to get the kids used to ordinary voices again instead of the myriad Reg could conjure. He had regaled them with stories of his life and the adventures that had befallen him. The one about being locked out of his room naked in a boarding house in Margate had been a highlight and the kids squealed with laughter for hours that day at the very thought of an adult 'in his nudey'. There had been a poignancy as they toasted Claire and then the delight of telling the children all about their gran. It was a privilege to mark the continuity of their little capsule of genes.

Time was surging on, though, quicker and quicker with each year, and Andrew was feeling it for his dad. Reg was a proud, independent man and that was obvious just to look at him. But there was no getting away from the fact that he was also elderly. Andrew caught it in tiny grimaces as Reg's bones cricked into the day, the rheumatic ache he confessed to while predicting rain, and a slight stoop in his gait when he was tired. As long as he was working, even in the fits and starts of any actor's life, he was active and therefore alert. When the time came for that to end, Andrew and Heather would make provision for Reg in the garage they intended to convert, and which they hoped he would agree to live in. Andrew didn't like the idea of his father rusting in the Grove, or anywhere like it. He didn't think John's lifestyle would suit looking after their dad. Reg's place was with them. Hopefully, that was all a long way off yet. He knew it would be one belter of a battle when it occurred, but Andrew was aware that he was half Reg and half Claire and as far as he was concerned that gave him double advantage in the stubbornness stakes. He liked to call it persistence, but Heather corrected him every time. Stubborn, pig-headed, dogged were all suggested instead. He blamed his parents. He looked at his own brood and saw their peccadilloes. Blame the parents.

★ ★ ★

261

Max had visited on Christmas Eve to give Milo a book about clouds and some washable deck shoes. Susie was so grateful she invited him over again a few days later and told him to bring his new girlfriend. She immediately regretted it but somehow knew he wouldn't take her up on the invitation. To see them all together again made Susie sad for the past, and a future that could never be. She blamed the time of year for making her sentimental but couldn't escape the notion that she had made herself get over Max a little too speedily. She hoped this one wasn't going to come back to bite her at an unguarded moment. He made his excuses and promised to call by in the New Year.

The Vines had open house for a few days, when they weren't visiting Sophie and Phil or paying duty visits to those who'd hosted them during the year. Susie's new neckpiece excited much comment. It was a gold chain with an outline of a heart hanging from it also in gold and studded through with a dozen tiny diamonds. She didn't want to know how many pieces her mother's new credit card had been blown away into but she wore it gladly. It was as close to a sign saying 'I love you' from another that she had ever worn.

With the turn of the year imminent the three amigos in the Clapham apartment wondered if they should make resolutions, then decided not as nothing precipitated disappointment and failure more than big promises that were always a little too ambitious to keep. Susie thought about her year and reckoned it could have been worse. True, her father had left her mother, her mother's beloved dog had died, Susie had broken up with her long-time boyfriend, but all told not a disaster. Milo was healthy, so was she and her sense of humour might return any day now.

She tried to think about a career trajectory but it descended into individual thoughts about her clients. She had some regrets there. On more than one occasion she had shoehorned an actor into a job, usually one they didn't want to do. None of the enforced situations had done any harm but sometimes she had to admit the client was probably above what she had convinced them to do. Oh, there were many good reasons she could cite, like the chance to work with a certain director or company, but in the end it was an elaborate form of entrapment and she wasn't proud of it. She needed to watch that. It was all very well wanting to keep her talent employed but the work should fit the client appropriately, or challenge them in the proper way. Some of the ones who'd had a hard year needed to have their self-esteem underlined and propped up. She would see to that. She would also be a lot more proactive with seeking out possible future projects. Some of her clients needed prodding to write for themselves as they became lost in other people's work. These were a restless bunch whose creativity needed channelling. She knew who they were and she would start on that strand pronto. She had found *I-Dentity* and through Jay Burns the movie *Highway*. He had kept that to himself, the cheating shit, while simultaneously trying to steal her project. She intended that he would regret that. Both projects were moving on in the New Year.

Her mobile rang and a nationally recognisable voice said, 'Hi, Susie. I hope you don't mind me calling you on your down time but I just wanted to wish you a happy New Year.'

She was astounded again that John Forbes would want to contact her, to pursue. It made her feel good. He made her laugh. He actually liked her and, more, he seemed to desire her too. Would it be so bad to see him socially now and again? Probably. She had a warm feeling just thinking about him.

★   ★   ★

Reg had invited Margaret for New Year's and they kept it simple. They drove into London early, dumped the car and headed to a splendid lunch at the Savoy. Replete with food and good cheer they scanned the television schedule, chose a film they both knew to watch and settled into the sofa with champagne on ice to toast another one down. By this stage Reg was a dab hand at manoeuvring a wheelchair. Margaret assured him he'd be up to buggies next although they were a lot more difficult to manage. He pointed out that she would look ridiculous in one.

They discussed *The Summer House* excitedly.

'It's strange and wonderful to be looking forward to a good job again,' Margaret said. 'Well, any job at all for me. I thought I was done.

A lot of people cannot see beyond my chariot and the fact that I live in a retirement home.' She chuckled. 'That title is probably a tad off-putting.'

'It does seem to suggest a cessation of work,' Reg agreed. Although they reminisced about old times, they tried to remind themselves that the old days weren't always good.

'It's hard not to miss them sometimes,' Reg pointed out. 'So much has changed. We're dinosaurs now and each year there are fewer of us. I sometimes worry when I'm performing with young actors that I'll be doing it in a style that disappeared with Garrick and stick out like a sore appendage.'

Margaret laughed. 'So much of my acting style is fake,' she said. 'I speak with a clipped accent but I'm actually from Cornwall, so I should have a natural burr to my speech. Did you know that?'

Reg shook his head.

'My family were fisher folk, so they looked on me as having run away to the circus. In fact, it was just dumb luck that a travelling theatre company came to our town and needed locals to swell the ranks, otherwise I might never have known that an ordinary mortal could strut their hour upon the stage.'

They toasted the fit-up theatre companies. They toasted fakery.

'Do you think about dying?' Margaret asked.

'Yes, whenever it's unavoidable.'

'I don't know about you but I find it frightening. I can't understand how it all just stops. I suppose, when I'm being positive, I

265

imagine it will be like going to sleep and never waking up. At least I hope it will be that way. Being largely chair-bound doesn't help of course. I feel I'm wasting a lot of precious time by being stuck in the damn thing. I want to be able to whiz about the place with as much vitality as I can muster. There are days when I could burst with energy and I cannot expend it on a good hike.'

'One does slow up, however, ambulatory or not.'

'And one takes on the face of someone else, an older person. When the younger generation looks at me, it sees an old hag. Inside I'm still vibrant and certainly a lot sprightlier than this poor visog lets on. My mind is still awhirl. I question more than I ever did. I am hard to please and intellectually as rigorous as ever. Or so I like to think.'

'Oh, you are, Margaret. I wouldn't fancy the chances of any deluded unfortunate who tries to put one over you.'

They toasted intact mental faculties.

★ ★ ★

John Forbes was an urbane man. He had tasted of many of the world's delights both legal and not. He had done things he might not have wanted his parents or children to see but had always treated everyone he met with the respect they deserved. And he paid the going rate. So why did he feel so dirty now? It might be that he was succumbing to the sentiment of the season, letting the sanctity it held get to him. He was a lapsed churchgoer, after all. Or perhaps integrity had come to the fore.

He had not been able to get Susie Vine out of his head. He felt lonely and horny. So, he fished out a discreet-looking card bearing a London number and little else. When asked he requested a curly-haired, petite brunette.

The girl was exactly as ordered. A lovely young woman called Kitty. She was educated, interesting and very beautiful. She was no Susie Vine, but then she never could be. She was her own self. Kitty. They drank wine and when it came to crunch time John had to admit that all he could continue to do was talk.

She shrugged politely and had the good manners not to say that it was his money and he could spend it as he saw fit. He had done, by credit card, during the initial call to the escort agency.

'There's no need for you to stay,' John told her. 'I don't want to waste any more of your time.'

'Not at all, it's been a pleasure.' She sounded as though she meant it.

As she shrugged into her coat he asked, 'Why do you do this?'

'I'm a student. I have bills.'

'What do you study?'

'Drama.'

'Ah.' Great, she was training to be an actress. Just my luck to get a drama student. 'The fees are ruinous,' he sympathised.

When she was gone he wondered if he would some day see her play a high-class hooker. The portrayal would undoubtedly have a ring of authenticity, couldn't not. At least she hadn't asked for his autograph. He finished the bottle of wine. Like water, he had found the lowest level. Let it be a lesson that there were places he could not go any more. The New Year was almost upon him and he sat, alone in a sterile apartment, wondering how he had come to this pass. He lifted the phone and dialled another number. 'Dad, can I come over?' he asked. 'Great. See you in twenty.'

When midnight came, John, Reg and Margaret toasted seeing another year through from start to finish intact. They hoped to make it through another. They raised a glass to absent friends. Then they toasted the future.

John looked at the older people and thought about how precious time was. I will make Susie Vine want to be with me, he vowed.

★ ★ ★

Moments after midnight a flurry of calls came through to Clapham. Chloe and husband were in Chittenham with Alistair at the Cock and Feather. The phone was passed between Susie and Valerie. When Susie spoke to her dad he gave her his best for Milo too then said, 'And do continue to look after your mother, dear. She's . . . ' he seemed stuck for the correct words ' . . . worth it.'

'Dad, I think that's the least of it. Anyhow, shouldn't you be saying this to her and not to me?'

'All in good time,' he said and rang off. His attempts at both praise and mystery were so off the bottom of the scale as to be immeasurable, Susie thought.

Lola rang, drunk, to issue her usual battle cry. 'I am a small, dark, hairy thing. No one will ever choose me.'

They were off for another ride on life's merry-go-round.

11

The morning started with attitude. Frost glittered, picking out details, and the refracted light emphasised the newness of the year. Susie was filled with purpose. Betty had scheduled a staff meeting to herald in the New Year. She had news to relay. Susie was determined to make the most of whatever decision the boss had come to. There was a skip to her step, in spite of the vicious cold. Her cheeks were glowing as she got into the elevator to take her to Arland and Shaw and she caught sight of a happy face smiling back from the reflective walls. Going up, she thought. Valerie had set off early to get together any paperwork needed. She swore she did not know what Betty had planned. Susie believed her.

All of the faces around the staff table showed a strained excitement.

'We've been somewhat under-strength since Burns left us in the lurch. That has opened a few vistas. But really it's a no-fucking-brainer. I have decided we should expand. To this end I have been in talks with another smaller concern, a one-man operation really and he's agreed to join us. He has a big Irish list as well as a solid representation of Brits and also some directors and designers. His factotum is about to start a family and he's not sure she'll come back to work so it's a perfect time for him to join Arland

and Shaw. I have his list, accounts and an overview of his set-up for you all to study. He is solvent, witty and easy on the eye.' She was twinkling as she gave that last nugget. 'He will move in later this week. As to our own end of things, I have talked to Nell and we have decided to follow a long-range plan she's had for years now. She will head up a literary agency under the Arland and Shaw umbrella. It's bound to be a slow burner but it does mean that we will be something of a one-stop shop from now on. I hope you approve.'

Betty was clearly puzzled by the laden silence that had emerged.

'You haven't told us the name of the agency that's joining,' Mitch explained.

'Oh, didn't I? Silly old fuckwit. It's Karl Fox.'

Susie stopped breathing and wondered had she heard properly. She felt heat generate in her cheeks and her tummy mangled into a small ball. Around the room her colleagues were energised by the announcement. Betty had pulled this stroke off with style, showing again why she had been so successful for so long in the bear pit of the entertainment world. For Susie, one fact spread through the room, leaked over her, drowning her gently: Karl Fox was the chosen one.

'He has Surab Khan,' Lola whispered, breathless with excitement, 'who is only the hottest man on the planet.'

'He's pretty hot himself,' said Mitch. 'I could listen to that Irish accent of his all day long.'

'You will from now on,' Susie managed.

Susie Vine and Karl Fox had a past that no one at Arland and Shaw knew about. Only a tiny handful of people knew their history. They hadn't had a proper conversation in fourteen years. She would waggle a greeting at him at functions then remove herself from any danger of talking to him. She couldn't bear to get too close to the man. He provoked a violent reaction in her. How would she cope?

'I'll leave you all to digest this. If anyone wants to talk about it I'll be in my office.' Betty left.

They were quiet for a few minutes, formulating their opinions, thinking of queries. Then Dave said, 'I presume this means a name change. Karl Fox is coming in on the highest level of management. There's no other way it would be attractive to him. We'll have another boss.'

Susie felt as if she'd been kicked in the stomach. She was the most senior agent at Arland and Shaw after Betty but she had no claim on the company, as she was an employee not a director. She was going to work for Karl Fox.

'The writers are coming,' Lola intoned. 'What's the collective for them? A misery of writers?'

'A pleasure of playwrights,' Nell announced.

'A ponce of playwrights, more like,' Lola scoffed. She'd once dated a writer of zeitgeisty works and was less than complimentary about the species ever since. According to her version she never got a word in edgeways with his groanings about life, work and the cruelty of the Muse. 'Plus he was always borrowing money and conveniently forgetting to return it. When I dumped him I robbed his first edition of *Waiting For Godot*, which nearly killed him, I'm delighted to report. Must hunt it out and see if it's worth anything.'

'Is it in French or English?' Nell asked with a self-satisfied glint.

She'll have to be watched, Susie thought, or she may turn into a monster. This new department might go to her head and they didn't need another Jay Burns in the office. It occurred to her that Karl Fox might be a pig to work with too. She had no idea what his style was. There was nothing she could do about any of that for now, so better to enjoy the simpler pleasures while they stuck around. When he arrived they would deal with any horror that might accompany him. She knew it was foolish to expect the worst, but she could see no other way.

The collective bug hit throughout and all morning the office rang with new suggestions. Valerie pinned the best to the board by the coffee machine. 'A neurosis of actors' was a great favourite, along with 'a dash of designers' and 'a command of directors'. Betty added 'a score of composers' as she paced by doing a particularly tedious radio deal for a client. 'Might as well get some exercise while this arse is going on,' she explained. 'Is it me or do all contract departments speak incredibly slowly?' she whispered to Susie. 'It's taken twenty minutes to get through incrementals on audio clips and all that we've added to the actor's fee is five pounds ten.'

'That's millions in dog years,' Susie pointed out.

'It's death by fucking pedantry.'

'I guess they want to make sure you have no comeback after the deal is done. They're being very, very certain you understand.'

'Yes, they're making me feel a bit too special and challenged. I might get a bit snappy now and that's the last thing anyfuckingone wants.'

The staff was taken up with how best to divide the office space to accommodate the new departments and personnel. In the end nothing was changed and everyone remained happy. They hoped Karl Fox would want to keep the basic open plan of radiating offices.

'He'll have a window to his back, which will make him feel he still has options,' Lola said, wickedly.

★ ★ ★

Milo had a sweaty journey to Morning Star. He was apprehensive about seeing Rafe, who was surely recovered enough to return to school. He hoped Vince hadn't changed his mind over the break and decided to follow a vendetta on behalf of his younger brother or the family honour. Streams of boys filed through the grey morning, heads down and reluctant to be there. The lights in the school windows seemed less beacons as hopeless gestures against the new term. Milo entertained a fleeting thought of skiving off, visit a museum or two, go to a movie. Even as he dreamed of escape he knew it would only postpone matters, much as he would have liked that. He would also be majorly dumped on at home and he was happy to be in the good books there at the moment. Best get the measure of this situation and then decide what action to take.

The classes gathered in their requisite areas of the gymnasium for Assembly, smelling of damp wool warming up. The air was foggy with boys' bad, morning breath. They endured an address by the headmaster, who was as pompous and boring as ever. He almost drained the good out of the Christmas holiday. Milo wondered how he didn't seem to notice hundreds of boys ignoring him. Probably didn't care, just took his wages at the end of the month and got on with it. A phlegmy cough started in one corner and passed in a round robin from group to group. It sounded like guts being thrown up.

Milo looked around in his immediate vicinity and caught Rafe's eye. He braced himself for trouble, but instead of malice he saw benign indifference. Actually it looked as though Rafe hardly registered his presence. Good, very good. That would do for a start. He wasn't going to rock the boat by speaking to Rafe, and it was a relief to know that the other boy wasn't likely to lunge at him with a weapon just yet. Of course he might just be biding his time till Milo's guard was totally down. He would have to be on his mettle at all times. It would be good to have eyes in the back of his head and maybe a few out the sides too. Humans were badly designed for danger.

Reg was about to plunge headlong into an early January depression when he heard the sound of a weighty thud onto his hall floor. Years before, Claire had bought and installed an especially wide post box to accommodate the delivery of scripts. Today it did not disappoint. The rewritten script of the film, *The Summer House*, lay on the Turkish runner they had bought on a holiday many years before.

The young auteur had been busy over the break and this was now a part Reg might have killed for, that any actor would kill for as a matter of fact. He had the immense satisfaction of reading the story knowing that it was re-created with him in mind. The script was gritty, upsetting and oddly moving. It was subtitled 'A Love Story'. Reg had never tackled anything like it and he could feel his nerves rise to the surface in a delicious mixture of fear and anticipation. The story centred on the relationship between a troubled young woman and her parents. She loves her father but, as dreams of her childhood become more frequent and detailed, she accuses him of abusing her when she was a child. It is moot as to whether the accusation is based on any factual event. In a daring and provocative scene she reverts to a childlike state and attempts to seduce her father, unleashing a terrible chain of events, which will see each of the trio suffer beyond endurance. It was edgy and difficult and over a contemplative cup of tea Reg became convinced that he was quite wrong for the part. He would never be able to carry this one off. A long and, in many eyes, successful career had never instilled him with confidence. With any extra knowledge or skill came the realisation that nothing got any easier. Margaret always said the day an actor was sure they could do a job was the day they ceased to be any good. He tried to let that bolster him but deep down he knew that this was the part that would expose him as a thorough fraud. He would need to do a lot of homework on this one and arrive word perfect and ready to take direction.

That was another worry. The director was young, a beginner. What if he didn't have the wherewithal to deliver the vision needed to realise this piece? It required a delicate, deliberate handling but with visual flair and the sort of chutzpah normally the metier of much more experienced directors. This youngster might have been able to write the words and suggest a strong story but could he translate that to a screen?

He needed to focus on positives. He was excited to think of working with Margaret on the project. She would bring a quiet and heart-breaking intensity to the part of the wife who deliberately chooses to know too little and do even less, until her hand is forced and an ancient sin visits destruction upon the family. He wondered who was cast as his daughter.

★ ★ ★

Would Karl Fox recognise her now, this groomed, controlled version of the girl she had once been? Where was the scattered handful with an opinion on everything, especially things she knew close to nothing about? I talk therefore I am, she would tell him. And what did she have to show for herself? There was Milo, the biggest plus to her life that she could possibly imagine. After that she was running into a blank. An engineer could point at a bridge and say, 'I built that.' A novelist had copies of books. She was not creative, as she once had been. What there was of her efforts then was largely forgotten. There were a few radio plays gathering mould in the BBC library and a shot or two in fading television shows that were never played any more unless to illustrate how jaded a time it was, how it had not stood the test.

Her theatre work was gone on the very night it was performed. Such was the nature of that beast. It existed only in the memories of those who'd seen and those who'd performed. That was its greatest loss as well as its greatest gain. It was transient but it had the chance to be mythical as it was remembered and embroidered down the years. No one bothered her much to tell her how wonderful her Hero had been in that long ago production of *Much Ado About Nothing*. How fitting.

She was a custodian now. It was potentially wonderful to guide and be listened to. To nurture talent and pave a successful way for it. But that would all be quickly forgotten when she was gone, either from the client's life if they moved management or entirely when she checked out. Her life was like a nice conversation, pleasant but easily forgotten. As a legacy it wouldn't even provoke the blink of a single eye years after she had forsaken this earth. She would leave a small genetic footprint in Milo, which would dissipate exponentially as time and progeny marched on, and of her achievements nothing would remain because they were not of any worth. I know just enough to be unhappy, she thought. I had a talent small enough to be of no use and a mind that realised this. That was the cruellest damnation.

★ ★ ★

She used to be able to remember the affair in forensic detail. That was just after it ended. It was to be expected then. At that point she felt she could never forget each and every exquisite, heartbreakingly beautiful moment. She revelled in the pain of the separation, and it heightened the sweetness of the love now lost. Over the course of the intervening years she began to pick out less and less detail and resorted to feeling the bigger sweep of the joy and agony it had thrown up. She wondered if it was right to call it an affair at all. An Affair was a time when people had a lot of inappropriate and satisfying sex but were destined to move on with or return to their normal lives. An Affair was impossibly exciting and made one lose weight and look tremendous, if a little tired around the edges from the fractured sleep and lovemaking.

That was her problem with calling it an affair, she supposed; she had not been returning to a husband or steady lover. Karl was it. He was the one she was with. There was no one else to go to. Affair had seemed a flimsy description, as if it was always doomed to end. Surely he was the Great Love of her life, she was just too stubborn to see it, and therefore she had lost everything. So it was much more of a tragedy than if a simple run-of-the-mill dalliance had ended. These were her justifications. These were the feelings she wallowed in.

Of course the ending was not the pyrotechnical marvel needed to prop up the losing of one's love in life. It simply fizzled away after an everyday sort of argument. Only that last time there was no reconciliation, no thrusting love and forgiveness in his bed. It took her a while to realise it was gone. They simply did not see one another. They spoke in intermittent, terse conversations on the phone without making arrangements to meet. She thought it was some sort of cold war, like many other times. He seemed gruff and unconcerned about her or her career. Well, she could take that till he came crawling back.

Many years later, with the power of mature reflection, she realised she had pushed him away deliberately. How could someone as beautiful as Karl Fox want to be with her? He was going to dump her when he came to his senses so she got in there first. Better to have the heartbreak earlier than later, that way it would be a lesser entity to deal with.

She partied hard and screwed around. It was gloriously nihilistic, freedom to do exactly as she chose on a whim and the time to regret it, if she so chose, at leisure. There were niggles. The sex was never as good as it had been with Karl but the thrill of the new was exciting, a fuel. At least, at first. She did miss that he had bothered to learn her body and what she liked to do with it and be done to. Somehow he had managed to engage her too. She never wanted to just lie back when she was with Karl. It was always better if both of them were together in rhythm and mindspace. His body flattered hers and vice versa. There was nothing they would not do for one another sexually and it all made perfect sense. They fitted together. Quick, drunken shags didn't quite step up to the mark.

Slowly, it began to dawn on her that he was not coming back as had been loosely planned in her head. In spite of her plan to get rid of him before he could totally annihilate her, deep down she'd hoped he'd fight for her. He didn't. By the time she realised this, the word was that he had another on his arm at openings and premieres. At the same time as his career was on an upward curve, Susie's was in stasis. Her pride would not allow her to beg for his return. Two could play that game, she reminded herself constantly. She would not be the first to crumble. She found herself briefly, but memorably, in Chris Falucci's bed. It was a time of abandon and limitless energy. He came very, very close to fulfilling her sexually. She remembered drinking a lot of champagne. Life was rolling by in an endless party and suddenly she was smacked right down to earth. Milo.

Denial was as loose a word as affair. It hardly covered how totally she ignored her predicament. She didn't tell Chris. She told no one. After the first realisation of the seismic change within her she pushed it to the very back recesses of her brain, as if it didn't exist as a situation and therefore didn't need to be clogging up cells. It festered quietly in her head just as the cells in her womb divided and expanded but she systematically pushed it sideways every time her brain told her she had to think this through. She had plenty of spare time to contemplate her future as she was short of work and could fill the days with plans for the baby. She did not. She refused to acknowledge it at all. Later, Sophie asked her if she had ever thought of a termination. She had not. She came to believe this was because she did not think about the problem at all, and that had been deliberate on her part so it looked as though she was in control. But she was well beyond the possibility of an abortion by the time she told the important people in her life the news that Milo was on his way and later she wondered if her mind hadn't been a devious organ. She left thinking about her state until such time as she had run out of options. She had to continue with the pregnancy. She wanted this baby.

At times she indulged in fantasies that Karl was the baby's father. The timing of the conception was wrong for this, off enough for her to know that she shouldn't let this fantasy exist. Perhaps it's my residual actor's brain wanting to tell a good story, she allowed. It was not. She was treading negative and dangerous ground. To allow these falsehoods even a mock-creative foothold might leave the faint hint that there had been a truth at their inception, a bit like gossip can taint a person forever long after a rumour has been disproved. She banished the madness. This baby would exist as himself, not some romantic glue to reattach two people perfectly capable of messing their lives up without a new one to blame.

Betty was told first. She had taken Susie on after her graduation show. At the time she was the envy of her class. She was the only one selected by Arland and Shaw. She wondered what happened to most of them. She avoided reunions now that she was an agent. It seemed prudent not to put herself in the way of actors trying to revitalise a career or failed troupers who wanted to return to the theatrical fold and saw her as the ideal way back in. She also wasn't sure how she would deal with the questions about her own acting career. Strictly speaking, she was one of the failed. There was no point in putting oneself in the way of unhappy musings on what might have been for the class of '87.

Betty was practical, something for which Susie would forever be grateful. While her head and body were seething with hormones and nausea, Betty could see an alternative future mapping itself out. She started Susie on photocopier duty, sorting post and general dogsbodying in the agency. Gradually, she allowed her to read scripts and do breakdowns. She went to shows and delivered reports.

'Duck to water,' Betty pronounced.

She was.

The ease with which Betty coped gave Susie hope that her parents might also take this news in their stride. That was a more fraught weekend as she battled all day sickness and the disappointed faces of Valerie and Alistair. Eventually she pointed out that she was practically in exile in London anyhow and the neighbours need never know of her scarlet shame if that was what was bothering them so much. They calmly pointed out they were more concerned about how she would manage with an infant and hold down a job. She loftily announced that women had been doing this for generations and, besides, she didn't live under Victorian strictures and there was such a thing as maternity leave, you know. It did give her pause for thought, however, and she made a note of it on her ever-lengthening list of things to ask someone about. Meanly, she allowed herself the thought that her parents were every bit as middle class as to worry about what the neighbours would think. When her bump began to show she stayed away, to spare them the rattling of their mores.

She did have to give them credit for one thing: a supplementary allowance appeared every week in her bank account. Come to think of it, her dad had set it up. It was discreet and a life saver. She had forgotten many of his practical kindnesses down the years. She had been so angry with him recently, with his cruelty to Valerie, she had wiped any points he'd accumulated from his slate. That was a rum thought process: as a parent he shouldn't be marked out of ten. She'd dread to think what Milo might give her if that was the case. Her dad had done his duty by her admirably and she had never lacked his love, however low-key it had seemed.

Susie held on to her temporary job as office assistant until her maternity leave. Even then Betty kept her busy with script work and when Milo was weaned she returned to Arland and Shaw.

Small incremental steps led to a more permanent junior position in the office. They had never taken her photo off the client wall so she waited for a crunch decision. It came by way of an offer of radio work from Chris, with whom she had an uneasy truce at the time. The day she turned that job down was the day she became an agent in earnest. She hardly noticed it happening as it seemed so logical. At home, later, she cried, but at that stage she could put everything down to vast bodily changes and therefore circumvent the sentimentalism or hysteria of chucking her life as an actor. When she came through the door the next day, the wall had one fewer head shot and the agency had one more full-time agent. She got a bigger desk and began to look for a mortgage. She needed to nest.

★　★　★

Break time held the possibility of a flashpoint with Rafe. Milo had settled into his regular seat for double maths and geography, which took him out of Rafe's eyeline as well as range for missiles. The strange thing was that Rafe seemed not to torture anyone during the morning sessions. He spent his time gazing out of the window onto the dull grey of the adjacent buildings and sky. From time to time he looked as if he was laughing to himself and that was nearly as worrying to look at as when his face was gurned into a hateful squeeze, precursor to many the wretched act. Milo dreaded what he might be planning in that head of his, ever more inventive ways of hurting people. This was the calm before the storm.

That was it, he decided. Rafe was calm, too calm, unnaturally calm. No good could come of it.

They headed back into English with Miss Fullerton and Rafe didn't bother to give her a hard time, which was mega odd because she was totally easy to make cry. What was going on? Milo wasn't sure he didn't prefer the old Rafe, the one he could read like a violent short story.

Then a terrible thing happened. Miss Fullerton picked out Milo in frightening detail.

'The headmaster tells me you recorded a radio play with the BBC before Christmas, Milo. Perhaps you'd like to use the experience to read this poem aloud for us?'

Oh God, it could not be worse.

Milo coughed and rasped, 'Can't, Miss, I've got a sore throat.' He didn't dare attempt the word laryngitis in case he made a mess of it and encountered more scorn than he could already look forward to after the teacher's awful suggestion. At that moment he did feel sick to the stomach.

'What a pity. Well, perhaps another time?'

Not till pigs are causing total gridlock in the skies, he vowed. Next they'd be asking him to read at Assembly and there was nothing in the world worse or more mortifying than that. Nothing, full stop. He sat as far back as the hard bench allowed, blending with the wood, praying for an invisibility cloak and dreaming of a time when people would stop talking to him or asking awkward questions. Anonymity was the best camouflage available. That had been his goal until now. Then he was accosted by an ugly thought. Did remaining anonymous mean giving up acting? He had enjoyed that very much and hoped his dad might have more for him. He was faced with a conundrum, a puzzle for which he could not see an obvious answer. He would think about it later. Bloody Miss Fullerton and her big, gobby mouth.

*　*　*

The new clients were displayed in the reception area and looked as if they had always been there. Valerie had interspersed them with original Arland and Shaw talent. A trained eye could pick out the different photographers who had snapped the essence of the actors. Or as Lola sarkily remarked, 'You can tell which hazy filters each of them favours to make those faces intriguing to the world and flattering enough for the actor to let us use the shot.'

'There are times when I feel you do not love your charges as much as they may love themselves,' Susie chided.

'Love, shmove. As long as they make with their commission, I'll blow smoke up their ass and play nice. Simple. Only rocket science is rocket science. Well, enough of them, now to me.' She took a deep breath and fired on all cylinders. 'Crazy Aunt Zelda spent Hanukkah wheeling men past, one with more infirmities than the last. She'd introduce them then whisper their diseases and taxable income. It was almost worth it for the laugh. Worringly, one or two seemed less than freakish, though I'll admit that was in comparison with the utter losers on offer. And they all made a living, which was irritating as I like to eliminate the destitute ones and trim the list down initially in that way. These are tense times for Lola, so watch my back. Speaking of which, I suppose it's fine that you sent Mitch to get me out of the clutches of Jay Burns even if I was having a great time, as it happens. All it meant was that I ended up snogging some mate of Mitch's later who was wondering if he's gay. He is. Another one off the list.'

'At least he was on and off in a nanosecond and didn't hang around wasting your time.'

Lola aha-ed at the truth of this.

Marty began the year with effusion, so Susie assumed nothing had changed drastically in his world.

From: marty@direkshun.com
To: Susie@arlandshaw.co.uk
Sent: 6 January 10.00
Subject: the movies

Happy New Year, Susie! Time flies when you're planning fun, eh? I hope you and yours had a wonderful holiday. I've been busy here trying to put our package together. We've decided to bring it to Cannes in February and I wondered if Craig would be available to be there with us. He is HOT right now and I think investors would love to see him in the flesh. We have seventy per cent of our funding but it's that elusive other thirty per cent that we need to nail down now. After that, I'll be proposing a summer shoot with a theatre release next January.

Simple, huh?

Let me know Craig's availability. It would sure help our cause to have him on the ground, and the Croisette, being wonderful.

Marty

Susie knew that the seventy per cent Marty's company had secured wasn't worth the paper it was written on without the final monies. It was always the magical final percentage that unlocked the main body of the capital on a film project. Still, it was hopeful and she would deliver them her client to help in the quest to make the project take flight. Plus, Marty had a track record of getting films made.

Every time she looked up, Susie expected to

see Karl Fox come through the office to take charge of his new station. It made her queasy to think that he would soon be a day-to-day feature again. She didn't know how she would react. Circumstances were so different now that it would probably make no difference whatsoever to her life when he arrived back into it. They were different people now. She squirmed to think of the roiling mass of insecurities that heaved under her studiedly nonchalant exterior then. She wondered if she was a more honest person now. Even if she did lie for a living, as she had informed Valerie. Was honesty merely a version of telling people what they wanted to hear, laced through with a few harmless truths?

Their last substantial argument had been over something typically trivial. She had promised to be at a certain place and arrived late and a little drunk. She had been recording during the day and had gone for drinks after work. He pointed out this was always the way with her, a loose grasp of responsibility, a tenuous notion of support. She blew up, starting with a particularly dirty, 'Always?' and moving on, one word leading to an illogical other. They drifted after that, both too stubborn to change or apologise. He began to see the woman who was now his wife. He hadn't really loved Susie after all. It nearly killed her.

So long ago, now. Another age. Other people. She barely recognised herself when she cast her mind to it. And yet.

She took in the others and realised they too were edgy about his imminent arrival.

Valerie led Nicky Ashewi to her desk with coffee and biscuits, which they both cried off, citing the previous week's binge eating and drinking.

Nicky was a stout, bright, pretty woman who was slotted mostly into mainstream character work but was a very capable, Susie thought brilliant, actress, able for much more. Casting and directors saw a plump female handy for the broad stroke of support rather than the leading roles in a production. It was a shame and very frustrating. Nicky also had brains to burn, though that wasn't always necessary or good for an actor. Some of the thickest people to tread shoe leather were splendid actors, possessed of a presence and cunning that made them unique and wonderful at their job. A lot of stunning-looking people were movie stars and couldn't act, but then they were not required to, as being a movie star and an actor were sometimes two different things.

'I have had a long, dark Christmas of the soul,' Nicky began, 'and I've decided I can't have another year like the last one. So, I thought I might try writing a one-woman show with the possibility of bringing it to Edinburgh in August. I'll still be available for any other work. I just can't bear being so idle and helpless.'

This was a constant state for most actors. The decision as to whether they worked was more often than not beyond their control. Someone else made the job and decided on whom to bestow it. Unless an actor had his own production company and employed himself, it was a matter of waiting around for someone to impress. Even making the work didn't always assure the actor of a job, as had been found out recently. A group of out-of-work actors wrote a television series for themselves, sold it to a network but were then made to audition for their own parts. Three out of the four failed to be cast. Gobsmackingly impossible, but true.

'Nicky, I don't know why you've been having such a lean time workwise. As you know, I think you're terrific and you've been so close to getting the jobs so often it's heartbreaking. I know you'd like to be playing bigger roles and I'd love that for you too. The bottom line for me is I want you to be happy and fulfilled. If this will help, I say go for it. Everything else is a bonus. Now, I have to warn you that Edinburgh is expensive and very few people who do it make a bean. In fact, a loss is generally what you can expect. It's often no reflection on the show, just the sheer amount of competition. So be prepared for that. We'll look at booking you a venue and arrange some London performances as a warm-up. That should concentrate you wonderfully. Deadlines.'

'A few voice-overs or an ad wouldn't go amiss either. I still need to pay the bills.'

'I hear you. And if you want to bounce ideas off me, or would like me to read anything, let me know. We'll build in pestering times for me to bother you and ensure you're really doing what you say you are. Deal?'

'Done.'

'Any inspiration yet?'

'Just the title, *Bless You*, seeing as I'm named after a sneeze. Actually I must mention that the name Nicky Ashewi would suit a bad panto, which my life story seems to be right now.'

'Oh no it isn't.'

'Oh yes it is.'

'Go write it down, woman. Don't tell me any more, show me.'

★   ★   ★

He arrived mid-afternoon and was halfway across the floor before Susie noticed him. She was finishing a phone call and laughing at a closing remark from the producer who'd called when she noticed a stillness in the air. The staff had stopped all activities and were staring. She experienced a moment of freefall as her mind came adrift of its moorings. This was ridiculous. She'd seen this man regularly ever since he walked out of her life. Why did this moment matter above all others? The weight of how much he had returned to her life was painful in that instant. I am going to talk to him, brush against him, endure him at work from now on. From here, right now, it looks like that'll be in perpetuity. A kind of perverted work marriage. That's the big deal, you fool. I really didn't need this latest complication, she allowed wrily.

He halted in mid-stride and flashed a beam of teeth that nearly finished Susie off. She fought for breath. He looked so good. 'Hi, everyone,' he called cheerfully. 'Apologies, my hands are full but I'll come by and say a proper hello when I've decanted all of this.' The voice was warm honey. Lola began to fan herself distractedly. He was wearing an immaculate navy double-breasted suit that emphasised his stature and made Susie want to take a bite out of him. The longing was painful. She was back to square one. This was the worst possible scenario. She was filled with the unpleasant feeling of impending unhappiness. Her work was the area she felt best about. It was a stable environment, which she controlled, to a large degree, but now she would have less power and the added complication of a palpitating heart and potential for lovelorn mooning at an unavailable man. It didn't bear thinking about.

She muddled through the afternoon, largely by leaving the office whenever possible. At the end of the working day a call went up to go to the pub to celebrate the new arrangement. It had become less and less of a tradition down the years as people began families, became attached or simply needed to go to an opening. Tonight even Nell came along. She blushed as she said, 'Babysitter,' breathlessly, the legend almost too much for her to overcome. She was bendy after one glass of indifferent Merlot and the colour settled in her face.

Valerie could not believe how vibrant the pub was. She thought of the Cock and Feather in Chittenham, which never seemed to deal in double figures customer wise. She remarked on this to Dave, who misheard the name as Shittingham and Valerie failed to correct him.

Susie could not lift herself from preoccupation. She was terrible company. When asked if she was OK, she croaked about a man on the Tube who'd breathed germs all over her and wondered disingenuously aloud if she was incubating a classic winter lurgy. Mitch, who was in love with his moped, sang the praises of the two-stroke engine and it was comforting to let his words envelop her. Hearing is the last thing to go, Susie remembered from somewhere. Is this what death will be like? she wondered. Me fading in a packed pub with a kind voice saying words I don't really understand and my colleagues beaming with happiness, unaware that I am about to slip away?

She was saved talking at any length to Karl by Nell who sloshed some of her second Merlot accidentally onto her jacket. She excused herself to the Ladies to dab off the small stain, followed by an abject Nell. 'It's honestly minuscule,' Susie told her. 'Now go back and make friends with our new colleague.'

'He's very dishy, isn't he?'

Susie laughed, very much in spite of herself. 'I haven't heard that word in yonks,' she admitted. 'Dishy,' she repeated. 'Yes, he is.' And so much more. Handsome, talented, vibrant, wonderful, treacherous. 'Married, too, with a brace of children or more.' She might have added, 'And a beautiful wife, some dogs, an Aga and a lovely house,' but she resisted.

She thought: I could have been that woman in the big house in Sevenoaks, driving our family around in the Espace.

But I'm not.

After Nell left the Ladies, Susie took great and calm care to fix her early-evening face. She had moved up a notch on the lipstick, darker kohl around the eyes and an extra spray of scent. She was ready for battle. Lola arrived and looked suspicious. Susie met her eyes as if without an apparent care. 'I reeked of Nell's red wine,' she casually palmed. That did the proverbial trick. Now to test her mettle in the fray.

Karl Fox was being amused by something Betty was telling the company and it suited him. He bent to kiss Susie's cheek and said, 'You smell divine.'

'Welcome to Arland and Shaw,' she returned, sounding calm and casual. She stayed busy ordering a company drink. They toasted Karl and themselves. And never once did she meet his eyes for more than a requisite three seconds. She felt herself watching the company from high above on the smoky ceiling of the pub and was happy not to notice any tension in any of them, especially herself. Perhaps I could have hacked it as an actor after all.

She was saved a celebratory dinner by citing Milo but left her mother to represent the Vine family. Outside, in a freezing London fog, she found a handy alleyway and gently puked up her wine and nerves. She wiped her mouth and the toe of one of her elegant shoes, popped two pieces of chewing gum and steered her exhausted self towards the station. All in all, she thought, this is only in the top ten most awful nights of my life. Top five was when you needed to start worrying.

'Oh, for fuck's sake, what am I at?' she said aloud, stopping herself in mid-tread. 'Tube, my arse.' She held her arm out to hail a cab.

She needed to hear a friendly voice so she phoned Sophie.

'The very person I was about to call,' her friend said. 'I am the bearer of huge news. Tash and Jan are pregnant.'

It was a relief to concentrate on other people's lives. 'That's wonderful. I never thought they'd actually do it.'

'It's more than that. They're both pregnant.'

'Surely not. I thought Tash had fertility problems.'

'She does. Or she's supposed to. Apparently she had a go with the turkey baster too for the laugh and to show solidarity with Jan and it worked! They conceived moments apart and presumably they'll have the kids at the same time too.'

Susie began to laugh. 'I honestly thought I had heard it all but this beats every other story into a cocked hat.'

'How are things with you?'

'Oh, you know, work-work-work. And Karl Fox has joined the agency.' She sounded so unruffled. 'We are now known as Arland, Shaw and Fox.'

The squeal from the other end of the phone nearly deafened her. 'It took you till now to tell me?'

Susie hushed her. 'You're one of the few people who knows what that means.'

'How did you not burst at the news? Honestly,

Susie, you are a mystery shrouded in enigma sometimes.'

'To me too,' she assured her. 'Anyhow, it's not that big a deal. It shouldn't be a problem after all these years.'

'Quite Jungian,' her pal adjudged. 'He thought synchronicity was at work in life and that our juxtaposition in space and time was not accidental.'

'Jeez, Soph, all that dope-smoking as a student really stood to you. And I'd call it more of a coincidence. Not a particularly comfortable one, granted.'

Sophie was on a poetic roll. 'A curve ball hurled out of time and space.'

'Great, now even the universe is having a go.'

Later, she hid out under her duvet, cursing her mind for stalling where it had. She was mistress of denying all thought of Karl Fox down the years but now she could taste him as clearly as the mint of her toothpaste on her tongue. Her skin itched for want of his touch. The longing to be with him was visceral, like an alcoholic racked with the craving for vodka. A feverish, addictive want gnawed at her gut. She had been surprised by so much of his proximity at the pub, his easy laugh, his elegant hands as they held his drink or gestured to make a point. She wanted to feel them running along her body, stopping to tease her, provoke her, lead her to a climax.

How could all of her years of strength be washed away in so short a time? She had hidden this inner world, locked it away to be left unvisited. It was the heart of her loneliness. No one was welcome here, least of all herself. She had been certain she was in total control of her life and pleasures. She was wrong. She shouldn't let this obsession take hold and yet right at that moment all she could do was fantasise about how it would play out when Karl Fox rejoined her waking day. Her mind thrilled to his imaginary presence. As she drifted to another level of consciousness she remembered his younger voice saying, 'I love you,' and sighed as she thought of her matching reply.

12

Reg always found it impossible to sleep the night before a job began. He woke on the hour every hour convinced he had set the alarm wrongly and would miss the time to get up. His nerves were frayed beyond endurance. He thought of how doctors recommended that one should avoid stress. This was impossible for a performer. On stage, actors were massively stressed by live shows every night, twice on matinee days. On film sets, quick decisions were made, and sometimes regretted for a career. Reg had sat on this script for six weeks, read it, worried it, consumed it. He was hopeful he knew it so well he could avoid the pitfall of making a wrong decision in the pressure of the moment on-set. That left the following day's read-through, scheduled for ten in a hall in Soho. He was better prepared than ever before for a job, but if he faltered during the initial run-through, he would lose confidence and be susceptible to everyone's opinion.

And that was before the dreaded admission that a script was subject to change from legitimate quarters after the actors' interpretations were offered up. The bally thing could change right up to a take, depending on all sorts of conditions and eventualities. Then it went to an editor and was well out of an actor's field of influence, unless they were very powerful and had final cut approval. Reg was not and did not. He was at the mercy of others for the major part of the shoot. He had to trust that he was being steered in the right direction and delivering all that he could to the part. There were pitfalls at every turn. He was already making his job more difficult by not scoring a good night's sleep. He should have taken a tablet. Too late now. His heart raced and thumped in his chest. He was hyper.

He had dreaded his medical examination almost as much. Time was when the BBC kept a few tame doctors in the building for this sort of thing but insurance medicals were now outsourced. He recognised the name of a doctor on the list that he had always been relaxed with but he was booked solid so Reg ended up attending a practice on Harley Street. He forgot to fill in one side of the questionnaire and, after waiting half an hour to be seen, endured some tut-tutting from a whippersnapper about the same. His felt his annoyance barometer on the rise. Usually he would have his blood pressure taken, step onto the scales and perhaps have a peek taken of ears, eyes and throat. Today, the doctor was thorough and scathing. Perhaps the investigation of minutiae was an unfortunate side effect of his age. Then the shit wrote, 'Satisfactory,' for Reg's general appearance, which Reg thought niggardly in the extreme. He muttered about Reg's weight but admitted his blood pressure and lung capacity were that of a younger man. It was altogether vexing and Reg wanted to leave with an epic put-down but didn't think of anything subtle or killer enough to say until he was well down the road. He walked to one of his favourite bookshops on Marylebone High Street and spent far too much money to displace his annoyance.

He assumed he had passed the ordeal, if not in flying colours then at least enough to be granted insurance to work, because his call sheet was delivered by courier, and a car arrived to take him to work on read-through day. The Harley Street quack had adjudged him fit to work and survive the shoot, so he welcomed the vote of confidence, the confirmation that he wasn't about to peg it in the terribly near future.

The company assembled, milling over teas, coffees and awkward introductions, nearly every visage showing the anxiety of embarking on a new challenge. He doubted anyone had got their full eight hours. Faces were lined with the apprehension that they might be the ones to let the project down. Everyone felt the same persecution. Reg grabbed a bevy and prepared to fail again but hopefully to fail better, à la Samuel Beckett's dictum.

The director gave a pep talk and said they should dive in. The reading went well. Then came the style talk. They would use the weather to do a lot of their work on mood. They would paint their picture using a palette of greys and threatening skies, introducing more colour for the vividness of the daughter's remembered story, then a riot of colour for the final tragic moments of the family's story. This relieved Reg on the visual front. He admired the work of the art director and director of photography and knew they would deliver the goods for their departments. He was steadily more impressed with the young man who had so maddened him in the hotel room late last year. David Glenn was a name to watch.

None of which did anything for Reg's confidence. He knew an army of people set up every shot of a movie and the last people who could afford to ruin that or waste time were the actors. That was the nature of the thing. Time was precious and expensive and once the shot was ready, it was incumbent upon the actors to be focused and prepared. There was only so much give or sympathy for mistakes.

Margaret took his hand in hers and whispered, 'I'll be the worst, fear not.' She knew his terror. She knew because it was her own.

★   ★   ★

A month and a half in, Karl Fox seemed largely at home in the office. Susie was not so calm. She had convinced herself that anticipation would be the worst part of his arrival at Arland and Shaw and that an overactive imagination was the enemy of nerves. So she had tried hard not to be affected by the fact that she would see Karl Fox every day but it brought with it an uncomfortable, nervous energy. She still hadn't managed the trick of not bolting when she thought she would be the only other agent in the office with him. It meant she was seeing more of the gym in the basement, which could be counted as a good thing. Equally, it illustrated that she hadn't dealt properly with his re-emergence in her life.

More worryingly, she wondered how much her presence at Arland and Shaw had affected his decision to join forces with the agency. Her mind disapproved immediately. That way madness lies, it warned. She should pay attention to the admonition. After all, now her devious thoughts were practically willing him to have chosen her. Those days were past. She could not allow the emotional silt to be churned up. In the bigger life picture he had chosen someone else. After so many years of denial she now allowed herself a brief wonder about why that last, silly spat had been the one that decided the whole round of the romance. They had always had passionate rows, why was that the decider? She would never ask him, of course.

Valerie spotted her discomfort and asked, 'Do you dislike him?'

'It's not a question of liking, or not,' she delivered. 'I didn't choose him as my boss so I'm finding it hard to adapt to that.' Which quelled any more questions from Val, at least for the moment.

Lola's unerring instinct for sniffing out disharmony was similarly dealt with. Susie even added, 'It's that he's not a straight replacement for Jay Burns but a whole different concept and I'm taking my time to figure out what I think of him.'

The year took on a strange stasis as many film productions were stuck in development hell. Her life felt a little like that too, as if it had ground to something of a halt. The warm and silly thoughts she'd had about the possibility of seeing more of John Forbes had been swept away by the return of her Great Love. All other bets were off while she worked a way to deal with this.

The first confrontation, when it came, was unexpected and begun by Karl.

★   ★   ★

Gregory told Milo he saw Rafe taking pills, stuffing them surreptitiously into his mouth when he thought no one was looking. This was a first. They'd seen him drink alcohol before, once even tried a slug of a vile, burning liquid that Rafe said was liqueur. Never again. It left a nasty aftertaste of sweet cherries in Milo's mouth and had given him a nearly instant headache. He still gagged to think of it and couldn't look a cherry in the eye any more. Milo shrugged. 'Whatever these tablets are, they're keeping him quiet. That's a good thing.'

'I guess. Bit weird though.'

'Like Rafe.'

'Yeah.'

'Has no one else noticed how zonked he is?'

'Maybe they have. But maybe he's supposed to be like that now. Like, maybe it's kinda medical.'

'Yeah.'

With that they abdicated any responsibility for Rafe. He was not their problem. He was far less of a menace than usual so that was good all round. Milo found it a relief to be able to ignore him. He realised he actually found Rafe tedious. What personality he had shown had been vindictive and uninteresting. It wasn't even a heroic but tragic flaw, like they were learning about in Shakespeare. The guy was plain toxic and best avoided. Milo didn't think there was a lot going on in Rafe's head at the best of times. Come to think of it, Rafe being quietly off his face probably was the best of times so no need to go poking noses in and upset the status quo by wondering why he was acceptably calm. Don't rouse the beast.

Adam looked lost but who cared? Milo didn't want to hang with him either, so he didn't. This was the best things had been in ages. As long as the spot on his cheek didn't multiply, Milo was close enough to happy for now.

★　★　★

Estelle Austen was the producer of *I-Dentity* and she had been busy. It proved the work inspiration Susie craved. She was fired up again. Estelle had secured some seed money from a small bank and some rich friends of her parents. Now, she was waiting on news of a grant from the Film Council and she'd had word that Screen South would give her money if the film was shot in its jurisdiction. She welcomed Arland and Shaw's involvement, along with the agency's valuable contacts and clients. She and the writer, Saul Hartog, had collaborated since their university days so they had a strong connection and their vision for the project was aligned and robust. She agreed entirely that Cannes would be the perfect showplace to launch it and seek investment. She had already got to work on a package and Susie was impressed with her handling of figures, prospective returns and the fact that already three major distributors wanted to talk when she put her package together. Best of all, Susie liked her. Estelle had enthusiasm, a splendid lack of bullshit, and a healthy sense of humour. She immediately declared that Saul was borderline socially autistic but said she usually passed it off as eccentricity which people found intriguing. 'Mostly I make sure he's washed and has brushed his teeth. He can get a bit distracted by the writing and he has no sense of smell.'

'A teenager,' Susie suggested.

'Mm, pre-teen even?'

'Gotcha. I have a male tweenie at home, so I understand.'

The biggest problem with Cannes, as always, was accommodation. Susie had snagged a room for John in a hotel, which was a miracle at this late juncture. She worried slightly that her persuasions in A-Level French might have led the manager to think he was on a promise come festival time. She had a room in a villa on the outskirts of the city. Craig Landor would be looked after by Marty and the *Glory Days* production. Which left *I-Dentity* to be sorted. Estelle amazed her by announcing she'd sourced herself a room, in a convent.

'I would never have thought of that,' Susie admitted.

'A Catholic upbringing is an amazing tool for

the future,' Estelle assured her. 'If only the French Jews ran a similar sort of asylum to this convent I'd have Saul sorted too.'

Susie looked across the office. 'I may have a secret weapon in that department. Lola,' she called. 'We have a mission, should you choose to accept it.'

★ ★ ★

Valerie had become accustomed to the cut and thrust of the London system. She had found it thrilling, liberating in her early days there. So it was a surprise to her when the sheer excitement of being in a crowd began to pall. Her conditioning was rural. She was accustomed to rolling green hills and charming streams. At this time of year she would tramp the byways through cowpats and windfall, letting the cold sharp weather clear her brain and exercising her dog. She missed his company. She worried about her garden. It was now that the weeds would try to colonise, slipping roots through the awakening soil, stealing space and nutrients, not unlike the hordes of city dwellers gasping for available air on the Underground or pavement on Oxford Street. She adored her job, that much was clear in detail, it was just that the concrete of the urban set-up was making her ache. She resolved to make time for a daily walk on Clapham Common. She needed to turn her back on what Lola called 'bucolic bollocks'.

She was travelling on the Tube to work, flicking through the newspaper, when a juggler type got on at Vauxhall and started to perform. She ignored him as she had no interest in juggling or magic, for that matter, and he seemed to be giving a bit of both, badly. She was reading an opinion piece, which pointed out that there were about three thousand attacks by dogs on mankind every year and that this figure did not go up just because it was being reported. The media were responsible for stoking up the populace perennially with lurid dog-bites-man reports. She felt sorry for the people who'd suffered but was thinking that owners should take more responsibility, as it wasn't the dogs' fault if they did exactly what humans had taught them to. She pulled herself up mentally. This was Devon Valerie going off on a rant. She would probably have got four days worth of chat out of just that one subject back then. But she was City Valerie now and had other things to obsess about. The youngster was still working the carriage. He had an easy patter and, to judge by the healthy chink of coins into his collection bag, charisma. He got close and Valerie felt something change. He was divine on the eye, a lovely voice and had bags of personality. There was also something oddly familiar about him. She took a punt and asked for his details. She covered it with a request about children's parties. The encounter with this lad had sparked the germ of an idea in her mind and she needed to check some details at the office.

★ ★ ★

Karl Fox had so comfortably integrated into the office setting that at times it took Susie by surprise to notice him there. Other times she couldn't get her mind off his presence. It was an odd state of play. Outwardly, each appeared unconcerned about the other. As far as Susie knew, Karl was unaffected by her. Though she imagined she saw a strange look on his face every so often. For her part she was glad to have stopped her hands shaking when she became over-aware of his proximity. Mostly she had. The worry for Susie was that it became almost comforting to have him there, to know what he was up to. That way she didn't need to be curious about him or his life. She had access to him for up to eight to ten hours a day. More than his wife, really. That offered a very odd sustenance. She should have known he would notice that, read her thoughts, tackle an issue. She had forgotten how direct he could be. It was a trait that stood to him well, certainly in his work. And at home? That was none of her concern. She imagined too much direct honesty could be a hard taskmaster to deal with in perpetuity. But what did she know? The things that passed between two people in a relationship were imponderable to outsiders. She sighed. Often for the two people at the core too.

He had been a theatre-company manager when she had first met him. He'd gone to the Edinburgh Festival from Dublin as the auditor of his drama society, fallen in love with the scene and headed to London afterwards to seek his fortune. He ran a happy organisation on very little money. He inspired enthusiasm and loyalty. He was good at his job. He was popular. Everyone loved the accent. Susie had worked briefly for his company, on a series of workshops for a new play. That was before they had begun to see each other. He had been helpful, good company, generous. He seemed still to be all of those things. And he still didn't shirk the hard questions. He advocated making the tough calls.

Why had she let a selection of non-events create an impenetrable void? It was a space they could no longer cross by the time she noticed it. But then, she was only half of the equation so he had to take some responsibility too.

She was sitting at her desk one Saturday, the office empty but for her and Karl Fox. He was deliberately letting a silence sit between them, she thought. Susie decided that she could match him. She worried that her breathing was unnaturally loud, like a dog panting. She concentrated on staying very still and quiet.

'Why did you not call?'

She had forgotten just how stunning his directness could feel, from the wrong end of it. He always said the only way to know something was to ask the right question, however prickly. Why did you not call? She knew he meant the long ago. Too late to hide now. So this was it. The Conversation. The Discussion they had never had. Her heart slowed, pushing against her tender insides, probing for escape. Every bit of her was an emotion, jostled now, hurt. A smooth marble stuck in her throat, trying to prevent the forbidden opening of the subject. Failing. She felt the manifestation of love reborn, an impossible equation to solve, too hard to tackle in the first place. It was the release of the stifled. In one crashing moment she thought, I am still in love with this man.

'I did,' she croaked. 'I did call.'

'No, Susie, you did not. I called you but you chose not to return those calls.'

'That's not how I remember it.'

'It broke my heart.'

Oh God. She wanted to crawl under her desk, away from this confrontation. Honesty is for easy things like bank details and taxes.

'You broke mine.' She wanted that to be the truth but it came out sounding petty to her ears, as if she was childishly returning an insult. She might as well have sung 'nah-nah-nah-nah-nah'.

'I took it that you didn't care.'

He was talking in a language she didn't want to understand, or speak in return. 'I was young. I was angry.'

'Are those good reasons?'

For what? For not fighting for a happiness I didn't even know I wanted? 'They were good reasons at the time.' Now they sounded like excuses. 'And it is true that I was young and angry.'

He nodded as if that cleared up something for him. 'It hardly matters now. I just wondered.'

And with that his curiosity seemed sated. She had been dealt with and dismissed. The case had been solved, a culprit named and order restored. But Susie wasn't finished. I was frightened of falling too far in, she wanted to yell. You were so beautiful and I was afraid you'd demolish me. How could I ever think you'd stay with me? Why would you? But these thoughts stayed silent and tearing her apart. However, he had opened the door, now he must deal with the consequences.

'Did you ever think of me?' She paused. It was hard to find the word to cover what she needed to say. 'Later?' she tried.

'Of course. And you're hard to avoid. London's small. Our business is a small world, ultimately.'

Her heart was making such a racket she could barely hear her words as she asked, 'And now?'

'I'm married, Susie.' He was definitely finished with the subject now.

'I'm not.' She was tugging still, determined to make something of this hers.

He shook his head. 'I'm not prepared to go there.' He looked disappointed in her. He might as well have added, 'You're better than that,' and finished her off altogether.

She panicked. There had been a terrible misunderstanding here and she had to clear that up. She had accidentally let herself down. She could not generate the words to correct what had been said. She had not been offering herself. She was simply pointing out that she had never married. That brought with it its own uncomfortable questions. Did it mean she was essentially still faithful to the ideal that might have been Susie and Karl? To think that meant she had spent most of her adult life avoiding other relationships in memory of what never was, could never be: the most redundant of all exercises.

She had called. Many times. She remembered his voice saying, 'Hello. Hello? Who is this?' in another place, without her, perhaps with someone else sitting by his side. Then she would hang up without speaking.

There, then, hardly able to breathe for the emotion he engendered in her, she knew she was still in love. Surely nothing but love could hurt this much? It was a relief to watch him leave. Her head sank to the desk and she left it there as she chanted, 'Oh God, oh God, oh God.'

★ ★ ★

Milo practised kissing on his hand. It wasn't very satisfactory. His lips were floppy and damp. Probably best not to lick his lips first, but hadn't he seen that in a movie and it was cool? He knew he should probably put his tongue into the other person's mouth when the time came so he darted it out and didn't like the sensation at all. He hoped it felt better in someone's mouth, though he couldn't begin to imagine what encountering teeth and another tongue would be like. A bit wet and slithery? While he was about it, washing his hands would be prudent before the next practice session.

He hadn't a hope with Isabelle. She was so far above him it was untrue. She was worldly and sophisticated. He'd made her a thank-you note with her Christmas gift to him but it was so cack he tore it up, then burned it for good measure in case it was ever seen. He practised his French accent in his bedroom. Rolling his 'r's only sounded like hawking up phlegmy spit. He knew all about phrases like, 'Voulez vous couchez avec mois ce soir?' — it was in a song, after all — but would never have the guts to ask. It was vulgar, anyhow, so that wasn't for Isabelle. Bet it's what I pronounce best, he thought, and it's less than no use to me. Sod's law. He had plenty of opportunity to say 'je t'aime' or 'je t'adore' but there was no way that he ever would. That would be to articulate the impermissible. There was no language for his feelings or circumstance. The most he could rise to was, 'Le ciel est bleu, n'est pas?' Well, the sky wasn't bloody well blue from where he was perched.

He could do with a few pointers. There was stuff he couldn't discuss with his parents. For example, there was no way he could ask his mum about Isabelle. He couldn't bear the earnestness he would see in her face, while he was waiting for her to laugh out loud into his face. Similarly, his dad would take it mega seriously but he couldn't bear the thought of him then sharing it with his mum and his wife. And he would. Adults just could not keep things to themselves. His gran wasn't a runner in the equation. She was way too ancient to approach. Mind you, she was likely the most sensible of them all. Still, it seemed too unnatural to try.

He thought he might phone Max and maybe have a man to man. He'd always said they could. Now that he was a bit removed from family life he'd have a good perspective and he wouldn't tell any of the others on him. He missed Max.

It was weird, really. There were too many

women at home and too many men at school. Not that he'd have liked a sister. No way. They were strange beings by all the accounts from the guys at Morning Star who had them. And any time he was in other homes and met them they were odd, very odd. Isabelle was different and not just because she was a Breton, and French, and older. She was special. She was a goddess. He hadn't a hope with her. His innards curdled at the impossibility of it.

13

Lola planted a haunch on Susie's desk. She was decked out in red, which Susie guessed was her way of dealing with the uphill journey that was a single life post Valentine's Day. 'Something's a-brewing,' she reported. 'No Betty, and Valerie is either doing her impression of the dependable, put-upon Sherpa or a dog with two dicks, can't decide which. I suspect a bit of both. Ideas?'

'Not the foggiest, though she did leave in an aura of mysteriousness this morning. No doubt all will be revealed at the staff meeting.'

It was still a no-show from Betty when they convened. The staff wondered why, except for Valerie and Karl Fox. Val passed out minutes of the last meeting and Karl announced that Betty would join via a conference call.

'I've hurt my leg,' came the familiar voice over the speaker-phone. 'It's a blasted nuisance. The fall itself was simple and silly, arsing about pruning a piss-poor clematis, of all things. I thought nothing of it, but when the bruising became entirely grotesque to look at I showed it to a doctor who told me I had cellulitis. As you can all imagine, I pointed out that I am too old to be vain enough to care about that. Porridgy thighs are the least of my cares. However, it turns out I have a sort of flesh-eating disease and have to put the damned limb up and not move it at all until the infection is banished, which could take

317

some time. So, I am dividing my clients between you all and hope you don't mind looking after them, however temporarily. Valerie has the list. I'd appreciate it if you could phone me individually later and we can discuss things further. Karl will chair meetings and I'll always be here on the end of the phone.' They heard a halt in her voice. 'I am so sorry. I want to be there very much, particularly as things are so exciting now that we're expanding and forging on.'

'The important thing is that you get well again,' Susie said.

The others hear-heared, all looking worried that Betty was perhaps more ill than she was letting on.

'I will, my dears. I am the original war horse.'

They signed off and got their first look at their list of new charges. Lola moaned loudly. 'I got Gertrude Vale. She'll never give in to the fact that she's mother material now. This should be a very aggravating ride for the Lola.'

'What's with the new title? The Lola?' Mitch asked.

'No reason, I just fancy it for a change.'

'Good enough,' he deemed. 'Oh, by the way, do call Jules. He's dying to hear from you. Really feels you made a connection, even though it's two months since you met up. I guess he's a bit slow on the uptake. Or you are. Whatever.'

'He was just using me to perfect his snogging technique,' Lola insisted. 'He's as gay as Christmas, which was when we met, which was why he was even further out of his mind than

318

usual and shouldn't trust anything he did then. That goes for everyone at that time of year. Still, I could always do with the practice myself and he comes without strings, I guess.' She gave a masterclass groan of despair. 'How has this happened? The last thing I need is another fairy friend.'

Susie's list was a surprise and she didn't know whether she found it a pleasant one or not. She had been issued Reginald Darwin, which was wonderful but there, also, was the name John Forbes. It had an oddly trippy effect on her. She couldn't take him on, though. Working together was going to exacerbate any potential problem so Susie decided to talk Betty into shifting him to someone else for the duration of her recuperation. She dismissed the tingling to see his name written on the page as a warped agently pride at nearly handling John Forbes' star career.

Valerie buzzed through. She could barely conceal the glee in her voice. 'I have someone on the phone looking for a Susie Vile. I'm guessing that's you.'

Great, everyone's having a go now.

★ ★ ★

John Forbes wasn't good at being alone. This surprised him. If asked, he would always have posited the idea that being alone was nirvana. From a distance it had always seemed that time alone, without others hanging out of him, would be ideal. It was about having choices. When he lived at home he had to row in with the dynamic of the house. He was dependent on others' schedules, their aspirations, their moods. He had looked forward to the personal chaos of having no one else to consider in his immediate surrounds. Now his choices could be based on as little as a whim. He only had himself to please. There was no come-back, no familial reproach. He could choose to do or not to do. But that was indeed the question. What did he do or want to do, or not do? Now he was at large and he was not at all sure what he should be up to. He was a man slowly running out of ideas.

He sat in his apartment watching television for hours, catching up on programmes he'd missed and the careers of people he knew, but even that palled after a while. Plus there was a lot of shit on the box. His home or, that is, the place where he lived was not unlike an anonymous suite of rooms in a hotel, without the staff to clear up and make the bed each day. Or the room service. So, he had all of the banality but none of the perks. He doubted anyone would walk in and immediately identify the place as his. Or if they did, it must surely mean he was a lot blander than he had previously suspected.

There was still some work to be attended to. He had scripts to read but few engaged him. He went out to studios to do post-production voicework on the Roundheads series. He recorded a radio advertising campaign for the Inland Revenue. But at home again the longed-for moments alone stretched into emptiness. He could not relax. He felt crummy, wasted. He needed a purpose. He had the upcoming trip to LA, certainly, but again that was work based. Looking at his life he wondered if he was just his job. That seemed to be his only definition. Other actors had alternative strings to their bows. Some wrote, some baked amazing cakes, some did charity work. His life was a selfish, single-themed bore. Without his work he was nothing.

He couldn't seek out his father now as he was out on a job. Of course, while he'd been filming his Roundheads drama he had rarely thought of how his dad was passing his down time. And it did feel a bit down from this perspective. He had let his father get out of sight and therefore out of mind. That was cruel and unthinking. John knew he had a propensity for careless abandonment. His ex-wife would call it more, no doubt.

He wondered about being single. The answer to his loneliness, if it was indeed that, was not a partner, though he would have liked the company. Perhaps that was why he had fixated on Susie Vine. John had initially seen her as earnest, a measured entity. That had intrigued him. But over time he felt her energy, her masked humour. Her careful modulation was an aphrodisiac to him, hiding, as he thought it did, a tenacious spirit and keen mind. He wondered about this. He thought he was looking for love but maybe what he needed was a personality. Harsh, but true?

He shook himself. He was creating a pernicious agitation out of nothing. This was just a fit of existential angst. That was the trouble with being an actor: you had to get inside a fictional character's head. You searched for what made them tick. As a result you lent yourself to a lot of armchair analysis and this could seep over into real life. In the end a character might also do something purely for dramatic purposes, to urge a story along, and with only the vaguest of motivation. He remembered a moment of his, in a play at the National last year, isolated and praised by all as a psychological insight into a tortured soul, whereas he knew he had simply lowered his voice for dramatic effect and to highlight the noise before and after. Leave the pretence to the stage, or the screen, he warned himself, and enough of the hysterical psychobabble.

He was bored, fed up, simple as that. John Forbes needed to learn how to be. By himself. For himself. He could be of no use to anyone else until he did that. And maybe he should get out more. He'd set up some lunch and dinner dates with friends and catch up on the news or even some juicy gossip. It was all right to laugh, without having to explain it to the nth degree. It was all right to relax.

★ ★ ★

Susie had to be proactive with the events life was chucking up at her. She needed to remove the obstacles she could do something about. She put it to Betty that she didn't think she could be of service to both John Forbes and Reginald Darwin.

'Nonsense, dear. You are the most senior agent

322

at Arland and Shaw after myself. You are more than up to the challenge. And I will be here to advise. I just can't be with the clients physically. John will need someone to go to Los Angeles with him, as scheduled, to settle him in and to handle meetings with American agents and so on. That person is you. Valerie tells me that Milo has a routine that she could well handle for a few weeks here and there so I do hope that won't hold you back.'

Susie bit her lip. Valerie was interfering. She was one step ahead of the posse in the agency, as witnessed by the big revelatory staff meeting about Betty's injury. She had guarded the information on that very closely. On the other hand she was sharing far too much by way of detail and information about Susie's situation. It was tantamount to Valerie offering up what she thought Susie's opinion would be or assuming her reaction to a situation. The adage of mother knows best was about to be nipped in the bud. Valerie would have to be talked to. Susie was feeling boxed into a corner not of her own choosing. Valerie was overstepping the mark. On top of all else, Susie was a more senior figure in the organisation and didn't need the receptionist second-guessing her and changing the course of her working life to the extent that she was.

'I know you've been there before but it would be good to go back and make more contacts.' Betty continued, unaware of her agitation. 'There's also Cannes.' Betty sounded tired and Susie felt bad to be bothering her with details. 'I had hoped I might have mended by then but my

323

doctor tells me this infection is a bugger to shift and can take an age to bog off.'

Susie tried another route. 'It might be good to give Karl one of yours. He would be great for John Forbes. And it would integrate him even more into the agency.'

'That had occurred to me but as it is he handles a lot more clients than anyone else, so it's not really a runner. Besides, John Forbes asked for you.'

Ah. This man was definitely pursuing her. The idea of him positioning himself to get her time and attention gave her a butterfly flutter of excitement. She worked hard to convince herself it was purely professional. She capitulated by saying that they would give matters a trial run and if either felt the arrangement wasn't working out they could move on. She was determined to offload John Forbes onto one of the others as soon as possible. He was all she did not need right now.

'I'm sure you'll rub along nicely,' was Betty's verdict.

'We'll see,' Susie said.

★　★　★

She had a boyfriend! That was all she could talk about. Milo couldn't stand it. Worst of all, this new guy on the scene was English. If he'd been French, Milo could have taken solace in the fact that they had a language in common and so on. But an ordinary, flesh and blood, English bloke was too much to take. She couldn't stop talking

324

about him. Garee said this and Garee said that with the emphasis on the 'ee' in Garee and a languid roll of the 'r', which actually made the bozo sound interesting and sexy (whatever that was supposed to be when it was at home). If the quantity of giggle and downright laughter he elicited in Isabelle was anything to go by, then this fellow was also comedian of the year. Milo wanted to die.

He retreated into his shell and tried to become dispassionate about this awful turn of events. She chattered on, a relentless retelling of a very boring story about how Garee made a big faux pas and then got out of it with charm and grace and, wouldn't you know it, really good humour. As he watched from the inner reaches of his mind, Milo got to thinking, and that was most uncomfortable. It was a wonder, his mind said, that she hadn't had a boyfriend before this. The terrible truth was that she probably had and hadn't mentioned it. Why would she share with a kid? Perhaps the last lad wasn't as fantastic as this Garee obviously was, so she'd had nothing much to boast about. She was clearly besotted now. She could not shut up. He hadn't a hope. He'd never had a hope. He was a child in her eyes, who was fast becoming spotty, sweaty and smelly, the worst combination of any of the S words. He was going on thirteen and she was nineteen going on twenty. She was so out of his league he wasn't even two divisions below, he was playing another sport altogether. He had walked onto a football pitch and played beach volleyball, in a bikini. He had been a fool and what's more he had made a fool of himself publicly.

The only way through this was to try to hate her. He would find a fault and exaggerate it, then detest her for it. He tried to think of a whiny quality in her voice but, although it was relating detestable Garee-based trivia, it was still the singing of an angel. Her face was animated, her dark brown eyes sparkling with the joy of new love, her curls tumbling about her cheeks and neck like velvet waves. At least she bit her nails. He tried to focus on that, to beef it up into an unforgivable flaw. Didn't work. Here was the thing: she wasn't interested in him. She was paid to look after him when his mother wasn't there. His mum might as well have pimped her for him. Cruelly, he thought that's what she does anyhow, sells and buys people. It was worse than pimping, though, and he knew it. The worst fact was: Isabelle was paid to *baby*sit him. His heart was a pain in the middle of his chest.

★   ★   ★

The Summer House was filming on location in south London, in the grounds of an estate that had all of the set-ups needed readymade. Reg had sounded excited when he talked with Susie by phone about the shoot. They were moving fast and word was good from the editor and producers. He was enjoying the process, his mind agile and engaged. He was up at six every morning and filming most days. In the evening he learned lines for the following day. He was on the dry so as to be as sharp as possible. She wished all of her clients had this man's work ethic. Acting was one of the professions where there was no retirement age. Anyone could work, as long as they were able or wanted to. Valerie had beaten retirement, Susie knew, even if the arrangement had been foisted unexpectedly on her. She had been saved from calcifying and was thriving on it. Susie wondered if she'd have the inclination to work when she got to that age.

The day was grey and misty. Trees lined the road solemnly, waiting for a breeze to liven them. She could see lights in the distance, a plucky glow amid the drab, damp weather. Caravans were parked in rows along the edge of a field. They were Pilgrim wagons in formation on the Frontier, braving the elements, fending off all attacks. This was the last human outpost before the end of the world. Figures huddled under an open tent, drinking tea and eating buns. She was in time for elevenses.

Introductions were made and Susie furnished with cakes and a strong coffee. The atmosphere was happy but concentrated. A producer paced in the distance, talking on a mobile. He stopped, looked at his phone and fiddled with it. Then began to walk around looking at the screen, holding it up to the air now and then.

'You never know where you'll run into our people out here,' Reg said. 'The signal is erratic and it seems only one person can have it at a time. So they all chase around to locate it in the first place then form a bit of a queue to use it. The circus moves on again when the magic does.' Reg frowned. 'I don't know why he keeps holding the phone aloft. It's not as if he can get himself up to the handset if the signal is two feet above him.'

'Perhaps he thinks that very act will be a technological butterfly net and capture the signal.'

'Do you know, that must be it.'

They passed a series of closed doors, each bearing a name. Reg grinned. 'Always reminds me of Amsterdam. Behind each door is a new delight, and all available for hire.'

'You are a very naughty man with a very naughty mind.'

They settled into their refreshments.

'I hope you're being well looked after,' Susie said.

'Oh yes, fear not. I have very little to bitch about. We're moving quickly because the cast is small and they just love it when the weather is dire as it really suits the piece. There is very little waiting around.'

'And the work?' It was high risk to ask an actor this in the midst of the shoot, lest they be despairing altogether, but something about Reg allowed Susie to ask such a hard question.

'I hope I'm not quite as bad in it as I think I am,' he responded, with typical modesty. 'I've settled for a little accuracy. I'm convinced I am not good enough to play this role, but there have been no complaints so far. Touch wood.'

Later Susie watched a scene where Reg's character realises his wife's betrayal has ruined his daughter, and his world, already fragile, crumbles into a thousand tiny pieces. The close-up of her client's face portraying the man's agony was almost unbearably beautiful, a work of art.

'He's like that the whole way through,' the director whispered to her. 'Fucking amazing.'

And he doesn't think he's good enough, she thought, and wouldn't believe he was even if he was told.

14

Gregory showed them the trick. 'It's science, in a way,' he said. He had purchased a litre bottle of Diet Coke and a packet of Mentos, then told them all to step back. He popped a mint into the bottle and a geyser of liquid sprayed up into the air, a good six feet.

Milo pronounced it 'Wicked' as did most of the company. Rafe was quiet but his eyes shone with twisted interest.

'It's something about an ingredient in the mint grabbing the bubbles in the Coke and shooting it out. Surface tension of liquid and all that.'

They ate the rest of the mints and poured the Coke down the drain as it was flat after discharging its power in the geyser. Gregory confessed to Milo that he'd learned the trick from his sister, Vonda, who was a nutter 'but good, you know?'

At lunch hour Rafe went to the shop and bought the same ingredients, but this time a two-litre cola. He didn't bother with an open space. He gathered the class in their room. Gregory wittered that it would be better to stick to just one mint as he wasn't sure what the result of more would be, though anyone there might have hazarded a good guess, having seen the earlier spectacular using just the one.

'Leave if you're scared,' Rafe said.

Curiosity got the better of everyone except Toby Williams, a spec-faced, four-eyed wimp according to Rafe, who berated him loudly as he left. 'He's gone to snitch on us so I'll make this quick.'

True to his word, Rafe opened the bottle, stuffed four mints in and stepped back. The geyser hit the ceiling and sprayed the entire company. There were guffaws and squealing. Boys were saturated in the sweet, sticky residue. The room was ruined. Brown liquid stained walls and desks. Maud appeared at the door.

'What the hell happened here?' he bellowed, making 'hell' seem very like 'fuck', they agreed later.

The last thing any boy would do was welsh on another. Faced with this wall of silence, Maud reddened to heart-attack level and roared a lot more. No one uttered a word and as Rafe was as shifty-looking as the rest, there was nothing to single him out. Maud announced that not only would they have at least a week's detention, he would personally make their lives even more miserable at phys. ed. classes *for the rest of their lives*. No one doubted his intent or ability to carry this out. They stood, damp and tacky, studying their shoes intently, still awed by the wonder of the experiment and trying hard to feel as guilty as they should.

★ ★ ★

Susie couldn't avoid John Forbes for long. She was his interim agent and owed him a duty of representation. She had to engage. There was no need to be nervy. It was perfectly normal for two people to get on well and he was a pro, like herself, who surely realised that the work was the most important thing. Now he sat opposite her, expensively clad, shod and scented. He looked like a god. She remembered an article calling him 'the thinking woman's totty'. He was certainly the stuff of posters and calendars and Susie knew that both were available for ready money in newsagents throughout the land. He wore his hair somewhat longer than usual, his sideburns showing flecks of silver, which only added to the mystique. She wondered if he had made a special effort for her, then immediately banished the thought. If she were totally honest she would have to admit she had taken quite a lot of care with her appearance that morning herself, as it was important to look very lovely now that her ex-lover was also working in the office. It wouldn't do to let the side down. She always dressed well, she was just a little more diligent today. And yes, she had been mindful of her new client's visit.

John Forbes' dark grey eyes held her in a balanced, quizzical stare and she found the scrutiny somehow enervating. If they had been in different circumstances she would have returned it quid pro quo, but this was business and that was not possible. Lola teased her that she never noticed men coming on to her any more.

'That's the root of your problem: you're giving out the wrong signals, or no signal at all, which is even worse than issuing wrong or confusing ones. If a man is confused, he'll give up. They don't have staying power like women, well, like me. Especially when faced with a brick wall or a crumbling one that doesn't seem worth the effort to get involved with repairing because the problem might run too deep, and involve stripping the plasterwork altogether and having to rebuild.'

Lola was on a major roll with the metaphors the day of that treatise. It had been exhausting.

Mindful of the wisdom despatched, Susie sat like a newly rendered, solidly constructed barrier and exchanged the pleasantries and promises of an über agent-superstar client set-up. John Forbes draped an arm over the back of his chair and hoped he didn't have a bit of drool on his carefully selected Paul Smith shirt and pullover. Then he took the arm back to rest at his side because he thought he probably looked like a prat.

Across the room, Karl Fox looked on. Was he showing too much attention for a casual observer? She didn't think she could handle that problem rearing its head today too.

'Have you been avoiding me?' John Forbes asked.

'After Los Angeles, I'm hoping that we can help sell *I-Dentity* at Cannes,' Susie said, ignoring his question totally. 'Betty says you have given permission to attach your name to the project.'

John Forbes rumbled a 'Yes'. He really did have the most amazingly textured voice.

Chocolate and claret with flinty tones of possibility and rumpled bedlinen. She supposed he was a notorious swordsman now that he was shot of his wife and children. He was certainly a flirt, not that she disapproved of that in a man. She wouldn't tolerate it in a business associate, though, unless it involved getting more money on a deal for a client.

She ruffled some pages on her desk for show. 'Good.'

There was a hiatus.

Close-shaven, strong jaw. Well-maintained physique. This guy was quite a package. He had to be: he often played an ideal, or an aspiration. It wasn't just the actresses who could lean over the desk and say, 'Susie, three words: maintenance, maintenance, maintenance.' John Forbes had to look after himself too. And how.

'Well, I can't think of anything else we need to discuss. I'll confirm the American meetings and schedule and get back to you. And I'll keep you abreast of the Cannes end of things.'

She squirmed at her use of the word 'abreast'. Cop on, she told herself, you're not seventeen.

Karl Fox came over to shake hands with John. Then he stood behind Susie and laid a lazy hand proprietorily, it seemed to Susie, on the back of her chair as they discussed Betty's injury and the new arrangements. She was a point of a triangle and for one blazing moment she felt used by both of these men. She stood to shake off Karl's hand and signal an end to John Forbes' time with her. She hoped they both noticed they had gone too far. She was given no indication one way or the other. It made her boil afresh. Where did these macho alphas get off using her to mark their territory? A small voice tried out the notion that she was overreacting but she was in no mood to listen to it. She walked briskly towards the exit.

Lola was giving a seminar on casting agents to Valerie as Susie escorted John Forbes off the premises.

'A good eye for the job but mad as a box of badgers and needs careful handling,' she was pronouncing. 'Happily, she's also good at thinking outside the box and beyond those badgers.'

'Felicity Byram,' John guessed.

'Top marks,' Lola confirmed. 'Hard to talk down as she has one magnificent set of bellows upon her, which is not bad for a hobbit.'

John Forbes laughed, genuinely amused by Lola. This was all the encouragement she needed.

'We call her the Truth Fairy, because she has such a loose arrangement with reality. Facts are whatever she decides as she goes along.'

Everyone looked set to have a nice little afternoon natter so Susie broke it up by asking Valerie to come have a word with her. Her tone had obviously communicated too much. Suddenly this was her mum, looking hurt and fearful. Susie couldn't bear it. 'Actually, it can wait. It's nothing, really.' She smiled reassuringly, let the company visibly relax and excused herself. She so needed to chillax, as Milo would say.

Rafe wanted to take it up a level, and he did. When he had gathered his audience he announced a feat of unimagined proportion. Then he produced the tools with which to garner their amazement. He had a small bottle of Coke and some mints. Milo had a bad, lurchy feeling in his tummy.

Rafe twisted the top off the bottle and poured some mints into his hand. 'Ready?' he asked.

The crowd murmured its affirmation.

'I asked if you're ready,' he yelled.

They roared confirmation.

He knocked back the mints and swallowed the drink. The crowd held its breath. Then he opened his mouth and spewed forth an awesome gush of fizzy vomit. Rafe looked as though a devil was quitting his system. The force of it knocked him onto his arse. Boys ran in all directions to escape the vile torrent.

'Oh, man,' Rafe groaned. 'I feel so bad.' He leaned on his side and heaved again, this time producing less and suffering more.

Vince shook hands with admirers. 'That's my brother,' he told them. 'He's fucking nuts.'

★ ★ ★

Lola had located friendly types, the Levis, who would put Saul Hartog up for the Cannes festival. 'There's a choice of yacht or villa.'

'I get the impression he's of the charming but eccentric persuasion of writer,' Susie said, 'so perhaps hidden in a building is best?'

'I can bring him out to the boat for some or other soirée,' Lola announced.

'Ah, and there I was thinking you'd be manning this London ship for the duration.'

'Nope. There's a good Jewish man available so I'll be staking a claim and getting on with things.'

'Don't you think it would be advisable to meet the chap first?'

'He's of the Faith and has talent. That latter detail already singles him out from the other dweebs on offer from my community. I'm getting nothing but positive vibes here.'

'Great. So why do I feel so apprehensive?'

'Susie, you have got to get jiggy with the positivity. Now, while you were gadding about in exotic film locations, Valerie uncovered a bit of shadow casting on behalf of the Truth Fairy. Avril Delamare was to be put on a heavy pencil for one of the Little Chef girl parts in *Highway*, our gay *Thelma and Louise* stolen from Jay Burns, but Avril also knows the director personally and when she mentioned it to him he said that particular role was cast, so far as he knew. So, Felicity's clearly up to some shenanigans with the deal and is using one of our clients as ballast if it goes tits up.'

'We don't like that.'

'No, we do not.'

'Last time I spoke to her about a similar problem she burst into tears, so I might not be the ideal candidate to deal with this.'

'That shall be my pleasure, tempted as I am to

set Betty on her. Anger is probably not best for the healing process so I'll leave her out of this loop.' Lola flexed her fingers in readiness. 'Oh, one other thing, which may prove that Felicity's finally flipped. She said she was very interested in calling back some lad called Ian Morton for the Brad Pitt type cameo. Seemed to think he's one of ours but he's not. Unless Karl's got some secret weapons squirrelled away.'

'Shouldn't think so.'

'Valerie volunteered to get to the bottom of that one. Actually, she seemed quite excited by it.'

'You don't say. Let me know how you go with the Fairy and I'll see if Valerie's got any developments to report.' An intuitive bell had rung in Susie's head. She steered around to the reception area and stood in front of the desk. 'Ian Morton,' she said, holding her hand out.

Valerie passed over a black and white photograph of a handsome young man. Colin Farrell meets David Essex, Susie thought. 'Feel free to explain,' she told her mother.

'Well, I was on the Tube earlier this week — '

Susie raised a hand. 'You have now officially gone too far. We need to talk.'

★   ★   ★

John Forbes expected meltdown of some sizeable proportion when he explained to his daughter that he was going abroad no matter how short the absence. He didn't think his ex-wife or son would give a toss. Sure enough, they didn't seem to. He based that on a fairly complete indifference to the news. He muttered about being glad to know they cared so much, to which Quentin gave a grunt and Roma sniggered. He felt like a big child.

'How's your game?' he asked his ex, hoping the question was laced with barb.

'Excellent,' she told him with a wide smile that confirmed he was at the same stage of development as an eleven-year-old.

He was relying on his daughter for satisfaction. The eruption didn't come. Flora was engrossed in a nail varnish tester and squawking into her phone. 'Shuh *UP*,' she urged one friend. 'NAO!' she exclaimed to another confidante. He rifled through some old tabloids to pass a decent amount of time on duty. Then he got ready to go.

Something in Flora's acquisitive head delivered the message that she should put her wedge-heeled boot in. She adopted her softest voice. 'Dad, I am so, like, broke. Can you leave me some money for when you're away? Like really enough to see me through 'cos I am so smashed after Christmas. I can get lots of credit on my phone with it to call you. And I need a new bag.' She made her eyes huge and imploring.

It would cost him if he wanted to avoid a scene and retain the affection of one family member.

'I can leave some cash with your mother and I'll bring you back an American handbag. How about that?'

This didn't meet her expectations. 'How could you possibly know what bag to get me?' she demanded. 'And *she* so won't give mc enough money to keep going.' A catch quelled her voice. She drummed up some tears then threw herself howling up the stairs. While she was on the move he caught her wail that no one understood her. She banged her bedroom door shut and when the reverberations died away and it was safe to travel again, John shouted, 'Goodbye,' and left. No one returned his valediction. He could imagine Quentin sitting in his teenage hovel making an L sign with his fingers and announcing 'Loser' at his exit. All John could think was that L was for lonely too. Feeling sorry for himself only made him even more pathetic, he decided. Back to Loser, then.

★　★　★

'You cannot go around picking up strangers on public transport,' Susie explained through gritted teeth.

'He had something. I could see that. And when I checked I saw that we had received his CV and headshot cold but hadn't yet replied.'

'Less of the we,' Susie warned.

'OK, I remember it coming in. I thought he'd be perfect for *Highway*.' Valerie wore the expression of someone who was misunderstood and felt an overreaction was being perpetrated against her. 'He did well. He got a call back.'

'That is so not the point.' Susie sighed harshly. 'As a matter of entirely idle interest, how did you

340

convince the casting director to see him?'

Valerie looked a little abashed. 'I said he was exciting new talent, then I used a phrase I'd heard from you. I said, 'Just take the meeting,' repeated it a few times while she was being negative, and that did the trick because she caved in.'

'I am gobsmacked, flabbergasted and generally speechless.'

'So now would be a good time to release more news?'

'Spin away. I have nearly given up on you. There can't be too much more that can shock me.' Be careful what you wish for, her brain clucked.

'I told Betty what I'd done and she said I should probably keep doing what I'm here for but also assist Karl if he'd like as he has so many clients to see to. I can handle some of the Irish clients who are still based in Dublin.' She began to falter when she saw Susie's face crease up. She couldn't tell if it was anger or further bewilderment. She decided to finish the sentence, as there seemed nothing else for it. 'Or something like that.'

'Oh. My. God. My mother is becoming a junior agent. You are sixty-six years old. You should be knitting tea cosies for the Women's Institute and going on day trips to closed-up tin mines. Do you have any idea how much stress you'll be putting yourself under? The family will kill me, if your antics don't first. Look at me. I have no life and you won't either from here on out.'

'I didn't have much of a life before this, as it happens.'

Susie put her head in her hands for momentary release from the maelstrom. Betty had no idea how complicated she had just made her life. Her mother would now work closely with her lost love. When she had regained a modicum of composure she asked, 'Do I have any other favourite phrases?'

'You're fond of 'I suppose, on some level', as in 'I suppose, on some level, we have to decide if this is the correct career move for you', along with 'at this moment in time' or 'in the broader sense' and you posh up your accent and lower your voice an octave for the Americans. Oh, and you quite like 'the reality is' too.'

'Jesus H Christ.'

'You've all got a patter. Lola is addicted to 'you're killing me here' for both clients and producers. Mitch likes 'not to put too fine a point on it'. And Dave uses 'I suppose it's true to say' a lot when he's playing for time. Karl has all of his Irish charm to use, and he does, along with fluffing up his brogue.'

'Have you discussed the putative-assistant plan with the very same Karl?'

'Betty cleared it with him and I'm awaiting instruction. Are you furious with me?'

'No, I'm not furious. I'm a bit frustrated, is all. I feel I have no control over anything any more, not at home, not here.'

'Perhaps you don't need to have so much control over things. Perhaps you should let things happen a little more organically.'

'That sort of anarchy might kill me right now. Control is about the only thing I can rely on, or could rely on. Now I'm not sure what's going on, in general and in lots of specifics.'

'You've always sought certainty,' Valerie said, 'ever since you were a child. It didn't always have to be correct, just definite.'

Was that the summation, then? Was this what her life could be reduced to?

'Right now I am definitely going for a run in the gym. Otherwise I might have to kill the next person who approaches me with a stupid offer or idea.' Gracious to the last.

* * *

Vonda was the wildest, craziest-looking creature Milo had ever seen or encountered. She didn't give a hang what anyone thought of her and made that plain from the outset. She was quite interested in the report of her adapted science demonstration.

'There are lots of things I don't mind doing,' she commented. 'But I sort of draw the line at making myself ill.'

They were all in agreement there.

'Unless it's to get off school,' she qualified.

'Well, yeah,' Milo said, glad of the common ground.

Vonda didn't seem to mind that they were boys; well, she was used to Gregory. Usually girls their age became snickering menaces or taunting vixens around boys, as far as Milo's experience went.

'I saw your school concert,' she told him. 'Wicked.'

Milo took in her brown eyes and coffee skin, her curls and perky nose. Yes, she was wonky and a girl and therefore *other* but she was captivating. There was one oddity he was finding difficult to come to terms with. Vonda was Greg's twin. This made Milo uncomfortable. If he fancied Vonda so much, did that make him gay for Gregory, even a little? This was a nightmare scenario. He sat as far away from Greg as possible in their den, worried that his confusion would lead to some terrible deed that would see him banished without possibility of return. And Milo did want to come back, to see Vonda.

Vonda. Her very name meant mischief and fun. The way she chewed gum was invigorating. She said she was crap at French.

15

Reg had hardly drawn breath after *The Summer House* wrapped. He went straight into a radio play and then almost on the back of it was asked to participate in an hour-long radio special about age and how the elderly are treated. It was to be recorded early on a Tuesday in Broadcasting House and he found he was nervous at the prospect of a factual intrusion into his world. This was uncharted territory as he normally said other people's words and tried not to bump into the furniture.

He jostled out of the Tube at Oxford Circus. It was nine o'clock and already London was buzzing. Preachers were setting up their microphones, getting younger and younger-looking by the day. Chattering Japanese tourists were already out taking photographs by All Souls Church in Langham Place. Behind the pillars of the rotunda, and clearly visible, some of the city's homeless were still asleep in their bags, rags and cardboard but this was either unnoticed or ignored by the photographers. What a strange world, he thought, pulling his coat tighter around him and scurrying on.

Outside the BBC, autograph hunters waited for the guests on popular shows broadcasting at that moment from within the building. They were a strange mixture, pale, as if they lived underground or generally out of the light, and

345

often carrying an injury. One asked him to pose for a photograph, though he doubted there was film in the camera. Another had a copy of *Spotlight*, the actors' directory, from years ago and wanted him to sign his page. As he gave his scrawl, and marvelled at the outrageously dated head shot, he had to ask, 'How did you happen to have my section?'

'Timothy Dalton is inside doing an interview,' was the reply.

'A happy accident, then.'

The man shrugged, quite nonplussed and said, ''Spose.'

Nothing like being brought down to earth.

He sat in the reception area of the studio, high above the ground, sipping bad Thermos tea and wondering what he had to say that would be of any interest to a listener. Yet, inside before the microphone and interviewer, he was unleashed. The hour was gone almost before they had dealt with the meat of the topic. They discussed the negative perception of the elderly, epithets like 'smelly old' as opposed to 'wise old' or 'generous old', which Reg hoped could be applied to him.

John Forbes sat over his morning coffee, mouth agape. He hadn't expected to be listening to his dad. When he got back from Los Angeles he was determined to spend time with his old man. He must make sure that Flora and Quentin saw more of him too. It was important that the children know their grandfather and appreciate what older generations could offer them.

John heard his father wonder if he was getting more cranky or intolerant, bemoaning lack of manners and grammar. 'Perhaps the world is simply changing, moving on without me.

'Of course I worry about our legacy to the next generation. I'm not sure what I'll be leaving behind: a planet in crisis, many more species under threat of extinction. That's all a great worry. But in essence I suppose all that any of us want is to be remembered, fondly, or at all.'

John heard his father's familiar and self-deprecating laugh.

'I am lucky,' Reg said. 'I will leave a little genetic detail behind. I have two sons and wonderful grandchildren. Not everyone is so lucky. And I suppose because I have lived at times before a camera, there are versions of me, or myself as others, to be savoured or seen long after I am gone. I have lived many lives, vicariously, through my work. But in the end, the one I've enjoyed most is my own.'

★   ★   ★

Rafe was totally weirding Milo out. He followed him around constantly. Whenever Mio stopped and stared, daring him to stop or have a go, Rafe just smiled. It didn't appear malicious but you never knew with Rafe. He'd had Christmas to think up new ways of pulling a bug's legs off. Milo had been one such bug last year, so who was to say anything had changed? Rafe's eyes were wide but a bit dead-looking. He had stopped talking to anyone, even teachers who asked questions. Again he made with the crazy smile and they backed off. Milo was certain they discussed it in the staffroom and decided to leave well alone. Gregory hadn't seen any more pills being popped but they agreed that he must be on something because he was little short of a zombie.

They were in the changing room after phys. ed. one day when Milo heard a whinnying laugh coming from the showers. Maud was roaring for them to get their lardy arses out and back to some education. They were a lazy bunch of sacks, apparently. Milo was sure Maud wasn't actually allowed to use that kind of language in front of them but he wasn't going to be a trailblazer and complain. As long as Maud didn't notice he was alive, life was moderately good. The giggling ratched up a level so Milo went to investigate. Rafe was sitting in a shower stall, rocking. He was laughing now, eerily without humour. As Milo grew closer he saw huge tears rolling down the boy's face. This guy was in trouble.

'Mate,' Milo said. 'We've got to get you some help.'

Rafe looked up and shook his head. He took a plastic Biro top from a pocket and dragged it along his leg. It dug deep into his flesh and a ruby welt and some blood appeared. 'That's better,' he said, to himself really. Then he calmly set about dressing, to return to the fray.

Milo wasn't exactly sure what he had just witnessed. He knew it was a deeply disturbed act. He worried that a baton had been passed to him and he didn't know what to do with it, or about it. He thought he might have seen the essence of unhappiness. He just didn't know. He was so not qualified to deal with this.

★ ★ ★

'Yes, I have my passport and ticket details,' Susie assured her mother. 'I am packed and ready but I don't want to go. How will you manage without me?'

Valerie and Milo stole a look at one another. 'I'm sure we'll do fine. Somehow,' Valerie said. 'You're only going for a week, really.'

'I've left all of the contact numbers you'll need on the notice-board and I'll email them to you when I get there so you have a spare copy, and you have enough money and so on. And I'm still going to be on the other end of the phone as usual.'

They heard the barp of a taxi waiting outside. 'Yes, yes,' Valerie said. 'We really have been through this a number of times.'

'Seven, today,' Milo agreed.

'Go, go, or you'll miss your check-in.'

They helped her to the pavement with her bags and trauma. She hugged Valerie and tried not to smother Milo with bear hugs. It was bucketing down so the farewell party returned to stand in the doorway as the cab pulled off. Susie waved through the back window but they were already a blur. The car was too hot and steamy. She thought she might be sick. Her head throbbed. She should turn around and go back. She was coming down with a bug.

The airport was stiflingly busy. Queues of

people snaked around the packed terminal area. She was glad to tuck herself into a lesser one for business travellers. She heard laughter and saw John Forbes charming a male and a female attendant. They hung on his attention. He looked around, spotted her and genuinely looked even gladder now that she was here. He dashed over to help.

'I'm out long before I normally saunter in because I wanted to make sure you were sorted,' he explained. 'All you need to do is to show my two new best friends your passport and we can repair to the lounge while they check you in.'

He moved her about on a whisk and before she could say 'I have to ring Milo and tell him the Rock is sitting opposite me' they were nursing champagne and chatting, cares dispelled along with the headache and the nascent bug.

'My life, or rather my work, is a lot like an airport: full of rushing and promises, bright lights and fragile dreams.' John laughed at himself. 'Forgive the cheap poetics, I think the drink has gone to my head.' Along with you, Susie Vine, he could have added.

They chatted easily and he was relieved that she had left work to one side. For her part Susie relaxed and enjoyed this urbane, amusing man, in between his signing autographs and posing for photographs. The Rock was similarly engaged and the two saluted one another, kindred travellers, gladiators, stars. Susie sent Milo a mobile-phone photograph of the American star because he was a big fan of *The Scorpion King*.

When they boarded they were shown to first

class. John turned to her and winked. 'A perk of the trade,' he said.

Susie laughed a lot in this man's company. She liked it. She caught the envious glances of the other passengers. Yes, I'm travelling with John Forbes and it feels marvellous. You would love it too, but sorry, he's mine for the next twelve hours. Longer. He's mine for the next seven days. The bubbles in her brain were loosening her rules but she really didn't give a rattle just then.

Later, after they'd eaten, they watched the same movie, they wore individual earphones and watched their own monitors but shared the experience, pointing out flaws in the logic or continuity errors.

'You were an actress?' John asked.

'For the briefest of anons. I wasn't all that good.' It didn't feel like failure to say this now.

'It's a mad job, really, as you know. Sometimes you look so busy but in reality the job was shot months beforehand and you're at home twiddling your thumbs, slowly going insane and waiting for the phone to ring. All smoke and mirrors. But so damned exciting when it's going well, and a bit terrifying no matter what.' He stretched a dead leg. 'I should take a walk but I'm kind of wrecked.' He yawned. 'Bedtime for the adventurers.' He turned and with a twinkle asked, 'Are you a member of the Mile High Club?'

Susie felt a tightening in her belly. 'You are no gentleman to ask,' she pointed out, trying to appear entirely suave with the question, feeling a flush light her face.

He quirked an eyebrow, mischievously.

'I may be,' she demurred. 'And you?'

'I may be.'

Side by side, they lowered their flat beds and Susie found herself trying to sleep head to toe with John Forbes, separated by a slim screen. She wished she'd packed a smarter set of pyjamas but Milo had given her this fluffy, pink pair with roses in the design and she'd wanted to bring a bit of him with her. John lay on his tummy trying not to moan aloud for the longing that Susie Vine was here with him, yet not. It was a different experience of the Mile High Club, the one where abstinence held sway. He preferred the more traditional route.

★   ★   ★

Valerie was fed up of her wardrobe. She had a choice of returning to Chittenham to retrieve clothes from there or start anew on Oxford Street. Chittenham involved a possible collision with Alistair, which she felt totally up to but, really, could she be arsed? Must watch her language; she was spending too much time around Lola and picking up too many of the wrong phrases.

Her Tube protégé had not been cast and she was not in a position to offer him formal representation, but she did tell him she would keep an eye out for opportunities suited to him. Any hankering she might have for agenting was assuaged by the assistant position to Karl and, besides, her hands were full running the office.

Lola buzzed through. 'We have trouble. Can you get all of the papers? Rod Ferguson has been busted for cocaine possession and we need to contain this tighter than a gnat's twat. Sorry, Val.'

'Oh please, don't be. You're at your granny's now, as they say.' She had to admit she'd never heard such a phrase. 'Susie will go mental,' Valerie observed, thinking she was picking up a lot of Milo's parlance too.

She dashed out and bought up the newsagents. There was nothing, as yet, in despatches.

'Not unusual,' Lola mused. 'We're lucky that Rod's real name is Rodney Wells, but there was another of those on the Equity books so he took his mother's surname for work.'

'Has he been bailed?'

'Not yet. I've got my cousin, Howard, on the case. He's a lawyer type and closed as the grave. Time to phone America?'

'Mmn. Why don't we email Susie instead and say the situation is under control and nothing to worry about.'

'Done.

'I made a call and found out that Rod's a hound for cocaine when he's in the money. That's why Jay Burns left him behind. He knew about the problem and didn't want to have to deal with it any more. Creep could have tipped us off. I didn't spend half enough of his money at Christmas.'

'Rod's modelling money came through,' Valerie said, 'which is why he's flush.'

'He can kiss that goodbye if the news breaks.

He'll be sued from here to kingdom come if the company find out about this.'

'Then we have got to keep it under wraps.'

'I think we shouldn't let it go beyond ourselves, Betty and Susie for the moment. Loose tongues might not mean any malice but this is a combustible one and I don't want it getting out of control.' She gave Valerie a sideways glance and said, 'Funny the way artist can sound like arses if you say it quickly,' and bustled off to save the day.

Valerie's heart sped along with the excitement of a crisis. She had never seen a line of coke up close, just in the movies. In fact she had never even seen marijuana, though she knew what a magic mushroom looked like. She regularly met the youth of Chittenham out 'shrooming when the weather was right. She didn't know anyone addicted to a celebrity drug but half of her acquaintances drank too much and munched on Prozac or Valium so she'd seen addiction up close. She liked Rod and resolved to find a way to help him. She took out the phone book and began to look up the numbers of clinics and specialists.

'What's this about Rod Ferguson?' Mitch asked as he arrived at the desk.

So much for containment.

★ ★ ★

He was washed and smelling of mint and cologne when Susie opened her sleep-clagged eyes.

'Morning,' he whispered.

How long had he been watching her? Had she snored? Had she shared secrets in her sleep?

'Morning,' she muttered, trying not to release her morning breath, feeling the parch of a slight hangover. She reached a hand to her hair and by feel alone could determine its crazy shape. She groaned and closed her eyes again. The trolley was already clanging for breakfast service so she puttered off to the loo and came back looking slightly less worn. Over herb omelettes and croissants they discussed *I-Dentity*.

'I love the questions it asks. Who are we? What is the self? What right do we have over ourselves and any other selves we might create? How can we maintain morality when science offers us so much that is tempting, dazzling, dangerous?'

His excitement was palpable.

'Do you wonder who you are?' he asked.

'Always, these days.'

He allowed her the time and silence to want to continue.

'I worry that I'm just my job. It's my personality, almost. Or so it seems at times.'

'I understand completely. I was thinking exactly the same thing recently. Pretending to be someone else for most of your waking hours makes you wonder if you're anyone at all in your sleep or the spare hours spent travelling from set to home.'

'I know I feel unworthy, somehow. A fraud.'

'Yes. Me too. A bit of a liar, I suppose.'

The jet engines hummed over their thoughts. They were in a muffled world, high in the sky, defying gravity and wondering who the hell they were, or what their purpose was.

'A glass of cheer would be welcome,' John said.

'It only postpones reality.'

'As an interim solution to an imponderable question it's not the worst.'

'We have to hit the ground running over here, so best not. God, I hate being so sensible.'

'No, you're right. Let the games continue, let the pretence roll on.'

'Let's fool some of the people all of the time?'

John gave a hollow 'Yeah' and they returned to their personal reverie.

The honesty had been more intense than undressing before the other. A shift had occurred.

As they came in to land, Susie said, 'Everything looks so organised from far away, up here, but it's usually chaos up close.'

'And be prepared to be a little appalled. No one tells you how ugly this place looks at first glance.'

John would stay with a friend in Laurel Canyon and Susie was booked into a hotel off Sunset Boulevard. He tried to persuade her to join him but she refused, having backed off into business mode again. Distance was a good antidote to the anarchy inherent in this trip. He left her off and mooched around while she checked in. He saw her to her room and mooched some more.

'Did you notice the people wearing head bandages down there,' Susie remarked.

'That's the quintessential LA sight around here. We're close to a busy plastic surgeon. Those are facelifts healing. Eyuw, as my daughter is fond of saying.'

'Precisely.'

'Though I don't think I'd rule it out entirely if gravity got too great a hold on my chops.'

'Are you serious?'

'Well, think of it, how is it that much different from having your teeth remodelled?'

'I guess,' Susie said, not entirely convinced.

They were both stalling his exit. He was standing too close. She looked into his eyes and knew that to be a mistake immediately. Emotion was too close, too unpredictable. To release it was not an option they could pursue.

'Susie,' his voice caressed.

She could feel his breath on her face.

'I think you should go, John.'

Thankfully, he did.

She sank into the bed, promising herself she'd check her emails in just a moment. All her mind could obsess about was John Forbes. Ridiculous, she admonished. I am in love with another man, Karl Fox. This is little better than a schoolgirl's crush. It was silly and without any dignity. As soon as her jet lag released her she would nip it completely in the bud. She had already let it get beyond her normal control.

16

Valerie introduced Rod Ferguson to Milo then left them to their own company while she prepared supper. Rod lounged on the sofa looking very cool but wrecked. He was the nearest thing to a rebel Milo had seen up close. He had stubble and a leather jacket and was a bit down-at-heel but mesmerising. Isabelle would probably have chucked Garee out if she caught sight of this guy. Eventually Milo's curiosity overcame shyness.

'So, like, my gran says you're in trouble for, like, drugs?'

''Fraid so.'

'What sort?'

Rod looked unsure about discussing the minutiae of Class A drugs with a minor.

'Is it smack?' Milo wanted to know.

'No!'

Milo waited for further information. He looked as if he had staying power.

'Oh, all right, it was cocaine.'

'Charlie.'

'Eh, yeah.'

'Isn't that, like, expensive?'

'Well, yes and no. Anyhow I came into some money lately so I went a bit mad and thought I could have whatever I wanted and it all sort of went to my head. It was a really stupid thing to do.'

'So my gran says. She says the cops found you

slumped in your car in your driveway in your underpants, like, out of it. She's really furious with you. Says you're, like, ruining your life and that you're better than that.'

Rod let his head fall into his hands. Too much reality was just too much for his system.

'Why do you take it?'

Rod wondered if Milo'd been set up by Valerie to interrogate him and make him feel even more of an idiot than he was.

'The truth is, it feels good, Milo. That doesn't mean I recommend it to anyone. It's not big and it's not clever.'

'Don't you feel good without it?'

'Well, yes, I do, but it makes me feel even better.' Does it though? he wondered.

Milo shook his head as if he didn't get it.

Rod grimaced. 'Can't fault your logic, buddy,' he said. 'You feel good for a while, but it doesn't last. And then you're filled with self-loathing.'

'Do you not like yourself?'

The young guy could really ask the tough questions.

'I'm not sure about that. Actors always have some excuse for messing up. We're a bit, I don't know, special like that. Or we want to be seen as special, maybe? But we're not that much different. Our problems are the same as everyone else's; we just have a sexier job. Or it looks sexier and glamorous sometimes anyhow.'

'Do you have a girlfriend?'

Was he going to tell him all he needed was the love of a good woman? 'Not at the moment. Do you?'

'There's someone I like. And I used to like someone else but she's, like, older than me and I don't think she knows or, like, knew and it was, like, hard. It felt good but bad too.'

How could he get so much out without appearing to move his mouth? Rod nodded. 'The older women can break your heart.'

'But this new one is, like, my age and even though she doesn't know that I like her I think she likes me and, you know, maybe?'

'Good luck, man. Go for it.'

Milo was on a roll now. 'There's this guy at school in my class that's doing stuff. It's tablets but we don't know what kind and I think maybe he's stealing them from his parents' medicine cabinet or something. I think he's really, like, messed up.'

'Do you think anyone will help him?'

'Dunno. No one really likes him enough to, I think.'

'Bummer.'

When supper was done and Rod was unpacking in Susie's room, Valerie filled Milo in. 'It's just overnight. I didn't want him going home in case the papers have got hold of it, though I'm hopeful they won't. Also if he's alone for the evening he might get weak. And he's promised to get help from tomorrow at a place I found for him.'

There was an unspoken problem hanging between them.

'Have you told Mum?'

'No. I'm not sure what I can say to her about it. I don't think she'd approve of giving Rod shelter here, in your home. And I think I should apologise for that to you, Milo. I just didn't know what else to do. And, of course, I'll lose my job if anyone finds out. It's a huge risk, I know. But I am certainly not asking you to lie to your mother so you must tell her what you feel is best.'

Milo thought about it. 'He's cool by me. We had a good talk earlier. And it is only for, like, one night? I don't think Mum needs to know.'

'A good deed in a dark world, Milo. Thank you.'

'No prob.' He shifted off to his computer.

Rod returned and sat waiting for another telling off. Valerie had not minced words earlier. He cleared his throat and said, 'I am going to beat this, even if it takes some kind of Pauline conversion.'

'Believe me, Rod, I'll even take a Philistine one if it means you're on the straight and narrow. You are no good to the agency half cut, or half arsed. Now go get a good night's sleep. Tomorrow we start again.'

★ ★ ★

The first question anyone in Los Angeles asked was, 'Where are you staying?' which roughly translated as, 'How much money have you got?' Susie quickly copped that everything meant something else. On an early occasion a woman declared, 'We were so worried about you,' but what she wanted to say was, 'You are so late!' The meetings with would-be managers for John were an education. Susie had rarely seen so much smoke blown up one, very fine, ass. John took it all in his stride, calm and seemingly comfortable with the hyperbole and hysterical praise.

'I *so* loved your (then they would fill in the show/movie/series). Wasn't that what you won your BAFTA for?' Ah, the power of the Award. 'I am *so* your number-one fan out here. We are *so* excited at the prospect of handling your career.' They rubbished other outfits in the most delicate of damnations. 'Well, of course, they've been handling (so and so) and we really think he is a *great* actor *but* he has made some poor decisions lately. We feel we would have gone with different choices.' And on and on.

And on.

Eventually all Susie could hear was, 'Please, please, please, choose me.' The meetings became more about the managers than the talent. John looked wrily amused. 'I have not had this much outrageous love made to me in decades,' he quipped, holding her eye and daring her to react.

They had hit the end of pilot season when all the new series were being cast.

'The actor I'm staying with does a couple of those a year,' John reported. 'Not one has ever made it to transmission so he gets all of the money and none of the opprobrium if the thing is aired and it's a turkey. Ergo a lovely house with pool in Laurel Canyon and barely a care in the world.'

'At the risk of sounding like the sycophants we're coming down with this week, that would be *such* a waste of your talent and I couldn't bear it or forgive myself for letting it happen on my watch. I want to see you work and to enjoy your and the public's reaction to the good things you do.'

He stalled and looked sideways at her. 'Thank you, Susie. That's quite a compliment.'

'It's the truth. I meant it. I believe in you. Now let's nail you some top management out here.'

It was good to be on an even footing with him again. They had their roles: he, the client; she, the agent. All was as it should be.

She was a lot more worried about what was occurring at home. Rod Ferguson was in a scrape and Susie couldn't get the details from the office, which made her suspicious and agitated. She flung out emails from her Blackberry but was fobbed off every time. They might as well have written, 'Look, over there, a lion!' She was skilled at spotting evasion: it was Milo's favourite tool. From what she could glean, Rod had been caught with some drugs but according to Lola this was no big deal and had been buried quicker than most ingénues' Hollywood careers. She was going to have to trust that it was all in hand.

'They say five thousand hopefuls arrive into Los Angeles every day hoping to make it in the business,' John said. 'Most end up waiting tables and starring in porn movies.'

'City of Angels,' Susie warbled. 'And Agents. And some very startled eyes.'

'Yes, everyone over twenty-five has had them done, and this bright sunshine really picks that up. Not to mention the gnashers, which come on a roll. Honestly, after a fire, dental records would be useless for identification: everyone's bought their teeth from the same place. It's Plastic Paradise. I think that's another reason the Brits and the Europeans stand out, we tend to have imperfect features and crooked teeth.'

John's host threw a party in his honour at the pad in Laurel Canyon. It was attended by the elite of a certain cache, and the downright curious of an even higher bracket of 'type', a power list unexpected in the host's home normally but who appeared for a chance to press flesh with the latest, hot, Blighty export and check out what all the fuss was about. He made sure to have her at his elbow at all times. He simply introduced her as Susie and she never quite got the opportunity to bleat 'agent' before their gaze moved on. She indulged him in this but made a note to reprimand him later. In truth, she reminded herself, if they'd been listening to the jungle drums as they should, they would know he had an English female agent running Rottweiler for him. And that was her.

They stuck to fizzy water as an impression had to be made and hardly anyone drank alcohol in public any more. They left the obvious drunken raucousness to an up-and-coming Irish hunk who was, against all LA odds and mores, a great hit with the company. She enjoyed the looks of incredulity that shot her way all evening. How could she have landed a treasure like John Forbes?

Susie was rigorously quizzed by the umpteenth wives of the myriad movers and shakers. They couldn't believe her hair was . . . words could not describe. Susie tried to fill in the possibilities, which ranged from alive to dangerous to natural. A tall, peroxide blonde, sucked, tucked, buffed and blow-dried to within an inch, gave a moue of horror. 'Do you mean that's in vogue in London just now?' She clearly had a mouthful of warm sick at the thought. Susie could have sculled a white wine. Or sculled the wife? That held a certain attraction. She formed the opinion that 'natural' was a condition that could be cured, and had been by most of the attendees. She, on the other hand, was a barbarian. Vive la difference, she thought, bring it on.

Those who came to have a look smiled and gripped her hand then looked over her shoulder for someone more important to talk to. When they did, they saw John and decided to stay within range. She toyed with some, asking questions such as, 'What are you enjoying at the moment? Release-wise?' They then had to decide what to throw their weight behind, to choose a particular movie or studio. It was fascinating to see some of the wriggles this precipitated. No one wanted to nail their colours too clearly to a mast in case that was the wrong thing to do in the company they were in. It was like herding cats to get an opinion out of them. The higher the status of the individual, the clearer the opinion. Those in power weren't half as afraid as the minions below them.

A burly man cornered John and began to talk business. He ignored Susie. His wife took up her case, obviously conditioned to remove the fluff while her bulldog husband did his thing. John reached casually back and rested a hand on her waist. It amused him that there was such a line of differentiation between social and formal and the sexist way the sectors were marked out. Any woman there to do business was thought to be a prostitute or a bulldyke. The others were the wives who were there to discuss treatments, the disgraced of the divorce courts and the latest yoga guru on the block. It was thoroughly, splendidly fickle.

The host had included many of his friends of yore and they were loose and fun. They also drank wine, which marked them out from the movie set power brokers. They were a ragtag of elderly actors and actresses, which meant they were over thirty years of age, some of them over fifty, which was so ancient as to be almost beyond numbers for an actor. There was a helping of writers too. They took to the comfy couches in the Den and screeched with drunken good humour. They were having a ball. They finally gathered at the window to watch the stiffer guests leave, all of whom chose ten thirty to a cue no one else noticed or understood, like geese suddenly taking to the air and leaving for the winter.

John grabbed a bottle of champagne and invited Susie to follow him. He led her to his room, which was really a guest suite complete with outdoor jacuzzi, as Susie discovered. He

366

popped the cork and said, 'Thank fuck they've gone. Have you ever met a more uptight bunch?'

'They're serious about what they do. They have to be. They're responsible for vast tranches of money, belonging to other people usually.'

He looked incredulous.

'All right, I'll come off duty for a while,' she conceded.

'I hope some of them have gone home to drink some fine claret, loosen up and enjoy their short lives. And they will be short if they don't relax.' He guzzled back a tumbler of champs and began another. He flipped the switch on the pool and said, 'Fancy a dip?'

He had to be joking.

He wasn't. Susie began to stutter excuses, mainly that she didn't have a swimsuit, unspoken was that she was not ready to be viewed partially naked by John Forbes. He pointed to a row of costumes ready to be used by the guests. She waved her hands, warding off the ridiculous suggestion, spilling some fizz on herself. John gave an exasperated sigh, stripped off and got into the jacuzzi. There was no mistaking that the man had talent in a lot of areas, at least one of which the public might never see. When she finished blushing, Susie took in the scene. She felt like a square. She looked into the sky to glean some wisdom from the stars. She didn't find an answer but thought, I won't be bested by this situation. I've done some things in my time. I'm a woman of the world. She struggled into a bathing suit while trying to keep her day clothes on till the last moment. Then she dipped quickly into the broiling water. She sat opposite John, leaning her head back on the side and trying to remain still and perfectly comfortable-looking.

She closed her eyes and let herself enjoy the sensation of the hot water pummelling her body and the alcoholic bubbles rush through her. Something about the quality of the water changed and when she opened her eyes it was to see John above her, holding tight to the sides around her head, poised for a kiss. She gasped, not so much from shock as the hot desire she suddenly felt. Her legs, of their own volition, wrapped themselves around him. She felt her costume roughly pulled from her body, then John thrust into her, his breath on her ears as he whispered need and joy. She tried to concentrate on a point of light within her, the place where pleasure lived and would explode from to invade her body. They finished quickly. Without speaking he carried her to his bed and made love to her all over again, his lips searching her and finally crushing her mouth in rapture as they came again.

She woke at four and decided to slip away. Her mind was a mixture of guilt and delight. Her heart thundered at the night's memories. She would figure out how to process it all later. The tines of a hangover began to spread in her brain so she went in search of water. She passed through the Den where one of the older actresses still sat, nursing a bottle of tequila.

'End of an era,' the woman muttered, her American accent making era sound suspiciously like 'error'.

Adam was Rafe's mate and should have been the only one to ride shotgun for his latest stunt. But he was afraid of how it would end. He sought out Gregory and Milo and convinced them to come to the bicycle shed. Some primitive sense of allegiance made them follow the boy. They found Rafe sitting on the ground clutching a can of lighter fluid. He wore a demonic expression on his face.

'Hey, you pussies, come to see my new trick? You're all too scared to try this, so I'm going to. I am the Man.' He cackled, an actual witchy squawk. He was a picture of dissolute, unnameable rage. Milo could practically taste how unhinged this guy was. It frightened him. They were going to be in so much trouble because of him. And what if he died?

'Rafe, you don't need to do this to impress us,' he said. The others murmured agreement.

'I'm not doing it for you tossers.' He looked at the top of the can with its different coloured plastic attachments for filling lighters of all sorts. 'See you later,' he said, then took a mighty whiff of the fluid through his mouth. Seconds later his eyes rolled back in his head and he pitched sideways, out of it. Then his body exploded into a fit like an epileptic might experience. They had seen it happen to Patrick Burke in Year 7, and that had been spectacular and truly scary. The important thing was to make sure he didn't swallow his tongue, Milo remembered. Also he might hurt himself if he thrashed into the bikes parked in the shed. He roared at Adam to go get help. He bent in to try to get Rafe lodged on his side while he jerked around. As he did so, Rafe's leg shot out and took Milo's from under him. He went flying through the air and hit his head against a concrete upright as he fell. A twinkling mist filled his sight and a pain began to rip through his head. Then he saw the ground moving very quickly towards him as his vision dimmed and he passed out.

★　★　★

Susie had six missed calls, all from Valerie. She knew immediately that something had happened to Milo. She pressed a trembling finger on the speed dial. She had been missing in action when her family needed her. Dear God, please don't let anything bad have happened to my baby. He is my life. She felt nausea rise and worried that she would faint. Far away the phone rang in London and Valerie answered. 'Don't worry,' were her first words. 'Milo had an accident at school, trying to help another boy, and he's been kept in hospital as a precaution.'

Susie began to scream out questions.

'Please, Susie, calm yourself. He is in the best place and he's fine. He is conscious and has a bit of a bump on his head and two black eyes that he's rather proud of.'

'I'll be on the next flight home.'

'That's exactly what he said you'd say and he said to tell you that you don't have to come back.'

'How entirely ridiculous. Of course I have to come home. I'll call you later with my travel details.'

Her phone rang immediately she ended the call. It was John. She stopped any talk of the night before by announcing her decision to go.

'Don't you think you're overreacting?' he asked.

She hadn't told him her reason. She almost laughed at how trivial it was compared with the situation at home. 'No. No. My son has been hurt in an accident. I have to go. This has nothing to do with . . . ' Descriptive words were probably a waste, so she didn't bother with them. 'You know,' she finished, making sure he knew that was a full stop on the subject.

'I'll go with you to the airport.'

'There's no need.'

'Yes, there is.'

'Right, well.' She didn't have the energy to argue with him. 'I'll give you your schedule for the rest of your visit.' Clear prose, clear signals. She was going to put them back on their formal business footing. It would have been better for her purposes not to see him but she didn't know how she could avoid it.

Twenty minutes later her insides churned to see him in her doorway. She had willed herself to be totally calm but instead there was a tectonic shift that threatened to propel her into his arms. Last night had been a terrible mistake and she mustn't compound it. He was fresh and showered. He smiled warmly and made to kiss her. She deflected him by twisting her face and offering a cheek. He was too good an actor to look anything but unfazed. In fact, he was very confused. He had hoped they would continue their obvious connection. He was crazy about this woman. Looking at her pack he had an almost uncontrollable urge to sweep her suitcase off the bed, ease her onto it and make love to her again. He could feel her distress and was distraught not to be able to help in a more tangible way.

Susie's senses were warm and liquid and she tried hard not to let her shaking body show her turmoil. She had muddied the situation unforgivably. It could never be allowed a repeat. She sighed and looked at him as he gazed out of her window, concentrating hard on something in the road. What a pity it all was. He was a lovely man.

They had checked her in and were making their way towards the departure gate when she decided to buy some magazines. *Vanity Fair* had a Hollywood issue and *OK!* would be the ideal chewing gum for her brain. She flicked through it out of habit and was stunned to see a photograph of her and John in an On The Town section. They were standing outside The Ivy, where they had lunched three days ago. He had placed his hands on her shoulders and she was laughing at something he had said while staring into his eyes. The attendant blurb said hunky English actor, John Forbes, had lunched à deux with a friend and everyone present said they looked very intimate and oblivious of those around them.

She remembered the day well. The lunch had

been quite funny. They were surrounded by the Set. Thin women lunched with other Important Wives, probably without eating anything but a leaf of lettuce and sipping a glass of still water. Agents and producers sat alone at tables to be seen and heard. Susie recognised all of the language. One was settling up the credits for a client, braying, 'We're going with first position there, single card, before the title.' Susie had taken a call from a busy woman who sounded like a character from a comedy TV show. She had requested a résumé and show reel for John and it had been sent. Susie doubted the woman was aware that she had dialled Susie and not the other way around.

'I know who you are,' she announced, sure, staccato, Jewish.

'Oh, good.'

'I know who you are, it's about the English boy.'

'Well, yes.'

'See? I know who you are.'

'Yes.'

'This is about the contracts.'

'No.'

'No? Well then, who are you?'

She had related it word for word to John afterwards and they spent the meal remembering the call and laughing without needing to go through it again. It was a most splendid illustration of weird and wonderful Hollywood and why people became hooked and never got over it.

Standing in an airport terminal, going home to

her injured son, it was an uncomfortable sensation to see them in a gossip column, but most unsettling was how they were together in the photograph. Susie was shocked to see that they looked like a couple in love.

She left the newsagent in a daze, just as John Forbes finished a phone call. She heard him say, 'Please don't be like that, Flora. She's just my agent.'

This hit her like a sharp slap across the face. She was stung by the diminution of her status, though it was what she thought she'd wanted: to be just his agent. Now the title pained her. Her cheeks flamed with the twin betrayals of her own stupidity and John Forbes' fickleness. She wanted to sink to the ground and cry and disappear.

I am just his agent.

It also meant the publication had hit the news-stands at home.

She thanked John formally and watched him leave before going through to sit in the ordinary departures area, this time, surrounded by strangers that she didn't have to make an effort for. She let her face fall as far as it needed to. She wanted to vomit out her worry for Milo and regret at her foolishness. She had made a mistake and now was undergoing a cosmic punishment, visited on her innocent son when it should have happened to her. She hated that she had enjoyed herself so much. It was amazing that she had, considering she was in love and always had been with Karl Fox. At that moment she couldn't quite recall his features, had to concentrate hard to get past John Forbes' face, his body. I am just his agent, she reiterated. A look from a fellow passenger let her know she was talking aloud.

She took out her Blackberry and began by rote to go through the least important of the emails she'd received. One company wanted Craig Landor to take part in a reality television show where the participants learned a new and difficult skill — cordon bleu cooking, in Craig's case. Her reply was practised, automatic. She was tempted to add the truth, which would have read:

Hi Moira,

I have spoken to Craig about *The Skill* (lie) and he is going to pass (truth). Thanks for thinking of him (lie) but he feels that he would not be able to come up with stuff to cook (truth) and would waste viewers' time (which this programme will anyway).

Best (lie)
Susie (truth)

The first of her fat, juicy tears hit the tiny keyboard as she pressed Send.

★ ★ ★

Milo was tiny and pale, lost in the white hospital bed. Worry crossed his face when he saw her. He was expecting a telling-off. She was the one who deserved that. She had been at a party when she was needed. No, worse than that, she was in a client's bed. Far worse.

Valerie looked from one to the other. 'I'm not sure who looks worst here.'

'I haven't slept since I heard,' Susie explained.

The journey had been filled with a litany of unwelcome images: Milo hooked up to life support, Milo dead and in a box. She was haunted by the feeling of him growing in her while she was pregnant and the oddness of having a being so other within. She relived the surge of love and relief when he was born; the aching pride at his perfection; the sense of dedication to him, which she had now reneged on. She was glad of the only available cramped seat in the economy cabin, which refused to allow her sleep, as she feared her dreams would be apocalyptic enough to make her cry out.

'I'll pop and get us all a nice drink,' Valerie said, leaving mother and son to time alone.

'I hear you were brave.' Susie touched Milo's hair, pressed a kiss onto her hand and onto his face. She hoped he could feel her love. It felt as if it might crush her with its force. 'You tried to help Rafe.'

'Yeah. Got a bit of a knock for my trouble though.'

'I'm proud of you.'

'I thought it would be good to help, a good deed like Gran sometimes does.' He looked as if he'd let something slip but Susie couldn't even guess what. 'You didn't have to come back, you know.'

'I did, Milo.'

'You so didn't, Mum, but it's good to see you.'

He fell asleep as she held his hand.

Valerie returned with two scalding cups of tea. 'Thanks, Mum.'

'Wait until you taste it,' she warned. 'You won't be so grateful then.'

'No, I mean for being here.'

Valerie wrinkled her nose. 'You probably have your father to thank for that. If he hadn't left I might not have ended up in London.'

'Mysterious ways,' Susie said.

'Quite. I rang him, you know. I suppose I needed to tell someone what had happened.'

And you couldn't reach me, Susie thought.

'It was like a strange reflex action,' Valerie went on. 'He wanted to come to London but I scotched that. I hope you don't mind but I don't think I'm ready for that yet.'

'You do what you think is best, Mum. I'm not much of a counsellor on personal relationships.'

'How was LA?'

'Interesting and insane.'

★ ★ ★

Vonda was appreciative of his trials. 'That Rafe is a mentalist,' she said. 'You were mad to get involved.'

Milo felt a swell of pride. His ears were hot. 'I had to,' he explained.

'This is groovy.'

'The hospital? Yeah. I'm going home tomorrow though. Will you come and see me there?'

Both Gregory and Vonda said 'Yes' at the same time so that was a success, as it didn't look like he'd asked Vonda especially.

'Do you think they'll take him out of school?' Gregory asked.

'I hope so,' Milo replied.

'Bet he ends up in a loony bin,' Vonda said.

'I don't think that would be a good thing,' Milo's mum said as she came back into the room. 'He needs some help, not to be locked up.'

'Lots of help,' Vonda said. 'And he is actually a nutter. He nearly killed Milo.'

'I think that might be an exaggeration,' Susie said.

Milo was glad to hear that Vonda thought his deed so huge. He was now the stuff of legend.

Susie wasn't so sure the little girl's assessment was so far off. She was sick to think of harm coming to her boy. From now on Milo would be her focus. He was her main responsibility. Milo was her life and she was quite sure she would do anything for him. In comparison with that everything paled. She had her work, she had her family and these precious gifts were all she needed.

17

Lola waved a copy of *OK!* under her nose and asked, 'Would you like to explain this?' The photograph taunted her again.

'Nice try, Lola, but as you can see that is merely an agent and a client enjoying a laugh together. Sorry.' Smooth and in control Susie was outwardly calm and magnificent, even had a wry smile around the edges of the mouth, while inner Susie was roiling.

Time would ultimately erase the shame and she certainly wasn't going to dredge up any public reminiscences of the American trip. Her priorities had returned full time to Milo, and anything she needed for herself could wait. In fact, the less she wanted from life the better. The fallout from expectations was always acute so why go bothering it?

John Forbes proved a gentleman. He rang to say he was back and to inquire again after Milo. These queries were easily dealt with. He wondered about calling by the office. Susie stressed how busy they were but that it was always nice to see him.

'Nice?' He had a mental joust on his end, if the pause he took was reliable evidence, and added, 'I'm not sure what it is I've done.'

She might have melted at the sound of his confusion, picturing too his features crooked into a frown, but even this far along it was hard to shake the feeling that she had been a fool. She had compromised herself and that would never sit easily. She rang off, citing work. Karl Fox strode by. For a moment she felt helpless. There was too much she had let get away and she needed to wrest her life back.

She threw herself into preparations for Cannes. She decided to fly over and back twice only, rather than stay for the duration of the festival, which Lola had opted for. It meant she could spend more time with Milo. It also kept the French visit on a firm business footing. She accompanied John to screenings or meetings but everything was entirely formal and proper. She ensured they were surrounded by industry colleagues at all times and kept the schedule so busy there was no time for delving into the personal.

Lola announced, 'The Warthog is to die for, so I am in hot pursuit. He's clearly worthy of me talent-wise if he can write *I-Dentity*, so no worries there. Yes, he's a bit timid but that's a plus as I have enough chutzpah for us both. Most importantly, he's totally Jewish, which is tops.'

'Do you not think this may muddy your work?'

'You really need to loosen up on the whole business front. You are becoming a dried-up old maid, and I don't mean that in a good way. Yes, this festival is work, but you know what, Susie, the chances of anyone dying if one of these movies doesn't get made is slim. Look around you. We are on the Croissette with the great and good of the movie world. It's glamour and falsehood and romance. It's showbiz, for fuck's sake, not cancer research.'

Lola had a completely new wardrobe and was determined that the world would see it. She arranged invites to parties, one of which coincided with Susie's second visit. She couldn't avoid it easily, as it was being thrown by the people Lola had found to put up Saul Hartog and it would be too rude not to acknowledge their help.

'They also have money they're interested in investing in film so it's a splendid opportunity to network,' she explained.

'Which we could do without the partying.'

'I'll pretend I didn't hear that.'

Craig Landor was attending and asked her to arrive on his arm. He would inevitably have a starlet on the other so Susie got out her best frock and did a full belt and braces on her make-up. She didn't know if John would attend also but felt she couldn't check. If she asked him and he said no, she would have to include him; if she didn't ask him, she had to live with the uncertainty. And an ever so slight disappointment, she was dismayed to find.

'I have a question mark over you and John Forbes.'

Susie had no gumption left to fight, especially a force like Lola. 'What would you like to know?'

'Why the long face since you got back from LA? And don't even try citing Milo to put me off.'

'We had a bit of a misunderstanding, that's all.

It's not important. The sun in Los Angeles fried our brains, is all. Besides, I heard him on the phone tell someone called Flora that I'm just his agent so that made things crystal, which they always were really.'

Lola laughed. 'I know you pride yourself on looking after details, dotting your i's and crossing the t's of a contract, but you miss so much of the real stuff, Susie. Flora is his nightmare teenage daughter who cannot accept that he is not coming home to pamper her. If she can't have her daddy, on her terms, no one else will.'

Susie couldn't process all of the information. She was dipping in and out of her own brain coverage. The signals were confusing.

'Oh, for crying out loud, woman, I could smack you very hard right now.' Lola drummed her exquisitely painted nails on the wooden railing they were leaning over. 'Remember that phrase the actors have, DCOL?'

Susie nodded. 'Doesn't count on location.'

They looked out at the twinkling lights of Cannes, all mesmerising promise and adventure.

'We're in France, Susie.' Lola left her to it.

He's here, Susie thought. Lola's asked him. She snapped back to reality and the fact that she was on an early plane out in the morning. She grabbed her purse and left without thanking their hosts or saying goodnight to Craig. As she rounded the gate at the bottom of the drive and started for her hotel, she saw a car go by with John Forbes in the back. He was talking on his phone and didn't see her. She should have felt relief. They had missed one another. Instead she was hollow. She listened to the cicadas sing happily, all the way back to base. She sat on the bed of her rented room and wondered if she should get drunk. The sequins of her pretty dress glittered, mocking her with their possibilities.

★　★　★

John Forbes decided it was time to make his apartment a home. He bought some paintings, framed nice photos of his children and lashed them to the walls. He began another record collection (Roma had hung on to his last one). He did up his spare bedroom so that Flora and Quentin could stay over if they wanted, which they never did. He spent more time with his dad. But he could not distract his mind from thoughts of Susie Vine. He could feel her still, under his fingertips and lips and deep in his heart. It made him ill to think that he might never again make love to her but he didn't think pushing her was any answer and at least as long as she had to contact him about work, they were still communicating. Then Betty came back to work and his opportunities to talk to Susie were severely curtailed.

'How did you find the interim working arrangements during Betty's absence?' he asked his dad.

'Most satisfactory. Susie Vine has a fine eye for detail. For instance, she polished up my *Summer House* contract because Betty hadn't had time to finish it and I was very well treated. And she's done me a few smaller deals that I have no

383

complaints about. I've also found her easy to talk to and pleasant company. How about you?'

'I adored working with her.'

This was more than was necessary and Reg mulled it over.

'You're lonely, aren't you, son?'

'No more than any of us.'

'Sometimes we need to be courageous, even if it doesn't yield the result we would like. At least we haven't whiled away precious time wondering what might have been. That is perhaps the most futile activity available to mankind. We only get one shot at this life. Better to be sure even if it also means being a little sorry when the outcome is unsatisfactory. There is not enough time in this life that we can waste any of it.'

'You make it sound simple.'

'Perhaps it is.'

'I'll think about it.'

'You should.'

★   ★   ★

'Garee' had broken it off with Isabelle so she cried a lot. It made Milo squirm even more than he had when he had thought her the most beautiful woman in the world. Now she was mostly liquid, though never quite a snotty heap like Jason Philips when he'd fallen off the vaulting horse in the gym. Milo didn't know what to do with her. He couldn't really sit her on a sofa with his arm around her and go, 'There, there.' It wouldn't be appropriate. He was seeing someone else, at least in his eyes, and it could be classed as unfaithful to pay so much attention to another woman. He was trying to glean pointers on romance and relationships from afternoon movies, a lot of which were in black and white and probably a bit old fashioned for now but a chap had to take what he could get and work with it. He tried to be a gentleman. He made Isabelle lots of tea and fled to his room, whenever possible.

He wondered how Vonda felt about him. He knew she liked him. But was that enough? Actually, it probably was because he didn't want to have to tackle any of the funny stuff like kissing. The best he could hope for was to impress her with derring-do. She was well happy with the Rafe incident and ending up in hospital on the back of that was certainly heroic in her eyes. But that had been months ago. Now they were facing into the summer break and he needed ways of meeting up. He was getting good at darts, which was an asset, as Vonda liked a game of those too. They could play with Gregory and it was a nice disguise for Milo's feelings. He could be with Vonda yet not seem like it was a big deal. Cool was everything.

The other thing he was really handy at was sailing. He had won some prizes lately, even one really big trophy, and everyone was suitably impressed. His mother had been shocked, really. She hadn't realised how good he was. Milo tried to be laid-back about it but he did stress that it was for him alone in his little Topper. No one else had helped. He'd got this all by himself. Then the Royal Yachting Association offered him membership and he thought he might pass out with happiness.

'There's this bit in the form, right?' he told his friends. 'And it says, like, that when the Olympics come round here in London I have to be available.'

Vonda did a quick tot. 'You'll be eighteen then.'

'Yeah.'

And when I'm eighteen I'll be able to kiss you properly, he thought. He couldn't wait.

He looked at Isabelle and wondered if he'd look that old too when he was her age. Maybe Vonda wouldn't fancy someone who looked that ancient. Or maybe he should avoid crying as much as the French girl did? That seemed to pile on the years.

★　★　★

Cannes yielded the finance for both *I-Dentity* and Marty's project with Craig Landor, *Glory Days*. The productions had moved on and it was time to do deals and get ready for the shooting work to begin. Days at the office were still odd due to Karl Fox's presence but Susie built in the misery of working with the man she could never have and let herself wallow in it whenever she needed an outlet for pain. In actual fact, she found Karl magnificent to look at but a little one-dimensional to deal with. He was showy but the substance was obviously kept for his private life, if there was much there at all any more. But he still had the ability to make her heart race if she rounded a corner and encountered him unexpectedly.

Lola was on to her, as usual. She could sniff out discomfort and intrigue like a trained dog. 'Why do I feel there's more to you and him than you are letting on?'

'I don't know, Lola. Why do you think that?'

'Perhaps our Susie has a crush on Mr Fox?'

'I don't have the time or the energy for that sort of folly.' Afterwards, she realised this had been the utter truth. It made her feel old. And the use of the word folly only added to that.

Susie set about negotiating contracts. She loved the nuts and bolts of a deal. Marty had a budget of five million dollars and he opened with an offer of one hundred and fifty thousand dollars as Craig Landor's fee. Susie was actually looking for a quarter of a million and countered with a request for three hundred and fifty thousand.

'We love him,' Marty said to that. 'But no one else has a clue who he is over here.' There was a pause. 'One seventy five.'

'Two fifty.'

They settled on an up-front fee of two hundred thousand dollars. Then came Susie's favourite bit: the details.

'In terms of profit participation, I propose five per cent,' she said.

'Of the producer profits.'

'No, of the film.'

'We could discuss corridors of recoupment, with a floor and ceiling built in?'

'Marty, you can build a whole house if you

387

want, but it's the film profits that I need here.'

'Two and a half.'

Susie laughed. 'OK. Two and a half per cent of some money is better than five per cent of none.'

All decent agents preferred box-office bonuses because of their transparency and the term 'as reported by *Daily Variety*' turned up as a norm in the contracts.

'Now, to the bumps,' Susie continued. 'I think we should agree a series of one-hundred-thousand-dollar bonuses from fifteen million at the box office upwards, in increments of five million. And we'll need to settle on some for awards too. Can we say fifty grand each for the Golden Globes and BAFTAs and seventy-five for an Oscar?'

'We'll only pay for wins, not nominations.'

'Done. We'll wait for the long form contract to deal with facilities, travel, premieres and so on. Finally, Craig's credit is a single card, first position of the cast.'

She had done well. Marty had new respect for her. Craig Landor sent flowers and champagne.

Karl Fox spotted the deal memo on the fax machine and read it. 'Jay Burns is right about you,' he said. 'He told me you were a shark.'

'Glad to be the subject of discussion,' she muttered disingenuously.

She was surprised not to feel more fulfilled. She should have been high with the exhilaration of doing a good deal but she couldn't find the satisfaction in it. And the report of praise from an ex-rival via an ex-lover did nothing to lift her.

Betty was still using a stick but looking better

than she had in ages. It was only on her return that the staff realised how much of a gap there had been without her. She gave cohesion to the office. They didn't feel under siege any more. Karl now had time to relax and spread. Susie found this strange and somewhat annoying. He had been a caretaker yet one of 'them' as they pulled together while Betty was away, but with her return he was clearly onto a management level with her. Susie felt like an undergraduate. Dissatisfaction welled again. She now worked for Arland, Shaw and Fox, and that was not the company she had joined thirteen years before.

★　★　★

'The place will be so quiet without Milo,' Valerie said.

It was a subject Susie hated to think about let alone put into words.

'Still, it's only for a month,' Valerie continued. 'He'll have a lovely time with Chris and Corinne and his . . . '

'Other family,' Susie finished and burst into tears.

'I'll call Sophie.'

Milo was to holiday in France with Chris and clan. Susie was treating it like an impending bereavement, something she couldn't even explain to herself. Valerie watched sympathetically, thinking of her own experience of domestic life rent asunder. This was a milder version of that, for sure, but her daughter was feeling it keenly all the same. He's not going away forever, she wanted to say. You'll survive. But she knew that from where Susie was viewing the problem, there was no solace.

'Susie, you are having a bit of a meltdown,' Sophie said. 'Let it all out.'

'I don't know why this is the thing to set it off.' She gulped repeatedly. 'Maybe it's that he's never been gone for so long before. It's like I miss him already and he hasn't even left. I can feel the gap and he's still here.'

'Are you sure that's all?'

Valerie sidled off, knowing her daughter wouldn't open up properly while she was there, which she found sad. Her place was elsewhere in the scheme of things.

'How's work?'

'Impossible. It's just all getting to me. I feel like I don't belong any more and I don't know why. It's not just Karl working there.' She pulled herself up. 'Well, that's stupid thing to say for a start. He doesn't just work there, he owns part of it. I work for him.'

'Is that what this is about?'

'No,' she wailed. 'I don't know why I do it any more. I don't know where the benefit is. What good is it? What good do I do?'

'Susie, not to put too fine a point on it, you are having a crisis of confidence. You're questioning your identity, your own self-worth.'

'Of course I am. I have no identity. I am my job. That's it. My self-worth is built around a false construct that is now falling apart. I am no one without that frigging career. There is no Susie Vine beyond the agent, or beyond Susie

Vine the mother. I'm only labels. Why are you smiling?'

'You are having the classic mid-life crisis. Textbook stuff.'

'How do you bloody well know?'

'I studied to be a psychologist, remember? Then I became a wife and mother, and sometimes I think that's all I am. Those are my labels.'

'Why has this one thing put me over the edge?' Susie asked.

'Milo going away leaves you without your camouflage, perhaps. You have no one to hide behind.'

'It makes me so unhappy.'

'Be sure that is what's making you unhappy. And if it's not, you have to do something about it, for yourself, not for anyone else. Get selfish. Get sorted. And give yourself a break.'

★   ★   ★

Reg's mind flitted about as he drove to the retirement home. He had gathered lots of travel books to take to Margaret. They had agreed that a holiday would be an ideal reward for their hard work on *The Summer House*. Reg was keen on Kiev but discovered it was hilly and that would be a problem for the wheelchair. Now he hoped to convince her of Moscow. They could wander the streets looking like old spies who'd been abandoned by their country of birth and forgotten by the new Russia. They would quote Chekhov and announce that they 'Must go,

Moscow'. They would look heroic and practise their accents. They would drink too much vodka and cause a stir.

He had a pair of cufflinks left him by his father, still in their box made of holly wood. He laughed to think of an actor having something made of that. They were by Fabergé, platinum and sapphire, with sequenced numbers and bearing the legend St Petersburg, Moscow, London all in Russian. It seemed a sign that Russia was a destination that had always been waiting for him. He had worn the cufflinks at his wedding, his sons' christenings, important events in his life. He would pass them on through the family, a small inheritance that would instigate the retelling of his visit to Moscow once. It would grow in each version and become a family legend as much as the cufflinks were an heirloom.

The quality of light on the journey fascinated him. A sharp sun beamed its brilliant, hard, light through the tree branches and telephone poles, forming patterns and rhythms as he sped along. He wondered if this was a problem for those prone to fits. He remembered notices in theatres warning whenever a strobe light was to be used in a production, as it might engender an attack. He wondered if this was a similar danger. He had noticed it on train journeys before and knew that to close one's eyes didn't do much to mask the flickering.

The news on the film was good. The editor and director were pleased with how it was cutting together. There would be a viewing for cast and crew very soon and he was going to suggest to Margaret that they go on their trip hot on the heels of that.

There was the large oak, with its ribbons and tributes to the dead. Its leafy branches reached outward to grant charitable shade and upward in joy to the sky. He was thinking that it must be many hundreds of years old when he noticed that he was doing close to a ton in mileage. He was going faster than he should so he pressed his foot to the brake, a little too brusquely because suddenly the car was behaving strangely and he wasn't in control any more. The vehicle began to spin. His eyes spotted little cat paw prints on the bonnet and he had the thought that they were like a fancy, bespoke paint job. The trunk of the magnificent oak was in the way of the car's trajectory. There was no avoiding it. He was in a slow-motion play of the final moments of his life, as he saw car and tree bole smash at each other. There was no pain. There was no sound. Pages of the books illustrating the treasures of Moscow fluttered through the car's interior, promising mystery and minarets. Reg felt his soul lift. It took one twirl around the tree, turned upwind in the last throes of his life and was gone.

★ ★ ★

John Forbes called his brother Andrew with the news. Then he rang Susie Vine. He began to cry and by the time the call was finished she was standing beside him at the morgue door. He enveloped her and wept into her hair, breathing

393

in her comfort and breathing out his grief.

'We had just got to know one another again,' he said. 'We had time to spend together and we did. What if we hadn't? He would have gone not knowing how much I loved him.'

'That didn't happen, John, so don't beat yourself up with it. He was a happy man and so proud of you.'

She stayed by his side as he made arrangements, quietly offering any support he needed. She saw him home. Visitors and family came and went. Susie answered the telephone and organised food and wine. No one except John took any great notice; she was the agent come to shore up the gaps. He didn't see that. He saw a soul mate. He hoped she could see that in him. Later, they cuddled together on top of his duvet, clothed but hardly noticing. He talked about his dad and his mum, about life and death. They talked of ideals and waste and how time was cruel. Later, after midnight, they crept under the covers and held each other tight. That was all the closeness they required then.

The office was stunned and working on autopilot. Phones rang overtime. They took messages of condolence, dealt with friends wanting to know what had happened, others just wanting to talk, to reason through what couldn't be explained or fully understood. Betty was inconsolable.

'He stayed with me all through the thick and thin of it,' she sobbed. 'He never doubted me, even when I made stupid mistakes on a deal, as I did at the start. He was wholly loyal, when it was neither fashionable nor profitable.'

'And you to him. He loved being your client, your friend.'

'I hope he knew how cherished he was.'

'He did, Betty.'

'Oh, you should have seen him in his youth. He was a blade, cutting through the dross. A brilliant actor. Such a talent. Right to the end. I talked to the director of *The Summer House* and he's predicting awards for Reg. That's how good he is, was.'

'He always will be,' Susie said. 'We have so much of his work left to us. He will always be here, entertaining us.'

His memorial was packed. Drawn faces were etched with loss and sorrow at the snatching of such a modest and wonderful human being. Andrew read from Shakespeare, quoting from Julius Caesar, a part Reg had played with the RSC in the seventies to great acclaim:

Nature shall stand up
And say to all the world
This was a man.

John finished from Hamlet: 'Good night, sweet prince, and flights of angels attend thee.' Another line from Reg's repertoire.

Stories were told, rich and necessary, as all of his vast array of acquaintances and colleagues remembered him. There was tea and sandwiches laid on by the family so that people could mingle and praise their fallen comrade.

'He would have loved this,' Andrew told Susie.

He put his arm about her shoulders as she cried. 'Please don't worry about him. He had a great life. He was fulfilled. He went out in his prime. He made a difference. Which of the rest of us will be able to say that at the end?'

John's hand remained in hers throughout.

★ ★ ★

It was important to set things straight. Reg's death had lent a perspective to events. She felt she must confront the past in order to get on with the future.

'Why did you not come for me?' she asked Karl Fox.

'You made it clear you weren't interested.' He wasn't cowed by the question nor did she expect him to be. His Irish background gave him an ease not shared by some of his English counterparts. 'I was mad about you, Suze, but you didn't want me.'

Suze. No one else called her that. She actively discouraged it. Because it had been his name for her. But this Suze was a woman now gone, disappeared over time.

'It was all so long ago, I'm surprised you're even curious any more.'

'I guess I wanted closure,' she said. 'It's the season for it.'

He left her to conjugate the information. He was right: it was all so long ago. It didn't matter any longer. It was a rite of passage and instead of moving on Susie had carried an empty, unsubstantiated feeling around with her for years. It had informed all of her other relationships. She had been longing for a phantom life, long ago extinguished, made impossible to re-create by the intervening time and events. She had wasted a large part of her life. The thought made her light-headed.

★ ★ ★

Vonda and Gregory came around to see him before the French trip. They were going to their gran's farm in Cumberland at much the same time. None of them was massively pleased at parting but no one wanted to be the first to admit that.

'It's just a change, for a while,' Milo said, feeling very mature.

'Yeah. Will you miss me?'

Gregory looked pink at his sister's question. He started to throw darts at the board as if practising a round.

Milo cleared his throat. 'Yeah. Course. You?'

'Yeah. Only a month anyway, like you said.'

'Yeah.' He felt some part of him would burst with tension.

Greg handed him the darts. 'Your go.'

They had afternoon tea and Isabelle insisted they speak in French to prepare Milo. It was weird but fun.

'Your accent is really good,' Isabelle told Milo.

'I used to practise it,' he admitted, without explaining why.

Vonda pecked his cheek goodbye, leaving a burn behind on his startled face. After he closed the door, he put his fingers to the spot. It was hot and dry, which augured well for a real kiss. He pressed the fingers to his lips. It felt good.

* * *

'I don't want to run out on you so I thought it best to discuss my plans,' Susie told Betty. 'I still haven't forgiven Jay Burns for what he did. I didn't want to put myself into that category.'

'To be honest, Susie, I've been expecting you to do something like this for a long time.'

'Really? Should I take that as a compliment?'

'Do.'

'Obviously, I'll be more a manager than running a big agency. I will start with six to eight clients and see how I go. I want to keep things small.'

'You're worried about taking people with you, I suppose.'

'Yes.' This was the bit she had dreaded. 'I don't want to look like I've left you in the lurch or for you to feel that I have or that I have stolen clients.'

'Susie, just tell me who the lucky fuckers are, then go about your business. You are my prize pupil and I'm glad to wish you luck and to help you where I can.'

'Craig Landor, Rod Ferguson and Nicky Ashewi will be my main clients from here and the others are just starting out and have only just approached me for representation. One of them is about to leave drama school and she serves me pizza regularly in Clapham. Small world.'

'You have my blessing.' Betty actually looked as though she was filling up. 'I'll miss you.'

'You're not upset, Betty? I really couldn't bear that.'

'Of course I'm fucking upset, you nincompoop, but only to lose you.' She daubed an eye. 'Besides, you are leaving me a lot.'

'So I hear.'

'Yes.' Betty was crowing. 'I get to keep Valerie.'

'You really are a tough old bitch. OK, you drive a hard deal but you do get to keep my mother.'

★   ★   ★

Nicky Ashewi's show stormed the Edinburgh Festival and was awarded a Fringe First by *The Scotsman* newspaper. It was an autobiographical account of growing up in the Midlands in the nineteen seventies. Her stories were full of fun and self deprecation. Best were her accounts of her father's obsession with Jaffa Cakes, their dog, Tonto, who snarled and sang in equal measure to the *Saturday Night Fever* track 'More Than a Woman', and the fact that her brothers taught Nicky to dismantle and reassemble their grandfather's World War Two service revolver, which always put off prospective boyfriends.

Susie went to her dressing room to congratulate her. 'You did it. I am so proud of you.'

Nicky was swamped by well-wishers. She introduced Susie as the woman who got her there.

'Nonsense,' Susie countered. 'She got here on the steam of her own talent.'

'As opposed to the steam of my own piss which would have been about as useful if I hadn't had Susie to push me to write the thing and book such a great venue.

'I've had interest from various TV producers,' Nicky told her.

'I'm not one bit surprised. I've had calls from some of them and I've arranged meetings around the Television Festival while I'm here to follow those up.'

They went to the Assembly Rooms bar to celebrate Nicky's success. Across the room Susie saw Jay Burns. He smiled broadly at her and nodded. She acknowledged him with a raise of her glass, then, like two sharks encountering one another in the ocean, they veered away in opposite directions, displaying the finest of professional courtesy.

EPILOGUE

It was late February when they visited Reg's grave to admire his newly finished headstone and to show him the BAFTA he had been awarded for his mesmeric performance in *The Summer House*. John Forbes had taken time out from filming *I-Dentity*. He held Susie Vine's hand, grateful to have her with him, wondering what she had made of his suggestion that they buy a house and live together. Lola stood opposite, wearing a very bright wedding ring, next to Saul Hartog, who now seemed taller and more handsome. Betty read a small speech and finished with, 'We loved Reg. We miss him. We could mourn him but how much better it is to simply rejoice that he lived.' Andrew and Heather had brought their children who were fascinated by the BAFTA, with its dramatic mask, and full of questions about why it existed at all.

They began to repair to the inn by the river where they would lunch and tell tall tales.

'Make me go after an hour, no matter how good the conversation is,' Susie warned John. 'I'm booked to mind Tash and Jan's babies.'

He laughed. 'The twins.'

Valerie and Betty took turns to push Margaret La Bute's wheelchair along the smooth straight avenues of the cemetery. Flora and Quentin chased after their younger cousins. The air was filled with the happy sounds of Reg's friends and family.

John stopped to kiss her. 'I don't think I will ever get over you, Susie Vine,' he whispered. 'I am so lucky.'

They kissed again.

'I think they arrest people for making out in public places,' Susie said, breathless and happy.

She looked back to wave one last time. Reginald Darwin's name and dates shone proud in the dappled sunlight, and below them the actors' legend, 'Resting'.

We do hope that you have enjoyed reading this large print book.

Did you know that all of our titles are available for purchase?

We publish a wide range of high quality large print books including:
Romances, Mysteries, Classics
General Fiction
Non Fiction and Westerns

Special interest titles available in large print are:
The Little Oxford Dictionary
Music Book
Song Book
Hymn Book
Service Book

Also available from us courtesy of Oxford University Press:
Young Readers' Dictionary
(large print edition)
Young Readers' Thesaurus
(large print edition)

For further information or a free brochure, please contact us at:
Ulverscroft Large Print Books Ltd.,
The Green, Bradgate Road, Anstey,
Leicester, LE7 7FU, England.
Tel: (00 44) 0116 236 4325
Fax: (00 44) 0116 234 0205

THE WOMAN ON THE BUS

Pauline McLynn

It was a typical Tuesday evening in Kilbrody. Cathy Long was on her way to collect her drunken father from the pub. Ozzy O'Reilly was in the graveyard, watching the Dublin bus through his binoculars. Charlie Finn was pulling pints for the stragglers at the bar when it hit him: he was bored. And that's when the woman from the bus walked through the door. Ruth Treacy's arrival is anything but boring. And her extraordinary behaviour is soon the talk of the town. It seems that she's here to stay — for a while, at least — and the effect she has on Kilbrody's inhabitants will change some of them for ever.

RIGHT ON TIME

Pauline McLynn

Every second counts for private investigator Leo Street on her latest case. She must find a missing teenager in the drug-fuelled streets of Dublin before it's too late. But with a watch that's stopped and a biological clock that's taken over, it's not going to be easy. Leo's irrepressible sidekick Ciara, her mischievous mutt No. 4, and Ciara's gorgeous twin brother Ronan, lend a helping hand. But can they track down the missing girl and save the day, or will a case of bad timing put all their lives at risk?

WISH YOU WERE HERE

Mike Gayle

After ten years together, Charlie Mansell has
been dumped by his live-in girlfriend Sarah.
All he wants to do is wallow in misery, but
mates Andy and Tom have a better idea: a
week of sun, sea and souvlaki in Malia —
party capital of the Greek islands. But
Charlie and his mates aren't eighteen any
more. Or even under thirty. And it shows. It
isn't the cheap beer, the late nights or even
the fast-food that's the problem. It's girls.
And life. And most of all . . . each other.

NO STRINGS ATTACHED

Clare Dowling

Judy is getting married on Saturday and it's going to be the happiest day of her life if it kills her. It's a military operation, but it'll all be worth it because marriage is for ever, right? But the night before the nuptials, fiancé Barry goes missing. Then his credit card shows up two days later in a nightclub in the south of France. A case of cold feet? Or worse, is it because he's being frog-marched up the aisle? Fanning her fury and grief is Lenny, Barry's best man. Lenny argues that relationships aren't permanent and that commitment ruins romance. With her fiancé romping around France, Judy just might be in the mood for a little romance — with no strings attached, of course . . .

SUGAR DADDY

Lisa Kleypas

Liberty Jones fell in love with Hardy Cates when she was fourteen and he was seventeen. However, Hardy wasn't going to let love stand in the way of his ambition to escape the poverty of his childhood. He left town — and Liberty broken-hearted. But, being a survivor, and determined to improve the lives of both her and her baby sister, she moves to the big city. There she finds a job and an unlikely friend in billionaire tycoon Churchill Travis. But though Churchill's son, Gage, believes she's a gold digger seeking a sugar daddy, their relationship goes deeper than most people think. Then, just as Liberty and her sister begin to feel settled in their new home, Hardy comes back into their lives . . .